Friend of My Enemy
Benjamin Eric Hill

AN [e-*reads*] BOOK
New York, NY

Copyright © 2002 by Benjamin Hill
First e-reads publication 2003
www.e-reads.com
ISBN 0-7592-5373-0

The friend of my enemy is my enemy.
—Arab Proverb

Table of Contents

Chapter One   1
Chapter Two   8
Chapter Three   20
Chapter Four   27
Chapter Five   33
Chapter Six   46
Chapter Seven   53
Chapter Eight   58
Chapter Nine   60
Chapter Ten   69
Chapter Eleven   73
Chapter Twelve   79
Chapter Thirteen   85
Chapter Fourteen   91
Chapter Fifteen   95
Chapter Sixteen   104
Chapter Seventeen   108
Chapter Eighteen   118
Chapter Nineteen   120
Chapter Twenty   125
Chapter Twenty-One   130
Chapter Twenty-Two   139
Chapter Twenty-Three   144
Chapter Twenty-Four   151
Chapter Twenty-Five   158

Chapter Twenty-Six   167
Chapter Twenty-Seven   173
Chapter Twenty-Eight   177
Chapter Twenty-Nine   180
Chapter Thirty   183
Chapter Thirty-One   189
Chapter Thirty-Two   192
Chapter Thirty-Three   195
Chapter Thirty-Four   201
Chapter Thirty-Five   205
Chapter Thirty-Six   213
Chapter Thirty-Seven   216
Chapter Thirty-Eight   223
Chapter Thirty-Nine   226
Chapter Forty   230
Chapter Forty-One   235
Chapter Forty-Two   239
Chapter Forty-Three   247
Chapter Forty-Four   252
Chapter Forty-Five   268
Chapter Forty-Six   274
Chapter Forty-Seven   278
Chapter Forty-Eight   286
Chapter Forty-Nine   294
Chapter Fifty   298
Chapter Fifty-One   302
Chapter Fifty-Two   310
Chapter Fifty-Three   319
Chapter Fifty-Four   330
Chapter Fifty-Five   334
Chapter Fifty-Six   344
Chapter Fifty-Seven   352

Chapter Fifty-Eight   358
Chapter Fifty-Nine   361
Chapter Sixty   363
Chapter Sixty-One   365
Chapter Sixty-Two   370
Chapter Sixty-Three   373
Chapter Sixty-Four   376
Chapter Sixty-Five   392

One

September 24, 2000

For Christina Goryeb it had been a week like many others. A morning talk show appearance on Monday in New York to attract interest for her latest book, *Women of Palestine, Hope for the Future.* A pair of closed-door evening fund raisers on Thursday and Friday in London and Rome for refugee children. In between she'd met with State Department officials about the current Arab-Israeli conflict, taught her classes in international relations and Middle Eastern studies at the University of Virginia and met with her boards of directors of foundations she served on in Washington, D.C.

She'd scheduled a visit to an orphanage in Jordan, but on impulse canceled it when she reached Rome. She hadn't thought beyond that. No one knew she was in Tel Aviv, not even her husband. She told the taxi driver to take her to the Institute for Biblical Archaeology.

It had been five years since she'd seen Chaim Asher, yet the memory of that man lingered in her thoughts like the fragrance of a fine wine. Five years earlier, she'd been drawn into his life. Now, it was happening again. Their love affair had been an aberration driven by shared danger. It was foolish to want to revisit that time.

Those days seemed so long ago, yet it seemed to her that nothing fundamental had changed in Israel. Civil war still simmered with Palestinians on the West Bank, while an embattled Israeli Prime Minister's hopes for peace foundered on the rocky shoals of Middle East politics. Arab and Jew still passed silently on the streets as if the other did not exist. Meanwhile, day laborers from Gaza still crowded like cattle into open trucks every morning to be driven to construction sites in Arab neighborhoods where they built new homes for Jews to live in. Israeli settlers down from their fortified hilltops in the West Bank to shop or work at their day jobs in the city, slung M-16 assault rifles on their shoulders for protection.

Once again, she read the letter in her hand, the one she'd read so many times in the past week.

"Do you remember your last law clerk, the old school teacher?" her Palestinian cook had written. "I have the sad duty to inform you he has died." Fatima included a short clipping from a back page of the Arabic daily *al-Kuds*. It said the body of Achmed Bikfaya, formerly a school teacher from Jenin, who'd also been employed by the noted Palestinian lawyer, Christina Goryeb, had been found hanging from a rope in her dusty Ramallah law office. A slip of paper in his pocket said "Here I once knew happiness." The article ended with "Mrs. Goryeb, who immigrated to the U.S. five years ago, has dual U.S.-Israeli citizenship."

This was absurd, she thought. Achmed Bikfaya was a fiction devised by Chaim Asher.

She had thought she no longer loved him.

After she'd fled Israel to live in the U.S., they'd exchanged letters, the kind of letters, old friends write each other, newsy and platonic without a hint of the old passion. Two months ago, out of the blue he'd sent her a post card showing the King David Hotel in Jerusalem.

"Remember—," he wrote.

That was where they'd made love for the last time.

"Always," she wrote back.

His letters had formerly been written in English, for the most part, their common neutral language. Now he wrote exclusively in Arabic, her language, no longer waiting for her response. His letters came every week, then every day, overflowing with yearning and adoration. She felt flattered but she was alarmed as well. There was something missing in these passionate letters—she didn't hear Chaim's steady voice in them, at least not the man she'd known. Instead, he complained that all his zest was gone, that he wasn't interested in his job anymore, or even in his life. And then, he wrote that he had to see her. Either he would come to Virginia or she would go to Jerusalem. "You need to visit your family in Palestine. Ramallah, is now governed by the Palestine Authority. No one will harm you."

Immediately she regretted the impulse that had led her to encourage Chaim.

"Chaim," she wrote,"for the sake of my daughters, what happened between us is past and must never happen again. Let us remain good friends, always."

She expected a polite letter of apology, a pledge to never again let his feelings for her go beyond the bounds of friendship. A week went by and then another without a letter from Asher. One day she realized he'd never write her again and pushed thoughts of him out of her mind.

But when she got Fatima's letter telling her the old clerk, Bikfaya, had hung himself, she cried.

Had she been his only life line? She couldn't believe he'd kill himself over an old love affair. Besides his dedication to Israel wouldn't permit suicide. It would be desertion.

She wrote the Palestine Authority for details of "Bikfaya's" death. A courteous reply in Arabic came by return mail from a Captain Kabir. The Palestine Authority had no record of the incident described by *Al-Kuds*, he wrote. He had discussed the matter with the newspaper's editor and discovered the Bikfaya story was merely gossip from the *souk* that had been written up by a free lance reporter.

That "free lancer" knew things about her only Chaim Asher would know.

Had Chaim faked the story to lure her back? It was manipulative and oblique, but he was capable of both, especially if he'd become mentally unbalanced.

She had no idea how to contact him once she had arrived in Israel. For his mailing address he used a Tel Aviv post office box. She wrote him that she was coming but when he didn't meet her plane, she'd tried to find him at his old *kibbutz*. His friends said he had gone away but wouldn't tell her where or when.

Then she remembered his superior at the Institute. Mekor, a hard and cunning man, but perhaps in light of the past he would be sympathetic to her.

Christina stepped from her taxi into the hot suffocating Middle East sun and glared at the glass and concrete office tower on King Saul Boulevard. Two lines of Hebrew on a plaque at the entrance said *Institute for Biblical Archaeology*. The ugly, familiar knot twisted in her stomach, and she paused for a deep, calming breath before climbing the broad stairs of the Haddar Dafna Building.

A dusty green Volvo station wagon tore around the corner into the square, tires squealing, veered toward her, and skidded to a stop at the curb. Christina recognized the driver as Mekor's trusted assistant, Gilda Sderot. Mekor in the rear seat was crystal cool under a frayed Panama hat. He wore a thin white cotton suit and an open-necked sky blue shirt.

"Get in Mrs. Goryeb," Gilda said.

Mekor opened the rear door and slid over to make room for Christina. His shoes were muddy as if he'd just come fresh from a dig.

Reluctantly, she got into the car.

Gilda drove off through the crowded streets of Tel Aviv at high speed. They went northward out of town past the Sde Dov military airfield until it picked up the coast highway to Haifa.

"So who gave you our phone number?" Mekor said with a dangerous smile.

"Chaim Asher, during that stinking business with B'nai Ha'eretz."

Mekor looked straight in front of her.

"Can you help me contact Chaim? Mekor. I must see him."

"Asking favors, Mrs. Goryeb? You're lucky we let you live," said Gilda.

"That's enough Gilda," Mekor said. His face was as impassive as the brown leather of the shoulder holster that peeked out of his coat.

"Asher's no longer with us, Christina. I haven't seen him for several years."

She faced him directly, eyes flashing. "I didn't come back to this accursed place for sentimental reasons. I'm worried about Chaim's health. I think he may have suffered a nervous breakdown. Either that or else he's dead."

Gilda's laugh was harsh. "By now he's found another woman," she said. "Remember, I've known him longer than you."

Christina snatched the *Al-Kuds* clipping out of her purse and shoved it under Mekor's nose. "Who else but Chaim could have written that?"

Mekor rubbed two fingers on his chin as he studied the news clipping. Only two people besides Christina Goryeb had known Achmed Bikfaya's true identity, himself and Asher.

"Did anyone in your immediate family know about you and Chaim?" he said.

Her eyes grew distant. "My daughters and house servants must have suspected something. But no one else."

"Let us suppose for a moment a careless word spoken here or there. Eventually, your secret could have hissed through Ramallah's *souk* like the flame on a fuse."

"Palestinians are my people. I have no enemies here. This is my home," he said.

His glance was thoughtful as though she was a piece of an intricate puzzle.

"In the U.S. you are the voice of moderate Palestinians. For this you would not be universally beloved among your people. Islamic Jihad or a similar terrorist organization may have written this to discredit you and your efforts."

"I doubt that very much," she said coldly. "Perhaps you'd better read these." She handed Mekor a small bundle of letters.

Mekor muttered as he read one of them. Mawkish, almost childish. What had happened to Asher? he wondered. Had the man's brains finally turned to shit? Good men went to pieces in his line of work. Iron men, men like Asher. A famous neurologist from Hadassah Hospital had once described it to Mekor as "delayed shock syndrome." It was usually brought on by the things men like Asher did, like strangle a sentry with a nylon garrote or drive a stiletto up under his chin through the roof of his mouth and into his brain. When you're that close, he's not just a target in a gun sight; you breathe in his breath, feel his death throes. Shock was often aggravated by the loss of loved ones or close comrades, the expert had said. American soldiers suffered from delayed shock years after the Vietnam War had ended. One of their psychiatrists had warned Mekor that Asher was acting strangely but Mekor had discounted the warnings. Asher had always been a moody bastard.

Mekor reached in his coat for a pencil. "Do you have a phone number where I can reach you, Mrs. Goryeb?"

Christina gave him the number of her home in Ramallah where she was staying. "How long will it be before I hear from you?" she said.

"Soon, very soon," he said. "Can I keep these?"

"Certainly. Thank you for helping me."

"You can thank me when we find Asher alive. Where can I drop you?"

"The Central Bus Station in Tel Aviv would be fine."

They rode back to Tel Aviv in silence. No wonder Asher had fallen so hard, thought Mekor. She was a beautiful woman. She wore no make-up and did not need to, for she had that rich olive skin that glowed with a golden sheen of health and vitality. There was a hint of gray in her lustrous curly dark hair, cut short. An American style. Her lush black eyebrows that showed no sign of being plucked. Her white, perfect teeth that glinted between soft parted lips. Her dark business suit barely concealed a sensational figure, equal to any of the star chorus girls he had seen in the cabarets of Tel Aviv.

As they drove up to the bus station, she turned to him. "I value your judgment," she said. "Please give me some advice."

The directness of her eyes, that charming smile.

"Be careful, Christina. I can no longer protect you in Ramallah."

* * *

At six o'clock in the evening, traffic was heavy on the street below, as crowds of office workers headed home. Mekor lit his 60th cigarette of the day and coughed violently. He closed his eyes for a moment, feeling the pain burn in his chest and dart out his arm.

Gilda shook her head. "Those Marlboros are killing you, Mike. Don't expect me to cry when they hook you up to the oxygen tank."

Ignoring her, he studied the letters Christina had given him.

"I don't believe Asher wrote this drivel," he said. "These are the letters of a school boy."

"If he didn't, who cooked up all that shit about Bikfaya hanging himself?" she said. Besides he wrote her in Arabic. That's what he'd do if he really wanted to impress her."

"How do we know if this is Asher's handwriting. All I have here to compare it with are reports he wrote in Hebrew which is nothing like Arabic. The only way to be sure is to find the bastard." Mekor's voice was a blast of anger as though it was her doing that Asher was inaccessible.

Gilda gave him a sympathetic smile.

"Why, you don't know where he is either," she said.

She glanced at her watch and rose from her chair. "Are we through, Mike? I'm having supper with someone tonight."
"That poor bastard," he said. "Yeah, we're done."
"Don't worry. We'll find him, Mike," she said.
She left him reading Asher's old reports on his computer terminal.

* * *

The sunset glinted on the blue Mediterranean through a gap in the Samarian hills above Tel Aviv, suffusing everything with warm glowing light. A gentle breeze caressed Christina's cheek as she sat in the garden of her beloved home in Ramallah eating supper with her younger sisters, Najat and Janine. She had not seen since them since their mother's funeral. She could almost see traces of her in Janine who sat tall and straight in their Maman's place at the head of the table giving orders in a low firm voice to Fatima to serve them coffee and baklava. She's sitting in my rightful place and I am but a guest in my own home, Christina thought bitterly. Najat, the youngest still had the giddy and carefree laugh of a school girl though she was a married woman with children.

"Whatever happened to Achmed Bikfaya, my old law clerk?" she asked Najat. "Do you see him around anymore?"

There was a moment of uncomfortable silence.

"He vanished right after you went to America," said Najat. "We never saw him again. I think he was in love with you."

Janine interrupted. "He was a very disturbing man," She gave Christina a steady look. "The Jews were watching you so closely at that time. There were ugly rumors in the *souk* that you were a traitor. That you had taken a Jewish lover," She spoke softly. "You never said much about what was going on, Christina. Now, you can tell us what happened five years ago. We have a right to know."

Christina felt a thump, a flutter in her chest as if her heart were turning over. They'll find out anyway. They always do. She took a deep breath. Where to begin?

Two

On that day the Lord made a covenant with Abraham, saying, 'To your descendants I give this land, from the river of Egypt to the great river, the river Euphrates, the land of the Ken'ites, the Ken'izzites, the Kad'monites, the Hit'tites, the Per'izzites, the Reph'aim, the Am'orites, the Ca'naanites, the Gir'gashites, and the Jeb'usites.
—Genesis 15, 18-21

In April 1995, on a lonely hilltop at sunrise, before an altar of stones, Mordecai Ben Yusuf, a gaunt, red-bearded man in black prepared a sacrifice. In his arms was a baby lamb. He was the spiritual leader of B'nai Ha'eretz, an Israeli settlement in the occupied West Bank of the Jordan River, the land where the biblical Kingdom of Israel flourished two millennia ago. In his arms was a baby lamb. A large brightly colored *kippa*, the knitted cap worn by religious Zionists, covered his flowing auburn hair. Bound to his forehead with a black strap was a *tefilin*, a leather box containing the *Sh'ma*, the prayer from Deuteronomy of God's oneness, and his right arm was bound with a similar phylactery. With his striped prayer shawl, long black robe and blazing blue eyes he looked like one of the Prophets of old.

Hear O Israel: The Lord our God, is one Lord.

Behind him, the men of B'nai Ha'eretz, the Children of the Land, knelt in the dry grass.

Sentinels with rounds chambered in their automatic rifles, stood with their backs to the group as they scanned the hostile hills, missing nothing. They too dressed in black, wore striped shawls, leather phylacteries and knitted *kippots*.

8

B'nai Ha'eretz was a "Torah City" of ultra-Orthodox Jews. On Wednesdays at dawn, like this one, they met on this hill for sacrifice and prayer. Fifty men gathered before the Rabbi, young men in their twenties, middle-aged men, and old united by the common dream of building the Third Temple. They practiced a form of Judaism that had not existed since the Romans destroyed Jerusalem. A Judaism with a priestly class, animal sacrifices, and, most important, rebuilding the Temple.

Lifting up the lamb as an offering to God, Rabbi Ben Yusuf looked out over a landscape of rocky hillocks, green valleys, and steeply terraced slopes, and felt a deep sense of kinship with his surroundings, certain in the knowledge that two millennia ago, his ancestors walked these same hills, performed these same rituals, and uttered these same prayers. Stone-built Arab villages surrounded by flocks of sheep were visible in the dim light at the foot of a distant mountain. A tinkle of goat bells from the vineyard below broke the stillness. Ben Yusuf lowered the struggling lamb to the altar and cut its throat with a commando knife. A thin jet of blood stained the corner of his prayer shawl. As the lamb's life drained out, he walked around the altar, holding the lamb so that blood ran thick and red over the stones, and marked each side with blood. He placed the dying lamb on the altar of stones, then knelt and clasped his bloody hands.

"Lord of the Universe, Maker of All Creation, O God of Abraham, hear our prayer," he said in Hebrew. "Thou who gave this Land to Abraham, Isaac, and Jacob: Galilee, Samaria as well as Judea. The Abomination that calls itself the Government of Israel does not lead Thy Chosen People. Those cowards say Samaria and Judea is not our country, that we're refugees and thieves who have stolen this Land and we live here only by the grace of *goyishe* American charity. This is a despicable lie. *We* are Your Light unto the Nations. The Lord will not forsake His Chosen People nor abandon His Covenant."

"Amen," cried the fifty. "Great is the Lord."

"The time of the Messiah draws near. He comes as we speak, even as new disasters daily threaten His arrival. Already has this Reign of Iniquity, surrendered the Lands of Sinai, Gaza, and the city of Jericho to the Arabs. Now, in the dawn of our redemption, they would give up Samaria and Judea! The Third Temple must be built. Israel's borders must encompass Samaria and Judea."

Rumbles of discontent came from the men assembled before him.

9

"Lord, give us courage to save your Land from the Abomination so that we may build the Third Temple," cried Ben Yusuf.

The men of B'nai Ha'eretz skinned the lamb. Over a fire built in a discarded 5-gallon kerosene can they roasted its meat for breakfast.

* * *

Three hooded figures wearing tiger fatigues and carrying AK-47s slipped quickly and quietly like shadows from one hiding place to the next on the hillside below.

Golani, saw them first. They were so close Golani could see their teeth.

Ben Yusuf had dubbed him "Golani" for wearing the bullet on a chain around his neck, and for his boasting about attending Camp Meir, a paramilitary summer camp in New York's Catskill mountains, where he had been trained by members of the Israeli Army's elite Golani Brigade. The paper targets he had trained on back at Camp Meir were black and white. He had never shot at a man before. These weren't men. They were the enemy. His hands shook as he raised his M-16, aimed at the mouth of the nearest guerilla and squeezed the trigger. The hooded face disintegrated in a spray of blood and bone. The body collapsed, the limbs jerked spasmodically and were still.

Immediately the two remaining guerillas returned fire. Golani dropped behind a big rock as AK-47 bullets buzzed past him on all sides. The rest of the men of B'nai Ha'eretz took cover too, diving behind olive trees and boulders on the crest of the hill. Gunfire rattled and popped all up and down the settler's positions on the ridge. The vacuous roar of the AK-47s drowned out the firing of the lighter Uzis and Galils and American M-16 assault rifles, the settler's weapons. Golani looked up to see a small dark object arc toward him. He barely had time to hit the ground again when the grenade fell in the rocks close by. The shock wave from the explosion hit his back like the slap of a great hand. Two more blasts followed in quick succession. Miraculously Golani was unharmed except for a loud ringing in his ears. He shook his head and waited for the guerrillas to advance but instead the two guerrillas disappeared down the hillside.

* * *

The settlers came out of their places of concealment slowly. Ben Yusuf bowed his head and thanked God none of his men were harmed. He watched the two guerrillas melt into the stony landscape as they dragged their dead comrade by each arm. The limp body flopped like a rag doll. The attack was an good omen; it would make the men more receptive. Time was running out.

Shlomo Arendt, a small bull of a man with wide shoulders and a heavily lined face stood cradling an M-16 behind an olive tree near Ben Yusuf. "They took the body so I doubt if they'll be back soon," he said. "But they'll be back."

"Whatever they do, whatever they plan, God, the Shield of Abraham, will protect us," said the Rabbi.

Recently, two machine gun toting settlers had been disarmed by the Palestinian Civil Police in Jericho. A bad sign since most settlers carried automatic weapons given to them by the IDF, the Israeli Army, in order to protect themselves against attacks. Israeli settlements expanded, checker board fashion, across the occupied West Bank, Gaza Strip and the Golan Heights during the past decade, when the Likud party had been in power. But Likud lost the 1992 election to the Labor Party led by Yitzhak Rabin and Shimon Peres. Now, Yasser Arafat, the Palestinian leader who once advocated the destruction of Israel, was negotiating a self-rule agreement with Israel as head of an entity called the Palestine Authority. If that wasn't offensive enough, "Peace Now", an organization started by reserve officers in the Israel Defense Forces, called for removal of settlers at Hebron, Nablus, Jericho, Netzarim, to be followed by evacuation of all the larger settlements.

Under agreements signed by Prime Minister Yitzhak Rabin, the Palestinian leader, Yasser Arafat, had limited authority over a small fraction of the West Bank that included six of his seven largest towns but he had no control over land designated by Israel as a military zone and considered necessary for its security. The West Bank was now a battleground between Jewish settlers and Palestinians intent on building a homeland.

"The *non-frum*, the unbelievers, are our greatest threat," thought Ben Yusuf.

Etzel Meyerson, the Rabbi's assistant, squatted beside the fire, carving roast lamb and forking the pieces into a serving bowl. Earlier, the

Rabbi and Etzel had mapped out their strategy. Faithful Etzel with his darting black eyes and pock-marked face, was another bright boy from Ben Yusuf's old Brooklyn neighborhood, Borough Park. By the fire, Golani, the new volunteer from Crown Heights, Brooklyn, proudly brandished his M-16. His blue eyes gleamed with excitement.

"Let's give the Arabs a real bone to choke on," Golani cried.

This was a promising start.

Ben Yusuf assumed the guileless look of a teacher inviting comment. Speaking to Etzel, he raised his voice slightly so the rest of the men could hear him. Ben Yusuf used his voice like a musical instrument, adapting it appropriately to suit each occasion, speaking in Yiddish rather than Hebrew as most secular Israelis would have done. Among the Orthodox and ultra-Orthodox Jews, Hebrew was reserved exclusively for worship and prayers.

"Israel is still the Likud's country, Etzel," he said with calm assurance.

"One well-timed massacre of Jews by Arabs could cost Rabin a vote of confidence in the Knesset," Etzel replied.

Yitzhak Rabin, the Labor Prime Minister. An anathema, clinging to power by a narrow majority.

Ben Yusuf raised his eye brows slightly but continued to chew.

"A no confidence vote would mean new elections," said Golani falling in step.

"New elections and a new Prime Minister," added Etzel. "A Prime Minister like Bibi Netanyahu who would not give the Land away."

"And what if he loses the election?" said Ben Yusuf.

"No," said Shlomo. "What if Bibi wins and turns on us?"

Ben Yusuf glanced at Shlomo again. Shlomo, who had been with him since *Yammit*. This time the stakes were much higher. Etzel wasn't sure about Shlomo.

"*Nu?*" Ben Yusuf said with mock bitterness. "Where is the *Intifada* when we need it?"

A guttural ripple of laughter moved through the men.

Eight years earlier Palestinians had taken to the streets in a revolt called the *Intifada*. Now all was calm except for periodic attacks like the one the settlers had just witnessed.

"We taught the Arabs how to be victims," said Shlomo. "We taught them how to kiss ass with the American press."

When Etzel offered Ben Yusuf a bowl of lamb scraps, he gently refused.

The Lord will not abandon his Chosen People.
"Something must be done to rouse the Arabs," said Golani.
"We don't have time to bait Arabs," said Ben Yusuf firmly.
Golani stared at him. "What are you saying Rabbi?"
Etzel answered for Ben Yusuf. "Every Arab we kick gives Rabin another reason to dismantle the settlements and take away our weapons. The Hebron Arabs went on a rampage after Goldstein, but you didn't hear their leaders howl for a fight."

On the eve of Purim in 1994, Baruch Goldstein, an ultra-Orthodox Jewish settler and physician, born and raised in Brooklyn, New York, walked into the Tomb of the Patriarchs in Hebron, a place venerated by Jews and Muslims alike as the burial place of Abraham, Isaac, and Sarah. Inside the massive 2,000 year old building, once a Jewish temple built by Herod, and now a mosque, Goldstein raised his M-16 and gunned down 29 Muslim worshipers before he was overpowered by the survivors and was beaten to death.

"Those Arabs in the Hebron mosque were plotting to kill Jews," said Golani.

"I thought Goldstein was the only Jew who was killed there," said Etzel, who could not resist gently baiting this youngster.

"Goldstein heard the *muezzin* up in the tower cry 'Death to the Jews' not 'Allah be praised', when he called Arabs to prayers. So he got the jump on them. Goldstein was truly following *Halakhah*. If someone plans to kill a Jew, you kill him first. That's *Halakhah*," said Golani. "The Arabs have murdered 90 more Jews since Hebron. The government is too soft on them."

Halakhah, Jewish ritual law.

Ben Yusuf reflected that Golani was a member of the synagogue in Brooklyn that adopted B'nai Ha'eretz as its Israel "twin" and sent money, lots of it. Golani's uncle was a member of "COJO", the powerful Council Of Jewish Organizations, an agency that sent hundreds of thousands of dollars to Israeli settlements, including B'nai Ha'eretz. COJO was the key to winning tens of thousands of American Orthodox Jewish votes, assuring that 3 billion dollars of American foreign aid would flow annually to Israel.

"The blessed Goldstein celebrated a perfect Purim," Ben Yusuf said calmly. "He became *kedoshim*, one of the holy martyrs; his was a perfect Jewish death."

Golani stood his ground. "If our enemy is not the Arabs, who is it, then, Rabbi?"

"God has many enemies," said Ben Yusuf. "But at this moment God's chief enemy is Yitzhak Rabin.

Prime Minister Rabin's High Court had dispersed Orthodox Jewish Councils in Haifa, Jerusalem and Kiryat Tivon after they refused to admit Reform and Conservative rabbis. The Rabbi spat out his words.

"Rabin wants us to pass for *goyim* like the American Jews with their pathetic Conservative and Reform synagogues."

"Rabin is a weak old fart," said Golani.

"He backed down when we protested relocating Hebron's settlers. Didn't he refuse to let the smallest settlement be abandoned?" said Etzel.

"It's just a trick," said Ben Yusuf.

He was merely repeating gossip, but in the supercharged atmosphere of B'nai Ha'eretz, rumor provoked hours of feverish debate. He raised a hand for silence.

"Let me tell you why Rabin really changed his tune," he said in confiding tones. "He needs every settlement to trade for Arab concessions when the final filthy deal is struck!"

Golani seemed unconvinced, but one of the other men nudged him.

"See, we are pawns," he said.

Ben Yusuf gave Shlomo a significant glance.

"Who can we trust? You remember Yammit, Shlomo. That's where we were double crossed by Menachem Begin, 'Mr. Historic Rights' himself. One of Likud's founding fathers. What irony!"

Shlomo responded with a sardonic chuckle.

Ben Yusuf turned to him. "Shlomo, if you had to choose between the Land and a soldier's boot kicking you out, what would you do?"

"I'd fight," Shlomo said without hesitation.

Ben Yusuf nodded knowingly. He looked around the meeting slowly at each man in turn, as they stoked their pipes and lit their cigarettes. He could smell the tension in the acrid smoke.

"I prayed for guidance," he said. "I went to Kiryat Arba where I lay across the tomb of the blessed Goldstein. His spirit spoke to me."

Goldstein was buried outside Hebron near the giant Kiryat Arba apartment house and shopping complex next to the baseball field in Meir Kahane Park. A concrete slab had been poured over the grave to keep Goldstein's body from being stolen. Ben Yusuf waited in line twenty minutes with a noisy crowd who lamented and embraced the simple head stone, and left piles of small pebbles beside it. Some prostrated themselves on the concrete slab. When his turn came, Ben Yusuf lay face down on it and began to pray. At first he heard nothing but his own thoughts, but then the Voice came up through the fresh concrete. Ben Yusuf lay still, not daring to breathe. Not two feet away, a stout woman with a day-glow orange Kodak Instamatic camera chipped tiny pieces out of Goldstein's head stone. Ben Yusuf was astonished that she did not hear the Voice, but it spoke directly to him and no one else.

Remember Joshua. Trust in the Shield of Abraham.

"Golani speaks the truth," said Ben Yusuf. He made his voice deeper, as if Goldstein were speaking through him. "*Halakhah* is higher than Israeli law. Trust in God."

He took Golani's hand and brought him forward to sit beside him in front of the men. Etzel gripped Golani by both shoulders. Golani's eyes shone as he was swept up into the timeless moment, past connected to present in an unbroken chain of heroes and prophets.

In a low energetic voice and with animated gestures, Ben Yusuf wove the last magic strand into his web.

"The *non-frum*, they who serve the Abomination, lack our strength. We have Torah while they are Godless," he said. "Joshua led an obedient people to drive the Ca'naanites from the Land through trust in the power of God. So must we rebel against the Abomination and reconquer the Land. The time has come."

Ben Yusuf's men responded with cautious cheers, something less than the whole hearted endorsement he had hoped for. Could he ever expect them to do more than talk? It was easy enough for them to drive into an Arab village at night and fire a few bullets in the windows, or ignite a plastic milk jug of gasoline under a car. But the thought of Jew fighting Jew was sobering. All settlers were active duty members of local militia units, and thus part of the Army. The instant they rebelled, they stood to lose everything, and they knew it.

"What do you propose Rabbi?" asked Shlomo.

Etzel was supposed to ask that question, thought the Rabbi. Belatedly, Etzel came to life.

"We will defend our homes if the Army comes," he said.

"Taking on the Army is a pretty tall order, Etzel, considering they are the ones protecting us from the Arabs," said Shlomo.

Golani jumped in. "But if we hold out long enough, people will see that our cause is just."

"Maybe, but a divided *Yisroel* is a weak *Yisroel*," said Shlomo.

Golani looked crest-fallen.

Lift up thine eyes unto the Lord, O Savior of Yisroel.

Ben Yusuf turned his fiery blue gaze on Shlomo.

"*Yisroel* is still the Likud's country," he said softly. "Our people will rally in a time of crisis. If we hold, the Army will see the truth and they will refuse to drive us out. Then the people will overthrow the government of evil. We will be the spark."

Shlomo remained silent. Finally he said, "At the right place, at the right time, it might work."

"Others would see and follow us," said Etzel with mounting enthusiasm. "We'd be heroes, not traitors."

Ben Yusuf gazed out at Baal Chazor, the mountain where God gave the Sacred Land to Abraham and all his descendants until the end of time. "Our settlement is on a hill. It would be easy to defend," he said finally. "Not like Yammit."

* * *

More than a decade before, the Army demolished Yammit, a settlement in the Sinai Desert, because it violated the diplomatic accord with Egypt reached at Camp David. Rabbi Ben Yusuf and members of B'nai Ha'eretz drove down to demonstrate. They'd climbed up on the roofs of the shabby pre-fab houses and waited for the bulldozers. It was a stand off until TV cameras showed up; then soldiers stormed the houses and forcibly removed the demonstrators. The experience left scars. For weeks the settlers argued furiously in favor of fighting the government until the government paid them handsome compensation for their loss. They decided that Menachem Begin had sold out for American aid.

Subsequently, Ben Yusuf and his followers became involved in the aborted attempts to blow up Dome of the Rock, the Muslim shrine built on the site of the Herod's great temple. Had the shrine been destroyed, three hundred million Moslems would have called for a holy war against all Jews. Perhaps that was why the plot came to the attention of the Mossad, Israel's elite intelligence service. Ben Yusuf was arrested along with the other conspirators, tried, convicted, and sentenced to three years in prison. After he completed 18 months he was released. During those months in prison he had planned his next move. He would build a city out of his hamlet of 300 residents in the heartland of the fertile Samarian hills north of Jerusalem. And he had.

Ben Yusuf's thoughts were interrupted by a question. "But Rabbi, doesn't fighting the Army mean we'll be the bad guys?" The question came from Arbel, the Naval reservist, a cherub-cheeked man with a short military hair-cut.

Nobody liked to do the dirty work thought Ben Yusuf in disdain.

"It is our special job to be a little nasty," he said. "Future generations of Jews will be grateful somebody stood up to that traitor, Yitzhak Rabin, and finally created a safe place in the world for Jews. So if the Army tries to take our homes, we fight."

"But isn't it murder to shoot other Jews?" said Arbel.

"It is prevention," Ben Yusuf said gravely. "*Halakhah* gives us no choice but to act when the lives of Jews are threatened. Those who try to force us from the Land of *Yisroel* mortally wound the entire Jewish people. They deserve to die. Does anyone doubt this?" Ben Yusuf's challenge was met by silence. "Good, then we agree."

"We'll need heavy weapons to have any chance against the Army," said Shlomo.

The subject of weapons was something Ben Yusuf did not want to discuss at the meeting. He looked around slowly before his eyes rested on Shlomo.

"We don't need special weapons," said Ben Yusuf. "Trust. That's all we need. Trust in the Shield of Abraham."

Shlomo said, "Even so, I know a man who may be able to help."

God was with them after all, thought Ben Yusuf.

* * *

The meeting broke up shortly afterward. After Shlomo spoke briefly to Ben Yusuf, he dawdled for a few minutes while the Rabbi went with the other men down on the rocky path. Shlomo tossed a stone thoughtfully in his hand. The Rabbi was right, he thought, *Yisroel's* greatest enemy had always been the tender-hearten hypocrites within, the ones who would one day try to give it all back to the Arabs. He wondered if he had promised too much by proposing to supply the weapons to the Rabbi, enough weapons to hold off the Israeli Army. He lived a double life, presenting two faces to the world. One was an artful mask, the face of a dedicated civil servant who lived among fanatics to keep an eye on them; the other was his true self. He twisted his muscular body like a spring, and threw the stone high into the sky. The hot dry breath of the desert to the south mingled with wisps of cool air from the surrounding hills. Its warmth stirred the cicadas into song. After a few erratic bursts of buzzing they settled down to a steady drone. Shlomo walked through an abandoned vineyard, past a watchman's tower, and on through the ruins of an Arab village where fig trees grew. He came to a steep gravel track near the perimeter fence of the B'nai Ha'eretz settlement. Above him, apartment blocks made of pale pre-cast concrete panels, decorated with gaudy little turrets, parapets, balconies and rounded bays were clustered on a rocky ridge behind gleaming circles of razor wire that topped a chain link fence. Sixty-one apartments had been built, with plans to build 68 more. With their TV antennas, tiled roofs, and solar hot water heaters, the modern factory-built structures looked oddly out of place in the biblical landscape; but the settlement was a modern self-contained community, a concrete fortress with homes, schools, shops and stores that could defend itself against an attack by anti-tank rockets. In the parking lot, he watched the men of B'nai Ha'eretz climb into their cars. Wives and children waved good-bye from windows and balconies as the men headed off for their jobs in nearby Jerusalem and Tel Aviv.

Shlomo followed the road up to the settlement's gate, nodded to the sentry on duty and made his way through the parking lot to his car, a battered black Citroen *Deux Chevaux*. He bent down and looked under it. A man in his position could never be too careful about Arabs. Arab workmen were employed everywhere in *Yisroel*, even in West Bank settlements like B'nai Ha'eretz. He opened the Citroen's hood, poked around, peered under the seats, and stuck his nose behind the dash board, paying particular attention to the ignition switch. Nothing seemed out of the ordinary. He started the two cylinder engine and drove to the settlement's gate. He waved to the guard and bumped down the rocky hillside. Eventually the road came out at a two-lane highway. Here Shlomo turned east and drove through the hills.

Fifteen minutes later he came to Ramallah, a Christian Arab town a few kilometers north of Jerusalem. He drove into the *Manara*, the town center, from which six main streets radiated like petals on a flower. The graceful traffic circle had become an ugly spider web of road junctions after the Army occupied Ramallah, but practical Shlomo could have cared less. He turned off on Shari' Irsaal, Radio Boulevard, and pulled up at the front gate of Taggart Prison. A sentry waved him through. Shlomo parked his Citroen in the Shin Bet compound at the rear of the prison and jumped out, carrying his *tefilin* stowed in a small velvet bag. The early morning air at 900 meters above sea level was almost chilly but the sun hung like a bloated red disc on the horizon promising heat. Shlomo hurried toward a low doorway at the end of an alley between two high concrete block walls. Over the door was a small white sign with black Hebrew letters that said *Sherut ha'Bitachon ha'Klali*, General Security Services (GSS). He nodded to a clerk at the front desk and signed the duty roster. Then Shlomo strode purposefully down a narrow corridor that was flanked on both sides by office doors. On the right post of each door was a *mezuzah*, a tiny white painted case fastened head high, containing the same prayer as did the *tefilin* phylacteries. Shlomo stopped at his door, touched its *mezuzah* with two fingers.

Thou shalt love the Lord thy God with all thy heart, and with all thy soul, with all thy might. And these words which I command thee this day shall be upon thy heart; and thou shall teach them diligently to thy children, and shall talk of them when thou sit in thy house, and when thy walk by the way, and when thy lie down, and when thy rise. And thou shall bind them as a sign upon thy hand, and they shall be as frontlets between thy eyes. And thou shall write them on the doorposts of thy house and on thy gates.

I AM THE LORD THY GOD!

In the middle of the door was a small plate bearing the title of the occupant in Hebrew: Shlomo Arendt, HEAD OF ARAB AFFAIRS, GSS.

It was time to put on the mask again.

Three

Christina felt her husband's eyes follow her as she hung his brown tweed sport jacket in the big oak closet that rainy April morning in Ramallah. Yes, he still loved her. Their separation had been as hard on him as for her. She felt sure he would stay in Palestine now. Standing in front of the wavy, cracked mirrors on the old-fashioned wardrobe she hesitated, overcome with the memory of the night before. A slim, elegant, unhappy woman looked back. She had hoped last night would be different. She shook her jet black hair out over her shoulders and down her cloudy white night dress. If only he had not drunk so much *jot*. The anise-flavored arak brandy made his breath smell like licorice. He had taken her roughly with no more regard than a soldier takes a prostitute, leaving her aching, sore, unsatisfied and full of anger she dared not express. Not if she wanted him to stay with her and her daughters in Palestine.

Looking out the open window beside the wardrobe, she welcomed the spring rain. The dull drizzle would spread carpets of wild flowers over the dry Samarian hills and tinge them with a hint of green for a few brief weeks before the summer heat scorched the grass tawny brown. Christina remembered that this was the day she was to attend a funeral of one of her clients at the Palestinian refugee camp of Jalazoun, north of Ramallah. The camp was a conservative Muslim environment, so out of respect she reached in the wardrobe for an *abaya*, the traditional black gown with its white *esharb* the head shawl worn by many Palestinian women.

As she watched Richard's reflection in the mirror, he raised himself to sit with his back against the ornate brass head board. She couldn't help but notice how soft his body had become. It had to be the unhealthy American diet. When she married Richard he had been strong, well-built with a hawk-bridged nose, dark liquid eyes and neatly trimmed black beard. Now, his waist was padded with excess flesh and his once fine face seemed slightly pudgy. The self satisfied expression on his face made Christina turn to face him directly.

"What are you smiling at?" she said.

"You won't have to dress like that in America," he said.

Christina stiffened.

"But we are in Palestine, my darling," she said.

He got out of bed and took her hands. His eyes searched hers intently.

A cold shiver raised goose bumps on her skin at his touch.

He kissed her roughly, shoving his tongue deep into her mouth, his breath still foul with last night's *jot*.

"No!" she said and pushed him away.

"You know you like it like this." His voice was cool but the hand he put on her wrist hurt.

She slapped him hard.

An excited look came into Richard's eye as he felt his left cheek. His hand opened her night dress, ran up her leg, over her thick pubic hair and came to rest over her left breast.

Christina closed her eyes and prayed it would be over quickly.

He bent over, lifted her off her feet. Held her in his arms as though she were a sack of flour.

"Don't do this, Richard," she said. "You are killing our love."

He stopped her words with another fierce thrust of his tongue. When she did not respond to him, he threw her on the bed. She landed hard, her head banged against the ornate mahogany headboard. She writhed away, attempting to evade him but he pressed her back to the mattress. His hands rudely forced her legs apart and felt she was dry. He spat into his hand, and rubbed saliva into the soft folds of her flesh at the meeting place of her thighs. Coarse and crude like a peasant she thought. The man she'd taken in defiance of her family. The father of her children.

She uttered a sharp cry as he entered her. His full weight was on her, grinding her into the bed. She could barely breathe. She stared at the ceiling, feeling helpless, furious, humiliated. His buttocks moved rhythmically with what felt like a vengeance. To her surprise her body betrayed her.

He laughed and leaned down to grasp one of her stiffened nipples in his teeth.

"See? You love it when I take you like this."

He ran his tongue over the taunt nipple, and Christina moaned, running her hands up and down his back, urging him on. She felt the glowing unwelcome warmth in every part of her body, her feet, her stomach, her breasts.

He gave a hoarse shout and she felt his body stiffen in release.

Christina was despondent as Richard rolled off of her. A somber frightening wrongness pervaded her, a dark impenetrable mist, stealthily closing in on her. Richard had never treated her this way when they'd lived together in Palestine. America had not only made him soft but domineering and crude, as well.

Richard sat up in bed and lit a cigarette.

"We need to talk about our future," he said. "Georgetown University has made me an offer and I have accepted." He paused to give her a chance to let the implication sink in. "I am now a full Professor in the School of Foreign Studies. With tenure."

For a moment neither of them spoke or even breathed.

"I have also purchased a 4-bedroom house near Washington for us, and a new Mercedes automobile," he said.

She swallowed hard. As if he'd read her thoughts, he reached out more tenderly this time.

"The past two weeks have been pure enchantment, Christina but we cannot live apart like college students who only visit on holidays. We must never be parted again."

"What about the offer from Bir Zeit University?"

She was an adjunct professor at Bir Zeit but he would be Department Chairman.

She forced herself to look up into his eyes. She saw his familiar look of stubborn pride mixed with anger.

"You shouldn't have gone to the trouble," he said. "You know I can no longer abide living in Occupied Palestine," he said.

"But you just said you loved me, that we must never again be parted."

His face went pale.

"Christina, even your love can't make me live in this dreadful place."

She tore herself out his arms.

"What do you mean even my love isn't enough? I am your wife. You are father of two half-grown daughters. This dreadful place is your home."

His face was drawn and filled with misery.

"You are my home, not Palestine. You could have joined me in America. Yet you insist on living in this poisonous land, exposing yourself and our daughters to the humiliation, the curfews, the intrigues, the beatings and the killings."

The grandfather clock in the hallway began to chime the hour.

"The Jews will not drive me from my home and the home of our ancestors," Christina said.

"No one is trying to drive anyone out of anywhere in the U.S.," he said gently.

He tried to touch her chin but she jerked her head away, her eyes glinting up ominously.

"Americans are innocent and greedy. They have no culture," she said. "They are a shallow people. Not really a people at all. All anyone cares about in America is cars and TV sets."

"Perhaps that is true," he said. "But in America, there's no Occupation. No one cares whether you are a Palestinian or a Jew."

"Our children will lose their connection with who they are, with our family, with our land," she said.

Her family could trace their lineage two millennia to the earliest Christians. Her Mother's family, the Haddadeen, wealthy aristocrats, descendants of one of the eight clans who established Ramallah in the 16th century. They owned substantial properties in Jerusalem, Eilat, Jericho, and Nablus. Her father's people, the Rantisis, had clever minds and were school teachers, doctors and lawyers. The faiths of both her parents reflected an ecumenicalism of more than a hundred years of Western missionary work in Palestine. Her mother was a devout Anglican while her late father had been a Lutheran. There was an uncle who was a Quaker, an Aunt who was a Presbyterian and numerous Eastern Orthodox cousins.

"In America, our daughters wouldn't suffer the sacrifices they must make now," Richard said. "Living here is robbing them of their joy, their youth. We could have a safe comfortable life in America, Christina."

She thought of her father, a respected Palestinian lawyer, no longer living. She recalled his clear intelligent eyes, deep set in a lofty forehead, and the indomitable will behind them. "*Samdeen*, stand firm," she could hear him say. "Don't give in."

"Don't speak to me of humiliation, curfews, and intrigue, Richard. I'm an attorney, I defend Palestinians before the military courts of the Oppressors. I know what it is to feel shame and dishonor. And what it is to fight back. With honor and dignity. And sometimes, we win."

Richard sat down on the edge of the bed.

Without knowing why, she sat beside him and drew her knees up inside her night dress. She hugged them tightly while she listened to his rapid Arabic, her mind empty of thoughts. His barely heard words beat softly on her ears, like the rain outside their window, begging, pleading, and tender.

She paid no attention until he spoke the names of their daughters, Aminah and Muna. Then she gazed into his eyes and was annoyed to see them bright with tears. Finally he spoke.

"Let our daughters grow up in comfort and safety," he said. "If you must stay here in Palestine, let them go to America with me. They are becoming like you. Rigid, self-righteous, willing to sacrifice everything for your bloody cause."

A hot swift current of anger ran through her.

"Our children are safe here, Richard," she said firmly. "The *Intifada*, the uprising is over. Jews and Palestinians are weary of violence."

"I hope you are right," he said quietly. "But there are fanatics enough on both sides to keep the fires burning,".

She could taste triumph. He was retreating.

"If you go back, you go alone. No amount of comfort will repay our daughters for losing their birthright."

Instantly, she regretted her words.

Richard faced her. "I refuse to sacrifice my life for Palestine," he said. "You are free to do as you like, but if anything happens to our daughters it will be on your head. You are a chauvinist and a fool."

"And you are a survivor with no honor," she shouted.

After that there were no words.

Richard dressed, packed his suitcases in silence. Calmly he closed the door of the bedroom behind him. Christina tried to stand but her limbs were limp and unsteady. She stared out the window at the rain that fell softly on.

The full enormity of what she had done did not hit her until the sound of his footsteps down the living room steps died away. Richard would never return to Palestine. He as much as said the Occupation had turned her into a hardened fanatic, willing to risk everything for her cause. How he must despise her. She pounded the bed helplessly with both fists, consumed with rage at a world that forced everyone to choose a single side. When she felt calmer, she dressed and went downstairs to the living room.

The scent of jasmine from the vine growing over the front gate outside the windows filled the air. Her mother, Leilah, sat on the divan, her stout figure concealed in a black *abaya* trimmed with silver thread and worked on a piece of embroidery stretched tightly in a small hoop.

"The girls are outside telling Richard goodbye," said Leilah. "He's waiting for a taxi. You can still catch him if you hurry."

"We've already said our goodbyes, Maman."

Leilah's steel blue eyes peered shrewdly at Christina over her gold rim reading glasses.

"I thought Richard might stay this time," she said.

"I did too."

"Did you quarrel?"

Christina nodded. "Our usual fight. He refuses to live here. I refuse to live there."

"There is nothing more worthless than a coward," said Leilah.

"Richard's no coward. He has our children's interest at heart. We simply disagree."

Leilah shook her head. "If he really loved his children, he'd stay in Palestine. Those Goryebs are no better than rootless peasants and they blow with the wind. I will always wish you had made a more appropriate marriage."

"Please, my Mother. Not another word against my husband," said Christina.

A breeze billowed the lace curtains around the louvered inside shutters. One of the shutters batted against the wall and Christina went quickly to fasten it.

"How proud your father would be of you," Leilah said in a more conciliatory voice.

Christina watched Richard as he stood by the front gate with their daughters, Aminah and Muna. He bent down to kiss each girl on the cheek. Still smiling, he looked up and saw her.

The vision of his pale, tormented face would always afflict her, and the memory of his harshest words would echo in her heart in the hard months to come. If any harm came to their daughters it would be on her head.

Four

Twenty-six kilometers north of Jerusalem in the Samarian Hills, near Ramallah, a crowd of students straggled out the gate of Bir Zeit University past Hamad Taleb, who sold hot *sfeeha*, spicy sweet meat spread on flat round pastry, from the charcoal-fired oven of his yellow push cart. In his Ray-Ban sunglasses, a red and white checkered *kaffiyeh* draped around his head, a black nylon wind breaker, and scuffed white Nike jogging shoes, he was a familiar sight. He waved at Eyad Sallet, one of the students he knew well.

The young man's large brown eyes were troubled.

"Try my *sfeeha*, it will cheer you up," Hamad said and held out a pastry.

Eyad shook his head. He wore a hand knit blue sweater over a clean white shirt, and held his books stiffly under one arm.

"Yesterday *al-Yahud*, the Jews, confiscated my father's house," he said. "They claimed he did not have a building permit. That house had been there 40 years."

"It grieves me sorely to hear this, my brother" said Hamad.

"Now I must leave my studies and find work so my father can build a new home," said Eyad.

A quarter of a million *dunams* of West Bank land had been confiscated by Israel since the Oslo accords were signed in September 1993. Hamad pulled at his wispy beard, the ritual tugs of mourning.

"The two things a man cares about most are his woman's honor and his land," he said. "If a woman is violated it is the end of the world. If his land is confiscated it is the same thing."

He glowered when he saw the dark-haired woman in western dress, who approached them.

"Khantarish," he muttered. The word meant shit, literally the lowest grade of hashish.

Eyad turned. "Oh, good afternoon, Professor Goryeb," he said with a smile.

"Eyad, I am outraged to hear about your father's home," she said. "Promise me you will do nothing foolish," she said.

Hamad shook his head. "*Khantarish*," he muttered under his breath. "Collaborator.

Pointedly she ignored him. "We missed you in class, Eyad. Today we talked about Ghandi. With civil disobedience we can defeat the Jews."

Hamad leaned over his push cart and said calmly, "Civil disobedience works only in English speaking countries with English law, and English guilt."

Christina could no longer ignore his menace. She seemed unpleasantly surprised as though a jackal had spoken. "Violence only brings more violence," she said. "We've already lost three generations of young men fighting the Jews."

Eyad gave her a ghost of a smile. "I'm sorry," he said quietly. "I will be leaving Bir Zeit so I can help my family."

"You must not leave school now. Scholarships are available," she said. "I will help."

"There is nothing you can do. Can you give us back our home?"

"No," she said. "Not now. But with nonviolence we could regain our land."

Hamad watched Christina disappear down the street. "Your fine Professor *Khantarish* is either a fool or a traitor," he said contemptuously. Then he smiled. "But even now, she is helping us without realizing it."

"In what way?" said Eyad.

"It would be better if you did not know," Hamad said. He offered Eyad *sfeeha* again.

The young man took the pastry Hamad offered him and licked his dry lips. "When the Jews bulldozed our home, my father also said 'Do nothing. We are powerless," said Eyad. "But I must act or I will suffocate."

"Islam is your father and your brother," said Hamad gently.

Eyad's eyes were distant as he chewed his *sfeeha*. He handed his books to the sweet meat vendor. "Take these and sell them," he said.

"Come to the mosque," said Hamad.

* * *

The al-Umma mosque was a small hewn stone building in Ayna Nub, a Palestinian village in the hills near Ramallah. The group, a Muslim youth club, had no name or formal organization and few people outside the mosque knew it existed. The youth club's activities centered around the al-Umma mosque where its members did everything as a group, a band of brothers. The mosque was their second home, a sanctuary from the monotonous grinding poverty. Hamad selected each member carefully. He took only children from the poorest families with many mouths to feed, families where 16 people lived crammed into two rooms with no kitchen or bathroom. These youths like thousands of others were angry at their parents' tacit acceptance of Israeli military rule over the West Bank of the Jordan River that had been captured by Israel from Jordan in 1967. In 1987, the youth of the West Bank took to the streets with stones and sparked the *Intifada*, the mass Palestinian revolt. After two years, the *Intifada* subsided, but the fury remained available for someone like Hamad to shape it for Allah's purpose.

In the back room of the mosque, Hamad watched Eyad take his place with thirty young men and boys who squatted around Sheik Karaeen, the blind old man who sat cross legged on the dusty floor. Hamad, who sat at the Sheik's right hand, casually checked each face looking for danger signs, an averted face, or eyes that did not meet his.

Most returned Hamad's gaze with unwavering loyalty but the response of two young men gave him cause for concern. He whispered in the ear of the Sheik.

"Who among us has been harmed?" said Sheik Karaeen. His thin voice was barely audible but a dozen hands waved in the air as his sightless gaze traveled around the room.

Hamad pointed to the first young man whose look alarmed him.

"I was arrested twice and twice wounded as I threw stones at the soldiers," said young man proudly. "The second time I was struck in the leg by an exploding bullet."

"You were brave. And the first time?" said the Sheik.

"A policeman broke my collar bone with his club so I could no longer throw stones."

The Sheik nodded and Hamad motioned to the second young man.

29

"The day before my final examinations from high school The Jews detained me for three months for no reason. I was unable to graduate and my studies were delayed for another year. Now I sell vegetables and chicken feed in the market," he said.

Hamad smiled. They were reliving the days of the *Intifada*, the beatings and days of torture in the Shin Bet detention cells. They had been boys when the *Intifada*, broke out. They had seen more than their share of bloodshed and pain.

"*Imam*, tell us again what Heaven is like," pleaded the boy who had been shot in the legs.

They never tired of the Sheik's answer.

"A place of indescribable pleasures," whispered the old man. "There are rivers, trees and green fields everywhere, eternal happiness, all that we wish for but do not have."

"To kill oneself is the quickest way to Heaven," said the boy who sold chicken feed.

"My son, to die for a frivolous reason is a sin," said the Sheik. "But to kill yourself for Allah, is the death of a martyr."

"And the reward of a martyr?" said Eyad Sallet.

"It is written that such a man will receive 70 virgin brides," said the Sheik.

Hamad stared at Eyad with blazing eyes. "The soil of all Palestine is *Wakf,* Holy Muslim Property," he said. "The Zionist state is an affront to Allah."

Eyad hesitated and then stood up to declare himself.

"*Jihad,* the Holy War of Islam, is my personal obligation," he said.

"My son, you will be the next to enter Paradise," said the Sheik.

* * *

In a dusty cinder block garage in East Jerusalem, Eyad Sallet removed his white cotton shirt while Hamad, measured his chest with a tailor's cloth ruler. The cool early morning air raised goose bumps on the young man's smooth brown skin.

"Ninety-six centimeters," murmured Hamad. He measured and cut broad strips of gray duct tape, laying the strips out in six parallel rows on a wooden table with the adhesive side up. Then he carefully positioned sticks of dynamite on them.

"Keep them in place," he said.

When he was finished, Eyad bent over the table and embraced the belt. Hamad secured it around his chest with more duct tape, gathered the fuse wires into a neat bundle and connected them to an firing device he had made from the electronic flash unit from a 35mm camera. He taped the device to Eyad's waist.

The young man rebuttoned his shirt and slipped into a blue denim jacket. Then he walked outside and picked up a bicycle. He exchanged a final handshake with Hamad, pinned on a *yarmulke* to pass for a Jew and pedaled off into the pale dawn.

He rode slowly at first because it was difficult to see. He headed west down the Nablus Road through stands of tall cypress trees and umbrella pines. As it grew lighter, he gathered speed. He went past the heavy buttressed walls of St.George's Cathedral, then the U.S. Consulate at the intersection of Agron Road, and finally the Garden Tomb of Jesus before he reached the busiest part of East Jerusalem in front of the Damascus Gate of the Old City. Here lines of Palestinian buses disgorged passengers from villages and towns in the hills of the West Bank. Shop keepers were throwing up their metal shutters and setting out baskets of produce, hanging shanks of lamb, putting fresh fish on ice and arranging pickles, cheeses, poultry, and fresh-baked breads. The air was redolent with the clashing scents of exotic spices. Eyad paused before turning right on Sultan Suleyman Street. He pedaled on for about 500 meters, paralleling the crenellated stone walls of the Old City until he reached Jaffa Road where he turned north and crossed that invisible boundary called the Green Line. It marked the old border between Jordan and Israel. His long legs pumped steadily uphill for more than a kilometer. He rode past the tall buildings and a police station, weaving through the swarms of people at the shopping malls near the intersection of King George Road. He dodged shiny new European and Japanese automobiles as he went by Zion Square and the neighborhood of Mea Sherim, where groups of men dressed in black gabardine and wore black fedoras or heavy Russian fur caps and spoke a guttural Jewish tongue that was not Hebrew. At the top of the long hill, he reached his destination, Jerusalem's Central Bus Station. He dismounted and wheeled his bicycle toward the people swarming around the station.

Someone shouted his name. A jolt of panic coursed through him. An Israeli soldier in army fatigues with an M-16 slung over his shoulder motioned for him to come. Eyad did not know the soldier's name but the soldier knew his.

"Let me see your ID card."

Eyad realized this was the same soldier who had stopped him the previous day when he made a dry run. He looked fiercely at his goal, the masses of Jews standing by the lines of orange and white buses from the Egged bus cooperative. If he ran toward them, the soldier might shoot him down like a dog and his sacrifice would be in vain. However, the soldier might also check his card and let him pass. With anger mixed with sadness and frustration, the boy slipped his hand into his shirt, and felt for the two buttons on the top of the firing device. He pressed the first and heard a faint whine. It rose swiftly in pitch, then became inaudible. The device was now armed and ready with sufficient voltage stored in its capacitor to ignite the fulminate of mercury fuses. He handed the soldier his blue ID card and waited.

The soldier glanced at the card and said, "Come with me." He grasped the boy's elbow roughly.

Eyad thought of Paradise and smiled. He touched the second button and in an instant, both he and the soldier passed from existence into oblivion.

Five

The remains of a shredded human hand were thrown on the sidewalk in front of *Yediot Ahronot*, Israel's largest daily. Pressed in the dead fingers was a crumpled note that unfolded read: "There is no peace with the sons of monkeys and pigs. The Lions of Allah triumph over the enemies of God." DNA testing established that the hand belonged to Isaac Eban, the soldier who died in the explosion.

* * *

Gathered around a bonfire on a warm Mediterranean beach, a small group of American tourists relaxed over grilled lamb, salad, and wine after a hard day's labor on the *kibbutz*, Gan Geneva. The air carried the scent of orange blossoms from a grove that was laid out in neat rows behind the dunes. Bottle-green waves crunched softly on hard packed sand as twilight faded into starlight. A tall man in a white shirt rose, a mandolin cradled in his arms. He strummed a few cords and the crowd grew silent. Then he strummed the mandolin again and began to sing:

Come then, my love,my darling, come with me. The winter is over; the rains have stopped; in the countryside the flowers are in bloom. This is the time for singing; the sound of doves is heard in the fields. Figs are beginning to ripen. Come then, my love; my darling, come with me.

Although there was a broad smile on his lean sunburned face, his pale eyes hinted at a distant sadness.

The sweetness of the tall man's song spoke to Christina Goryeb of Palestine, her Palestine. Her nostrils drank in the faint odor of wild flowers, anemone, cyclamen, squill, and thistle, borne on the warm breeze that came from the Samarian hills to the east. The odors mingled deliciously with the smell of orange blossoms. A thrill ran down her spine and she shivered as if the breeze had suddenly cooled.

This land she loved passionately was like *'akkoub*, the delicacy Palestinian women prepared from the heads of milk thistles that grew in the dry hills. Women bloodied their hands for hours peeling away the thorny husks to extract the small thistle meats that men ate greedily in minutes. She had given Richard a rare treasure, her ancestral home in Palestine, a treasure that she devoted all her time and energy to safeguarding. Why couldn't he love this land the way this singer did? This Jew. His unbuttoned white shirt revealed a flat stomach and thick chest muscles covered with short dark hair.

Christina reclined on a beach blanket, her fine tanned legs revealed by her pale green cotton sundress, her eyes and thoughts hidden behind large black sunglasses. The dress, one of her favorites, had been purchased at Ibiza on a vacation with Richard several years before.

Normally, Christina would have turned down her friend, Naomi Litvin's invitation to visit the *kibbutz*, but Richard's departure had left her lonely, troubled, and in need of distractions. Christina had not told Naomi about her argument with Richard, but Naomi must have sensed something was wrong, for she seemed more solicitous than usual yet she did not ask about Richard. With affection, Christina watched Naomi spread lotion on her red, easily sun burnt arms. Naomi, with her guileless face and prematurely gray hair was one of the few Jewish lawyers who represented Palestinians before the military courts of the occupied West Bank. The *kibbutz*, Gan Geneva, was one of Naomi's clients. A longtime peace activist, Naomi worked to build bridges between Israelis and Palestinians. Although Christina approved of Naomi's bridge building activities in principle, she had no desire to socialize with the Oppressor. Naomi was her only Jewish friend, and although Naomi insisted there were many Jews like herself, Christina suspected Naomi was a rarity, an endangered species.

Two American college girls in wispy bikinis sat opposite Christina and Naomi. Christina watched and listened. Although her English was excellent, she was reluctant to converse with anyone she did not know well, and she did not wish to reveal that she was Palestinian. The girl in the iridescent pink bikini who had introduced herself as

Melissa, leaned forward, confidingly. Her brash yet naive manner reminded Christina of the dreadful American comedies that were often aired on Israeli television.

"Wow he's hot!" she said.

"Do you think he would talk to us?" said her friend Debbie, a tall, dark-haired girl in an equally iridescent turquoise bikini.

Naomi smiled indulgently. "I'll invite him over for you, when his song is over," she said. "He's a dear friend of mine."

When the song came to anend, the tall man put down his mandolin.

"That was written 30 centuries ago by King Solomon," he said. He pointed to a young man adjusting a small reflecting telescope mounted on a tripod. "And tonight, after the moon sets, Elohim will show you where stars are born."

Although he seemed to address the entire crowd, it felt to Christina as though he was speaking especially to her. This tall, pale-eyed Jew was a professional charmer, a skilled entertainer, she decided, and looked away.

Naomi beckoned to him to join them. Christina watched a wave crash into glints of foam as he approached.

"Chaim Asher," Naomi said, "I want you to meet my friends, Melissa and Debbie who've come all the way from Los Angeles, California."

"Shalom." Asher shook each girls' hand.

"And this is my friend Christina," said Naomi.

Christina removed her sunglasses to study his face. He had a face with strong bone structure, dominated by expressive hazel eyes above high cheek bones, finely formed nostrils and full lips. A small scar near one corner of his mouth gave him a look of vulnerability and distinction. Asher's handshake was warm and firm.

"How good of Naomi to bring you here," he said as if meeting Christina was a rare, unexpected and personal pleasure.

She felt her cheeks grow warm and realized with a shock that this was the first time since her marriage she had looked upon a man other than her husband with desire.

Asher next turned his attention to Melissa and Debbie. "Have you been enjoying your visit to *Yisroel*?"

"Not until we came to this *kibbutz*, Hiram. Can I call you Hiram?" said Melissa.

"Only if I may call you Marissa," he said.

Christina noticed with amusement that Chaim Asher's hazel eyes did not flicker to Melissa's pert breasts, even though she arched her back to toss her shoulder-length sun bleached hair out of her green eyes. Well, thought Christina, he was probably used to having young women throw themselves at him all the time.

"The name is C h a I m." Asher's voice was teasing and gentle.

"Ha-Ha-Hiram," said Melissa.

"No, say 'Chaim' as you clear your throat," he said.

Melissa tried again.

"Much better," said Asher. "So, how do you like our *kibbutz*?"

"It's a great place to visit," said Melissa. "My parents back in L.A. think of Israel as this mythical country. The Promised Land. Like it's the Land of Oz or something. The place where we all should yearn to be."

"Next year in Jerusalem, eh!" said Asher.

"To tell you the truth Chaim," said Melissa, "I'm a little disappointed. Everything is so small and old. You can't get a decent cheeseburger anywhere."

Christina felt a twinge of sympathy for Asher, and wondered what he would say to this young dissatisfied customer. She realized she was evaluating his demeanor the same way she studied her clients. Looking for the surface details to reveal the truth. A lawyer's curiosity. No a woman's curiosity.

He burst out laughing. His laughter had a pleasant resonance. Christina wanted to hear him laugh again.

"So you are homesick already?" he said.

"I guess," said Melissa.

He raised an eyebrow at her. "Well, this isn't America," he said briskly. "And why did you come, Debra?"

"To discover my Jewish roots," said Debbie. Unlike Melissa, she spoke without flippancy.

"And did you?" Asher asked.

Christina was suddenly curious as to what this dark haired girl would say.

"The synagogues here are all Orthodox. It's like the men are the more significant people before God, and women don't count for much," said Debbie. "In America we're mostly Conservative and Reform. Women are rabbis."

Asher smiled broadly. "Conservative and Reform is something dreamed up for America. In *Yisroel* you don't have to go to synagogue to be a Jew."

Debbie hesitated, as if trying to decide whether to say something or not.

Asher prompted her, "What else did you discover."

Debbie shrugged. "Everyone here drives like a maniac, they're nonchalant about red lights, and they're routinely rude."

"Well, we're a fierce people," said Asher.

This time, Christina thought, his laughter sounded almost mechanical.

"Crazy is more like it," said Melissa. "Everyone I see has a pistol in his coat pocket."

Naomi did not smile. "With deadly enemies all around, many Israelis carry weapons to be safe," she said. "But other Israelis like myself do not believe guns are the answer. Only a just peace with the Palestinians will bring *Yisroel* genuine security."

"There's no need to alarm our guests, Naomi," Asher said. "You are safer here than in your own most dangerous country," he added.

Beneath his smooth badinage, Christina heard an undertone of persistent distress.

Debbie broke the uncomfortable silence that settled over the group. "Melissa almost got us thrown in jail," she said. "It was her idea that we sneak into a women's barracks on an Army base in the middle of the night."

Melissa shrugged cheerfully. "Isn't the Army the soul of Israel?"

"Lucky for us, the guy from the American Embassy who got us out of jail suggested we visit a *kibbutz*," said Debbie. "And that's how we came to Gan Geneva."

"Those poor girls in the barracks, sleeping on straw mats on the floor, said Melissa. "Here, at least you have beds with clean sheets in separate rooms."

"Do you have your own room, Chaim?" said Debbioipe.

Asher shook his head. "A small one. Most single men and women and all the children sleep in dormitories."

"It's so beautiful how everyone shares everything at Gan Geneva," said Melissa.

Goodness, thought Christina, a grown man without a home of his own. Although there was a thin gold wedding band on his left hand, she sensed his marriage was dying or dead, that he remained chained to it out of duty and honor, and his unhappiness was as deep as her own.

Debbie turned to Naomi. "What do you think about the peace talks with the Palestinians?"

Although Christina and Naomi had spoken frankly in private, she was unprepared for Naomi's response to this American girl.

"There is no true peace process," said Naomi harshly. "The Palestinian people will continue to resist until they shake off the occupation."

"Boy, are you ever a pessimist," said Melissa. "I think Israel's bending over backwards for peace."

Christina felt the familiar hot spark of anger rise within her.

"Naomi's right," she heard herself say. "The agreements will merely turn Palestinian towns into prison camps."

Asher gave her a thoughtful look.

"What are you talking about, Christina?" said Melissa. "The Palestinians are getting the West Bank. I heard it on CNN."

Asher lifted a calming hand. "The Palestinian Authority will govern its own towns and villages. But, as Naomi and her friend say, there will continue to be friction."

As he reached to place more driftwood on the fire Christina stole a glance at his forearms. Thick and muscular, they were covered with fine golden brown hairs. What was more troubling to her was that several times she had found his hazel eyes focused on her, and how much she had enjoyed the sensation. She was not unaware of her beauty, but, surrounded by her family and involved in her work, she had never encouraged such attention, had found it an unnecessary distraction. The political debate reclaimed her thoughts.

"Hasn't Israel agreed to withdraw from the West Bank?" said Debbie.

Asher said, "We're leaving the major towns. For security reasons, though, we retain control of the roads, highways, strategic Palestinian villages and, of course, the settlements."

Naomi's voice trembled. "And the Army and the settlers will continue to remind Palestinians who is on top and the Palestinians will fight back, which will play into the hands of killers on both sides."

"What about that famous handshake two years ago in Washington?" said Debbie.

"Mere window dressing," said Naomi bitterly. "Gaza has $40 million of donor aid that it cannot spend because *Yisroel* will not allow raw materials like cement to be brought in. Traffic in the West Bank is halted at over fifty checkpoints. Vegetables going to market must be taken off at the border and reloaded on Israeli trucks."

Christina wondered if Asher would deny this or attempt to explain it away but he remained silent.

"So why are the Palestinians still being harassed. Why?" asked Debbie.

No one answered her.

If Deborah's and Melissa's reactions were shared by other young Jewish Americans, thought Christina, perhaps there was hope for her people after all. These brash American girls were no different from idealistic young people everywhere, no different than she and Richard had been. They too desired honesty and were impatient with illusions of their parents. Even Asher's hollow chuckle and his silences seemed to betray his realization of a dream turned nightmare.

"Did I say something wrong?" said Debbie.

Asher said carefully, "Our people are split between those who say they want peace with the Palestinians and those who want to rebuild our historic homeland."

"Historic homeland?" said Naomi mockingly. "Chaim, please! Jews haven't ruled Palestine for over 2,000 years. Our claim to it based on Genesis is ludicrous. If you believe Genesis, the Land of *Yisroel* extends from the Nile to the Euphrates rivers. So why should we stop with Palestine when God gave us Egypt, Jordan, Syria and Iraq as well?"

"Many in those countries are afraid they're next," said Asher.

His smile was gone, replaced by a look of grave abstraction.

"Chaim, I take it you are not in favor of kicking the Palestinians out?" said Debbie.

Christina did not wait to hear Asher's reply. Her heart racing, she picked up her beach bag and rose to her feet. She had to get away, disturbed by the impossible longings that this man stirred in her.

"Where are you going," said Naomi.

"I'll be back," Christina murmured. A walk on the beach would calm her. She had no intention of returning.

Briskly, she strode across the wet sand, staying just out of the wash of the waves. The Mediterranean was calm and silvery, bathed in moonlight. A line of low clouds circled the horizon. Away from the heat of the bonfire, the cool night air raised goose bumps on her bare arms. She walked on slowly, enjoying the feel of wet, hard sand on her bare feet.

Presently, she heard light, feminine laughter and then a low male voice. In the dim light she saw the two lovers embrace in the shadows beside a row of red and white striped beach cabanas. At her approach, they drew apart and slipped into one of the shelters, drawing the canvass curtains behind them. When she reached the end of the cabanas, she saw the yellow lights of the *kibbutz* village glowing thorough a gap in the sand dunes. Curious now, she entered the village. It consisted of white cottages in beside a sandy lane lined with eucalyptus trees, some large buildings including a dining hall, library and nursery. Farther along the lane she saw open-sided corrugated iron sheds where tractors and farm equipment were stored, a throbbing generator shed, and an old cemetery with slanting headstones. She looked back at the bonfire on the beach and heard the faint sound of singing. The beach party was still in full swing. The laughter of children caught her ear, and drew her to the nursery.

When she peered through the screen door she was astonished to see Asher.

He was surrounded by children, who listened as he read the *Little Engine That Could* in Hebrew. With great enthusiasm, he employed different voices and mannerisms for each of the engines, the Big Steam Engine, the Old Black Engine, and the Little Blue Engine. A little girl wearing pink pajamas sat on his knee, her face red and wet with tears. The child couldn't have been more than four years old, and her sobs rent Christina's heart. The child kept calling for her mother. From time to time, Asher interrupted his story to comfort her but without success. A six-year old boy in blue pajamas tried to pat the crying child on the shoulder but she only shrieked and pushed him away.

Christina opened the screen door.

"Let me hold her," she said. "May I help."

The children stared at the strange woman in their midst, everyone except the little girl on Asher's lap who rubbed her eyes with balled-up fists and continued to wail.

"This is our guest Christina," said Asher to the children. She is visiting with friends at our *kibbutz* tonight." Then he turned to her. "Your friends wondered where you disappeared to." Gently, he lifted the little girl into Christina's outstretched arms. "Her name is Sharona."

Christina pressed the little girl to her breast, murmuring words of reassurance. She felt the rigid limbs, the small heaving rib cage, the anxious drumming of a tiny heart. Gradually Sharona's sobbing subsided. Five minutes later she snuggled her head under Christina's chin.

The other children laughed as Asher puffed and hissed in imitation of the *Little Engine That Could*. "I think I can, I think I can, I think I can," he said. His arms pumped like pistons.

When he finished the book, one of the little girls handed him a well-worn copy of *Goodnight Moon*. By the time he reached the last page, all the children were asleep on their pillows.

Gently, Christina laid Sharona in the empty crib and drew the sheet over her. The little girl's eyes flickered as her thumb slid into her mouth.

Asher turned off the nursery lights as he left.

Christina followed him outside. The dry eucalyptus leaves rustled in the breeze as they walked toward the beach. She breathed in the sweet tangy air, redolent with odor of eucalyptus and citrus.

"You seem to be a man of many talents," said Christina after they passed out of the village.

He laughed softly, a genuine laugh this time.

"Sometimes I read to the children while the nursery attendants are at supper. Thank you for helping with Sharona."

"It was my pleasure," she said. "But the child obviously misses her mother. Do you really think it's wise to separate young children from their mothers?"

"Sharona's mother is dead," he said quietly. "An Arab tossed a grenade in her car."

Christina flinched. She wondered what this man would say if he knew she was one of them, an "Arab".

"Please don't misunderstand me," he said. "A *kibbutz* is a family. I slept in this same nursery when I was as young as Sharona. The whole *kibbutz* took care of me. Not just my mother and father, but everyone.

"What about Sharona's father?" she said.

"He left the *kibbutz*." There was a note of contempt in Asher's voice.

Like Richard, Christina thought. If anything happened to her in Palestine, Munah and Aminah had numerous, aunts, uncles and cousins to fall back on. Nothing in America would ever be able to replace such a family.

41

They had reached the orange grove. She looked up at the sky. The stars had grown stronger, gleaming bright pin pricks of light in the darkness above.

"Didn't you promise to show us the stars?" she said.

Asher laughed. "Elohim will do that. Tonight I'm off duty."

His face was little more than a moving shadow next to hers. Their hands touched briefly as they walked. She did not move away.

"Christina?" he said wonderingly. "You are a mystery woman. All I know about you is your name."

She laughed. The spell would be broken if she confessed she was a Palestinian. "Obviously, I'm not a Jew," she said. "I grew up in France. My parents were Algerians, *pied noire*." In her student days abroad, she had often been taken for French Algerian.

"But your Hebrew is excellent," he said.

She wet her lips, amazed at how easily the lies came. "I teach Middle Eastern Literature at the Sorbonne."

"So you are visiting *Yisroel*?"

"Just for a while. The summer classes begin again soon," she said. She hoped he would not to question her further.

A desert owl hooted in a nearby thorn bush. It launched itself into the air, flying so close she could hear the swish of feathers. The night breeze had grown cooler and Christina shivered under her sundress. Asher put his arm around her bare shoulders. She permitted herself to luxuriate in his warmth as though they were lovers or old friends. But they were strangers to each other, and this night she was a stranger even to herself.

He veered off the path with a rustle of small stones.

"Where are we going?" she said.

"It's a short cut to the beach." His eyes sparked in the moonlight.

She followed him to a deep depression between two sand dunes where salt grass grew thick and tall. Here the air was warmed by sand that slowly gave up its heat from the previous day's sun.

He lifted her hand to his lips, kissed it lightly.

"To the Queen of Sheba," he said.

"Ah, you are beautiful, my beloved, ah, you are beautiful! Your eyes are doves behind your veil... Your lips are like a scarlet strand; your mouth is lovely... Thy breasts are like twin fawns, the young of a gazelle that browse among the lilies...

His voice was gently ironic, acknowledgment of sweet complicity and rueful knowledge. The familiar lush imagery of Solomon's Song—such a potent cliché! Was it the promise of union between sacred and profane love, or merely the siren song of a randy old king with hundreds of wives?

"Is this where you bring all your conquests?" she said.

He didn't answer.

An uncomfortable silence fell between them.

She felt herself confronting the same thinly concealed sadness she'd sensed in him earlier on the beach. He was infuriating, like one of those cubist portraits where several aspects of the same face never resolved itself into a recognizable whole. She was angry at herself for letting him bring her to this spot. The whole day had been a mistake, this foray into enemy territory.

"I think I'd better get back to the others," she said.

"Please stay," he said. "And no, I do not routinely bring women here to ravish them. Where did you get such a dreadful opinion of Israeli men, Christina? Surely not from Naomi."

In his banter, she detected his desire to find out more about her.

"You mean it's not customary for married men to be flirtatious in Israel?"

"Not routinely," he said. "But you are still a mystery. From your remarks I know you are critical of Israel, like most of Naomi's friends, and then of course there is the matter of your husband. Does he let you wander off on strange beaches with strange men?"

She was caught off guard by that, then realized he had noticed her wedding ring.

She chose her words carefully, wanting neither to lie, nor to reveal any more to this compelling stranger. Wanting not to think of the difficulty that had become her marriage.

"We live apart," she said.

As she turned away he kissed her. The stubble of beard on his cheek prickled her neck with a delicious tingle. Her fingers gripped his shoulders and his hands moved inside her sundress. She let him feel the warm firmness of her breasts, gently tease her nipples, awakening lazy circles of taunting warmth. Yes, this was what she wanted.

"If you feel you must run away," he said. "I can't stop you."

But he knew she would stay.

Tenderly he unbuttoned her sundress and peeled away its green husk. Modestly she tried to cover herself with her hands while he paused to remove his clothes, and arranged their discarded apparel on the salt grass, spreading her sundress on top. The Ibiza dress. The second honeymoon with Richard dress.

He hovered above her supported on his arms. She waited for him to fall upon her as Richard would have, waited for the rough gestures of need and demand. Instead Asher's lips slowly made their way down her body, covering her breasts, her belly and then reaching her inner thighs, her inner lips. His knowing, appreciative tongue savored her as if she were a rare dish of *'akkoub*.

The heat mounted languidly to her pelvis, her armpits, at last enveloping her, completely drinking in her nakedness. She offered her throat to the stars. Now she was floating through an unmapped ocean. Her hands found his long, thick penis and guided it to her moist inner lips. He entered her with gentle strokes, then probed deeper until she let out a little gasp. Each hip thrust was unbelievably slow and intense. She clasped him tightly with her thighs.

"Chaim," she cried, no longer in control of herself, the pleasure almost too great to be born. A joy that had its own integrity, unlike any she had experienced. She was no longer floating. Her back arched and she cried out as she climaxed. A maddening fire inside her burst loose in an explosion of light, color, and fury. Her hips jerked helplessly with each new release.

In a moment, Chaim too uttered a deep cry.

For a long time they lay still together, naked, in each others arms in the moonlight.

Christina leaned over him on one elbow, her fingers moved idly thorough the soft, flat hairs on his chest.

"I must see you again," he said at last. His face seemed as ardent as a schoolboy's.

She willed herself to calmness, formality. "Chaim, I can't," she said. "I'm married. I have a family."

He kissed her lightly on the lips.

"May I call or write?"

"Please don't Chaim," she said.

Now the spell was broken. Asher watched her while she put her clothes back on and then he too dressed.

He smiled faintly. "The party will be ending soon, and Naomi will be looking for you," he said. He showed her the direction of the bonfire.

They returned their separate ways to the beach party. Asher was there when Christina arrived. The fire had died to glowing embers. Everyone was clustered around the telescope, heads uplifted to the sky.

"On a clear night, you can see Andromeda with your naked eye," said Elohim. He pointed to a constellation in the East.

"Where?" said Naomi.

Asher's arm pointed. "Look up from the stars that form that big box in the sky—there. The fuzzy patch of light is the galaxy. Look sideways, not directly."

"I still can't see it," said Melissa.

Before Asher could answer her, a black BMW 735i roared up and stopped on the sand about thirty feet away.

Christina raised a hand against the glare of its headlights.

"Asher," called a woman's voice imperiously.

It was a beautiful hard face framed by thick dark hair that leaned out the window of the BMW. The woman wore no make up other than dark red lipstick. She noticed Christina and looked directly at her, through her with the force of a laser beam to the back of her skull. Then she gave Asher a knowing smile.

"Get in, you handsome bastard," she said. "You look like you just got laid."

The door closed and the BMW backed away rapidly with a whine of gears.

"How could a man like that have such a ball-buster of a girl friend?" said Melissa.

"He didn't look all that happy to see her," said Debbie. "Besides, she may not be his girl friend."

"I'd really like to get to know him better," said Melissa.

"Go for it," Debbie said. "We're going to be here a few more days."

Christina did not see Chaim Asher again that evening, to her intense relief and vast regret. Later when she asked a member of Gan Geneva where he'd gone, she received a wary look.

"Chaim Asher was called away on a family matter," she was told.

Six

The tall young man did not seem to know he was being followed. He slipped through the crowd in Ramallah's *souk*, a thin, rangy figure, head cloaked in a checkered *kaffiyeh*, walking fast, intent on his goal. Stalls of silversmiths, craft shops, pastries, mosaic-tile floored barber shops, shoe stores, fruit and vegetable stands lined the narrow street. There were bolts of cloth, square tins of kerosene, plastic buckets, open sacks of curry, cocoa, sesame, pepper and all kinds of beans. Shop vendors in the *souk* hawked their wares at the top of their lungs. Every shop had a loud radio tuned to Radio Damascus. Without warning he turned and looked around. Almost hidden in the tall young man's hand was a tiny black transistor radio.

Ten meters behind, Ya'akov Kallenborg, an undercover Shin Bet security officer, paused nonchalantly at a vegetable stand to finger a tomato. He wore a green striped *jalabiyya*, a flowing Palestinian robe and carried a heavy staff. He smoked a hand-rolled cigarette of green tobacco. A wrist microphone in his sleeve was connected to a two-way radio concealed under his *jalabiyya*. Turning his face away, he muttered into his sleeve, "Our man smells a tail. He's got to be dirty."

He spoke to Itzak Naveh, the officer in charge of his Shin Bet undercover team.

"Stay with him, until Dopkin takes over," said Naveh in a bored voice.

Kallenborg could hear Naveh by means an ear plug that was concealed in the black *kaffiyeh* that he wore around his head secured by a two black thongs. Naveh himself was perched in a church steeple 100 meters away on the crest of a hill watching through powerful Nikon binoculars. A multi-channel radio that permitted Naveh to speak to any member of the undercover team was concealed in his pale cream suit. He posed as a tourist for the benefit of anyone who might come up to the belfry. On his head was a ridiculous blue cloth rain hat with a wrinkled brim. A copy of *The Lonely Planet Guide to Israel* stuck halfway out of his right coat pocket. From his vantage point, he could see down into every alley, courtyard and street in the *souk*.

Their suspect did not go far. He turned into the Jerash Hotel just off King Abdullah Street. Kallenborg walked past the entrance to the hotel, glanced in, and saw his quarry enter a phone booth.

"He's making a phone call," said Kallenborg over the radio.

"Fucking wonderful," said Naveh.

Kallenborg crossed the street and came back on the other side. If the Palestinian came out immediately, Kallenborg would loiter in the background, where he'd be less likely to be noticed. He passed Dopkin on the corner reading a folded copy of the Arabic daily *al-Kuds*. Kallenborg stopped in front of a carpet shop and pretended to admire the colorful rugs that hung for display on ropes. After a few minutes he began to grow anxious. Sooner or later the shopkeeper would come out and try to sell him a rug, and neither he nor Dopkin could speak Arabic well enough to pass convincingly as Palestinians. Although the streets of Ramallah were within sight of the city limits of Jerusalem to the south and patrolled by the Israeli army, a mob could surround the undercover team and hack them to pieces before help could arrive.

Suddenly Kallenborg saw a twelve year old boy dart in the door of the hotel. The boy wore a checkered *kaffiyeh*, a castoff field jacket, and army trousers that hung on his body like a tent. Dirty brown toes stuck out of his tire-tread sandals. He emerged seconds later with a black transistor radio in one hand. Kallenborg suspected this was the same radio as the one their quarry had carried.

Naveh saw the boy too. "Kallenborg, you take the boy," he ordered quickly. "Dopkin, check out that Arab in the hotel."

The boy rapidly ascended a flight of stone steps set in a narrow hillside alley. Kallenborg wheezed after him, perspiring heavily under his disguise. At the top of the stairs he found himself in an appalling slum, surrounded by a dense mass of tottering stone houses so old that they seemed ready to collapse on his head. Children swarmed everywhere in filth choked alleys, relieving themselves where they pleased.

Kallenborg did not look back; a bold demeanor was his best defense in a place like this. He spotted the small figure in the army jacket through a dark passage ahead, and walked fearlessly through the noisy, narrow, smoke-filled lanes. A dog barked behind a locked door and started another yapping. Somewhere a baby cried; whispers, groans and laughter came to him out of the shadows. He passed seedy outdoor cafes where bearded Arabs with sharp eyes sipped strong coffee and puffed on gurgling water pipes. These loiterers and vagrants no doubt saw his heavy staff and knew it could shatter bone. He also carried a silenced 9mm Beretta in a shoulder holster under his robe. From stinking street to stinking street he pursued the boy.

"Kallenborg, where are you?" said Naveh at last over the radio.

Kallenborg saw a faded street sign on the corner of a building with English and Arabic lettering, an artifact of the long vanished British Mandate. When he looked again he saw the boy disappear into one of the buildings that lined the street.

"Al-Fajr Street," Kallenborg said reading the English name. "The boy went into a house."

"Describe the house," said Naveh.

Kallenborg licked his lips. There were no address numbers on any of the buildings.

"Yellow stone, four windows with bars, and a roof that extends over the sidewalk in front," he said.

"Anything else?" said Naveh.

"A neon sign."

"Why didn't you say so?"

"It's in Arabic."

"So?"

Kallenborg knew only phrases of spoken Arabic; the glowing blue script was unintelligible to him.

"Grab the boy," said Naveh. "He's got something we want. I'm coming with the backup team."

Kallenborg drew his pistol. As he started to kick down the door, he heard the wail of a siren. It gave him the courage he needed.

Inside, Kallenborg found a bespectacled young Palestinian man wearing an sweater and slacks who sat at a desk behind an old Adler typewriter and a untidy stack of manila legal folders. When he saw Kallenborg, he jumped up in astonishment. Kallenborg noticed the

Palestinian was holding the tiny radio. He heard the sound of running feet and looked down the short hallway just in time to see the boy in the army jacket vanish through an open door into a back alley.

When his eyes returned to the Palestinian the radio was gone.

This young man was taller and heavier. He eyed Kallenborg's pistol and slowly raised his hands.

"Why are you doing this? What do you want," the Palestinian said in Arabic. The alarm in his soft brown eyes deepened.

Kallenborg gave him a feral smile as he stepped forward and grasped the Palestinian's lapels in both hands.

"That little fart was a runner for the Lions of Allah," he growled. "You're going to tell me why he come here."

"What boy?" said the Palestinian.

Kallenborg drew back his fist and hit the young man hard in his solar plexus. He doubled over as the breath rattled out of him. With the steel capped toe of his shoe Kallenborg kicked viciously at the young man's left shin. The bone snapped with a dry crack and he collapsed in a heap on the floor. Kallenborg bound the young man's wrists with thin plastic handcuffs. They had little razor blades in place of the usual ratchet mechanism so that they could be drawn up very tight, cutting off the wearer's circulation causing extreme pain.

"What's going on?" said Naveh over the radio.

Kallenborg stepped over the injured man, and sat down in his chair at the desk. The first drawer was locked but his eyes lit up when he opened the second. He took out the radio and examined it carefully. It was a smooth black plastic rectangle about 20 centimeters by 40 centimeters in size with rounded edges and corners. The controls were utter simplicity: an AM/FM scale in white numerals on the front beside the familiar General Electric logo, two tiny knurled plastic wheels on the right side for volume and tuning, a jack for an earphone but no speaker. Molded black letters on the back of the case stated the radio was a GE model 7-1627A, made in Malaysia.

"Kallenborg, are you all right?" said Naveh.

Kallenborg fumbled with the cover to the battery compartment. Behind three AAA batteries he found a slip of paper covered with tiny groups of numbers. He glanced at the Palestinian. The injured man met his eyes with horror. He knew what the paper was all right, thought Kallenborg with grim satisfaction. He started to put the paper in his pocket and then changed his mind. "Take these numbers down," Kallenborg said into the wrist microphone.

"Wait a minute—what are they?" said Naveh.

"It's a code I found in the radio," said Kallenborg.

"Read them to me."

Kallenborg read the number groups to Naveh slowly and again a second time to be sure he got them right.

"What happened to the boy?" said Naveh.

"I have captured another suspect."

"Sit tight. We'll be there in five minutes."

The siren was closer now but he had time to accomplish a little more. Kallenborg walked around the office. There was one large and airy room, with white-painted walls and two smaller ones, a kitchen and a lavatory. After a quick survey, he started searching in earnest for dynamite, fuses, and timing devices. The lavatory and kitchen were bare. In the larger room, Kallenborg rapidly went through the two desks and row of grey metal filing cabinets tossing papers, books and files in every direction. He opened the glass fronted bookcases that lined the walls and glanced thorough several tan leather bound volumes. They were in three languages, Turkish, English, and the newest, Hebrew. The ones in English were entitled *Regulations of His Majesty's Government In Palestine*. He tipped the bookcases over and they fell with loud crashes of breaking glass.

Kallenborg frowned at the framed diplomas and certificates that hung on the wall. Behind the larger of the two desks he found a collection of stylish women's shoes. He retrieved a piece of tissue from the waste paper basket. It bore the faint red imprint of a woman's lipstick. The window sills were adorned with potted geraniums and in the far corner half hidden by a changing screen hung an *abaya*, the black gown with its white *esharb* the head shawl worn by Palestinian women.

A lawyer's office, and from the looks of it, a woman lawyer. Men in predominantly Muslim Palestine rarely accepted the council of women, reflected Kallenborg. Surely this lawyer was a whore, some sort of Arab witch, who inspired young men to blow themselves up for the sake of Allah.

He rapidly reviewed his progress through the three rooms. The place was clean. He had done all he could here.

Kallenborg squatted beside the injured man on the floor.

"Give me your identity card," he said.

The young man stared up at him blankly as if he were speaking in a foreign language.

"You are required to carry your ID at all times," Kallenborg said. He turned the Palestinian over roughly and searched his pockets, causing him to twist in agony. He found the card he was looking for in a back pocket.

"Abu Awad," said Kallenborg reading the name on the blue colored ID card. "Who are you?"

There was a squeal of brakes outside as an Israeli jeep pulled up. Two border policeman in full battle dress armed with M-16s burst through the door followed by Naveh.

"Good work Kallenborg," said Naveh. "I'll take over."

Abu Awad glared at him defiantly.

Kallenborg rested his shoe lightly on Awad's broken shin. "I once knew a man named Gregor who won't cooperate until we stuck a wire up his ass. He glowed like a lamp when we plugged him into the wall," he said.

"Take it easy Kallenborg," said Naveh. "Did you do this? What a mess!" he said looking around. His eyes traveled to the framed diplomas and certificates on the wall. "Do you know whose office you just tore up?"

Kallenborg snorted. "Arabs are Arabs. Does it matter?"

"It may. This office belongs to Christina Goryeb. Her husband is an American citizen, an advisor to the American government."

Kallenborg shrugged. "So what?" he said. He thrust the message from the radio under Naveh's nose.

Naveh spread his hands in a gesture of resignation. "We've suspected Mrs. Goryeb for a long time, but our orders are to grab her only when her drawers are really down," he said.

"Isn't this enough?"

Naveh took the message from Kallenborg and smiled. "Get out of here you dumb Litvak," he said.

"What about him?" Kallenborg pointed at Abu Awad.

"Take him to Taggart Prison for questioning," said Naveh.

* * *

Later that morning, Christina Goryeb carrying her brief case and wearing her brown courtroom suit, pushed open the door of her office to discover overturned furniture and broken glass. Her law books and case files were strewn across the floor. All thoughts of the guilty pleasure she had shared with the handsome Israeli she knew only as Chaim left her mind. What remained was anger and a sense of shame. She had lain in the sand with one of the hated Oppressors. She had betrayed her beloved homeland for desire. Hands shaking, she carefully placed the briefcase on the desk and surveyed the damage. Later, when she was calm, she called Naomi Litvin.

Seven

It was an dusty old prison in Ramallah, built by a Major John Taggart of the Royal Engineers during the British Mandate as one of a series of fortified police stations that served as strong points during the Israeli war for independence. Israeli army personnel assigned to Taggart Prison on Irsaal Boulevard steered clear of the Shin Bet compound at its rear, on general principles, for no one wished to know what went on there. Naveh led the way to the interrogation cell, a small cubicle with white-washed walls. He switched on the lights. Through a barred window set in the door he looked in at Abu Awad who was strapped to a small chair in the center of the cell. Beside the chair was a long wooden table with more leather straps. Abu Awad still wore the slacks and sweater he had been arrested in. His head was covered with a jute sack soaked with urine. His legs were immobilized by heavy iron shackles.

Naveh turned to Kallenborg. "What have you done so far?" he said.

"The usual—the piss soaked hood, no lights, no food or water since we brought him in," Kallenborg said. "Do you want me to soften him up some more?"

Naveh shook his head. He opened the cell door and they went in.He jerked the stinking sack off Abu Awad's head and tossed it in a bucket next to the table.

Abu Awad flinched as the light struck his eyes. His face was pale and drawn but his air of self-possession infuriated Kallenborg. Most Arabs he questioned broke down completely after a good beating and hours of sitting in total darkness under the hood, but this one could prove to be more difficult.

"I demand medical attention," said Abu Awad.

"One of our doctors is on the way," said Naveh. "Unfortunately, he has been delayed."

Abu Awad eyed the rubber hose truncheons and whips made of electric cable that Kallenborg fingered on the wall.

"There's an excellent Palestinian hospital here in Ramallah. Take me there," said Abu Awad.

Naveh smiled. "No one cares what happens to terrorists, Awad. Besides we're not interested in you. It's your employer we want."

Awad returned his smile calmly. "Then you have made a mistake," he said. "Mrs. Goryeb is innocent."

"What does she do?"

"She is a lawyer," said Awad.

"How long have you worked for her."

"Two years."

"What are your duties?

"I'm her part-time clerk in the morning. I type, file, and prepare legal documents for her. I also run errands, and help locate and interview witnesses."

"What do you do the rest of the day?"

"I study law at Bir Zeit University."

Naveh nodded thoughtfully. "Such perfect cover for a busy terrorist, wouldn't you agree, Kallenborg?" He took a black transistor radio from his pocket and held it up for Awad to see. "Please explain how this came into your possession," he said.

Abu Awad shrugged. "A youth from the street ran into the office. He dropped the radio and ran out."

"And you picked it up," said Naveh.

"I couldn't leave it lying on the floor. I assumed the boy was a thief so I put the radio away. If the rightful owner came to claim it, I would give it to him."

Naveh sighed and dangled the coded message from the radio in front of Abu Awad's eyes.

"It is the truth, nevertheless," said the young man, averting his eyes.

"The boy could have chosen any door on Al-Fajr Street but he came to your door," said Naveh.

"Our door was open."

"How convenient." Naveh stared at Abu Awad for a moment, his lips pressed together in a hard line. Then he nodded at Kallenborg.

Together they hustled Abu Awad out of the chair and threw him face down on the table securing his hands and legs with leather straps.

As Kallenborg grabbed his injured leg, Abu Awad cried out. "If you harm me in any way, I'll show my injuries to the world. You will look like the Gestapo to your American keepers."

"No one cares about Arabs," Kallenborg said. He selected a rubber hose truncheon from the wall. Then he stuffed a dirty rag into Abu Awad's mouth. "It will keep you from biting off your own tongue," he said.

His first blow knocked all the breath out of the young man who writhed on the table trying to escape the savage onslaught. Straps held him in place. Kallenborg beat his back and shoulders for several minutes until at last Abu Awad's head slumped sideways.

"He's fainted," said Naveh. He lit a Marlboro cigarette and pulled the rag out of Awad's mouth.

Kallenborg threw a bucket of cold water over the unconscious young man. Abu Awad groaned as Naveh jerked his head up by the hair and peered into his dazed eyes.

"Who does Mrs. Goryeb work for? Tell me, and this will stop," said Naveh.

"No one but herself. She is innocent," gasped Awad.

Naveh spat.

"This is what innocent people look like, you filth." He thrust a photograph in front of Abu Awad's face. Kallenborg caught a glimpse of a charred body sitting upright in a burned out car. The neck was arched, the jaw opened in a silent scream, a blackened tongue protruded through cracked teeth. Skeletal fingers still gripped the half-melted steering wheel.

"She was the mother of two children until one of your friends threw a phosphorus grenade in her car."

Abu Awad closed his eyes and his expression remained impassive. "Hundreds of Palestinian mothers and children have been murdered by your soldiers too," he said.

"If your Mrs. Goryeb is innocent, why does she permit her office to be used as a letter drop for terrorists?" said Naveh. "Is she working for Hamas? Is it Islamic Jihad? Hizbollah? Or is it the Lions of Allah?" He let Abu Awad's head drop. "The next time you piss, you *mamzer*, you'll piss blood."

This time Kallenborg aimed his truncheon at the area over the young man's kidneys.

When Abu Awad passed out, Naveh said, "We'll try again later."

"We can beat him all day and he won't talk," said Kallenborg. "Let me try my way."

"Your methods are excessive."

"They always work."

Kallenborg's feral grin irritated Naveh.

"You make me sick," he said. "There's a big difference between you and me, Kallenborg. I do this work to save Jewish lives. You enjoy it."

Kallenborg shrugged.

"Why are Jewish lives more precious than others? We all have our excuses, eh Naveh? If you hated torture that much you could find another job."

* * *

The prison cafeteria where Kallenborg ate supper was a cramped, windowless room brightly lit and filled with noisy people. The place smelled of overcooked cabbage, cheap insecticide, and sweat. A smiling woman wearing army fatigues and thick round spectacles walked toward him carrying a metal tray piled with food. It was one of Shlomo Arendt's secretaries, the one they called "Delilah". She was corpulent with large breasts and broad hips. A prominent, hairy mole grew on the side of her fleshy nose. She was a *yenta*, a busy body who spied on Shlomo's subordinates and filled his ear with tidbits of gossip.

"Move over, Ya'akov," she said. "Every seat is taken."

Kallenborg detested her but there was no way to escape now. She smiled her thanks. Delilah's ample thigh and side of her breast pressed against him with motherly affection.

"Shlomo is so pleased with Naveh," she said through a mouthful of *kishke*. "Did he single handedly arrest all of the Lions of Allah?"

"Something like that," mumbled Kallenborg.

Inwardly Kallenborg seethed. Naveh had stolen all the credit for the day's work as he usually did. If he, Kallenborg, was going to get ahead in this organization he had to get around Naveh and have direct access to Shlomo.

"Come on," said Delilah encouragingly. "You can tell me what really happened."

He looked around quickly. An Arab busboy in a greasy apron cleaned a steam table on the counter a short distance away. "Well, technically, I shouldn't, but since you'll read Naveh's report anyway, you should know the truth." In a low voice Kallenborg gave her a brief account of how he had arrested Abu Awad that morning.

"So you were the one who grabbed this Arab, not Naveh," said Delilah. Her sweaty cheek pressed close to Kallenborg's ear. "Don't trust Naveh. He's soft, not practical enough. If you can make the Arab talk, go straight to Shlomo. You'll really help the organization and yourself. That's what I'd do, if I were you."

After supper Kallenborg stopped by the prison's electrical shop and asked to be supplied with three meters of electric cable, an Israeli three-prong plug and a rheostat. The duty clerk, a young woman in army fatigues, looked surprised.

"What do you need it for?" she said.

"To make an honest man," said Kallenborg.

She gave him a curious look but complied with his request.

He returned to Abu Awad's cell and stuffed a gag in his mouth. As Awad sat helpless, strapped in his chair, Kallenborg placed his feet in a bucket of water and completed his preparations.

"Now listen carefully," he said. "The wire I stuck up your ass is part of an electrical circuit. Ordinarily it carries a maximum load of 220 volts, 50 cycles. However, this device permits me to vary the flow of current in the wire. Let me demonstrate, then we'll discuss your Mrs. Goryeb."

Kallenborg's fingers turned the dial of the rheostat. Abu Awad gave a muffled scream and slumped in the chair.

Eight

The following morning, three men met in the Prime Minister's office in the Knesset Building. Shlomo Arendt stood stiffly in front of the Prime Minister's desk. Major General Mekor Ivry, the Director of the Mossad, sat in an arm chair on the Prime Minister's right. Shlomo's boss, the Director of the Shin Bet, was conspicuously absent. The Prime Minister, his back to Shlomo, smoked a Lucky Strike cigarette as he stared out the window. When he finally did speak, he did not turn around.

"This is bad for all of us," he said and shook his head. "Very bad. An Arab dies in detention while we're talking peace with Arafat."

Shlomo stared at the old man with ill-concealed contempt. As far as he was concerned, the Prime Minister and his Labor Party were weak apologists who were busy giving Samaria and Judea back to the Arabs—just as Shlomo's father had said they would after the 1967 War. Never mind that the Prime Minister was a hero of the 1948 and 1967 wars, a retired major general who had been Prime Minister once before and who now served as his own Defense Minister.

"There were other Arabs in his cell," Shlomo lied. "We're interrogating them now to find out who killed him."

The Prime Minister he wheeled around angrily. "Just what I need, more dead prisoners on my hands. May I remind you only moderate pressure can be used when interrogating prisoners, and special permission must be obtained from my Committee."

"What do you want us to do with Mrs. Goryeb?" said Shlomo.

"Just keep an eye on her," said the Prime Minister.

"These are exceptional circumstances. I request permission to interrogate Mrs. Goryeb, without limitations," said Shlomo.

He handed the Prime Minister a typed memorandum which he read through quickly. He reached for his pen and scrawled his initials after the "disapproved" line and added the date.

"Fool," he growled as he gave Shlomo the paper. "Your own request tells me this is a woman who's seen as a moderate. And her husband lives in America. I will agree to this only when we have irrefutable proof she is a terrorist. Then, no one will care what happens to her."

His icy blue eyes bored into Shlomo.

"And if this Goryeb turns out to be a terrorist, your intellectual giants have alerted her. If she's dirty she'll be even more careful. That will make her more dangerous. I'm turning this entire matter over to Mike," said the Prime Minister. "You'll assist him."

Mekor looked triumphant.

"The Mossad has no experience with domestic security. This case belongs to the Shin Bet," said Shlomo. "There are those in the Knesset who will oppose your decision."

The Prime Minister's eyes glittered. "I give the orders, Shlomo. You follow them. I've shot men who didn't."

He turned on his heel. "One more thing—Shlomo, make sure my denial is fastened in the front of Goryeb's dossier where none of your idiots can miss it."

"Can we question her?" said Mekor.

"Use a light touch, Mike. If this Goryeb dies without my permission I'll have your balls for *sheshkabob*. Put a good man on this job, someone with a light touch and a brain," he added.

Nine

The two men sat at a plywood table in Taggart Prison wearing telephone operator's headsets. Twenty young Israeli women in fatigues sat quietly with expressionless faces at adjoining tables that lined the white washed cinder block walls of the *shicklut*, a military intelligence listening post. They wore headsets too, and each was equipped with a computer terminal. These women were *marats*, the listeners who monitored phone conversations in the occupied West Bank.

"I like to think of myself as a patient hunter," said Kallenborg to his newest colleague, Chaim Asher of the Mossad.

"Well if you are so good at your job why haven't you arrested the Lions of Allah?" snapped Asher.

Chaim Asher, the Mossad *katsa*, or case officer, assigned to find the Lions of Allah had met Kallenborg only an hour before, and already detested the man. Kallenborg spoke several languages but poorly. Asher suspected Kallenborg had no natural aptitude for intelligence work but possessed a sadistic streak. The man did not look frightening with his slight frame and wire rimmed glasses. His skin was tanned a mottled reddish brown, the tan of a thin-skinned blond man who lives out in the desert sun and his initial manner was diffident, as if unsure that he had the right to take up anyone's time. His close-set watery blue eyes moved around the room. On his wrist was a 23 *kamhr* Poljot, Russia's answer to the Rolex. In his hand was a well worn paperback.

"Shlomo told me you were pulled off the Eitan case," said Kallenborg. "So tell me, who killed our good Judge?"

Asher did not rise to the bait. "The Lions of Allah are a lot more important right now than the Eitan case. A soldier was blown to bits at the bus station in the heart of Jerusalem. How long have you been working for Shlomo Arendt?"

Kallenborg shrugged. "Two years."

Asher's gaze returned to the paperback book in Kallenborg's hand. "What are you reading?"

Kallenborg started to turn the book over so Asher could not see its title but Asher snatched it out of his hands.

The Hasamba stories were a popular children's series. "*Hasamba Fights Black September?*" Asher read the blurb on the front cover. "The Hasamba kids help the Army fight terrorists," he chuckled. "Those Hasamba kids are so smart and clever the PLO never has a chance."

"I'm reading it to improve my Hebrew," said Kallenborg stiffly.

"I haven't read this is one yet. Do you like it so far?" Asher rifled through the paperback.

"It's a bit juvenile for my tastes."

"Really?" Asher smiled. "But they're great stuff! You should try the older ones. Hasamba takes on the British, then the Nazis and the Arabs. I read every one in the series when I was a boy."

"Well, maybe we should call in the Hasamba to help us on this case," said Kallenborg in an unnecessarily loud voice.

The *marats* all tittered.

So that was it, thought Asher. Kallenborg was playing to the young women in the *shicklut*. Well, two could play this game.

"Your Hebrew could use some improvement, all right," said Asher. "Where did you say you came from?"

"Lithuania."

"I asked for an experienced agent and Shlomo palms off a Litvak immigrant on me."

"I'm a Jew," said Kallenborg defensively.

"If you say so. What did you do in Lithuania, Mr. Ya'akov Kallenborg?"

"I was a detective."

Asher's cigarette stopped mid-way to his lips.

"So, who was your employer?"

Let's see if the bastard admits it, he thought.

"The Federal Security Service, USSR," Kallenborg said quietly.

"Ah yes, the Second Chief Directorate of the former KGB. Tell me, what were your job duties?"

A note of pride crept into Kallenborg's voice. "I directed 35 Special Agents, organized and conducted investigations for state companies, supervised and inspected temporary detention facilities," he said.

"I'm surprised they let people like you in the country," said Asher.

"Every Jew has the right to live in *Yisroel*," said Kallenborg.

"But a KGB officer, a Jew?"

"My mother was Jewish," said Kallenborg. "Besides Shlomo thinks I have talents," he said.

"Oh, for the Shin Bet, I'm sure you do," said Asher.

"But I'm not good enough for the Mossad, eh?"

"You may be a Jew but how do we know you're not a Russian mole?"

"So I'll never be trusted, is that it?" said Kallenborg.

"You don't know the difference between police work and gathering intelligence and you don't know much about *Yisroel*," said Asher.

Kallenborg curled his lips. "Enlighten me then, oh komrade, about the proper duties of the Shin Bet and the Mossad."

"The Shin Bet is responsible for domestic security," said Asher. "The Mossad carries out special operations."

This was an oversimplification; as in other countries, the jurisdiction of Israel's various intelligence services was left deliberately unclear. In addition to the Shin Bet and the Mossad, there was Aman, the largest service that handled military intelligence, as well as the Sayret Matcal for commando raids, Lakam for scientific spying, and the Liaison Bureau which helped Jews escape to Israel from Russia.

"Well obviously the Lions of Allah case is an internal security matter," said Kallenborg. "I don't see how the Mossad should be involved."

"Shlomo didn't tell you?"

"He said you'd be working with me."

Asher's expression was almost angelic. "The PM took this case away from your sainted boss. My instructions are to conduct a special operation with your help. I'll need you for local information and I need some Shin Bet credentials."

Kallenborg was obviously displeased. "You'll want me for more than credentials," he said. "I can interrogate suspects and extract information."

"Your kind of expertise I don't need. That the Palestinian boy you were questioning knew where the Lions' dynamite comes from. Too bad he died before you found anything out."

"The boy had a weak heart," said Kallenborg.

Asher didn't know what infuriated him more, the lie or the smile on Kallenborg's face that insinuated he could count on Asher to share in the joke.

"Your heart would stop too if you had an electric wire jammed up your ass. But then you might be the kind to find it rewarding."

Kallenborg chose to ignore the insult. "My methods always work."

"But the boy's dead and that's a little awkward, don't you think?" said Asher. "Now our only lead is that lawyer he worked for, Christina Goryeb."

"She knows a lot more than the boy. He was just her tool. Pull her in for questioning," said Kallenborg. "She'll start talking."

"Let me see her dossier," said Asher.

Kallenborg dropped a bulging manila file tied up with a green cloth tape in front of Asher. "*Bon appetit*," he said.

When Asher opened the dossier, his was the heart that stopped. The face above ID# 990672461 was the face of his lovely, mysterious Christina.

He still thought of the woman as 'his Christina', although she'd made it clear she wanted no further part of him. Naomi refused to arrange a meeting, or divulge Christina's whereabouts. "She doesn't want to see you, again Chaim," Naomi had told him. "She's not the type of woman for you." Yet he had trusted fate to bring them together. He had known then she was not Jewish—her name told him that much—just as the wedding band on her left hand had told him she was married but he had never dreamed she was Palestinian. He made love to her and she had lied to him. He, a Mossad *katsa*, had believed woman's lies. He had let his guard down.

"Do you know this woman?" said Kallenborg.

"No," Asher said.

He skimmed the dossier's pages, assessing the extent of the damage. He thought about excusing himself from the case. Christina would recognize him the moment she saw him, and she knew where he lived. Gan Geneva would be an easy target for her revenge if she was in fact the terrorist Kallenborg said she was.

But what if she wasn't?

Asher had often staked his life on his instincts about people. He was seldom wrong. His instincts told him Christina was no terrorist. He studied the dossier carefully.

"What makes you think this woman's dirty?" he said finally.

"We've been issued warrants to shoot on sight on less evidence," said Kallenborg.

"Then you will find this interesting," said Asher. He read aloud from a memo at the front of the dossier.

Carmi Gillon
To: Director, General Security Services

From: Shlomo Arendt
Head of Arab Affairs

Subject: Special Permission to Interrogate

Christina Rantissi Goryeb, is almost certainly a member of the terrorist network known as the Lions of Allah.

She was born in Rehavia, West Jerusalem in 1958, the eldest daughter of Darwish Rantissi, an Arab lawyer. She studied at the Beirut Arab University. After completing her law degree, she undertook a two-year apprenticeship in the office of Raja and Fuad Shehadeh in Ramallah, a hotbed of Arab radicalism, before working with Jawad Boulous for an additional two years. Early in 1990, Mrs. Goryeb established an independent practice also in Ramallah.

She professes to hold moderate political views and is involved in the Peace Now movement. Her husband, Richard Goryeb, a naturalized American citizen who works in Washington, D.C. is involved in Arab fund raising in the U.S. and actively lobbies the American government against *Yisroel's* interests. Mrs. Goryeb provides legal services and representation to street fighters who are accused of security violations before the IDF's military courts in Samaria and Judea. She is a strikingly beautiful woman who misleads our judges, unduly influencing them to rule against the GSS, thereby placing *Yisroel* at great risk.

As a routine precaution, she was put under surveillance, however, no visible links to terrorists could be established until a few days ago. A GSS undercover officer discovered a coded message in her office. The partially decoded plaintext is addressed to the Lions of Allah.

I recommend that she be interrogated using "moderate pressure" as permitted by the guidelines of the Landau Commission.

Approved:_____

Disapproved:_____/s/_____Yitzhak Rabin_____
Date: Nisan 25, 5755

"The PM disapproved the use of pressure in any interrogation of her," said Asher.

Kallenborg shrugged. "We can use pressure; we just don't tell anyone. Coddle a terrorist and you will be the next one they kill."

"That's assuming the person you torture is a terrorist and not some dupe who was in the wrong place," said Asher.

"All Palestinians are terrorists one way or another. None of them are dupes," said Kallenborg.

That was when Asher knew that he'd stay on the case. If he didn't, his Christina would surely be killed.

Kallenborg rummaged in his pockets and brought out a package of Players cigarettes. He ran a finger affectionately over the letters "JPS" embossed in large intertwined gold script on the rich chocolate brown cover. There were smaller gold letters too that he touched, letters which said The House of John Player, Nottingham, England.

Asher watched Kallenborg toy with the package of cigarettes. "A Litvak with expensive tastes. You're definitely not like Shlomo's other men," he said. "Where do you live?"

"I have an apartment in Tel Aviv."

"Nicer than your old home in Vilnius?"

"Oh, much better. It's on the beach," Kallenborg said, "How about you?"

"I live on a *kibbutz*," said Asher.

Kallenborg gave a sour laugh. "At least we have one thing in common."

"What can that possibly be?"

"We're both secular socialists."

"I was raised a Zionist," said Asher. "It's not the same thing as your communism."

"So were your parents Holocaust survivors, or what?" said Kallenborg.

"We were here before that. My grandparents came to Palestine in 1902 to escape the *pogroms* in your Russia where Jews were slaughtered by the thousands."

Kallenborg's hand waved contemptuously. "Jews never called this place Palestine. We're taking back the land the Arabs stole from us."

A Litvak who doesn't know history, thought Asher. "Wrong again," he said. "Palestine was a province of the Ottoman Empire when my grandparents came here. It didn't become *Yisroel* until 1948."

"When did British rule start?" Now Kallenborg sounded genuinely curious.

"The British took over Palestine in 1919 from the Turks under a mandate from the League of Nations and promised to make it a Jewish National Home," said Asher. "But then, they quickly reneged on the deal."

"I suppose that was when the Arabs started killing Jews," Kallenborg said.

"The Arabs started raiding our settlements in 1905 when more and more Jews fled Russia. But still the first Jews were welcomed by the Arabs. They liked our Jewish gold. My grandparents bribed their way into Palestine with gold. They paid gold for the worthless land along the coast that became our *kibbutz*."

"I take it you don't like Arabs?" said Kallenborg. His voice had become hard and preemptory.

"They're no better and no worse than other people," said Asher.

"But you've spent your life fighting them."

"We had peace with the Arabs once, we'll have peace with them again."

"So you're a peacenik after all?" said Kallenborg.

Inwardly Asher twitched with annoyance. "I don't hate Arabs. They're human beings just like the rest of us. When I was growing up, I remember Israel was 'a light unto the nations'. We were to be an example for other countries to follow. I try to keep that in mind."

Kallenborg looked around the *marats* before he spoke.

"All that changed once the world saw Israeli soldiers beating Palestinians on TV," he said.

The *marats* remained silent, engrossed once more in their own work.

After a moment he said in a low, almost conciliatory voice, "Well, at least you're still living the socialist ideal."

Asher's smile was ironic.

"On the contrary, my *kibbutz* is run for a profit." he said. "We entertain tourists."

"Why do you need the tourists?"

"We need their dollars. I fear the day of socialism is done," said Asher.

"So what is your job there?"

"We pick oranges, vegetables, weed the gardens and the vineyard. I also help entertain the tourists. There is a nature walk and at night, we have a campfire, sing songs, and look at the stars." He drummed his fingers. "I don't know how much longer we'll be able to see the gas clouds in Orion."

"Why not?" said Kallenborg.

It was obvious to Asher that once again, Kallenborg was feigning interest but maybe he'd learn something.

"Light pollution from Tel Aviv, the new neighborhoods and factories."

"Why do you stay on with the Mossad?" Kallenborg said. "You sound homesick."

"I like my work," said Asher.

"We communists used to say that too."

"I'm protecting the only country where Jews can be safe," said Asher.

"That's the U.S., not here," said Kallenborg with a smirk.

Asher felt his face redden. "The Holocaust happened once, it can happen again."

"Not in the U.S.," Kallenborg said.

"The United States is like Germany in 1939," said Asher earnestly. "When it gets too hot for Jews over there, they'll come home to *Yisroel* where they belong."

"You're crazy. Nothing bad has ever happened to Jews in America. Besides, American Jews are so rich they can keep us afloat."

This time, Asher had no answer for Kallenborg.

One of the *marats* turned away from her computer screen. "Mr. Kallenborg, we're intercepting a call from Christina Goryeb. Do you want to listen in?"

"Where is she speaking from?"

"Her home," said the girl.

Asher glanced at a large video monitor that showed the streets of Ramallah in blue outline. Colored icons marked the positions of suspects he was tracking, based on the latest reports from police, under-cover teams, prisoner interrogations and informers. Overlapping orange and yellow rectangles down in the *souk*, the Arab market, indi-cated a meeting between two suspected agitators. Some distance away was the blinking red triangle that represented Christina Goryeb. She was in her home on Irsaal Boulevard.

"Who is she talking to?" said Kallenborg.

"Sounds like her sister."

Kallenborg cursed happily and began to smack his fist into his open hand.

Ten

Three days had passed since the Shin Bet had torn up Christina Goryeb's office and detained Abu Awad for questioning. The fury she felt had subsided to a dull numbness. Dressed in a thin blue cotton wrapper, she stood at the second floor window of her house drinking spiced coffee. She spoke to her sweet-natured youngest sister, Najat, on the telephone.

Najat had made festive plans for their day. Christina let herself be beguiled.

"And, after we take the children to services at St. George's Cathedral, what should we do?" she asked.

"We could drive out the Nablus Road. Perhaps a picnic lunch," Najat murmured. Her voice was soft and musical. "Wine. Stuffed grape leaves?"

"Stopping where?"

"The olive grove near the Garden Tomb of Jesus. The olives are in bloom."

Christina smiled slowly. She could see children playing in the dried brown grass on a hillside amid gnarled trunks dusted with white petals while she and her sister lay on a rug in the shade, gossiping tranquilly and nibble at their food. "Flat bread and *baba ganoush,*" she said.

At that instant an eerie monologue on the phone line in Hebrew interrupted them. "Wait a minute," a harsh man's voice said. "I thought Jesus got buried in a church but she said garden tomb. How did he get buried twice?"

"*Ah*-lo! We're on the line," Christina cried angrily. Abruptly the voices vanished. "Did you hear that, Najat?"

"Hear what?"

"That man. That was a man's voice."

"I heard nothing."

"He said 'garden tomb'. It was as if he were eavesdropping."

She was certain the men on the telephone were not the result of an accidental malfunction. The hard knot of fear returned to the pit of her stomach. The men's' voices grated on her. It was not so much the words as the tone. Contempt, contempt was in their minds. Directed at her, of course, and at Najat. Hissing contempt because they were Palestinian.

"It's probably the Shin Bet," said Christina.

"Has there been any word on Abu Awad's release?" Najat asked.

"I'm afraid not. I've been to Taggart Prison every morning with his mother to beg to see him."

"Maybe he is being held in the Russian Compound or Petah Tikva," said Najat.

"I went there too. Nobody will even admit Abu Awad is being detained. They hate me because I dare to stand up to the Occupation."

Christina shivered. As she took another sip of coffee and willed herself to remain calm. Warily she looked up and down the broad avenue that ran in front of her home. It was lined with date palms and old hewn-stone Arab buildings. Across the street, an old woman with a white head shawl sat staring at her from an open window. Even though their eyes had met, the old woman did not wave or nod, and she knew the old woman would sit motionless in her window all day long, except when her daughter-in-law took over. Those two saw everything that happened in the neighborhood. There was nothing unusual in this behavior; her other neighbors stared out their windows too. Next door on her left, a side-walk cafe was just setting up. Two street sweepers bent over their work with languid movements outside her front gate. One wore a Coca-Cola T-shirt and dungarees, the other had on dirty white pants and a blue denim jacket. In her neighbor's chicken yard next door, a rooster crowed. It was going to be a beautiful day. Her anger subsided.

"What will you wear today?" asked Najat.

Christina cradled the receiver on her shoulder and moved to an old-fashioned wardrobe next to the window. "I'd really like to wear an *abaya* for comfort but a suit would be less conspicuous." The black Palestinian gown with its white head shawl would increase the risk of an ID card check by the police. Israeli ID cards had a magnetic strip on the back like a credit card which made running a security trace on the holder as simple as using American Express. Although she and Najat were Israel citizens, their cards were different from those of Jewish citizens. The sisters' cards said "Christian" under the box labeled "Nationality" instead of Israeli. She did not want to be stopped by the police when she was with her children.

"Not one of those ugly brown suits you wear to represent clients?" said Najat.

"Of course not. Hold on—" Christina thumbed through several garments on hangers. She took one out and modeled it before a mirror. After she did her hair, a touch of make-up, some eye-liner and stylish sun glasses would transform her. She would be striking. Yes, this had possibilities.

"For you I'll wear my cream silk suit," Christina said.

After her phone conversation with Najat, Christina felt happiness return to her. She looked around her spacious peaceful bedroom with affection. The only sound was the ticking of the grandfather clock. No one was up yet. Her children were still asleep and the servants were out of sight. How she adored her home. It had been built by a Muslim trading family in the 1920's when Palestine was under British rule. The rambling two-story structure with its thick stone walls and flat roof was light and airy. There was also a harem where the women had been relegated. After Christina acquired the house, she decorated its walls with gay water color prints, and gleefully filled the harem with law books. She had copper wire screens placed in the windows to keep out insects. Pipes for hot and cold running water were also installed, together with a modern septic system.

The previous owner was a bottled gas merchant whom she had represented last year before an Israeli military court in Taggart Prison. Despite her solid dissection of the evidence trumped up against him, he was found guilty and deported to Jordan. After the trial, he could not pay for her services so he made her a gift of his house.

The echo of running footsteps outside interrupted Christina's thoughts and she went quickly to the window. At the far end of the avenue a young boy raced in her direction. Behind him, in the distance, she could make out two men in a white Peugeot. They seemed to be slowly following him. Her mood darkened.

As the boy came down the sidewalk, mouth agape and chest heaving, she recognized him as Afif Rubez, the youngest son of her family's cook, Fatima. Afif pushed aside the tall iron gate and knocked hurriedly on the front door. Christina went downstairs to let him in.

"In fifteen minutes you will receive a summons, " he panted. "The Shin Bet came to your sister's house."

Another summons! Why today, on Sunday, of all days. Today, when she and Najat had planned a picnic for the children? Why bother her sister? It was utterly amazing. She could not even take sunshine and fresh air for granted. Hot tears sprang to her eyes.

"Run away," the boy said bravely. "I will throw stones at the soldiers when they come."

She took him in her arms and hugged him tightly. Then she drew back and held him at arms length.

"You must do nothing," she told him sternly. "Your mother still needs you."

The boy stiffened and gave a nod. His eyes were filled with the familiar mixture of shame and fury.

In a moment a police whistle shrilled outside, followed by a loud hammering on front door. A harsh male voice bawled, "Shin Bet! Open Up!"

Christina froze. She was wearing only a wrapper, her hair was uncombed. No make-up either but there was no time for that. The door was shaking. She knew what the Shin Bet did to the houses of Palestinians who didn't cooperate. Palestinians grimly joked that the Star of David on Israel's flag would be replaced by a bulldozer rampant on a field of debris. Undoing the lock, Christina angrily flung open the door to confront her tormentors.

Eleven

Kallenborg took a deep drag on his cigarette before grinding it under his heel. "Christina Goryeb?" he asked in a soft Players-scorched voice. Behind Kallenborg waited a detachment of Israeli border policemen in green berets with Uzi submachine guns at the ready.

"You know who I am," she snapped and glared over his shoulder.

He smiled hesitantly and handed her a typewritten sheet of paper. She snatched the summons from his hand and began to read.

"Come with us," he said putting on his KGB Major's manner.

She thrust the paper back under his nose. "You've got the date wrong," she said calmly. "It's effective tomorrow. Come back then."

* * *

A few paces away, Chaim Asher watched the scene from his seat at a Formica topped table in the sidewalk cafe. He wore black trousers and a frayed brown sports coat with clean white shirt, open at the collar. Under his coat was a Beretta 93 R mini-submachine gun. He steeled himself to face Christina. His heart pounded. He'd been compromised, his cover blown. He would have preferred to be any place else in the world. With grim satisfaction, he wondered how she would react. Now it would be her turn for the unwelcome surprise.

When he heard Kallenborg say, "I can detain you without a warrant," he rose. If Kallenborg kept farting around, a crowd would gather and things would get ugly. They had better pick up Christina Goryeb quick and sweet, he thought. He put a 10 *shekel* note down on the table to pay for his *shwarma* and coffee. The policeman moved aside to let him through the big iron gate set in a high stone wall that surrounded her house.

"Excuse me," Asher said with exaggerated courtesy addressing the woman behind Kallenborg.

In her flimsy lavender bath robe, with her jet black hair uncombed, and her unblemished olive complexion, bereft of make-up, Christina Goryeb was as hauntingly beautiful as he remembered her from that evening at Gan Geneva. The sight of her moved him deep inside in a way that frightened him. If he was wrong about her it would be the fatal mistake of his career.

She clutched the lavender robe closed with her left hand as she met his eyes.

"I'll handle this," Asher said to Kallenborg.

He had a sick feeling in his stomach as he spoke, "We don't demand that you accompany us, Madame we request it." He took the summons from Christina's outstretched hand and pulled out a pen. "Incorrect date? It's just been corrected."

Using Kallenborg's shoulder as an impromptu desk, Asher wrote in Sunday's date, and said to Kallenborg, "You wait for me here. I'll be inside. The lady should be properly dressed."

Asher put the summons back in Christina's hand and gestured toward the door. She didn't budge. He pushed her front door open wider and walked into her house, knowing she'd have to follow him. As she did, he closed the door behind them.

In the dim vestibule illuminated by a single naked light bulb, he heard a movement and dropped to one knee, his Beretta drawn.

A young, dark haired girl wearing yellow stripped pajamas stumbled forward into the light rubbing sleep out of her eyes. Christina Goryeb bent down to put her arms around the girl and spoke soothingly to her in Arabic. As she did, her robe fell open, exposing her pretty breasts. Asher remembered the crescent shaped birth mark beside her left nipple. As she covered herself she glared at him fiercely. Then she slapped him.

"So you are a policeman, not a minstrel!" she said in a mocking voice.

He stood up and gingerly rubbed his cheek. "And you are certainly not French," he said quietly.

"You wrecked my office, kidnapped my clerk, and tapped my telephone. Why?"

He felt anger that she'd connect him to Kallenborg's actions, that she'd think he was no better than that ex-KGB thug.

Carefully he returned the Beretta to its holster.

In a moment an older girl in white pajamas appeared. She stared at Asher with unfriendly curiosity.

These were Christina Goryeb's children, Asher realized. "No one lives in this house except women and children," she said. "I'll come with you to answer your questions. But first I must get my things and speak to my children."

As she disappeared through a pair of double doors, Asher followed her. The doors opened into a large bright courtyard.

Asher was surprised.

He had never been in a wealthy Palestinian's home before. Like many Jews, he had assumed all Palestinians lived in squalor. He knew whole families, including uncles, aunts, cousins and grandparents were packed into small stone or mud-brick hovels in the villages. It was even worse in the Gaza Strip where many lived in shacks of wood and tin. In this house there was a beautiful silence and a sense of peace. Keeping alert, Asher walked around the courtyard. Warm pale light flooded down from above. On one side of the courtyard was a sunken fountain full of lily pads and ornamental carp, while in the center a graceful tamarisk tree spread toward the light. He passed by a little alcove and noted the wooden dais within. Perhaps it was here that a sheikh from the nearest mosque had sat only the previous evening conversing with the men of the neighborhood. Fueling plans for subversion and espionage. He noticed an etched bronze *nargileh*, a water pipe for smoking tobacco or hashish, resting on an inlaid table in the middle of the dais. Its fire pot was empty gathering dust.

Christina Goryeb was probably telling the truth about no men in the house.

Through an archway Asher caught sight of her as she disappeared with her children up a stone staircase that ran up one wall of a spacious high-ceiling room. He galloped up the stairs, taking two at a time. They led to a wide balcony that looked down on the room he had just come through. Through one of several doors that opened onto the balcony, Asher saw Christina speak to an older woman in a night gown, whose gray hair was plaited into a long braid. The old woman turned to give Asher a look of hatred and scorn. The she took Christina's daughters quickly into her room and shut its door.

Christina Goryeb turned to Asher and said, "I'll need five minutes to dress, Mr. Policeman," and closed the door behind her.

He was left alone on the balcony. He found himself intrigued by the combination of the old-fashioned Palestinian house, and this Westernized Palestinian woman. The room below him was comfortable and feminine. Compared to the Spartan *kibbutz* where he lived, this was a luxurious palace. A Japanese color television set sat on a low table before a wide divan. Flowers in a vase decorated an elaborately carved table against the wall. On the divan was a copy of the English language *Jerusalem Post*. Behind the divan on a Persian carpet was a half-finished Monopoly game with play money arranged in little piles along the edges of the board.

A library lined with books opened into the room below, and through its open door he spotted an inlaid roll-top desk with a telephone. He went back to the bedroom door and listened. The sound of a hair dryer came faintly through it. Did he have five minutes or ten? Asher bet it would be more like ten. When he got down stairs he made a bee-line for the desk. He was looking for magic phone numbers. Phone numbers with area codes in Jordan, Libya, Syria, Lebanon, Iran, or perhaps even Iraq. Phone numbers that could be tapped for leads. There might even be magic pieces of paper lying about, papers that when decoded with the proper key would reveal information about the next shipment of explosives.

Beside the phone he found a rotary card index, a green blotter, two yellow legal pads, a drinking glass holding sharpened pencils, and an electrified antique lamp. He thumbed through the index cards. Mostly the listings were in Ramallah and Jerusalem, but a few phone numbers were located in the American capital, Washington, D.C. He noticed a redial button on the telephone and pressed it. A woman answered in Arabic. Asher recalled that the last person Christina called was her sister. He hung up without speaking.

Above the desk on a shelf were some feminist novels in English, a dense tract by the American philosopher Herbert Marcuse, and two books by Haim Be'er, an Israeli novelist, one of Asher's favorites, who wrote about life in an Orthodox Jewish neighborhood. In a row of pigeon holes, he found statements from Morgan-Stanley, an American investment manager, as well as canceled checks, receipts and bills from local shops, and personal letters bearing a return address in Washington, D.C. from Richard Goryeb.

The letter was written in flowery high-flown Arabic with a blue felt tip pen that left an untidy trail of blots. It began with a cry from the heart. "Once again I beseech you to join me in America," Richard Goryeb wrote. "I understand and respect your love for your family, friends and the duty you feel toward Palestine. But if you cannot bear to leave our native country, our daughters deserve the chance to grow up in America, free from the Zionist Oppressors. I miss all of you terribly. Have the girls received my presents yet? The stuffed giraffe is for Aminah and the baby gorilla's for Muna. You would be very proud if you could see me today. Through our good friend, Professor Said, of Columbia University, I have obtained an introduction to the American Secretary of State, and now I am on intimate terms with the man. In fact, I am involved in a remarkable new policy initiative with the State Department. The support of Israel is more expensive than the Americans can now afford, and Israeli brutality toward Palestinians has finally eroded public support here. The Palestinian cause most surely will be furthered by my important work, and I regret that I cannot not tell you more about it. Although your work in Palestine is important too, you can do much more for our fellow Palestinians if you come to America."

Asher put the letter back in its envelope and returned it to the pigeon hole with the other letters. He came out of the library and sat down on the divan in front of the television and pretended to read the newspaper. Richard Goryeb's letter revealed a number of interesting things. The man cared about his family. He wanted his wife to live with him in America. Christina Goryeb could have left Palestine anytime she chose. She stayed—Why? And the language seemed oddly stiff for a man writing to his wife. But Richard Goryeb's message, Asher realized, was not for his wife alone. He was writing to people like Asher and Kallenborg. All foreign mail going in and out of Israel was opened and read by postal inspectors. Richard Goryeb had written "Zionist Oppressors" to make sure the inspectors woke up when they ran across his letter. Richard Goryeb was telling the Shin Bet that he now had friends in high places who could make a lot of trouble for Israel if they bothered his wife and children. And perhaps his wife, Christina, realized this too. But did Richard Goryeb really know the American Secretary of State or was he bluffing? Mekor had warned Asher that Christina Goryeb would require careful handling. He wondered why, if she could live in America with her husband, did she chose to stay in Ramallah? Did she defend poor Arabs accused of crimes out of a sense of noblesse oblige, or was she in reality a terrorist?

A shadow fell across Asher's face and he looked up to see Christina Goryeb waiting for him. She was dressed in a brown linen suit and carried a small attaché case.

"Open that case, please?" he asked.

"Certainly, Mr. Policeman," she said.

Inside he found two candy bars, a paperback mystery, pencils, a pad of paper and a copy of Military Order 378, Rules of Procedure for Dealing With Individuals Accused of Security Violations. But thankfully no little plastic bag of explosives and a detonator. He motioned to her that she could close her attaché case.

"You were expecting something perhaps, more volatile?" she said. "I am so sorry to disappoint you."

He took her arm firmly and they walked slowly through the house. Before leaving the courtyard she turned and looked back. Her eyes rested briefly on every detail as though she were committing it to memory and bidding farewell. Then she went with Asher. Outside he handed her over to Kallenborg. Surrounded by a phalanx of border policemen they walked to the white Peugeot at the curb.

Twelve

The Shin Bet compound was at the rear of Taggart prison. Kallenborg led Christina through a door at the end of an alley. His grip on her arm was harsh and unpleasant. Asher walked a few steps behind them. Inside the prison, Kallenborg paused at the front desk to sign a log. The next stop was the desk of another official, a young man who glanced at Christina with limpid curiosity and signed a brief statement. She read it over Kallenborg's shoulder and shuddered. It was a certificate that affirmed she was in good health and her life was not in danger, a document that was required for admitting new prisoners.

Her heart sank. It meant she would be questioned and detained. She would be temporarily imprisoned without a trial, just like the Palestinians she represented in the perfunctory hearings before military judges at Taggart. She knew full well what else to expect. Over 350 Palestinians were held under administrative detention orders ranging from a few weeks to one year in a dozen Israeli prisons and military detention centers, the largest being Ketsiot in the Negev Desert. Kallenborg led the way down a narrow winding hall to a windowless compartment that served as an interrogation room.

Florescent lighting hummed overhead providing brilliant illumination that reflected off the room's white-washed cinder block walls. The strong odor of disinfectant rising from the damp concrete floor made Christina dizzy and faintly nauseated. In the center of the room was a long wooden table with two folding chairs and a telephone. A utility toilet without privacy screens projected from the back wall. Immediately she regretted the coffee she had drunk earlier that morning.

Kallenborg and Asher sat down in the chairs.

Christina was left standing facing them. If seemed inconceivable to her that she had made love to one of these men, had cried out in ecstasy, and then later in private, cried for shame. Resolutely she placed her attaché case down on the table as though this was a courtroom, and she was representing a client. A client who had to idea of the charges against her but knew them as false.

Kallenborg rubbed his jaw and eyed her for a moment. Then he picked up the phone and said softly, "This is Kallenborg. Bring me Christina Goryeb's dossier." As they waited, he stared at her coldly. Despite the wave of panic that swept over her, she did not display any fear. Instead, she returned his stare with frank interest.

"I recognize your voice. You are the one who listens to my telephone conversations, aren't you? And I'm sure you are the one who detained my clerk, Abu Awad. Where is Abu Awad? Where is he?" she said. "In the strongest terms, I protest this harassment."

Abruptly Kallenborg looked down. He began scratching his left forearm, then his right and finally the back of his neck. He produced a plastic bottle of lotion and dabbed some on the welts that were raising on flaky reptilian skin.

Asher looked away. He seemed embarrassed to be in the same room with Kallenborg. Good, she thought, let him be embarrassed.

An orderly in a dirty uniform entered the room carrying a bulging manila file tied up with a green cloth tape. Kallenborg snatched it from him and extracted a document.

"This is a detention order," he said crisply. "It states that you, Christina Goryeb, are a suspected terrorist. Your imprisonment is required to safeguard the public order and security of *Yisroel.*"

Christina's knees felt rubbery. Her worst fears were confirmed.

She heard herself say in her courtroom voice, "That is utterly ridiculous!"

Kallenborg paused. Asher's head turned in her direction.

She wondered what they were waiting for. The detention order had been read, but they were not leading her away to a cell. That meant Kallenborg and Asher *did* have questions to ask. The detention order was a bluff to secure cooperation. Even more significant, the Shin Bet was not going to beat the living daylights out of her to extract information they needed. She felt a surge of confidence.

"Why are you doing this? You know I am not a terrorist."

Kallenborg coughed. "Our information is confidential."

"Show it to me," she said.

"I cannot show you anything."

"Because it was gathered using wire taps and paid informants?" she said.

Kallenborg lit a cigarette.

"Blackmail and torture then?"

He blew a cloud of smoke and squinted. "Security rules prevent me from showing it."

Christina's assurance grew. She pointed a finger at Kallenborg. "Your case against me must go before a judge within 96 hours. Military Order 378 requires this. Also, I request a legal representative be present with me and I request that a record of the proceeding be kept."

"You are mistaken." Kallenborg's face turned red. "Neither a lawyer nor a record are required."

"Even your military judges like a little due process," she said calmly. "I represent Palestinians accused of security violations—."

Kallenborg interrupted her. "Palestinians, Palestinians. There is no such thing as a Palestinian. There are only Arabs. You are an Arab!"

"Your government is negotiating self-rule agreements with people who call themselves Palestinians. Is that not true?"

"You are out of line!" Kallenborg screamed. Then Asher whispered something to him. With an effort Kallenborg seemed to check himself.

Asher went out of the room and came back with another folding chair.

"Sit down, please, Mrs. Goryeb. I'd like to ask you a few questions," he said as if nothing had happened.

Christina smiled. So Asher was one who played the good cop, she thought. His tone was apologetic. He might have been gently accusing his grocer of selling weevils in the flour.

"May I see your identify card?" he said.

Reluctantly Christina removed her ID card from her wallet and gave it to Asher.

He examined it and looked at her with surprise. "This says you are a citizen of *Yisroel*. Where is your residence?"

She gritted her teeth. "My home is in West Jerusalem. I also have a house in Ramallah," she said.

"You mean you have two domiciles, one in *Yisroel* and one in the West Bank?"

Was this a thinly disguised threat to take her Israeli citizenship away because she lived in Palestine and not in Israel?

"No. My legal residence is 105 Azza Street, Rehavia, West Jerusalem. I was born there, my sisters were born there and my father was born there. We are all citizens of Israel."

He flipped quickly through her file and stopped. "Where do they reside now?"

"One sister still lives in Rehavia with her husband. My other sister lives in Ramallah. Our father died two years ago."

"And your mother, Leilah?"

"She lives in Ramallah with me."

Asher's eyes narrowed. "I see. May I have your vehicle registration please?"

"I don't presently own a car. However, I do have an Israeli driver's license."

"Let me see it, please."

She gave him her driver's license.

Asher stared at it and shook his head. "This is most irregular."

Christina shrugged. "There's nothing unusual about owning a house in Palestine."

Asher put her ID card and drivers license on the table in front of him. When she reached to take them he put his hand over them.

"A message was found in the possession of your law clerk, Abu Awad," he said in a stern voice."

Christina remained silent.

"The message refers to the Lions of Allah," said Asher. "You are a citizen of *Yisroel*. Do you know it is a crime for you to communicate with a terrorist?"

Christina nodded slowly.

"I represent Palestinians falsely accused of crimes, not terrorists," she said. "However, just because someone sent a letter to my clerk— and all sorts of people do write asking me to represent them—does that make me a terrorist?"

"We have the message nonetheless," Asher said.

"I know nothing about the Lions of Allah. I never heard Abu Awad mention them." She gave Asher a fierce look. "And where is Abu Awad?"

"I'm afraid you will have to ask Mr. Kallenborg," said Asher.

Kallenborg glared at Asher. "Abu Awad was found dead in his cell," he said. "It is most unfortunate."

The meaning of Kallenborg's words hit Christina like an electric shock.

"MURDERERS! CRIMINALS! FIENDS!" She slammed her hand down on the table. "He was a scholar, his hands were not stained by stone throwing. He was no more a terrorist than I am." Then in Hebrew she said to Asher, "You are no better than the Germans who butchered you. You built a museum to commemorate your dead. Yet you kill us in the same way."

"You and I agree Abu's hands were white," said Asher quietly.

Christina looked at him in disbelief. She dried her eyes with a tissue from her suit pocket.

"What are you saying?"

"Abu Awad was an unlikely terrorist. But you unfortunately are a different story. My colleague Mr. Kallenborg believes the message Abu Awad received was intended for you."

"That's impossible."

A look of ineffable sadness came over Asher's face.

"Mrs. Goryeb, if you don't cooperate with this investigation we will blow up your house."

Christina was speechless.

No one said anything for a moment.

Asher said, "The Shin Bet will investigate and report that a Ramallah terrorist blew herself up making a bomb."

"You may murder me the way you murdered hundreds. Steal our land, steal our lives, you'll never break us," Christina said.

"Let's start with who is buying sticks of dynamite," said Asher calmly.

"I refuse to be bullied," said Christina.

She opened her brief case, took out the paperback mystery, and pretended to read it. She glanced up and caught Asher and Kallenborg exchanging angry looks.

"Very well," said Asher.

They both got up and left the room. Kallenborg turned out the lights and Christina heard him lock the door behind him.

She was left alone in total darkness.

At first she was aware of nothing but a smothering emptiness. Then a soft pulsating throb seemed to fill the entire room. She realized it was her own pulse. She stood up, aware of an uncomfortable pressure in her bladder. The toilet must be only a few feet away. She could hear the faint sound of water running in the tank and went toward it in the darkness with hands outstretched. She found the toilet and relieved herself.

While she was sitting on the toilet, the door was suddenly opened, the lights flashed on and Kallenborg stood in the doorway.

"Are you comfortable?" he said. Then he extinguished the lights and closed the door.

The interrogation lasted all day.

Sometimes Kallenborg and Asher left her locked in the room with the lights out for an hour or more. Periodically, one of them opened the door, flipped on the light switch, and stared at her for a few seconds.

It was after sunset when they released her. Asher said finally: "If you change your mind, call us." He gave her a slip of paper with a phone number on it.

"Now, please return my ID card and driver's license," she said.

Asher stared at her as if thinking it over. Then he handed her the cards.

Thirteen

In the main square of Ayna Nub, a Palestinian village in the hills near Ramallah, Asher jockeyed through a crowd of religious Muslim women, their heads bound tightly in white *esharbs* with Kallenborg at his elbow. Asher and Kallenborg wore charcoal grey *jalabiyyas* and covered their heads with checkered *kaffiyehs*. A ragged black suit coat over his *jalabiyya* completed Asher's disguise.

Today Kallenborg's presence was even more irritating than usual. Kallenborg chewed *bizr*, salted sunflower seeds, and spat the empty hulls noisily on the ground. It took all of Asher's willpower to keep from snapping the man's scrawny neck with one swift rabbit punch.

"The nerve of that woman!" Kallenborg said. "The day after we release her, she's out here inciting a riot."

"Be still," said Asher.

Kallenborg hissed in his ear.

"This particular village is politically very active," Kallenborg said. "If I were you, I'd pick her up now, before we have a real mess on our hands."

The old Palestinian man next to them eyed Kallenborg suspiciously.

"Keep your voice down," Asher said to Kallenborg. "I want to her what she's saying."

"I can't believe you let that bitch defy you. She ought to be in a detention cell with a piss-soaked hood over her head. After twenty-four hours, she'll gladly tell you all she knows about the Lions of Allah. We don't have time to waste on surveillance."

"Shut up," said Asher.

He knew Kallenborg was goading him, hoping to cause him to make mistakes. Then Kallenborg could complain to his Shin Bet boss,

Shlomo Arendt, who would in turn would use Asher's blunders to discredit the Mossad. Asher turned his attention back to the people on the podium, and his mind on the disturbing problem of Christina Goryeb. If she were a terrorist, would she be found at such a gathering? Of course not, he wanted to think. Still, this gathering was perfect cover for a sophisticated terrorist.

He turned his attention to Mrs. Goryeb's companion, the tall woman grey-haired woman in a blue dress, and recognized Naomi Litvin but he was not altogether surprised. The two women sat at a table with a small bony man with clever dark eyes. Broken columns rose behind them, marking what had once been the front of a Roman building. Mrs. Goryeb and the man wore traditional robes. His hand rested on a staff. Naomi leaned toward Christina and they became engaged in an animated conversation. The two women were obviously close friends as well as colleagues. Would Naomi Litvin trust a terrorist, or did her desire to build bridges blind her to danger? Guileless Naomi, with her commitment to waging peace and her stubborn faith that Israel could survive if only reason could prevail. As though reason played any part in the life of Israel. Kallenborg interrupted his thoughts.

"I've seen that old nanny goat speak at 'Peace Now' demonstrations," said Kallenborg. "Naomi Litvin, who wants to give our Land back to the Arabs. That gnome next to her is the village *mukhtar*. The mayor. Too smart for his own good."

Now Naomi handed Christina a thin green book. Asher tried to read the title but it was too far away. Knowing Naomi, the book had to be poetry. Christina reached in her purse and pulled out a red volume.

"What shall I put in my report?" said Kallenborg. "The suspect exchanged messages with a dissident at a political gathering?"

Asher shot him a look of disgust.

The mayor reached for the microphone on the table. "Welcome to our *nawada*," he beamed sweetly. "We Palestinians have long known the value of learning, so I know you will take heed of our distinguished guests, Mrs. Naomi Litvin and Mrs. Christina Goryeb."

Silence fell over the crowd as the grey-haired woman drew the microphone to her.

"What do you want most?" Mrs. Litvin said in fluent Arabic. Her voice was strong and clear.

For a long moment the crowd was still. Though she was Jewish, Asher sensed the crowd recognized her as an ally. Finally, someone cried, "Our own country," and the whole audience burst into wild applause.

Over the hubbub Kallenborg said to Asher, "What rubbish! Arabs wait on Jews, sweep the streets, and lay the bricks and mortar. They are born slaves."

"You've been listening to Shlomo Arendt," said Asher.

"Shlomo's right, you know. We should get rid of the Arabs, remove them from our sight," said Kallenborg.

Mrs. Litvin held up her hand and waited until the applause died down. "Occupied Palestine is a small place. No abundance of natural resources is to be found here. No oil, coal, gold, not even much water."

A country as poor as *Yisroel*, thought Asher.

"Without natural resources how can roads and towns be built, how can people be fed and clothed?"

"Allah will provide. He is most great!" cried a young man at the front of the crowd. He wore a black *kaffiyeh*. Asher noticed the austere old man lying on a pallet next to him.

Kallenborg followed Asher's gaze. "That's Sheikh Karaeen from the al-Umma mosque. He's the one who keeps the village hot heads stirred up."

Another crazy bitter old man, thought Asher.

The sheikh's harsh face reminded him of the old black clothed rabbi who scolded his mother one day in Jerusalem for not covering her arms as she sold vegetables from their kibbutz. Asher had been so angry at the rabbi for insulting his good natured, hardworking mother, but she just laughed. "Pay him no attention," she said. "He's a crazy, bitter old man. Just a relic from the ghetto." His mother had thought such people were harmless, eccentric, a form of life that would wither away when exposed to sunlight. Mrs. Litvin deflected the heckler with the same cheerful guile.

"God is indeed most great!" agreed Mrs. Litvin. "He has provided you with many gifts and the greatest gifts of all are the minds and talents of your people."

There was another outburst of cheering and clapping. Someone shouted, "Our minds are the oil well!"

"Yes, and if you and your children drill wisely, they will produce riches," said Mrs. Litvin.

The crowd settled down to listen and Asher breathed a little easier. "I say 'children' but many of you think I refer only to your sons. I speak of your daughters, too. They, too, must know where their abilities and skills lie. They, too, should prepare for jobs and careers. They, too, can be engineers, doctors, lawyers. Whatever they wish to be."

Looks of confusion swept around the square. The sheikh raised himself on one elbow and whispered to his young companion.

The sheikh's young man called out, "You cannot do man's work with flour on your hands. Women should stay at home and let men do the talking."

A slow fire rose in Asher's brain. "Women should stay at home," the Orthodox rabbi had yelled at his mother, then spat at her.

Mrs. Litvin smiled patiently. "Education is important for both daughters and sons. I would like to introduce you to a Palestinian mother of two daughters. She is Christina Goryeb, a lawyer from nearby Ramallah."

All eyes were on Christina as she poured a glass of water from the pitcher on the table. She took a brief sip.

"I owe a great debt to my parents. My father prayed for sons and my mother gave him three daughters."

Women in the audience clucked sympathetically.

"Yet his daughters were just as precious to him as sons would have been. He sent us to the Friends Girls School in Ramallah. Afterward we took degrees at the University. Two of my sisters are surgical nurses in the Ramallah hospital, and I am a lawyer. We married strong Palestinian men, and now we are raising our children."

Sheikh Karaeen beckoned to his companion. The young man leaned down, listened and sprang up.

"You say women are equal to men?" he shouted.

"I say women must have equal rights," said Christina, "because we make equal contributions."

Asher found himself cheering silently and was mildly surprised.

"Does that mean women have the right to do everything men can do?"

"Certainly," said Christina. "The more women can do the better off we all are."

"Then Sheikh Karaeen says you are immoral in the eyes of Islam," shouted the young man.

Mrs. Goryeb fired back. "If Shiekh Karaeen says that I'm immoral in the eyes of Islam, let him say it himself to my face. Over 3,000

Palestinians were thrown in military prisons when our people rose up against the Occupation. I volunteered to help, as did Mrs. Litvin and other women lawyers. Without us, your brave sons would be still rotting in a detention camp. We defended Palestinians accused of crimes before the military courts. There is nothing immoral about providing schooling to girls."

This woman had a special courage, thought Asher. Where did it come from? She had nothing in common with the crabbed Moslem cleric, yet both were Palestinian, both of them *Yisroel's* sworn enemies.

His sworn enemies.

"The *Intifada* showed us that we can hold our heads up," shouted the sheikh's young man. "We will never succeed if our women are defiled by unworthy thoughts."

"Many brave deeds were inspired by the *Intifada*," said Christina. "Still after two years we were forced to retreat. Would you like to know why?"

"Zionist oppression brought us to our knees," he said.

An electric shock went snapping through the crowd. Heads twisted and bobbed, arms began waving, voices raised shrilly for the right to be heard above other voices.

The mayor seized the microphone and banged his staff on the table. "Please let our speaker continue," he said.

Christina waited.

"Zionist oppression was only one reason the *Intifada* retreated. But another reason was our own Palestinian factories. How tired we became of buying their cheap, shoddy products!" she said. "They had no incentive to make good wares. Ignorance, superstition and greed are what keep us under the heel of the Oppressors. Judging from the grand houses our Palestinian factory owners built, huge fortunes were made. Our boycott of Israeli merchandise had eliminated their competition, but no one looked after the public interest. The third reason is that the *Intifada* retreated because we began to quarrel among ourselves, again. We Palestinians must use our heads. We will need educated men and women who can work together to build a new Palestine."

Was this the speech of a terrorist, he wondered. Would a dangerous rabble rouser blame anyone other than the 'Zionist Oppressor' for Palestinian woes? A woman of valor, he thought with admiration.

The sheikh's young man jumped on the podium, put his hands on the table and leaned over Christina. He shouted, "As a Christian woman you have no right to tell Islamic women what is good for them." He turned to the assembled women and yelled "Do not listen to this blasphemy any longer."

"I am a Palestinian," cried Christina.

Asher heard scattered hisses directed at Christina's accuser.

The mayor's eyes flashed as he rose to his feet. "Young man, I do not know who you are and I care even less to know. You have been discourteous to me and my guests. Let me offer them an apology on your behalf." He brought his staff down on the table with a sound like a whip cracking. "Now Go!"

As one person, the crowd chanted "Go! Go!"

The mayor addressed the crowd. "Let me conclude our nawada with a little story." He took a sip of water. "There was once a very beautiful clock that sat on a little pedestal in Ramallah's City Park. You could reach up and move the hands because it sat on a short pedestal at eye level. The clock was made of the finest materials and by the best craftsmen, but it never kept the proper time. So the Mayor of Ramallah, took a chair and sat by the clock to see for himself what was wrong with it. Do you know what he found? Every Palestinian who passed by, set the clock according to his own watch."

Scattered laughter broke out among the crowd but the major held up his hand.

"Wait, there's still more. The Mayor of Ramallah, knowing he could not change human nature, had the clock removed and presented it to the Mayor of Tel Aviv where it was installed in the center of the city, very carefully, still on its little pedestal. But it didn't keep time there either. Every Jew who passed by set it by his own watch."

A storm of cheers and laughter broke out around Asher. He had heard the joke before.

Kallenborg nudged him. "That was quite a performance," he said.

"The mayor's a smooth operator," said Asher.

"No. I meant Goryeb."

"You believe she had another motive in mind?" said Asher.

"Of course. Don't you see what she did?"

"She defended herself in a tough situation and did a good job of it."

Kallenborg sighed. "Look, she knows we're watching her. She just put on that show to fool you."

Asher shrugged. "I have a different theory," he said.

Fourteen

Christina Goryeb returned to Taggart Prison that afternoon to interview her latest client. She had exchanged her *abaya* for a tan linen business suit, sun glasses and a trace of eye-liner. In one hand she clutched a charge sheet; in the other was her wine colored leather attaché case. The familiar feeling of dread and revulsion descended upon her, twisting her stomach into hard knots. I must be insane, she told herself. Only the day before she had stated to the despicable Chaim Asher and his loathsome partner, that she did not represent terrorists. In a few minutes she would be speaking to a boy accused of being one. How she wished she could have refused the case but it was an obligation. Daoud Rubez the accused terrorist was also the eldest son of her family's cook, Fatima.

A giant guard took Christina to a holding cell into which twenty Palestinian youths had been crammed. They wore blue jeans and dirty cotton shirts and stared sullenly at her through the bars. The odor of urine, sweat and disinfectant assaulted her nose.

"Rubez," bawled the giant.

No one moved.

"You have five minutes," he told Christina, and left her peering into the darkened cell.

A hand shot out of the wall of bars at the sheet in her hand but she jumped back in time. Daoud was thin and tall. He was seventeen years old, but he had the broad shoulders of a grown man. She had not seen him since his first remand hearing, eight days before. She gasped as Daoud moved into the light. A piece of tape held a square of gauze on his forehead, barely concealing a nasty purple and red gash where a rubber truncheon had landed. The Israeli Supreme

91

Court issued an injunction every three months that barred Shin Bet interrogators from torturing prisoners. Beatings were administered nonetheless, although now they were reserved for Palestinians who were suspected of being terrorists. The Shin Bet always identified the few who died as "leaders" of terrorists groups or "collaborators" who died of injuries inflicted by other inmates in the same prison. She hoped they had not beaten a confession out of Daoud or forced him into changing his account of what happened.

"I may be able to obtain your release," said Christina. "You are scheduled to appear before Judge Avram Weinberg next Monday, Daoud. We need to go over your testimony to prepare for it the hearing."

He looked away avoiding eye contact.

"It is not honorable to have a woman speak for me," said Daoud. "I must have a man."

"Unless you can find an attorney who will work for nothing, I'm the only one you can afford," she said with a grim smile.

"It goes against honor," he said.

She turned to walk away. Very well, she thought, I am released. But she knew better.

"Wait," he said in a low voice.

She realized the bravado was just a mask to hide his fear.

"Do I speak for you or not?" said Christina compressing her lips.

"You may speak for me, Madam," said Daoud, humbly this time.

"Then listen carefully," said Christina. "The Shin Bet is required to report to Judge Weinberg on your interrogation so that he can determine if a further period of detention may produce new evidence."

Daoud gave a harsh laugh.

"I did nothing," he said.

"The charge sheet says you are suspected of being a member of the Lions of Allah," she said. "Are you? That's very serious charge."

"I'm not worried," he said.

The other boys in the cell stared at Daoud and his eyes flashed defiantly. Christina was immediately apprehensive.

"That's not what I'm asking you now. Are you a member of the Lions of Allah?"

He shook his head. "I told you before, I am one of the *shabab*." The *shabab* were the young stone-throwing freedom fighters of the *Intifada*.

Christina gave a sigh of relief. "Were any of your *shabab* friends present?"

"I was alone."

She glanced at the sheet. "What were you doing at the springs outside Ayna Nub at 10 o'clock at night?"

"Weeding my Mother's garden," said Daoud. "She grows tomatoes, eggplants, and squash," he added.

She lifted an eyebrow at Daoud.

Fatima's garden provided vegetables for Christina's table. Was he implying that she was at fault for his predicament? "Let me guess," she said. "The police arrived just as your hoe uncovered a box of bullets?"

"I said before, I was only pulling weeds."

"But you broke the curfew," said Christina.

"I worked all day in East Jerusalem," he said. "The moon was strong and evening was the only time I had to help my Mother," said Daoud.

"What sort of work do you do in East Jerusalem?"

"I am a bricklayer."

"Who did you work for?"

"Rosenbluth and Sons."

"Would Rosenbluth speak well of you?"

"He seems satisfied with my work."

"Then I will ask him to testify."

"Do you think Judge Weinberg will hold that in my favor?"

Christina did not want to raise his hopes prematurely. "This particular Judge is his own man. Now tell me what the Shin Bet did to you?"

Daoud trembled, involuntarily. "The Monster interrogates me night and day."

The Monster, the giant guard who brought Christina to Daoud's holding cell, was the interrogator most feared by Palestinian prisoners.

"He beats me and shakes me like a rat until I faint. Then I am forced to stand for hours in a cell the size of a chimney with my head covered by a urine soaked hood. Sometimes he locks me in rooms that are freezing cold or steaming hot. He sings to me, '*Tahqiq layl w'nihar, hatt al-inhiyar*', interrogation night and day, until the breakdown."

She felt a cold fury but no surprise. Stories like this were all too common in her practice. "When do you sleep, Daoud?" she asked him gently.

"A few hours every four or five days in this cell."

She glanced at her watch. There was time for a few more questions. "Do any of your friends work for the Lions of Allah?"

"No. Our leadership forbids dealings with men like the Lions."

"Were you carrying a weapon?"

"No. We fight the Oppressors with stones, not bombs."

"Have you ever smuggled arms or explosives?"

"No."

"I suppose the Monster demanded that you sign a confession?" said Christina.

"Yes, but I would rather die than sign a lie."

"If you are innocent you have a good chance for release with Weinberg. But be polite and hold your temper when you appear before this judge. If he thinks you are a trouble maker there is nothing I can say that will help you."

The look of fear was back in Daoud's eyes. She saw the Monster was padding toward them.

"Tell my Mother I am well and brave," whispered Daoud. He shrank away from the bars.

"Your time is up," the Monster said to Christina in a voice that seemed to come from out of the ground.He turned to Daoud. "You will see death in your next interrogation, but you will not die."

You will not have him, she thought fiercely, prepared once again to fight with dignity and honor. And sometimes we win, she'd told Richard. Sometimes she won.

Fifteen

Overhead, a paddle fan barely stirred the sultry air in Christina Goryeb's law office. Christina herself sat behind her old Adler type-writer working on Daoud Rubez's petition, while her sister Najat sat beside her. They lunched on the cucumber sandwiches Najat had brought. The sisters looked enough alike to be frequently mistaken for each other from a distance, or by people who didn't know them well, but Najat was more gentle and conciliatory, her voice was softer but her opinions were as firm.

"I don't know how you are going to clear your name if you don't know what you've done wrong," said Najat. "Besides, you and the girls should go to America and be with Richard."

"That's what the children want, and it would be safer for them," said Christina slowly.

"Oh, go to America, Christina!"

Christina shook her head. "The truth is I don't think the Shin Bet will let me. One of those Shin Bet men parks down the block in an old Fiat and follows me wherever I go." She pointed out the window. "Look at that!"

"What is the matter?" said Najat.

"That money changer across the street was never there before and now he's glued to that spot under the cinnabar tree. I'm sure he's another one paid to spy on me."

"No Palestinian is safe or free here. The Jews watch all of us. They want to be rid of us. Just because they spy on you doesn't mean they'll stop you from leaving," said Najat.

Christina came close to her sister and said in a low voice. "Yesterday, our Mother received an anonymous note. It said: 'Why has

95

the honor of your family been stained? When will your daughter do what is good for her?'"

"Then you must take the children to the American Consulate and ask for visas," said Najat.

"Not yet," said Christina. "If I leave Palestine, the Shin Bet could retaliate against our family." A stubborn look crossed Christina's face. "Besides I'm not giving up that easily," she said firmly.

Najat refilled their glasses with iced tea.

"Maybe the Shin Bet hopes I'll lead them to whoever they are looking for," said Christina.

"But suppose they don't find anyone?"

"Then they will blow up my house," said Christina calmly. "That's why I must clear my name. The Lions of Allah are probably nothing more than a gang of adolescent boys who call themselves freedom fighters."

Najat looked away. The sisters finished their tea in silence. When it came time to leave, Najat embraced her sister with tears in her eyes.

"Christina, I'm so frightened."

"I'm frightened too. But we must keep our heads up. *Samdeen.*"

After Najat left, Christina went back to work on Daoud Rubez's petition, methodically noting weaknesses in the case against him. She was his only hope. For her, she realized, it was a hopeless situation whether she won or lost. The Shin Bet would believe she defended Daoud because she sympathized with the Lions of Allah and was one of them. Very well, she thought, let them, but at least she could win back Daoud's freedom. Perspiration trickled down her arms as she worked. Each time she pulled a page out of the typewriter and separated the copies, a tissue copy stuck to her damp forearm. When she peeled it off, faint carbon images of the letters remained on her skin.

The jangle of the little bell hanging over her office door, announced a visitor. In the doorway stood a boy about fourteen years old, with a checkered head dress pulled around his nose and mouth. His dark eyes, set in fine chiseled features, were hard and bright. There were hundreds like him in Palestinian villages. The boy's hard eyes darted around the office but he said nothing.

"Yes?" asked Christina. Surely he would be joined by his mother, sisters and brothers. Between much shouting and tears they would tell her about the father in prison and beg her to obtain his release. But there was something different about this boy.

"Where is Abu?" he said.

He glanced furtively over his shoulder at the money changer across the street, took a few steps into the room and closed the door behind him.

"Abu no longer works here," said Christina.

The boy's eyes widened. He slid into a chair beside her.

"We are being watched, woman," he said in a low voice. "The back door was locked. Give me the radio quickly."

"What radio?"

"The transistor radio you received. It is for me."

"I don't hold radios for everyone who happens to walk by," she said sharply.

"You must have one," the boy insisted. "Give it to me and unlock the back door so I can leave. Do it now, woman!"

Christina lost patience with this ridiculous boy.

"Out! Out! Get out!" she said, and pointed to the door.

The boy jumped up from his chair but made no move to leave.

"I'm working for Palestine," he said in the tone of a proud, disdainful Islamic male addressing a mere woman. "Hamad sent me."

Now Christina understood.

Chaim Asher and his Shin Bet associate thought the coded message in the radio was for her. Now, this street urchin expected her to have a transistor radio for him. A radio that must have contained a concealed message. So poor Abu Awad had been working for the Lions after all. Under her very nose! The steady flow of Christina's clients and their families would have provided him with an excellent camouflage. Well, she would put a stop to this business right now.

"Tell Hamad I must see him," said Christina.

"He won't come to you," said the boy.

"Where is he?"

"You will find him in the *souk*."

"Take me to him, then. I must speak to this Hamad in person."

The boy looked at her for a moment, then nodded.

Traditional clothing would be best to wear for a visit to Hamad. Behind a screen, she swiftly changed into an *abaya* and *esharb*.

When she came out, the boy was crouching at the window. The money changer across the street rose to his feet and moved out of the shadows that obscured his face. Kallenborg! He seemed to be speaking into the collar of his robe—which must conceal a police radio—and started to walk toward them.

"I'll get rid of that son of a whore," the boy said. "You leave by the back door."

"How do I find Hamad?"

"Meet me at Sayian, the carpet dealer's. Do you know his shop?"

Christina nodded.

Without any hesitation, the boy opened the door, picked up a stone, and threw it at Kallenborg. Then he raced off down the street in the opposite direction from the souk. She smiled when Kallenborg broke into a trot after him. Kallenborg disappeared into a side street, his robe flapping at his heels.

She bolted the front door. Opening the back door, she peered down the empty ally. She slipped on a pair of dark glasses and went outside. As she wheeled her bicycle to the head of the ally she heard a scraping sound, then a thud and a muffled oath. She recognized the voice. For the first time since the nightmare began, she felt like laughing.

Chaim Asher lay sprawled on the ground several yards behind her. He was wearing a blue striped *jalabiyya*. Beside him lay a crumpled *fez*. He must have fallen while climbing over the high wall that lined the back of the ally to spy on her.

He did not seem to recognize her in Palestinian garb.

She swerved to avoid a pothole, and sailed around the first corner she could find. She rounded the next corner too, narrowly missing a spindly legged donkey loaded with sacks of cement led by two men.

The street ahead was shady and quiet with buildings on both sides. Interesting and disgusting odors mingled in the air. A warm breeze rushed up under her gown and played on her bare legs. She pedaled past store fronts; a butcher shop where flies clustered on cuts of raw meat on hooks, and a grocer piled fat oranges in a stall. In the cafes, men poured hot coffee from tall thin pitchers into tiny etched brass cups. They did not bother to look up. She felt encouraged.

Ahead, two Israeli soldiers in a jeep shot out of a side street. Christina steered for a tiny alleyway to the right. Almost immediately her bicycle became air borne. A scream rose in her throat as she arced down a long flight of stairs. The bicycle hit the steps back wheel first, pitching her up and down in a series of neck-wrenching jolts. With each impact, the drive chain rattled loudly against its guard. She struggled to keep the bicycle's front wheel straight. Two small boys who played on the stairs looked up just as she flew past. Wobbling dangerously out of control, she reached the foot of the stairs where she careened across a busy intersection into the *souk*, and plowed into a soft wall of oriental carpets that hung over ropes on display.

The crowd of people at the corner bus stop broke into laughter as she struggled to extricate herself. She had arrived at Sayian's.

Sayian, an elderly Armenian, ran out from under an awning to help remove the rugs that had fallen down on her. Livid with rage, he berated Christina as he anxiously inspected each carpet. Murmuring thanks and apologies, she brushed the dirt and flies off her gown, and picked up the bicycle.

Christina retreated from the throng of shoppers to a side walk cafe in the shade of a olive tree across the street. She sat down at a table and ordered an iced lemonade.

Her eyes fell on a green swath of Arabic graffiti spray-painted across a stone wall beside Sayian's shop. It read: "The Lions of Allah protect our Land from the Zionist thieves! The hand of our enemy will be cut off!"

An elderly waiter brought her a glass of watery lemonade. She kept an eye on Sayian's shop. Where was the sharp-faced boy? Had he escaped Kallenborg? The direction she had seen him take was toward a maze of streets and alleys.

She sipped her lemonade slowly. Out of the corner of her eye she saw a young boy hand something to the elderly waiter, then disappear into the crowd of shoppers. The elderly waiter handed Christina a wadded dirty piece of paper. Smoothing it out on the table she read: "Ask at the carpet shop." Ask for what? she wondered. Ask for Hamad, of course. The trick of sending a different boy with a note increased her uneasiness, and when she paid her waiter, she gave him an extra tip to look after her bicycle. She felt light-headed as she crossed the street to Sayian's shop.

Sayian himself met Christina at the door, a sour expression on his face.

"I came to see Hamad," she said firmly.

Sayian scowled and peered up and down the street before motioning her to wait while he disappeared behind a curtain. Outlining the darkness in the back of the shop was the heavy wooden frame of a carpet loom. A row of sad-eyed little girls stared at Christina curiously in the dim light. They squatted on a plank suspended before hundreds of vertical woolen threads, knotting colored lengths of wool into the threads and trimming them to form the pile of a new carpet.

After a long interval, Sayian returned. He led Christina through a side door out into an alley. They ducked under long strands of hemp that were being twisted into rope by a gaunt Circassian man who cranked a primitive winding machine. Sayian entered another building. It had a dirt floor. Christina followed him along a dark passage lined with bales of raw hemp and heavy coils of rope cable stacked on pallets. Fat-toed lizards skipped in the dust at their approach. A revolting odor filled Christina's nostrils and she saw a fly-infested hole in the ground under a staircase that served as a latrine. As she and Sayian began to climb the stairs, she heard a mumble of voices in the room above. At the top they were stopped by a sleepy young man. His hands played with a green string of worry beads.

"This operation *al-Yahud* will not forget. This time we kill their children," said a scratchy tenor voice. "Damascus will be impressed."

She understood the implications instantly and her heart pounded.

An attack on the Jews was being planned. The Lions of Allah were tools of Assad, the Syrian President. These people were professional terrorists, not a mere gang of boys as she had supposed. Christina did not want to hear anymore. She hoped her face would not reveal her fear.

A lively gurgle came from the *nargileh* in the corner of the room where a group of coarse-looking men sat around smoking apple tobacco. A game of *sheshbesh,* a Turkish version of backgammon, was in progress. The men fell silent and turned to stare at Christina in an unfriendly manner. A short obese man in a soiled robe rose to his feet with surprising quickness. He wore dirty white Nike jogging shoes.

She recognized him instantly. He was the ugly man with the pushcart and Rayban sunglasses, the man who'd called her 'Professor Khantarish'.

"I am Hamad," he said.

He was the one who had spoken of killing children.

"You have something for me, *Khantarish?*"

Christina drew back from the insult as if slapped in the face.

"My name is Christina Goryeb. I am—."

Hamad waved his hands briskly. "Yes, I know. I know all about you and your two fine young daughters, *Khantarish*. Give me my radio now." "I have no radio for you," she said.

The fat man studied her with cool contempt. Finally he said, "In that case, what are you doing here wasting my time?"

As if by accident his robe fell open to expose a pistol, a 9mm Marakov. Christina had seen one like it when she defended a teenage boy accused of gun smuggling. She sensed that her best strategy would be to show the revolting Hamad deference.

"I need your help, *Effendi*," she said. "The Shin Bet is watching me."

Hamad gave a chuckle. ""Half of Palestine is watched by the Shin Bet. Now you are finally one of us, *Khantarish*; a second-class citizen in your own land. Now it's your own neck under the heel of the Occupation. Tell me, do you still believe this struggle can be resolved by peaceful means?"

"I am so overcome that I cannot speak," she said.

"You cannot speak, *Khantarish*?" jeered Hamad, "This is war. Do you understand?"

Christina lifted her head. "I came to warn you the Shin Bet intercepted your message."

It was Hamad's turn to be overcome and speechless. "How did they discover the radio?" he said finally.

"The Shin Bet told me a message was found on my clerk, Abu Awad. However, they said nothing about a radio."

Hamad cursed. "What did the fool tell them?"

"If you mean Abu Awad, he was tortured to death in Taggart Prison. I never had a chance to speak to him. I was summoned and questioned in Taggart two days ago."

Hamad's eyes were slits of suspicion. "Why did they release you?"

"They had no proof I committed a crime," she said simply.

"That would not stop the Shin Bet from throwing you in a cell," said Hamad. "No, I think you work for them, *Khantarish*."

She thought about telling him that the Shin Bet threaten to blow up her house, but stopped herself. It would only confirm his hunch that she had been blackmailed by the Jews, that she was compromised enough to be dangerous to him. He was a terrorist with ties to Damascus. She knew what he looked like, and where to find him. It would be in his best interest to kill her, she thought.

"If I were working for the Shin Bet, I would not be here, Hamad. I would give them copies of your messages and say nothing," she said.

Hamad looked around at the men as if to judge their reactions to her story. Finally he nodded. "That is what I would do too. Still, your release troubles me. It is most unusual. You must have influence, *Khantarish.*"

"I think not," said Christina.

"What did the Shin Bet ask you?" said Hamad.

"Many routine questions. No thanks to you, they believe I smuggle dynamite for the Lions of Allah."

Hamad seemed appeased.

"These messages are important to the future of Palestine. You took great risk to come and tell me these things and I appreciate this," he said.

"I thought it best to warn you personally, *Effendi,*" she said. "Perhaps it would be better to use a new address, somewhere more secure?"

He gave her a cunning smile.

"We need not worry. Your office on Shari' al-Fajr is still safe. In fact, it is safer than ever."

"I don't understand."

"Surely you do. You claim to have no influence yet I believe you must at least have friends who can cause trouble for the Shin Bet. So all they can do is watch you and wait. Tomorrow we circulate a rumor in the *souk* that the Lions of Allah know the Shin Bet is watching your office. Since the Shin Bet knows this is true, they will assume we will be afraid to use your office again for messages. That way we can continue to use your office under their stupid noses."

The sleepy young man looked up from the *nargileh.*

"So clever, Hamad," he giggled. He brought out a large sharp knife out of his *jalabiyya* and began cleaning his finger nails.

"I fear this is all too complicated and dangerous for me," said Christina, her heart sinking. Was there no way out of this web of deceit, violence, and death?

"Do not worry."

"No? But I'm the one the Shin Bet is watching," said Christina. "I'm the one they'll throw in prison. They'll blow up my house."

Hamad's amiability suddenly vanished.

"*Allah akbar*, God is great. He will not permit harm to fall on you or your children, but he has no mercy for those who do not serve him, *Khantarish*."

The sleepy young man drew the dull side of his knife slowly across his throat as he smiled at Christina. Then he mimicked slicing two younger, smaller necks beside her.

Sixteen

Young Muna Goryeb hummed softly, bent over a notebook on the cool earth colored tiles of the kitchen floor concentrating to blot out the currents of tension she felt in the room. She sketched tiny figures with a ballpoint pen. They wore virtually identical dresses. Nearby, at a granite counter, Christina carefully cut tomatoes and onions into thin slices but did not speak. It was Fatima's night off. Her aunts, Janine and Najat, and her grandmother, Leilah, helped to prepare a light supper of *meze*, an assortment of salads, pickles and fresh cucumbers. Thin loaves of flat bread baked on iron bowls turned upside down in the huge, Butagas-fired, brick oven on the back wall. Beside it was a modern gas range. Shiny copper pots and pans hung from a rack overhead.

"Tell me, what sort of man was this Hamad?" asked Leilah.

She wore a black *abaya* trimmed with silver embroidery and her bedroom slippers. A broken tile clicked under her lumbering tread as she went to the refrigerator.

"Fat, cruel and cunning, my Mother," said Christina.

"A Bedouin, do you think?"

Forty-five years of marriage to a respected lawyer had developed Leilah's skills in cross-examination.

"His accent was not Palestinian," said Christina.

"A Turk perhaps?"

Christina shook her head. "He spoke with a Damascus accent," she said reluctantly. She did not want to alarm her mother more than necessary.

"Then he must be one of those Syrian madmen," Leilah said. "They are the worst."

"If Papa were alive, he would know what to do," said Najat.

"Call your husband home immediately," said Leilah. "Your safety is his responsibility."

"Richard would just tell me to book the next airline flight to America," said Christina.

"I am ashamed for you," said Leilah. "Your father wrote pamphlets calling for one Arab nation with no boundaries. He would never dream of leaving our homeland."

Christina glanced down at her youngest daughter and her notebook. "Are you scribbling again, Muna?" she said sharply.

"They're my fashion designs, Mommy," said Muna.

Usually Christina didn't mind being referred to as "Mommy". Muna had learned the expression from American films that appeared on Israeli television. But today the word grated on her nerves.

"You should be reading instead. And I haven't heard you practice your piano either," she said.

Muna kept humming.

Christina frowned and looked across the room at a small blackboard on which her daughters' names were written in blue chalk, followed by three ruled columns of chores headed in Arabic, LESSONS, ROOM, and MUSIC. X's appeared in all but one of Muna's columns.

"Go practice your piano for a half-hour, Muna."

"I did it already."

"We didn't hear you. You must practice your scales."

Muna stormed out of the room. In a moment the sound of a piano echoed down the hall. Christina winced as Muna's fingers skipped hurriedly over the keys.

"Do it right," she said.

Aminah, Christina's older daughter, descended the stairs from the storeroom over the kitchen reading an American paperback romance. Christina had glanced through Aminah's book herself and had been irritated. Aminah's book reminded her of Tolstoy's *Anna Karenina* except that it took place in America and had a happy ending. The image of herself in the arms of Chaim Asher on the beach at Gan Geneva flashed through her mind like an incriminating photograph.

"Aminah, you don't have three X's," she said in a sharp voice.

"But I'm reading, Mother," said Aminah sweetly. "And it is English."

Christina rose to her feet. "Give me that worthless book. You must finish your lessons, clean your room, and practice your flute before you can play."

Aminah sulked. That was Richard's look, so stubborn and prideful. She was dark like her father, with his small even teeth, and the same thick eye lashes. She even set her jaw like Richard did.

"Give me the book," said Christina.

"Please don't take it away, Mother," Aminah cried. "I'll do my lessons right now. I promise." Then she smiled wistfully. "I so much like to read about America. Will we ever visit Daddy soon? I wish we could live in America like he does."

Leilah shot Christina a knowing glance.

"We do not belong in America. Palestine is our home," Christina said. "I want you to know who you are, to know your grandparents, aunts, cousins and uncles. Now give me that book." She held out her hand to take it.

"I hate this ugly place," Aminah cried. "I hate the soldiers, the curfews, the killing, and I hate you. I want to live with Daddy where it is safe."

Christina fought to control her temper.

"America is also a very dangerous country," she said calmly. "Students in the public schools carry guns. Washington, where your Father works is called the "Murder Capital of the World". Palestine is our home. We must stay here and we must fight to keep it. We cannot permit the Jews to steal it from us."

Aminah threw the book at Christina. Then she turned and ran out of the room.

Christina sat down, her eyes bright with tears, feeling the hot foul breath of the Occupation, the coercion, the manipulation, the constant twisting of the knife, making itself felt in every corner of her soul.

"I've got to do something, my Mother!" said Christina. "This ugliness has entered my children. They have no place to escape."

"But how was it any different for you?" asked her mother. "We are Palestinians."

"Remember Uncle Mukhtar's house," said Janine. "You used to escape from us there."

"Our house was so crowded all the time. You and Najat were such noisy children," said Christina. "I wanted to read in peace."

She remembered the interesting people who came to the old man's home to have him settle their disputes according to *sulha*, Islamic Law. How she'd admired his wise calm, his dignified bearing. He let her have the run of his library and did not laugh when she told him she wanted to be a lawyer and work for the good of Palestine like her father. The dreams of a girl come true, Christina thought. But now she was a hostage with no one to turn to for help, providing cover against her will to Syrian madmen who'd destroy her family, unless the Shin Bet blew her house up first.

"You were such a hermit," said Janine. "Always hiding in your books."

Finally Leilah spoke. "Uncle Mukhtar has great influence. Go see him tomorrow and speak with him," she said. "That's what your father would do."

Seventeen

Usually Christina ignored him as he followed her around Ramallah in his gray Fiat 124 but that morning, Asher suspected she was trying to shake him off.

When she'd left her house earlier, she nodded to him, the nod that had become part of their ritual. This morning, however, she glanced his way but did not meet his eyes as she usually did. Immediately apprehensive, he returned her nod with his usual melancholy smile, then started up the Fiat's engine and followed her at a crawl as he always did. His obvious surveillance was intended to unnerve her, to isolate her from other Palestinians, and pressure her into telling him what she knew about the Lions of Allah.

This morning, he remembered the smell of *her* and cursed under his breath.

He kept a wary eye out for assassins sent by the Lions; nonetheless he knew local Palestinians would not willingly reveal his presence to them. They knew what happened if an Israeli were harmed in their neighborhood. Any house that provided cover for an ambush was immediately blown up and bulldozed. The whole neighborhood would be harassed by the Army, and subject to curfews, tear gas, random house searches by soldiers. Family members would be detained by the police for rigorous interrogation that included beatings and torture. All the same, Asher was glad for the additional protection that Itzak Naveh's Shin Bet undercover team provided. They circulated quietly through the streets and alleys around him. Naveh's team included Ya'akov Kallenborg who posed as a messenger on a tiny Honda motorcycle.

His hunch about Christina proved right.

Instead of going directly to her office as she usually did, she detoured to her sister Najat's house. Five minutes after she arrived, he saw Najat leave the house and turn in the direction of Shari' al-Fajr. She wore Christina's light brown business suit and carried Christina's familiar brown brief case. Christina must have counted on fooling him but he noticed the difference easily. Najat, unaccustomed to carrying a heavy brief case, did not walk with Christina's graceful gait.

He parked the Fiat in an alley that ran behind Najat's house and got out. Looking around a corner, he watched Christina in a black *abaya* leave by the kitchen entrance and walk through the alleys to a side street. For a few moments his view of her was obscured by a donkey cart driven by a fresh vegetable vendor. Asher recognized the vendor as one of Naveh's men. The donkey cart passed by just in time for Asher to see Christina getting into an old Vauxhall.

Asher spoke into his walkie-talkie to Kallenborg.

"She's in a black and grey 1962 Vauxhall, blue license plate JP70263 headed west toward the traffic circle. Just follow her."

Then he turned and sprinted through the alleys, dodging around a peddler who carried his entire inventory of pots and pans on his back. Rounding a corner, he dropped his walkie talkie in a collision with a street sweeper and had to go back to retrieve it. He was panting with exertion when he got back to his Fiat.

He threw himself into the car's seat and switched on the two-way radio.

"Kallenborg, where is she now?" he said into its microphone.

A hollow crackle of static came from the radio and Kallenborg replied. "She just left the traffic circle. She's on Route 3 headed west."

Asher started the Fiat's engine and pulled away on an interception course. He radioed the military checkpoints around Ramallah, instructing them to delay Christina if she attempted to pass through their control but not to arrest her. When at last he caught up with Kallenborg, the road twisted in a southwesterly direction through hills dotted by Israeli settlements. Kallenborg's Honda could barely keep up with the Vauxhall which was 100 meters ahead and accelerating. Kallenborg hunched over the handlebars, in an attempt to reduce wind resistance, fell back as Asher's Fiat passed him.

Asher wondered what Christina was up to.

If she was headed for Jerusalem, Route 3 was certainly a roundabout way. The direct route, Route 60, ran due south from Ramallah. He accelerated until he was fifty meters behind her Vauxhall. It ran well considering its age, he reflected. His Fiat was at least as old as the Vauxhall, and the Model 124 was notoriously unreliable. If Christina pressed him hard, his Fiat might overheat, rupture a radiator hose and he'd be stranded at the side of the road.

His other problem was the traffic, mostly the new Israeli bourgeois commuting to Jerusalem or Tel Aviv from settlement apartments and Palestinian laborers seeking work in Jerusalem hiring halls. Christina easily passed a Palestinian bus slowly grinding up a steep grade. Frantically, he looked for an opening to pass but was thwarted by the oncoming traffic. When he was finally able to clear the bus there was nothing in front of him but the dusty grey road, the bright blue sky and the stony yellow hills.

She had eluded him, again.

He reached Ayna Nub, the small Palestinian village, without catching up with the Vauxhall. This was where the road forked north to Tulkarem, a larger Palestinian town or south to the settlement of B'nai Ha'eretz, one of the Torah cities. Asher elected to go north.

Five kilometers farther on, deep in the Samarian Hills, he came to a collection of rude stone huts around a well where a Palestinian blacksmith and his elderly assistant were shoeing a brown donkey. Asher got out of his car and spoke to the old man in a black *jalabiyya* who held the donkey's halter.

"Have you seen a grey and black car?" said Asher.

The old man stared at him vacantly.

"Have you seen a car?" Asher handed him a ten shekel note.

The old man nodded solemnly and spat an amber stream of chewing tobacco on the ground.

"When did it pass?" said Asher.

The old man turned to the blacksmith who was bent over with the brown donkey's hoof clamped between his knees.

"Zarb, my brother," he said. "Did we not see a car pass when your second wife came to the well to fill her jars, and the donkey who is blind kicked them so that now one of them leaks, and you laughed, for which she is angry with both of us?"

The blacksmith drove another nail.

"She will not be angry after tonight," he said with a lewd smile.

"When did the car pass by?" said Asher impatiently.

The old man screwed his eyes shut for a moment as if lost in his own head.

"This morning," he said.

"Where did it come from?"

The old man pointed north toward Tulkarem.

It was the wrong car.

Asher gave him another ten shekel note and leapt into the Fiat.

When he radioed the Ramot checkpoint near Jerusalem, he learned Christina had not passed through there. That meant that she had to be somewhere south on Route 3, he reasoned, unless she had doubled back toward Ramallah. Entering Ayna Nub, Asher saw a handful of elderly men in *jalabiyyas* with prayer rugs under their arms standing by the mosque. The Fiat careened through the intersection and roared south. He wanted to ask if they had seen a woman driving a car but there was no time.

As a professional he knew he should have excused himself from the case the moment he realized Christina Goryeb was the subject of the investigation. The sight of her face each morning was like a drug to him. He played back in his mind, the memory of making love to her on the beach, the memory of gently teasing the tips of her breasts, and of hearing her moan softly in pleasure. Until Christina, he had prided himself for his self-control and discretion. He was no monk, but he did not confuse physical desire with love, and he held his deepest feelings in reserve. He gave the best of himself for his work and did not curse his loneliness. A *katsa* was supposed to think with his brains not his balls. A *katsa* did not fall in love on the job, let alone with the enemy.

He knew what would happen to Christina if he excused himself. Mekor would assign another *katsa* to the case, someone "practical" like Ramon Boker, Gilda's latest *shmuck*, someone who would recommend that Christina be killed if she became inconvenient.

If Asher ever got out of this mess alive he planned to retire from the Mossad.

He had been thinking about quitting for years. He hated what Israel had become. The hatred started with the Lebanon War and the death of his son, David. More land, that's what Israel's Fighting Family really wanted. Every war had enlarged Israel's boundaries. Asher and his friends had been content to live in their *kibbutzes* and leave the Palestinians alone. Those new religious bastards wanted "God's Land, Jacob's inheritance," no matter how many Davids had to die for this dangerous sentimental hallucination.

The Fighting Family had killed his son, had destroyed the best part of his life.

* * *

When the Vauxhall's engine stopped running without warning, Christina's heart sank. She coasted to the side of the road pumped the accelerator desperately, and tried the starter several times, but the engine would not burst into life. She listened to the tick of hot metal coming from the engine as it cooled. A strong odor of gasoline filled her nostrils. The road vanished between two hills. Perched atop one of them she recognized the pre-cast concrete apartment blocks of an Israeli settlement. She couldn't expect any help there. Dismayed, she got out, lifted the hood, and leaned over the warm smelly engine. No loose wires or disconnected rubber hoses were visible, and she had no idea what was wrong. There was no alternative but to abandon Najat's Vauxhall and flag down a ride.

Several cars and trucks passed her without stopping. A dump truck with a load of hot asphalt pulled up behind her. She greeted the men who got out to help in Arabic. Abruptly they froze as a battered tan Volkswagen jeep rattled by and parked in front of her car. The blue and gold sticker on its bumper proclaimed THE LAWS OF TORAH COME BEFORE THE LAWS OF MEN. Christina's would be rescuers drove off quickly.

Four bearded men in army green bullet proof jackets left the jeep and approached Christina slowly. Automatic rifles were slung from their shoulders.

"What are you doing here?" a man with a pock marked face and darting black eyes demanded angrily. His Hebrew had an American accent.

"My car broke down," said Christina in Hebrew.

He grabbed Christina by the arm and shoved her into the Vauxhall. "Leave! Get out of here."

She turned the ignition key and let the engine crank several times. "I told you it won't start."

"Your carburetor's flooded!" he said. "Push the accelerator to the floor. Hold it there. Don't pump."

She looked at him blankly.

"Arab cow," he hissed. "Get out. I'll make it go."

As Christina hastened to get out of the car, her left toe caught in the hem of her *abaya*. She tripped and fell forward, landing on the pavement. Pain ran through her knees and right wrist. The men gaped at her. None offered to help her to her feet. In back she heard a screech of tires.

When she raised her head, she saw the familiar, pale-eyed, troubling face of Chaim Asher. His lips were curved in an ironic smile and he was dressed in a short-sleeved navy cotton knit shirt and khaki pants. Civilian attire. He flipped open his wallet to reveal a badge and an identification card to the four men.

"Shin Bet," he said. "What are you fine upstanding citizens doing?"

"This Arab cow is spying on us," said the bearded young man closest to Christina.

Asher's wallet disappeared as he lifted Christina to her feet. "And who are you?" he asked the men.

"We're the patrol from B'nai Ha'eretz", said the leader. He pointed to the settlement on the hill. "Watch duty. I'm Etzel Meyerson, patrol leader, at your service."

Pointing to Christina, Asher said, "Fix her car for me, will you, patrol leader Meyerson? It's a small thing."

The men from B'nai Ha'eretz looked at each other uncertainly.

"Hey, for the security of Greater *Yisroel*, why not," said Etzel with a smirk at Christina.

Asher looked at him coldly. "*Kisch mein tokus.*"

Christina rubbed her sore right wrist while the four settlers leaned over into the engine compartment. The stinging pain in her knees had subsided. If the settlers could get her car running again she might arrive at Uncle Mukhtar's on time provided, of course, she could lose Asher. He leaned nonchalantly against the side of his car. The youngest man tried one more time to start the Vauxhall's engine.

"No spark on the center lead, Etzel," the young mechanic said. It's a bad coil!"

"Well, you're out of luck," said Etzel.

"Do you have a spare?" asked Asher.

"No, they don't usually fail," said Etzel, "and we don't have money to stock extras."

The Vauxhall would not run. She would not be able to keep her appointment. She felt numb and miserable.

"We'll arrange for a mechanic to come later today," Asher told them. "Meanwhile, you men are responsible for keeping an eye on this vehicle."

Etzel gave Asher a mocking salute. "If there is nothing more we can do, we have to get back to B'nai Ha'eretz."

After lowering the Vauxhall's hood, the patrol drove off. Asher and Christina were alone.

"Arrogant bastards," he muttered to no one in particular. Then he noticed blood from her scraped knees on her abaya. "That must hurt," he said.

"It's nothing."

"No, we'll need to take care of it," he insisted.

Producing a first aid kit from the Fiat, he ordered Christina to sit in the passenger's seat. He pushed her robe over her knees with the manner of fact manner of someone accustomed to providing first aid. Deftly he cleaned the abrasions on both knees with a gauze pad. The thought that he could see her naked legs made her face burn.

"I'm afraid this will sting," he said before applying antiseptic.

She looked warily into his pale hazel eyes and saw sadness. Who was the real Chaim Asher, she wondered. Was he the policeman or the man on the beach? Unbidden, the memory of that night came back, treacherous warmth. A night of shameless pleasure, a lifetime of regret, she thought. Like a appalling drug store novel. She tried to smile as he smoothed band-aids on her knees.

He stood up. "Let's go," he said, in a business-like tone.

"Am I under arrest?" she said.

"Don't be silly, Mrs. Goryeb," he said. "I'm offering you a ride. Unless, of course, you prefer to hitch hike."

"You are on your way to Jerusalem?" she said.

"I happen to be, now," said Asher lightly. "Or wherever else you'd like to go."

"You followed me to my sister's house. I mean that's your job, isn't it, to follow me around?"

"More or less." Asher looked amused.

"Well, how did you turn up here so conveniently?"

He threw back his head and laughed. "Your little trick didn't work. Your sister doesn't walk the way you do."

His eyes flashed and the sadness in them vanished. He was clearly enjoying himself. She cast about for a plausible story to feed him. Something frivolous.

"I just wanted to go shopping in Jerusalem without the Shin Bet at my side," she said. "If it will make your job easier, Mr. Policeman, I accept your kind offer of a ride."

He laughed again.

He might not have believed her, but she had bought time. Of course, she would have to find some way to escape him after they arrived in the city. She gathered her *abaya* with all the dignity she could muster and pulled her legs into the Fiat, straightening in her seat as he shut her door. She noticed the gleaming electronic equipment nestled in a low console between the worn seats. Asher retrieved her keys from the Vauxhall and locked it. As he got into the Fiat he handed them to her, and she noticed his wedding band. He caught her eye and the melancholy look had returned to his face. Suddenly, she wanted to find out more about him, wanted to provoke his smile again.

"What will your wife say when she hears you have been driving around with a dangerous Palestinian woman?"

"My wife is dead," said Asher, in a flat toneless voice that left no room for further discussion.

He said nothing as he started the Fiat's engine. Its raspy growl filled the silence. A gust of dry hot wind through the open window blew a wisp of hair across Christina's eyes and he reached to brush it away with his right hand.

Startled, Christina pulled away and was immediately annoyed with herself for letting him know that he made her self-conscious.

She forced herself to speak.

"That night at Gan Geneva, you said half of your people want peace, Mr. Policeman. Do you remember?"

"I remember," he said.

"So, in which half do you count yourself?"

He shrugged, as though a heavy weight lay on him and he was stealing a moment's relief.

"The Gods have condemned us to live in this land together."
His voice was heavy with irony and sadness.
Suddenly she wanted to tell him about Hamad.
"Do you really think I'm a terrorist?" she said.
"That's what I'm trying to decide," he said seriously.
No, she could not confide in him. Her daughters would never live safely in Israel or Palestine again if she betrayed the Lions of Allah to the Shin Bet. And Chaim Asher, this moody and sentimental man who once made love to her, had also threatened to blow up her house.

To keep this land, she thought, each side had threatened to destroy her. Yet the land was hers as well, and she could not bear to leave it.

* * *

They did not speak again until the Fiat reached the outskirts of East Jerusalem a quarter of an hour later. The highway passed through the Ar-Ram checkpoint and wound through slopes densely packed with residential quarters before becoming clogged with a busy cobweb of traffic.

"There's a garage just ahead, to your left, Ghassan's," Christina said. "They have a tow truck."

Asher turned off and drove slowly through a narrow street. The familiar welcome sights of a bustling Palestinian neighborhood greeted Christina's eyes. As swarms of children ran up and down the stairs and in and out of courtyards, women scrubbed clothes. Bright cotton garments dried on lines between the buildings. In a barred window, an old man stroked his cat while he read. Some boys played marbles on a level patch of ground. Asher stopped in front of a line of cinder block buildings. Clustered on both sides of the street and up on the sidewalk, automobiles waited to be repaired. By the garage door, in a shower of sparks, a welder repaired an engine block that lay on a pallet of old tires.

Asher looked around. "Are you sure you want me to leave you here?"
"I'll be all right. You've been very kind", said Christina.
"Look, this doesn't look like a safe place to leave a woman alone."
Christina laughed.
"But the people here know me. I'll have Ghassan pick up my car. While he is mending it, I'll call a taxi and do some shopping. My car should be ready this afternoon."

Asher dawdled. He was obviously reluctant to let her go but she knew she had outwitted him for the time being. As she opened the door, she couldn't resist a parting dig.

"Is your concern for my safety a professional matter or is it merely personal?"

Asher grinned. "Strictly professional, Mrs. Goryeb. Enjoy your shopping."

Abruptly the phone in Asher's car rang and he lifted the receiver. "Ghassan's. Red and green sign. Cover the rear exits," he said.

It took no imagination to guess who he was talking to.

He'd trapped her again.

Eighteen

Christina watched Asher's Fiat disappear from view at the next intersection. She expected he would double back, wait down the block and follow her when she came out. She thought of sneaking out the back of Ghassan's garage but she knew Kallenborg would be waiting for her. There had to be a way to escape.

She found Ghassan leaning over the counter in his office, scowling at a pencil-thin young man. The garage man's dingy *kaffiyeh* was splotched with ketchup and car grease.

"Ghassan, my car has broken down," Christina said.

"It is always a pleasure to serve you, Mrs. Goryeb. Where do I find your car?"

She gave him directions and took a large bank note from her gown pocket. It was twice what the normal towing charge would be.

Ghassan picked up the money with alacrity.

"Can you have my car ready at five o'clock?" she said.

"But of course. Will you need to rent a car?"

The thin young man interrupted.

"I own a taxi, Madame, a splendid big American sedan." He pointed to a well polished white 1963 Mercury parked inside the garage. The Mercury's engine wheezed with slow, labored beat. Whatever repairs Ghassan had performed on it were obviously temporary.

Christina wondered whether she should risk an escape in this elderly taxi. She had nothing to lose and she was late for her meeting with Uncle Mukhtar. She gave the driver an appraising look.

"Do you know the Wadi el-Joz district?" she said.

The driver nodded eagerly.

"I'll take this taxi, Ghassan," she said.

She would ask the driver to drop her near Uncle Mukhtar's home. While he was settling his bill with Ghassan, she slipped into the back seat of the Mercury. Asher would not see her if she lay on the taxi's floor.

Triumphantly the thin young man returned and slid behind the wheel.

"We leave at once."

Nineteen

Izz Din Riad looked down at the flat brown roof tops of the Old City from his terrace garden. Where was Christina Goryeb he wondered, and why did she want to see him? Izz Din Riad, the Naqib al-Ashraf, Chief of the Prophet's Descendants in Palestine, wore a spotless white *kaffiyeh* over his dark suit with a carefully knotted silk paisley tie. His short white beard and mustache were neatly trimmed. With faintly imperial movements, he consulted the large gold Patek Philippe on his wrist. Christina was already a half hour late. Every minute of his day was accounted for by the timetable of the faithful. Sybil, his stout, white-haired English wife, cut long stemmed roses and handed them to a waiting gardener.

As he had every morning, the old Sheik rose at sunrise and kneeled upon a threadbare prayer rug, his most prized possession. Izz Din Riad was one of the wealthiest landlords in East Jerusalem. His mind was a myriad of subtleties. He possessed a quick, lucid intellect that had an uncanny ability to see into his adversaries' hearts. He knew that Jews were ruled by sentimentality and he knew what those sentiments were. He spoke to Jews as a Jew, to Palestinians as an Arab, and to American reporters as an Englishman. No one knew what went on in Izz Din Riad's mind except himself. As a young man he had dreamed of becoming a great Palestinian leader and had fought the Jews in 1948 when Jordan's Arab Legion led by the Englishman John Bagot Glubb, tried to prevent the Jews from seizing a land they believed was theirs in restitution for the Holocaust, a crime that Palestinians did not commit. But those dreams like the dreams of many Palestinians were never realized.

When his prayers were done, Izz Din Riad had performed the rigorous exercises that kept his sixty-eight year-old body almost as fit as it had been when he fought in the Arab Legion, alongside the British in World War II, against the Vichy French in Syria, and against the Arab tribes of Iraq who sided with Hitler. After a breakfast of coffee and toast with Sybil, he went to his study to read and dictate replies to his correspondence. At ten o'clock he walked to the spacious living room in the back of his house. Men squatted on its cool tile floors or sat on thick cushions placed around polished brass trays on low folding tables. Behind the louvered windows, shaded outside by acacia trees, in dim surroundings infused with heavy clouds of cigarette smoke, the sharp fragrance of Turkish coffee and the hiss of whispered discourse, Izz Din Riad would listen to his supplicant's requests with head bent and eyes closed until noon. Most Palestinians came to him with civil disputes, disagreements about business dealings, political alliances, grazing and water rights, land boundaries, family feuds, an amulet for a sick goat or donkey, the payment of a bride's dowry. His decisions followed *sulha*, Islamic law. There were others who consulted with him but about less mundane matters. At a quick nod from his secretary, Izz Din Riad would step into the adjacent room for a private meeting, or murmur advice cautiously on his cellular phone that he suspected was also was listened to by Israeli intelligence.

* * *

Sybil glanced curiously over Izz Din Riad's shoulder. "Christina Rantissi. What on earth are you doing?" she said.

She could never seem to remember Christina's married name.

Izz Din Riad turned to see Christina climbing down the garden wall and for a moment he remembered her as a young girl again, the daughter of Darwish Rantissi, a close friend who refused to let the Jews push him off his land. Having the run of his neighborhood with her best girl friend, Suha, the girl who lived next door. Climbing trees and walls, playing hiding and seek, swinging on ropes, dressing up Suha's cat in doll clothes, reading books for hours in the crook of an old olive tree in his garden.

The adult Christina, fear in her eyes, jumped to the ground and hugged him as he bent to kiss her cheek. "Oh, my Uncle, I am in so much trouble," she said.

When he looked at the top of the wall again he saw nothing there. "But you are always getting into mischief," he said with a slight smile. Patience would reveal everything to him in good time. "We delayed lunch, but when you didn't arrive we began to give up hope that you might come," he said. He pointed to a little glass-top table with bowls of food and rattan chairs on the veranda.

"Dear Christina, so good to see you," Sybil said in fluent Arabic. "But why on earth did you climb over the garden wall?"

Izz Din Riad said, "She is in some kind of difficulty. Let's sit down to lunch and she will tell us about it."

They moved to the rattan chairs around the table. Flower pots were arranged along the edge of the veranda, bleeding hearts, petunias, and more roses. The gleaming Dome of the Rock mosque rose in the foreground on Mount Moriah of antiquity and beyond it the minaret of the Al-Aqsa near the Wailing Wall of the Jews.

Sybil said, "The cook made your two favorite dishes, *tabuli* and *yabrak*."

Christina took small servings of each and a piece of thin flat bread.

"Is that all you are having?", asked the older woman. "You used to eat all the time."

"I'm really not that hungry."

"She doesn't have a young girl's appetite anymore," said Izz Din Riad.

"I should remember. You have children of your own now," said Sybil. "We never get to see enough of you. Is your husband still in America?"

"Yes."

"Will he be returning to Palestine soon?", said Sybil.

There was an awkward pause as Sybil with bird-like gestures poured black over-sweetened coffee from a pitcher into tiny handle less cups. There was a slight tremor in her hands.

"Richard has taken a position in a university in America," Christina said stiffly. He writes me that he is an informal advisor to the American government."

"Now tell us about this trouble you are in," said Izz Din Riad.

As Christina told her story, he regarded her thoughtfully but did not speak.

"This man—they called him Hamad—said he would kill me and my children if I did not continue to accept messages for the Lions of Allah," said Christina.

Sybil covered her mouth. Her hand tremor had become disturbing.
"My Uncle, you have many influential friends," Christina said.
"Perhaps you know someone Hamad might listen to."
"My friends do not usually conduct business with men like
Hamad," Izz Din Riad said, gently. In another part of his mind he considered the options, but with a sinking heart. There was a time he
could have set spies to work. These agents would find out who
Hamad was, and either bribe him to stay away from Christina, or
betray him to the Jews who would arrest him. There was a time when
Izz Din Riad would simply have had Hamad killed. But today certainly this Hamad did not act alone. Today, a man like Hamad would
be the leader of a military cell of a larger organization with influential
outside connections. Connections like Hamas, that was aided by Syria;
or Hizbollah, the Party of God, that was directed by Iran; or Islamic
Jihad, that received help from Palestinians living in American, or any
one of half a dozen other terrorist organizations with powerful
patrons. Sadly, these people were beyond his reach or powers of per-
suasion. It was always prudent to affect events without taking responsibility, even if friends or family were involved.

"One of my clients told me there is a secret organization that runs
the *Intifada*," said Christina.

The *Intifada* was never put down by Israel although it was less
active after 1992, its organizational structure was still intact.

"You mean the Orient House?" he said. "It's one of their poorest
kept secrets."

"Do you know anyone connected to it?" said Christina.

"I have a slight acquaintance with the man who organizes the
young stone-throwers, the *shabiba*," he said.

Christina's face brightened with hope.

The *shabab*, the mainstay of the *Intifada*, were organized into neighborhood clubs and their leader would be appear to be a valuable ally.

"Unfortunately, neither he nor the Orient House would be able to
help you with Hamad," said the old Sheik.

"Why not?"

He looked at Christina patiently.

"My dear, many groups with many objectives are fighting for
Palestine. The Orient House is a sort of sidewalk cafe where every
leader talks, and only some of them listen."

Christina took a sip of coffee, her eyes fixed on the old gentleman.
"There must be someone we know that this Hamad would listen to?" said his wife.

"I'm afraid there is not," he said and felt ashamed.

"What should I do now?" Christina said.

"My dear," he said, "I wish I knew."

"Well, I have some advice," said Sybil looking squarely at Christina. "This Hamad is not your biggest problem. You better get yourself to America, and do it quickly, or you lose that husband of yours to a pretty American girl. Whatever happened between you two?"

"My duty is here in Palestine," said Christina to Sybil. "My husband believes he can serve our cause better in America. He writes frequently, asking me to join him."

Izz Din Riad gave Sybil a sidelong glance. "It isn't easy to leave Israel, even for someone like yourself who is married to an American citizen," he said to Christina. "I would imagine the Israeli government wants to keep you here so they could find their dynamite smuggler." His eyes narrowed slightly. "A second possibility is—"

Christina interrupted him. "My Uncle, I know my predicament."

The old man raised a hand. "Hear me out, please." His face was inscrutable. "Suppose you cooperate with the Shin Bet by giving them copies of Hamad's messages."

"Become an informer? Never!! Besides Hamad would cut the throats of my children before my very eyes."

Izz Din Riad's smile was back in place and his eyes met Christina's. "There is a third possibility," he said quietly. "Continue to let Hamad use your office as a letter drop and tell no one."

"The Shin Bet will blow up my house," said Christina.

"The Shin Bet will not know," he said. "You yourself said they do not have any solid evidence against you, and they do not possess sufficient resources to watch you constantly. Certainly Hamad won't tell them."

"So the enemy of my enemy is my friend?", said Christina sadly.

"We all serve the same cause in different ways," Izz Din Riad said.

Twenty

Another perfect day on the Jesus Riviera, thought Gilda Sderot cynically as she looked out over the biblical sea of Galilee, from the Caesar, one of Tiberius's newest hotels. It could not be more than eight-thirty in the morning. White jacketed stewards straightened rows of cushioned lawn chairs beside the swimming pool where hotel guests, mostly American church groups with their pastors, would be soon working on their expensive sun tans. In the gravel paths that ran between beds of bright crocus and lilies, Arab gardeners bent to remove cigarette butts and camera film foils. Beyond was the long golden beach where more men raked and smoothed sand trucked in from the Negev desert, put up beach umbrellas, and tightened the ropes of bright colored beach cabanas. On the far shore were orchards and vineyards of old *kibbutzes* built in the 1930s while in the distance rose the dark volcanic wall of the Golan.

With mounting impatience, she watched Ramon Boker windsurf in lazy, oblivious arcs on the choppy blue water. For reassurance, she opened a small black compact and examined her face in its mirror. A striking face with heavy lidded eyes and full sensual lips stared back at her. The face of a powerful, young tigress. She held the glass closer searching for signs of wrinkles or blemishes. No, her skin was still perfect. Her dark eyes glittered like polished onyx flecked with gold. She smiled and the face in the mirror smiled back at her. That knowing, intimate smile could make grown men cream in their pants. Any man except Chaim Asher, she thought resentfully. The night she'd taken him to a nude Mossad swimming pool party, he'd been more than willing, avid with a ravenous intensity that matched her lust. But the morning after he was remote and cool as ever. I'd only bore you, Gilda, he'd said.

Gilda had already beckoned twice for Boker to come in, but he'd ignored her, deliberately, she thought angrily. *As if windsurfing was almost better than making love.* An inshore breeze blew steadily kicking up white caps that made Booker's surfboard vault into the air. He'd complained the other *katsas* called him "Gilda's schmuck" behind her back. Let them whine, she thought. Their jibes helped remind him she was the "horse" who helped him up the Mossad's promotion ladder. He yearned for the privileges and prestige that advancement would bring. The conceited young fool prided himself on all of his abilities. She found his compact well-made body irresistible and he knew it. With a surge of anger, she realized he wanted to see how far he could push her, how far he could tease her and still keep control.

"Boker," she yelled. "Get your *tokus* in here."

Now he hauled on the sail and turned in toward the beach, pointing the surfboard directly at her. He ran up on the sand and slid to a stop at her feet.

She frowned at him. "Why didn't you come when I first called?" she said reproachfully.

"The wind is great," he said.

"I'm cold, I want to go in," she said.

"So go in. I wanted to sail."

She slipped her hand under his trunks. Her finger gently probed the cleft between his buttocks, teasing. She felt his cock stir but he made a show of ignoring her so she gently squeezed his balls.

"Well, if you insist," he said with a tight smile.

Their room was on the tenth floor. It was luxuriously trimmed with white marble and brass, but the hotel's owners had cheaped out on the furniture, which was covered with imitation wood vinyl. He disappeared into the bathroom while Gilda poured herself a glass of the hotel's complimentary wine from the refrigerator. It was Carmel, another cheap touch that irritated her. If those tightwads wanted to buy Jewish wine, the least they could have done was buy Rothschild's, she thought. She went out on the balcony. The white marble floor tiles were warm, almost hot to her bare feet, from the morning sun. In a moment she heard the sound of water running in the shower. He emerged a few minutes later wearing a towel tucked around his waist.

"Why didn't you tell me you wanted to go to Copenhagen?" she said sweetly. "Did you actually think I wouldn't find out?"

"I didn't want to tell you until I got the job," he said.

"But why Copenhagen?"

The angry words poured out.

"For the same reason anyone with a brain in this place wants out. *Yisroel* is too small, too damned tribal, the Orthodox ram their crappy religion down everybody's throats."

"You were born here," said Gilda sharply. "This is your home."

Now she was Gilda, the patriot, the guardian of *Eretz Yisroel*.

"Look—just because I was born here doesn't mean I can't experience a wider life," he said. "There's a world out there, I want to live in it."

She didn't say anything for a while and he gave her a bleak look.

"Many Israelis want out," he said. "There is a 7-year waiting list to go to the U.S."

"Yes, but to *say* you want out when you work for the Mossad is treason!"

He stared at her defiantly. "If you feel that way, I might as well start packing my bags."

"Don't give me that look! I could transfer you to an Army unit in South Lebanon."

"Fuck me to tears!" He gave her a dismissive gesture.

"Your butt would be Jew-burgers if the Hizbollah ever found out you were an ex-*katsa*," she said harshly.

He went inside and sat down in the bed.

Relief flooded through her as she followed him. She stood in front of him gently stroking his hair. "Think about your career, Ramon. Next year Mike may assign you to *Al*."

Al was the ultra secret Mossad unit that spied on the U.S.

"Once assigned to *Al*, you'd be enjoying the good life in America instead of chasing Arabs around Europe."

He looked up with interest. "So what's the catch?"

"There is no catch, darling." She cleared her throat. "In the meantime, there is the Goryeb case which gives you a unique opportunity to do something under Mike's nose."

"My career, like the rest of me, is yours," Boker said slyly. He lay back on the bed, waiting for her to finish what she had started on the beach.

"Chaim Asher is blowing the Goryeb Case. He's lost his nerve and his reflexes. I'd love to turn you loose on Christina Goryeb. It would be a good chance for your to show Mike what you can really do."

"Is that all?"

"No," she said. "Undress me."

He slid to his knees. He unbuckled her belt. Her skirt slipped down easily around her ankles and she stepped out of it. He kissed her soft olive stomach, resting his tongue on her navel while he pulled down the elastic band of her silk panties to expose the mass of dark curly hair that covered her cunt. Gilda's face was avid with anticipation, lips parted and eyes wide her fingers fumbled with the buttons of her blouse. He bent to lick the inside of her left thigh. She rewarded him with a little side-step to give him greater access. He moved higher, his tongue barely grazing her skin until his face was buried in the nest of curls at the junction of her thighs. He smelled expensive French perfume and tasted her salty moistness as his tongue parted her cunt lips. The tip of his tongue targeted her clitoris. In for the kill.

"Ahh, God!" she sighed. She sat down on the bed, unhooked her bra. Her heavy breasts spilled out, silky olive with large raised brown nipples. Her ultimate weapon, he thought.

Quickly he pulled off his towel to reveal a gigantic erection. The head of his cock was smooth, bulbous, almost purple. Gilda took into her mouth, sucked on it greedily. He trembled as she ran her tongue under its circumcised tip. A delicious ache spread across his groin.

His eyes met Gilda's. She must really want me to stay, he thought.

"And now its your turn," she said sweetly.

He knelt between her legs again. She fell back on the bed, her legs wide apart. He licked her inner lips with his tongue, her cunt a banquet to be savored slowly.

Her belly heaved until she pulled him away and laughed.

"Let's fuck, tomorrow we may die," she said in a mocking voice.

He laughed wit her. "The motto of the Mossad," he said.

Of course Gilda would be on top, but that gave him more control. He adjusted the pillows behind his back and bent forward to take her stiffened nipple into his mouth. He rubbed it gently against the back of his front teeth with his tongue. She teased herself with his cock while her hips shifted in little rocking movements. Finally, she slipped him inside her. Her hot quivering cunt slipped back and forth on his bare groin. Now she rode him the way he'd surfed the sea. Watching the mesh of their sexual organs drove the pitch of his excitement higher and then suddenly he was afraid he'd come too soon, cheating her, earning her scorn. Quickly, he distracted himself by thinking of something he hated.

A scraggly bearded Hasid in a black suit screaming at Boker for driving his car on the Sabbath.

A wooden crate in Lebanon filled with butchered body parts dripping with blood that had once been Maronite Christians.

Gilda arched her back and dug her long manicured nails into his taunt buttocks. She gave a low lusty cry and his diversionary mental picture show stopped. She collapsed in his arms and he rolled her over. He fucked her with a vengeance until he too cried out.

"No Copenhagen *shicksa* can fuck you like this," she said triumphantly.

Twenty-One

Late that afternoon on Azza Street in Rehavia, West Jerusalem, when Naomi Litvin got out of her taxi and looked up at the golden-hued stone building where she lived. The heavy smell of cooking *kishke*, stuffed cabbage and *gefilte* fish hung in the air, and the iron manhole cover at her feet bore the inscription, "City of Manchester", a relic of the British Mandate and the early days of *Yisroel*.

Life had been intense and difficult when she was a child, but full of hope. She remembered her father, a surgeon at Hadassah Hospital, leaving home every morning wearing his spotless white tunic buttoned on the left side. In the warm evenings, her mother, Lillian, served glasses of cold tea and sandwiches of boiled tongue while everyone debated politics around the kitchen table, disciples of Israeli patriots like Ephraim Katzir, Menachem Ussishkin and Eliezar Sukenik. They were building a socialist utopia, raising their children free of the stifling ghetto culture of Eastern Europe. Their landlord was Darwish Rantissi, Christina's father. Naomi had grown up with the Rantissi girls as playmates, speaking Arabic almost as well as she spoke Hebrew.

She was troubled when she thought of Christina. She knew that Christina's marriage was no longer a happy one, unlike her own. Thoughts of Christina and the happiness of marriage inevitably led to Chaim Asher. She had sensed the mutual attraction between Christina and Asher the moment she introduced them; it was as though they were two halves of the same puzzle. She knew Asher through her connection to Kibbutz Gan Geneva, where he adroitly guided tourists through one of the surviving remnants of socialist utopia. Their conversations related to legal affairs, never personal matters, but she sensed the deep grief in him, and that he had built walls to protect himself from further pain. When he visited her office the day after the picnic on the beach to ask for Christina's phone number, he'd been jaunty as a schoolboy in love. She had withheld the number at Christina's request. A love affair between them would have been impossible. Love between a Palestinian and a Jew was doomed in a country where the only permitted passions were religious zealotry and tribalism. She realized she was allowing herself the luxury of despair. Despair, she told herself firmly, was out of the question. A Peace Now rally was scheduled that night. She hoped Yigael would want to go; she knew she had to.

As Naomi entered her apartment she was greeted by the mouth watering aroma of frying potato *latkes*. Her husband, Yigael in his army green T-shirt and fatigue trousers looked up from the kitchen sink where he was washing dishes. He had spent the past six weeks with his army reserve unit. He dried his hands and came out to greet her. She was so happy to see him, she could have cried.

"Well, hello," he said with a tired smile.

She embraced him. He smelled of stale Marlboros and sweat.

Naomi's mother, Lillian, nodded from the stove but Natan, Naomi and Yigael's fourteen year old son, seated at the kitchen table with his nose in a math book, as usual barely acknowledged her arrival.

"Christina telephoned," Lillian said. "She's coming over to talk to you."

"Did she say what it was?"

"No, but she sounded upset."

They sat down in the living room. Yigael handed Naomi a glass of wine and a piece of cheese.

"How I missed you," she said her hand resting on his. But we shouldn't get too comfortable, darling. There's a 'Peace Now' rally at City Hall, and we have to go."

She knew what he was thinking. He'd been sleeping on the ground for six weeks, eating bad food and dust. He wanted a shower and a shave, followed by food and sex, not an angry crowd.

"A rally? What for this time," he said with a notable lack of enthusiasm.

Naomi sighed. She could read him so well.

"We are protesting the expropriation of a Palestinian's land for new Haredim neighborhoods," she said.

The Haredim were a sect of ultra-Orthodox Jews. Yigael hated them for their arrogant intolerance of non-observant Jews.

"The cause can get along without us this time, Naomi," he said. "I'm beat."

Naomi frowned.

"Yigael, they want to send us into a war with the Palestinians that will never end. It will consume us, our children, all we care for."

Natan lifted his head from his math book. "Papa, you have to go," he said.

Lillian shot him a fierce look. "Get back to your homework, Natan."

Yigael's voice was laced with anger. "The Haredim don't recognize the Government of *Yisroel* and won't serve in the army that protects them," he said.

"So why get so upset? It will be useful for them to see how many we are." She smiled gently.

"You think they're like *Fiddler On A Roof*. Well they're not quaint, they're not harmless and I hate them," he said. "See, I'm losing my temper already."

Naomi bit into her cheese.

"You know, the Deputy Mayor in charge of city planning, is a member of the United Torah Party, she said."

"That blood sucking hypocrite!"

"If you feel that way, you really come to the rally with me."

There was a knock at the door. When Naomi rose to open it, Christina stood in the doorway, her head covered with a long Palestinian scarf.

"Come in. I'm so happy to see you. Come in," Naomi said.

"I need to talk to you," said Christina. "Privately."

That was when Naomi noticed that Christina's mascara was streaked. She'd been crying, and the Christina she knew never cried.

* * *

When the two women left for the rally, Yigael returned to the kitchen. It was a corner room, his favorite room in the apartment; cluttered and comfortable with peeling linoleum on the floor, and tall white painted cabinets that rose to the ceiling. The soft warm light of the afternoon sun shown through two large windows. Lillian removed *latkes* from skillet and piled them in a serving bowl.

"Let's watch the news," he said to her.

"Why not."

Yigael switched on the small black and white television on the counter. It flickered into focus just as the announcer said, "Recent protests by Jewish settlers raised new concerns in the army. Two hundred rabbis have declared that no soldier need obey an order to dismantle a settlement."

Yigael scowled at the screen.

"We won't have an army if soldiers can choose which order to obey," he said.

"Then we are finished," said Lillian matter-of-factly. She handed Yigael a plate of latkes and apple sauce.

The announcer moved on to the next news item. "Increased security will be provided at a 'Peace Now' rally this evening at City Hall where Prime Minister Rabin is expected to speak. Members of the Gush Emunim movement are rumored to join in a counter demonstration with Kach, Kahane Chai and Haredim supporters."

Kach had been led by the fiery Rabbi, Meir Kahane, until his assassination in New York City by Arab terrorists. The Kach movement was officially outlawed in Israel after one of its members threw a grenade into a 'Peace Now' rally, killing one person and injured six.

"I thought the Gush Emunim and the Haredim despise each other?" said Lillian.

"They still do, it's one of those stupid religious dispute," said Yigael.

Most of the religious settlers believed the End of Days prophesied in the Bible was at hand and they were its agents, an utter heresy to the Haredim who equated such doctrine with the false Messiah.

"Such charming people!" Lillian said.

Yigael rose to his feet and reached for his fatigue jacket.

"Aren't you going to eat more?" said Lillian.

"I better go to that damn rally."

* * *

Yigael walked briskly toward the central business district in Jerusalem. It was located in the triangle formed by King George Road, Ben Yudah and Jaffa streets. Kenyon Jerusalem, a sprawling multi-level shopping mall with vaulted glass roofs supported on chrome and steel, dominated the sky line. Late-model Subarus, Volvos and Mercedes-Benzes zipped past Yigael on the street. A throng of men in black suits, beards, and black hats moved quickly by on the opposite sidewalk, also headed for City Hall. He heard a far-away noise that sounded like chanting. Rounding the corner he caught sight of Naomi and Christina on the edge of a street crowded with demonstrators, thousands of them. Many of the demonstrators carried Israeli and Palestinian flags. There were also banners that said "One Nation Not Many Ghettos" and "Peace Now, Not Violence." He watched Naomi and Christina pause, as if deciding what to do. Then they joined in.

* * *

The route up King George Road was lined with security men and soldiers. Demonstrators walked in tightly packed bunches. Most wore modern clothing, slacks, jeans and skirts but mixed in the crowd were small groups of Israeli Arabs in traditional robes.

Naomi was worried. Christina had said so little since they left the apartment, and Naomi's concern mounted as she marched beside her friend.

Finally Christina said over the hubbub, "I've decided to go live with my husband in America."

Naomi was astonished.

"I never believed you'd give up."

"I am so very tired." Christina's glance was pure reproach.

Naomi laid a hand on Christina's arm.

"I am so desperately tired of this insane place," Christina said.

"Oh, Christina, of course it's insane." Naomi swung her hand in a wide arc. "But where else do you see Palestinians dressed like shepherds in the Bible, Jews like 18th-century Lithuania, and people wearing blue jeans and T-shirts."

"And all of them clawing at each other's throats," she said bitterly.

"Only the lunatics are clawing, Christina. Most people want peace like we do," she said with conviction. "We can't give up now."

But she saw the exhaustion in Christina's face and regretted reproaching her friend. Of course Christina needed to be with her husband now.

"Will you take over my client's cases?" said Christina.

Naomi took Christina's hand in hers with a gentle confiding grasp. "Of course I will."

They walked in silence.

Naomi tried to imagine Christina in America, unable to practice law, wholly dependent on Richard for the first time.

"The children and I will lose our souls in America," said Christina. "But if we stay we will lose our lives." She whispered the rest in Naomi's ear. "My law clerk Abu Awad passed messages for the Lions of Allah. The Shin Bet found out before I did, and they killed him. Now I'm under surveillance because they think I'm working for the Lions. Meanwhile, the Lions have threatened to hurt my children if I don't continue to let them use me."

Naomi stared at her speechless.

Christina continued. "The Shin Bet threatened me with prison but decided to let me go. They're trying to get me to inform on the Lions but I really don't know anything about them."

"I'll be your lawyer," Naomi said. "You can count on me."

"You'll be the first person I call."

Naomi thought some more. "Perhaps the Lions of Allah can be persuaded to leave you alone," she said.

"I asked Uncle Mukhtar to intervene with the Lions on my behalf but he is powerless."

"Forgive me for not understanding. Of course you must leave as soon as possible," said Naomi.

"We will leave on Tish B'av. Tomorrow I go to the U.S. Consulate for visas. The next day I present arguments at Daoud Rubez's detention hearing."

"I can argue that case for you."

"Thank you but no, I promised this one personally."

Above them loomed the vertical black and white stripes of the City Tower-Eilon Tower skyscraper. Here the procession turned on Ben Yudah Street and entered the Midrachov, the center of downtown Jerusalem where motor vehicles were prohibited. The outdoor cafes and small shops that offered street food, clothing, shoes, jewelry, and souvenirs were closed, their metal shutters pulled down. City Hall was around the corner on Jaffa Road. Suddenly more security men appeared wearing riot gear. Soldiers in full battle dress, observed the procession closely. Numerous Haredim men in black crowded along either side of the street. They shouted "God Will Punish the Blasphemers". The marchers responded by singing *The Song of Peace*.

Naomi joined in enthusiastically in the refrain. "Just sing a song of peace, don't whisper a prayer, sing a song of peace loudly."

Christina remained silent.

A flying wedge of West Bank settlers, bearded men wearing army jackets and carrying M-16's slung on their backs, pushed and shoved their way into the marchers just in front of Naomi and Christina. Quickly they linked arms and blocked the street. A vivid yellow Kach banner was unfurled in their midst and held high between two poles.

Naomi felt Christina's grip on her hand tighten.

"We must get away from here," Christina said.

They tried to turn and run but it was impossible to go against the flow of the crowd. The marchers pressed angrily against the wall of armed men. Under their onslaught, the human barricade began to fall apart. Naomi saw one or two marchers push through and run toward City Hall. Several demonstrators grappled with settlers and were thrown to the pavement. Naomi felt dizzy with fear. Riot police carrying plastic shields and rubber truncheons moved swiftly to separate the settlers from the marchers.

From the other side of Ben Yudah Street, a group of Haredim counterattacked. They wore yellow paper Stars of David pinned to their coats and chanted "*sodot medina mishtara*", secret state police. A beefy black clad man struck a policeman with both fists. The officer staggered and fell backward.

There were no longer any bystanders, Naomi realized. Everyone was drawn into the free-for-all. Naomi and Christina searched anxiously for an escape route. A teenage boy standing next to Naomi yelped as a stone struck him in the head. Another marcher, shoved from behind, collided with Christina and she went down. As Naomi helped her up, she noticed Christina's hands were bleeding. A man in a blue plaid shirt lay dazed on the pavement. People stepped on him, and Naomi could not reach him to help. It was all she could do to cling to Christina and keep her own balance.

A middle aged Haredim man with a reddish beard pushed his face at Naomi. Fury coursed through his body up and down like a big angry snake coiling and uncoiling inside the black cloth of his suit. His features were white and rigid.

"You self-hating Jewish piece of shit, politics is not for women!" he shouted at her.

He lowered his head and butted Naomi in the stomach. All the air rushed out of her lungs and she fell to her knees. She stayed doubled over, outraged, frightened, and racked with agony. Time seemed to stand still as she tried desperately to inhale. Her mouth worked gulping air, but her body seemed to have forgotten how to breathe. She wondered if she were dying, dimly aware that Christina was now struggling with the Harredim brute. And then she saw a familiar stocky figure in army fatigues.

Yigael!

He caught the red-bearded man by the shoulder, spun him around and hit him once very hard on the bridge of his nose with the edge of his hand. There was a soft popping sound and blood spurted out. The man crumpled up with a sharp cry of pain. "Don't hit me, again," the man groaned, shielding his face with his hands.

Naomi's lungs filled gratefully with air. Yigael lifted her in his strong arms. "Follow me," she heard him say to Christina. Naomi's head was pressed against his chest. She heard the rhythmic pounding of his heart as he carried her out of the crush toward the edge of the crowd. Now it was safe to cry. She sobbed uncontrollably, felt the hot tears run down her cheeks. Once they were away from the mob, Yigael put her down and wiped her eyes.

"Let's all go home," he said. "Christina you must spend the night with us so you can get some rest."

But Christina shook her head.

* * *

With white clenched hands Christina drove the Vauxhall slowly back to Ramallah. Had any day been longer she wondered. Although the return trip was much shorter than the winding road to the West that Christina had taken that morning, the journey seemed to last forever. The setting sun cast deep shadows in the hills.

Richard was right, she thought, and she was wrong. Even if many Israelis longed for peace, the violence she had just witnessed in Jerusalem pointed to darker times were ahead.

Rising in the mountains to the left, a lonely minaret marked the mosque built over the cenotaph of the prophet Samuel. A few minutes later she drove past the Semaris Hotel on the right, once the finest tourist hotel in Jordan, now used only as a lecture hall. When she caught sight of the Arak distillery she knew Ramallah was around the next bend.

Ramallah, her beloved, tragic, hopeless home.

Twenty-Two

Ten o'clock the next morning, Christina anxiously waited with a small group of Palestinians and Israelis in a room on the second floor of the U.S. Consulate for her name to be called. Her face was hot with shame for deserting Palestine. From time to time, a middle-aged American man with a neatly trimmed fringe of gray hair called out names and summoned people into an office at the end of the room. When they returned, their faces told what happened behind the closed door. The unlucky ones were grim and full of despair. One young man left weeping. The expressions of those who were going to America were jubilant.

On her lap was Daoud Rubez's petition. She looked down and re-read it for the third time. Tomorrow she would appear in Court to argue against his detention. She made a mental note to call Aaron Rosenbluth and remind him to appear as a witness for Daoud.

Where were Najat, Muna and Aminah she wondered? They were to have arrived an hour ago.

A stylishly dressed Palestinian woman with sad eyes sat next to Christina. The woman wore a red scarf around her shoulders and her fingers were covered with gold rings. Christina assumed the sallow-faced boy with the croaky adolescent voice next to her must be her son. He looked sullen and defiant.

The woman smiled at Christina. Christina realized she had been staring and looked away, embarrassed.

"Do we know each other?" the woman asked.

Christina introduced herself. "I come from Ramallah."

"I'm from Ramallah too. My name is Marid. I feel I should know you. Your name is familiar," said the woman. "Where are you going?"

"We're not leaving. I'm just registering my girls for their passports," Christina lied. She wanted to divert Marid's attention away from herself. "Are your neighbors upset with you for leaving?"

"Are you crazy?" Marid said. "They wish they were me. Anyone who can get out should get out."

"What does your husband say?"

"My husband is a civil engineer in Toledo, Ohio," said Marid proudly.

"Then you have nothing to worry about," said Christina.

"I am registering my son for his passport." Marid's handsome face contorted suddenly with fear. "I'm concerned for his education. The Shin Bet threw him in prison for three months, for no reason and he missed his final exams."

"It has happened to other boys, too," said Christina.

"Well, I'm coming back," said a stout businessman sitting across the room. He put down an electrical parts catalog. "I plan to return next month. I'm staying put."

"I'd like us to have our own Palestinian state," Marid said tentatively. "only I think it will never happen. Not in my lifetime."

When the door to the office opened, a rumpled Palestinian man with a drooping Turkish mustache came out, looking frightened. The grey-haired American called out, "Goryeb, Christina, Aminah and Muna, Goryeb?" His smile suggested polite disinterest.

Christina panicked. Najat and the girls still had not arrived. She rose to her feet.

"I am Christina Goryeb. My daughters, Aminah and Muna, will be here in a few minutes. Can you take someone else?"

He nodded and called another name.

What had gone wrong, wondered Christina as she went down the stairs to the ground floor. She felt like a rat in a maze, every direction she turned a barrier rose in her face. Outside, she stood in front of the Consulate blinking against the brilliant sunshine while her eyes adjusted.

"May I help you Ma'am," said a young African-American marine guard. His hair was cut very short and he wore a spotless crisp blue and khaki uniform. Strapped on his hip was a 45 caliber pistol in a highly polished black leather holster.

"I'm supposed to meet my daughters here," she said.

"Would they be the people you are looking for?" The marine pointed to small group of people a short distance away.

She recognized Najat first.

Two young Israeli soldiers were questioning her and she looked frightened. There was Munah, clutching Aminah's hand, tears streamed down the younger girl's face. Aminah stared sullenly ahead, her eyes bright with tears too. One of the soldiers held their ID cards in his hand while his companion spoke on a walkie-talkie. Automatic rifles were slung over their shoulders.

"I don't get it. Those two guys've been hassling the hell out of that lady and her kids," said the marine. "I can't see they did anything wrong."

"She is my sister and those girls are my children. They're here to get visas to go to America. Their father is an American citizen. Could you ask the soldiers to let them go, please?" said Christina.

The young marine licked his lips. "I'm sorry Ma'am. I have no jurisdiction outside this gate. American soil stops here."

He spoke into his walkie-talkie. "This is Lance Corporal Cleveland. We've got a disturbance at the front gate."

"What's happening?" said a soft American voice at Christina's elbow.

The grey-haired woman who spoke, wore a flowered skirt and sandals. The man next to her, who wore a single breasted tan tropical suit, seemed to be her husband.

"The soldiers won't let my daughters come with me. We're trying to emigrate to America," said Christina. She caught Aminah's eye and waved. Aminah whispered to Munah and the younger girl's face lit up with a smile.

"Maman!" she cried. She broke away from her sister and ran toward Christina.

One of the soldiers, the one who wore a *kippa*, lunged for Munah but she was too quick for him. As Christina put her arms around Munah, the other soldier who wore a stylish haircut and dark glasses motioned to her with his automatic rifle.

"Come over here!" he said.

The old woman in the flowered skirt said angrily to her husband. "I think we should talk to these brave little men, Barry."

"Don't get involved, Genia," said her husband quietly.

The old woman placed herself between Christina and the soldiers. "You should be ashamed of yourselves, treating women and children like this," she said in Hebrew. "What have they done?"

"Do not concern yourself. They are Arabs," said the soldier with the *kippa*. "This is a security matter."

"Security, bosh!" said the old woman. All these people wish to do is leave Israel."

The soldier with the dark glasses whispered in his companion's ear, who shrugged and returned the ID cards he held to Najat. Then they turned and sauntered away down the street.

"They stopped us for an ID card check," said Najat as Christina hugged her.

"It was bad luck that you just ran into some hard-headed Zionists," said Christina.

"My name is Genia," said the old woman in the flowered skirt. She held out her hand.

It felt warm and dry to Christina. "Thank you, for saving us," said Christina. "I don't know how we can ever repay you."

"You don't have to," said Genia and smiled. She turned to her husband. "Come on Barry, let's let these people take care of their business." As she waved goodbye, the sleeve of her blouse pulled up to expose faint blue numbers tabooed on her forearm.

Christina felt a gentle tug at her elbow. "Ma'am could you and your family come with me," said Corporal Cleveland. Behind him were three other smiling marines.

Christina beckoned to her daughters.

"Come, they are ready for us now," she said. They were escorted into the Consulate and up to the waiting room.

"See how politely the American soldiers treat us," Aminah hissed to her Mother. "I hate the Jews. They treat us like criminals."

They straggled into the small office behind the sitting room and the American closed the door. He invited them to sit down in white plastic chairs, and introduced himself as Mr. DeHart, one of the Consul's assistants. He opened a manila folder. "Your husband is Richard Goryeb a naturalized American citizen living in the State of Virginia?" he said.

"Yes," said Christina.

"Where is he employed?"

"Georgetown University."

"In what department?"

"I believe it is called the School of Foreign Studies."

"And his position?"

"Professor of Middle East Affairs."

"You and your daughters are applying for immigrant visas to the United States for the purpose of a family reunification?"

Christina nodded.

He took their passports from the folder, opened each booklet and verified them against their photographs. "Your visas have been approved, Mrs. Goryeb" he said smiling. He scratched out his signature with a pen on the stiff paper and tucked the visas inside each passport before handing them to Christina.

"Is there anything else I must do?", she asked.

"Not here," said Mr. DeHart.

She sighed in disbelief. Uncle Mukhtar had said it wasn't easy to obtain the visas but it had turned out to be so simple. A great weight lifted from her.

Suddenly Muna burst into tears. Before Christina could comfort her, Aminah threw her arms around her younger sister.

"We're going to live in America," she cried triumphantly. "We're going to be with Daddy again and we'll live like Americans."

Twenty-Three

In a tiny courtroom in Taggart Prison, later that morning, the military Prosecutor presented his case against Daoud Rubez. Christina kept her eye on Judge Avram Weinberg, a granite-faced man with close-cropped grizzled hair and a wrinkled colonel's uniform.

Judge Weinberg kept his eyes on the ceiling.

Daoud Rubez in leg shackles and handcuffs sat next to Christina. He twisted in his seat and let his eyes wander around the courtroom.

"Where is Rosenbluth?" he whispered.

"Keep still," she said.

She did not want Daoud to make a bad impression on Judge Weinberg. "Rosenbluth promised to come. I spoke to him yesterday."

The Prosecutor, a young spit and polish lieutenant in rimless glasses addressed Judge Weinberg.

"Daoud Rubez's guilt is written all over his face. As you can plainly see, he is a belligerent, hardened street fighter. He refuses to answer questions or cooperate with the authorities. We have information that he is connected with the Lions of Allah. The State recommends another week of detention to continue his interrogation."

Judge Weinberg's eyes never left the ceiling. "Goryeb for the defense," he called once the Prosecutor sat down.

Christina stole a glance at the back of the courtroom. Where was Rosenbluth? His testimony was crucial. She rose and addressed the bench.

"Your Honor," she said, "My client admits he broke the curfew. But there is no evidence he committed other crimes, no allegation or proof that he carried a weapon or threw stones. Daoud Rubez is a 17-year-old bricklayer who broke curfew to weed a garden. The Shin Bet has

144

already questioned young Rubez for over a week, shaking him, beating him and forcing him to go without sleep for days at a time to obtain a confession. This is not justice in a civilized country."

The Prosecutor was on his feet immediately. "Rubez was not beaten. This is an outrageous accusation. The GSS used only moderate pressure within the guidelines."

Christina stared at the Prosecutor for a moment. What was her word against the word of the GSS?

"Your Honor," said Christina. "To justify holding Mr. Rubez it must be shown that the defendant is a threat to public security because he is withholding information."

Judge Weinberg glared down at her. "What's your point?"

"Your Honor, the State has requested an extension of Daoud Rubez's detention for the purpose of further interrogation. No new information has been presented since the last hearing," she said.

A few feet away at another table a sharp-faced man in a decrepit blue blazer without a necktie whispered urgently into the Prosecutor's ear. His eyes gleamed above a bushy mustache. He clutched a thick legal file to his chest as if he were afraid Christina would snatch it away from him.

The Prosecutor waved his hands.

"Your Honor, may we approach the bench?"

A look of mild distaste appeared on Judge Weinberg's face. He motioned to the Prosecutor to come forward. Christina moved to join them.

"We have confidential information to discuss," said the Prosecutor to Christina. "You stay there."

"Your Honor, my client should know the evidence against him."

"Please sit down, Mrs. Goryeb," said the Judge sharply.

Christina remained standing.

"Judge Weinberg, when you ruled last week that the evidence against Mr. Rubez did not prove his guilt, I requested that you sign and date each page of the testimony against him."

"I did and I remanded Mr. Rubez for further questioning," said Judge Weinberg. There was a note of irritation in his voice.

"Your Honor, please be sure the pages you initialed are not being shown to you again," she said.

The Judge gave her a thin smile. "I can remember my own handwriting, Mrs. Goryeb."

The Prosecutor conferred with Judge Weinberg, whose eyes hardened as he turned the pages of Daoud's dossier.

"Are you trying to make a joke of this court?" He growled to the Prosecutor, "This is the same bullshit you showed me last week".

The young officer looked surprised. "We still have additional material to present if we could be given leave to bring it during a court recess. Could we have two hours?"

"I'll take it under advisement while I question young Rubez myself," said the Judge.

His gaze shifted to Daoud.

"I recognize a sanction should apply to you, Mr. Rubez, and I'm willing to give you credit for the time already spent in detention."

Christina prodded her client. Daoud rose to his feet painfully and put his hands on the table for support.

"Thank you, your honor," he said.

"I am considering your first offense, Mr. Rubez, the curfew violation," said Judge Weinberg. "We need to clear something up before I decide whether to remand you for further interrogation. Was there any reason why you couldn't weed your garden during the day?"

Daoud licked his lips. "I was at work, in Jerusalem."

"Remember to address me as 'Your Honor', Mr. Rubez," said the Judge. Who is your employer?"

"Rosenbluth and Sons."

Judge Weinberg turned to Christina. "Can anyone vouch for that?"

Christina turned her head and looked at the courtroom door one last time. She was about to shake her head when the door opened and a fat grey-haired man in engineer boots sauntered in. He wore jeans and a plaid shirt that bulged over a pot belly. The stump of an unlit cigar stuck out of the corner of his mouth.

"Yes, your Honor," said Christina. She beckoned to the fat man. "I call Aaron Rosenbluth."

"Get rid of that filthy cigar," said Judge Weinberg.

Mr. Rosenbluth looked unabashed and pocketed his cigar.

"Swear him in," the Judge said to his clerk.

The contractor took his seat on the witness stand.

Christina remained standing. "Please state your name and occupation," she said.

"My name is Aaron Rosenbluth. I build apartments for the Ministry of Housing."

"Are you on schedule with your contract?"

"Actually no, we're falling behind. We've got so many immigrants from Russia who need a place to live."

"Do you know the defendant?", said Christina.

"Rubez lays bricks for me," said Mr. Rosenbluth.

"Are you pleased with his work?"

Aaron Rosenbluth shrugged. "He is a good mason."

"Does he report to work regularly?"

"He shows up, at least he did until he was arrested."

"Does he leave early?"

"We're so busy nobody leaves early."

"Do you need him?"

"Certainly. The man I hired to replace him can't lay bricks in a straight line."

Judge Weinberg interrupted. "Mr. Rosenbluth, did you ever have any reason to fear Rubez?"

"No, of course not."

The Judge adjusted his glasses and flipped slowly through the pages of the thick file on his desk before looking up at the ceiling.

"Mr. Rubez, I'm looking at your police record; I see that four years ago you served two weeks detention for throwing stones at a policeman."

Now the Judge was watching Daoud. "Isn't that a fact?"

Christina waited, hoping Daoud would not complain that he had been shot with rubber bullets.

"I was 13 years old and foolish, your Honor," said Daoud.

Good boy, thought Christina.

"But you served another period of detention when you were fifteen, again for stone throwing. An entire month spent in prison that time. How do you explain that?"

Daoud remained silent.

"I'm taking note of fact that you managed to stay out of trouble during the past two years."

Judge Weinberg stared at the Prosecutor. "Do you have anything more to say?"

"Your Honor, the State is concerned about the risk to public security. Arabs, like Rubez, enter *Yisroel* to work on construction projects everyday. They work hard, they do a good job, but they leave small packages of dynamite under the seats of their buses on their way home."

"Do you mean to say every single Arab does this?"

"No, your Honor," said the Prosecutor. "But the Shin Bet believes Rubez has links to terrorists."

"Bullshit! The evidence you showed me is the same evidence you showed me last week," said Judge Weinberg. He transferred his gaze to Daoud.

"Mr. Rubez, I'm willing to overlook the Shin Bet's suspicions about you this time. But, I don't want to see you here again."

Judge Weinberg reached for his gavel and brought it down smartly. "Case dismissed!"

Surprised but triumphant, Christina hugged a stunned Daoud next to her.

"You are free, you are free," she told him.

He looked at her in disbelief.

"Thank you, your Honor," she managed to say to Judge Weinberg. Inwardly she didn't know whether to laugh or cry. The bailiff removed the handcuffs and leg shackles from Daoud Rubez and went to call the next case. Christina quickly put away her papers. A soldier, their security escort inside Taggart Prison, materialized at Daoud's side.

Outside the courtroom in the narrow corridor a familiar voice called out "Christina!" It was Naomi Litvin.

"How did you fare with old Stone face?" Naomi asked.

"We won!"

"I told you Weinberg's tough but fair," said Naomi brushing back a wisp of prematurely grey hair. "I've been meaning to tell you. Remember the poetry you loaned me? I feel guilty about keeping your books so long."

"Keep them as long as you like," said Christina. "They're yours."

"But I've already sent them back to your office! Look for a parcel."

* * *

Back in her office after lunch, Christina sorted through the mail that had piled up on her desk while she was preparing for Daoud's hearing. Lifting up some magazines and newspapers, she uncovered a parcel wrapped in butcher's paper. There was no return address. She guessed it was the returned books from Naomi Litvin. The package felt heavy and she wondered if Naomi had included some books of her own.

As she untied the heavy string that bound the package, she thought about her courtroom victory and wondered if she was giving in too easily to Shin Bet intimidation.

A victory like this did not happen often. But it was proof enough that one could bring about change without violence. One small step at a time, it had been done before. Ghandi drove the British from India. Martin Luther King had based his civil rights movement in America on Gandhi's principles. Israel was changing, slowly and painfully, but changing nevertheless. The present Prime Minister had been elected because he promised to bring peace.

Christina pulled back the wrapping paper. Inside, covered in newspaper were some red cardboard tubes. They looked like highway flares. She picked one out and read the warning in German and English that had been printed on the side: HIGH EXPLOSIVE HANDLE WITH EXTREME CARE. STORE IN A COOL DRY PLACE. I.G. FARBEN CHEMICALS, DEUTSCHLAND. She stared at the dynamite and her mouth dropped open with horror. Carefully, she returned the stick to the package and bundled it up again. Then she carried the package gingerly over to a small table near the door where Hamad's messengers picked up their mail and shoved it underneath.

She returned hastily to her desk, breathing air in deep gulps. The day was hot and flies swarmed through the open windows. Perspiration soaked through her blouse as she picked up a file and attempted to read the papers in it. She could stand it no longer. She put her papers away and locked her desk.

As she reached for her coat to leave, a young boy wearing torn levis and a black checkered *kaffiyeh* slipped into the room. He gave her a bored glance and went to the mail table. She watched in fascination as he moved with arrogant grace, lazy as a cat stretching in front of the fire, alert, about to spring and strike. He reached under for the package of dynamite, hefted it carefully, and retraced his steps to the door. Then he was gone.

She had helped the Lions of Allah smuggle dynamite.

Pain tore cruelly at Christina's heart like the claws of a wild animal.

She was about to lock the door when a voice called through the open window, "Good afternoon." She looked out and saw the postman. He handed in another parcel wrapped in brown paper and string. It was addressed to her in Naomi's handwriting. The books of poetry.

Friendship and poetry were not enough.

The reality was dynamite.

Twenty-Four

The tires on the big Volvo tractor-trailer screamed as Sabah Kaysoom negotiated the twisting curves on Route 3 west of Ramallah towards B'nai Ha'eretz. He was in a hurry but the narrow two lane road was not built for speed. The Volvo's suspension was not as stiff as the Russian Army truck he had practiced on and the gear shift had an unfamiliar pattern. He was in his early 30's, with an arched nose, heavy lidded eyes behind tinted aviator glasses and thick black hair. In the lobe of his left ear was a tiny gold stud. Behind him in the trailer's squat oval tank rode 10,000 liters of No. 1 diesel, enough fuel to supply a small town with electricity for a month.

Hamad had selected him because he was an ex-Syrian commando, he resembled the regular driver, Ariel Hirsch whose dirty blue overalls he wore, and he spoke Hebrew. The real Hirsch weighed ten kilos less. His naked body lay in a shallow grave dug in a ditch behind the oil depot in Haifa, his throat cut from ear to ear.

One faint worry disturbed Sabah: had Hirsch been reported missing yet? He had listened to the dispatcher at the oil depot over the truck's two-way radio until the signal faded after he reached Tel Aviv. Since then he had heard nothing but static. Did Hirsch have a wife, friend or co-worker who expected him to be a particular place and time after work? There was no way to know.

The afternoon sun was sinking as Sabah pulled off the highway and started up the hill toward the settlement. He passed a faded sign that read:

MINISTRY OF HOUSING PROJECT
B'NAI HA'ERETZ

Below this was a rifle thrust aloft by a clenched fist encircled with:

YESHIVAT EYAL

Eyal—The Only Way!—Sabah had been briefed, was a *hesder yeshiva*, a college at the settlement where young rabbinical students received religious and military instruction. That meant they served in the Israeli army and would be able to defend themselves.

The track wound up a dry hillside strewn with stones and clumps of tawny grass. Higher up, on a saddle between two hills, the fuel truck passed broken stone rectangles, the outline of what once was an Arab village. A red-haired goat foraged under some fig trees that grew outside the shattered walls.

To the untrained eye, the rocky hillside concealed nothing, but Sabah recognized the settlement's outer defenses, a mine belt, consisting of at least 5,000 mines placed in a kilometer long belt around the perimeter, with fields of fire cleared through the olive trees and boulders by bulldozers. Concertina wire loops curved away from both sides of the road. Above him, the settlement jutted up from the crest of a rocky ridge. The cluster of buildings, silhouetted against the afternoon sun, reminded Sabah of one of those ruined Crusader castles that dotted Palestine, reminders of an earlier time when Europeans tried to steal his land.

Behind the mine belt and wire Sabah Kaysoom observed an electronic fence with motion detectors, laser beam trip lines and infra-red sensors. A patrol road illuminated by mercury vapor lights at night, encircled the settlement.

The truck's engine began to labor as the grade increased sharply. He passed through another barbed wire barrier in front of which was an electrically fired Claymore mine squatting half a meter off the ground on a small tripod mount. The fuel truck lurched to a stop beside a sentry box outside a chain link fence that was topped with more concertina wire. Keeping his face in the shadows, Sabah handed Hirsch's ID to the guard on duty. Lightly he gripped the handle of his double edged commando knife. It was hidden in the loose sleeve of his overalls in a scabbard strapped to his left forearm, the only weapon he carried. Sabah hoped the armed settler wouldn't detect any difference in his face and Hirsch's on the ID card. Hirsch had visited the settlement only once a month. The guard, who wore a *kippa*, curled his lips slightly at the sight of Sabah's gold stud.

That ear stud of Hirsch's was pure luck. The stud marked him as a non-observant Jew, a pariah whom the religious Jews of B'nai Ha'eretz would avoid. It amused Sabah that the religious Jews seemed to hate their non-observant brothers as much as they hated Palestinians. Calmly he looked out the windshield while he waited for the guard to run a security check on his computer terminal, hoping that Hirsch had not yet been reported missing.

Sabah's mission was twofold, first to disable the settlement's power generators and then to look for defenses that he had been unable to spot with his binoculars. He had watched the settlement many times from surrounding hills through the flattened perspective of powerful East German binoculars. From his hillside lookout he had seen precisely where Hirsch had driven when he came to deliver fuel each month and what he did. Now everything seemed to leap out at him in three dimensions, pots overflowing with pink and blue blossoms on apartment house balconies, clothes lines that stretched from balcony to balcony, sagging under the weight of drying laundry, shrubs and well-kept lawns below, a brightly colored pavilion with a dance floor beside an Olympic-sized swimming pool, and a soccer field where children played—many easy targets for the vengeance of Allah. He also saw machine gun nests protected by sandbag breastworks, bunkers and trenches.

The guard handed Sabah the ID back and waved him thorough. He swung the tractor-trailer to the right and pulled up beside the generator shed where the fuel tanks where were buried in the ground.

Young men some wearing black hats and suits walked in small groups beside a modern hexagonal shaped building a short distance away. Sabah recognized they were the students at Eyal, the hesder yeshiva. A few armed settlers in green army fatigues lounged in trenches on the edge of the settlement, idly smoking cigarettes behind .50 caliber heavy machine guns protected by sandbags. None of them noticed Sabah. No one noticed him haul the thick metal clad neoprene hoses out of their trays on the sides of the trailer with a clatter. He had timed his arrival to coincide with the supper hour. He connected the hoses to the trailer's five dump valves and dragged the heavy metal nozzles over to the storage tank inlets. There was a faint gurgling sound of fuel flowing when he opened the dump valves. Mixed with the fuel now flowing from the truck were 500 liters of heavy syrup and

250 kilos of diatomaceous earth, a combination that would clog the filters and fuel injectors of the diesel power plant. It would take twenty minutes for the trailer's tanks to drain its lethal load.

The diesel generators would at first run rough and then within a few minutes would grind to a halt. Without electrical power the ring of mercury vapor lights that made night into day along the settlement's perimeter would be extinguished. The sophisticated electronic defenses would likewise cease to function. The settlement's defenders would be virtually blind.

The syrup had been diverted from a confectioner's shop near Ramallah; the fine earth had been stolen from a garden supply. Sabah had tested the mixture on the fuel system of an old Mercedes taxi in East Jerusalem, however, he wasn't certain of the correct proportions to use on a large scale. As a precaution, he had tripled the recipe that had ruined the taxi's engine. However, Sabah had to escape before the generators stopped and he had no idea when that would occur. If the generators failed too soon, *Al-Yahud* would have time to call their Army for help and months of careful preparations would be wasted. The first sign of trouble would be a cloud of black smoke from the exhaust stacks of the power plant.

When the attack was launched later that evening, Sabah would lead a squad to this bunker and cut the throat of every Jewish child inside.

Fifteen minutes passed slowly. He wanted to get a closer look at a nearby bunker in the center of the settlement that he had identified as the communal nursery where the children slept but he had to stay with the truck to be sure the underground storage tanks did not overflow.

As he checked the gauges on the trailer a tired voice behind him said, "You're late. We're nearly out of fuel. What happened?"

The speaker was short, bald and perspiring. He wore thick glasses, grease stained overalls and carried a pistol in a holster strapped to his hip. Sabah recognized him as the power plant's engineer. Sabah had seen him once through binoculars when he came out to smoke a cigarette with Hirsch.

"I got stuck in traffic," said Sabah.

A rough calloused hand with dirty finger nails gripped his hand firmly. "I'm Bernstein. Sorry, I can never remember your name."

His head was bare, not covered by a *yarmulke* or *kippa* which meant he was not a religious Jew. Sabah would have to talk to him.

"Hirsch," said Sabah.

Bernstein gave him a quizzical look. "You've put on weight, Hirsch," he said.

"My wife's taking a cooking class," said Sabah with a flash of inspiration. "She's angry if I don't eat everything she puts in front of me."

"Really? I didn't know you were married."

Sabah cursed himself silently for the mistake and gave Bernstein what he hoped was a knowing smile.

"Looking for something on the side, eh?" said Bernstein.

Sabah patted his pockets and found Hirsch's Marlboros. "How about a smoke?"

They lit up together.

Bernstein exhaled a thick cloud of smoke as he looked out over the barren hills. "I hate this place," he said.

Sabah nodded sympathetically.

"All the women are ugly and the Hasidim treat me like a *shaigetz*," said Bernstein. A *shaigetz* was a Christian, shunned as an outsider.

Sabah remembered the sight of a Jewish women shaving her head in an open window, one of the many strange things about *Al-Yahud* that his binoculars had revealed. After she had toweled her head dry, she put on a wig.

"I can't understand why anyone would take a beautiful woman and shave her head," he said.

"To make her ugly, of course, so no one will want her," said Bernstein. "It is the Hasid way. All I want to do is look, not touch. How can they stand to fuck their woman after they have made them ugly."

"Upside down all women look the same," said Sabah.

Bernstein laughed. "So Hirsch, where are you from?" he said.

"Haifa."

"That explains it—I couldn't place your accent. It sounds almost Arab," said Bernstein.

"Haifa has a lot of Arabs. I grew up in a mixed neighborhood."

"I can tell. And your father didn't have a nose for money either so we're both from the bottom of the barrel," said Bernstein. "Not like these Hasidim who have God's ear."

The gauges indicated the tank was almost empty. Sabah closed the dump valves, uncoupled the hoses and dragged them back to the truck with Bernstein's help.

"Why not stay and have supper with me. I haven't had anyone to talk to in a week," said Bernstein.

"Maybe another time. Someone's waiting for me in Tel Aviv."

"Really, what's her name?"

"Inga!" said Sabah with a wolfish grin. He tossed Bernstein the pack of Marlboros and walked toward the cab.

"Raise your hands and turn around slowly," said Bernstein harshly. Sabah froze. He felt the muzzle of Bernstein's pistol against his spine.

You're not Hirsch," said Bernstein. "Hirsch has four children and is devoted to his wife."

Sabah raised his hands, his right hand close to his left sleeve. He had to do this quietly; there must be no scream or gunfire.

Bernstein patted Sabah's sides to check for a gun, an amateur's mistake. In one quick movement Sabah drew his knife and plunged it right up to the hilt into Bernstein's neck. He gave the handle a violent twist. In silent horror, Bernstein stared back at him. His eyelids fluttered behind his thick glasses as he collapsed in Sabah's arms. Sabah eased the dying man to the ground and grunted as he pulled the bloody knife out of Bernstein's neck. He wiped the knife on the engineer's trousers and slipped it into his scabbard up his sleeve.

"It is the will of Allah," he said quietly. "*Al-ain bel ain al-sen bel sen.* An eye for an eye, a tooth for a tooth."

His only regret was that Bernstein had prevented him from getting a closer look at the nursery.

No one saw him kill Bernstein. The confrontation had taken place in the narrow space between the truck and the generator shed. Sabah looked for an empty barrel or crate in which to deposit Bernstein's corpse, then realized that if it were discovered, *Al-Yahud* would be alerted to the possibility of an attack. Grasping the dead man under the arms, Sabah dragged the body to the right door of cab and heaved it up into the passenger's foot well, concealing it under a small tarpaulin. He wiped his bloody hands clean with an oily rag and wiped the blood off the seat beside him but the interior of the cab still reeked of blood. He started the engine and drove slowly to the settlement's gate.

When he arrived, the guard was speaking to another Jew who gave Sabah a sharp look and held up his hand. Two cloth *"falafels"* on each shoulder of his uniform shirt identified him as an lieutenant in the

Israel Defense Force. He was blue eyed and his brown curly hair stuck out like a halo from underneath his *kippa*. An M-16 was slung over his shoulder.

"Are you Hirsch?" the officer demanded.

Sabah stared back as panic raced through his veins.

"Your dispatcher telephoned here," the officer said. "He's trying to contact you. Is your radio on?"

Relief flooded through Sabah. "I'm out of radio range. The depot's in Haifa," he said.

"You can use our phone to call back," said the officer.

Sabah looked at his watch. "The bastard just wants to be sure I filled your tanks. The depot's closed by now."

The lieutenant nodded accepting the explanation. "What's that funny smell?" he said wrinkling his nose.

Out of the corner of his eye Sabah saw a trickle of blood run across the floor of the cab from under the tarp. The cab smelled like a butcher's shop. "It's diesel oil," Sabah said quickly.

"It smells like blood to me," the lieutenant said. "Eli, come here and tell me what you smell."

The guard approached the truck and sniffed. He grasped the hand holds on the side of the truck's cab and put one foot on the running board beside the driver's window when his eye fixed on Sabah's gold ear stud.

"Unclean slave," he muttered.

He gave a self-righteous frown that the true believers reserved for co-religionists who strayed and stepped down.

"I don't smell anything, Avi," he said.

Sabah gunned the engine to imply he wanted to leave.

The lieutenant shrugged and the guard waved Sabah on.

Twenty-Five

Avidar Shoval, Shlomo Arendt's nephew was in charge of B'nai Ha'eretz's defenses. That night Avi sat in the settlement's command bunker watching computer screens that displayed the status of electronic sensors on the perimeter fence. He was a Lieutenant in the Army reserve, a veteran of the 1982 Lebanon War. The fingers of his right hand were mutilated by the Syrians when he was captured in the Bekaa Valley. Avi—everyone called him that—was not a religious Zionist, unlike his companions in the bunker, Dror and Yedvav, and most of the other settlers. He loved the rocky wheat fields, steep vineyards, and gnarled olive groves below B'nai Ha'eretz with a love for growing things, not for their place in legend or history. His faith was dutiful—he believed because his ancestors believed—yet he had an instinctive understanding of the qualities and failings of the dour Hasidim he lived with. With his candid blue eyes and contagious good spirits, he had the charisma to inspire a lumber yard full of fence posts to fight.

A few minutes later, Shlomo Arendt joined him in the bunker.

"Tired," he murmured. "A long day."

"Have you had supper, Uncle?" said Avi.

"I just got in."

"Drop by our apartment. Miriam will warm some meatloaf for you," said Avi.

"Your young bride does not need to be cooking for me," said Shlomo.

"It is the least we can do. You're the one who raised me, Uncle."

A rash of red dots winked sporadically on the computer screen that displayed the settlement's Western sector.

Shlomo tapped the screen. "What's this?"

"I've sent Lavon and Hur to investigate," said Avi.

His walkie-talkie squawked and he picked it up.

"It was a couple of goats," said Lavon's voice.

Avi pressed the transmit button. "Move them away from the fence," he said.

Through the bunker's entrance, the men heard a distant burst of automatic rifle fire. Avi picked up the walkie-talkie again.

"Next time use rocks, Lavon," he said. "We don't want to alarm the Rabbi."

"Caution makes you wise, Nephew. Have you read the story in today's *Yediot*?" said Shlomo.

"Which story was that?"

"*B'nai Ha'eretz, From Settlement to Torah City.*"

"No I missed that one, Uncle," said Avi.

"Rabin's Planning Commission leaked the maps of our proposed expansion," said Shlomo. "Now all the details are out in the open. These bastards will get the Arabs worked up again and they'll deny our application like they did last time. 'Sorry our hands are tied'."

"If Jews can't live here, they can't live anywhere," said Dror. He was a thin gangly Hasid from Williamsburg, New York."

"This is not a good sign," Shlomo agreed.

The lights flickered, dimmed to orange and then everything went black. Static crackled from the combat radio on the shelf above their heads as it switched automatically to battery power. Its dials glowed a luminous green.

"That lazy *shmuck* Bernstein," said Dror.

"I'm sure Bernstein'll have the other generator going in a minute," said Avi.

He found a flashlight and switched it on. They waited for the lights to go back on, cigarette ends glowing in the dark.

"What's taking him so long?" Yedvav said.

"That *shaigetz* probably drove over to Ramallah to sniff some Arab cunt," said Dror with a smile.

"I'll go check on Bernstein," said Avi briskly. "You two take the jeep and see if Lavon and Hur are all right. Make sure everyone is on their toes. We're vulnerable without the sensors and we don't have enough men to watch everywhere."

He stuck the walkie-talkie in his pocket and climbed the bunker's steps. Shlomo followed. Outside the lights of Matityahu, Nachliel and Kiryat Sefer, three smaller settlements on nearby hilltops, glowed reassuringly. To the east the lights of Ramallah illuminated half the sky. Candles and flashlights flickered in the windows of the settlement's apartments.

A deep imperious male voice called from a window, "The lights, what happened to the lights?"It was Rabbi Ben Yusuf.

"Generator trouble, Rabbi," Shlomo called back.

"How long will it take to repair?"

"I'm going to see Bernstein, now," said Avi.

"See to it that it's fixed," said the Rabbi curtly.

"I'm going to have a look around," said Shlomo to Avi.

The generator shed was dark when Avi opened its door and played his flashlight around. The two yellow painted Caterpillar diesel generators sat silent on thick concrete pads. The only sound that greeted his ears was the tick of cooling metal.

"Bernstein?" Avi called out.

He wondered how hard it would be to restart the generators himself. He'd seen Bernstein do it before. The stench of oil almost made him vomit as he made his way to the side of the nearest diesel. He found the red start button on its control panel and pressed it. The big Caterpillar diesel moaned as compressed air shot into its cylinders and rumbled into life. It ran erratically for a few seconds and then shut down. He tried to start the other diesel with similar results.

Where the hell was Bernstein? The Rabbi would fire the little bastard if he'd been out on the town again. Avi went outside and looked around. He heard an engine roaring on its way up the hill and prayed it was Bernstein's jeep.

He jogged toward the main gate.

The sound of the engine had a deep bellowing roar like a jeep that had lost its muffler. Standing beside the sentry box, he could see the chain link mesh that covered the main gate silhouetted against the glare of bobbing headlights. Avi winced as the lights veered off the road and then swerved back on again. Bernstein must be roaring drunk, again he thought. Avi hoped Bernstein would remember the gate was chained shut at night. At the last minute Avi realized the vehicle was a truck, not a jeep, and it was not going to stop.

With a deep labored groan, the tractor-trailer ripped the main gate from its posts and carried it along on its hood, crumpled and bent, for a few meters until the engine stalled.

It was the same Volvo tractor-trailer that had delivered fuel to the settlement barely two hours before. Avi jumped up on the running board and leaned in the driver's window. Slumped over the wheel was the driver, covered with blood, bleeding from a nasty wound in his neck. Avi ran to get the first aid kit in the sentry box. When he returned with a roll of tape and gauze pads, he lifted the driver's head and shone his flashlight on the man's face.

Bernstein's dead eyes stared back at him. The steering wheel was lashed with a piece of rope.

A bullet buzzed by Avi's ear and clanged off the truck's door post. He hit the ground and rolled over and over to get away from the truck. Another bullet smashed into the rocky soil by his side as he scrambled crouching to his feet.

The sniper must have an infrared scope, he thought.

"We're under attack," he yelled into his walkie-talkie to Dror in the command bunker. "We're under attack! Everyone to his station. Call the Army."

The .50 caliber machine gun below the main gate began to roar as tongues of flame came from its muzzle. Rounds of green tracer arched through the sky toward the suspected position of the sniper. As he ran toward the command bunker he heard a thud and was knocked off his feet by the concussion of a mortar shell which exploded as it hit the ground. Bits of shrapnel whined through the air.

Avi pressed his face into the dirt and covered his head with his arms. More shells fell, their explosions marched across the settlement like the foot steps of a demented giant, one after another for what seemed like an eternity. Then there was silence.

The walkie-talkie squawked."Post 4. Movement to our front," said a voice. Post 4 was the machine gun nest below the smashed front gate.

"Fire a flare," Avi said. He felt a hand on his shoulder. It was Shlomo, Dror and two other settlers with M-16s.

"We've got to stop them from coming in the front gate," Avi said.

Crouching low, they ran past the Volvo truck, Bernstein's coffin, toward Post 4. Avi heard a loud smack behind him like two hands being clapped smartly together. He switched on his flash light.

Shlomo bent over Dror who lay motionless on the ground. Blood and grey bits of brain tissue oozed from a hole in his forehead and trickled down into his sightless eyes.

"Take him to the infirmary," cried Shlomo to the other men.

"He's dead, Uncle."

They left Dror lying on the ground and dived over the sandbag breastworks of Post 4.

The landscape was illuminated by the unearthly white glare of a parachute flare, a false sun that oscillated back and forth 100 meters in the sky as it slowly descended. Shadows darted among the rocks below. Avi heard shouts in Arabic and the rapid pop-pop of automatic rifle fire. Flashes of flame stabbed the darkness.

A voice chanted over a loudspeaker in sing song Arabic: "The Lions of Allah bring death to *Al-Yahud.*"

The veteran Army reservists among the settlers calmly lit their Marlboros and fixed bayonets on their M-16s and fired at the flashes coming from the muzzles of the attackers. Thirty meters away, a line of about 10 guerrillas spaced six meters apart swept up the hill toward the main gate. One of the settlers beside Avi triggered the Claymore mine on its low tripod in front of the machine gun nest. A deadly hail of shrapnel from the exploding mine broke up the charge. Five of the surviving attackers dived behind rocks. Then the machine gunners kept the guerrillas pinned down with continuous fire. As soon as one parachute flare neared the ground, another flare climbed into the sky to take its place trailing a faint plume of sparks before it exploded into light.

Avi fed clips of ammunition into his M-16 stopping only to let the barrel cool. A young man wearing blue jeans and a denim jacket, broke cover and ran down the hill followed by another. An older man in a black *kaffiyeh* rose to his feet and waved his arms to rally his men. Shlomo trained his M-16 on the leader, fired two quick bursts and the man fell backward to the ground. The rest of the men fled down the hill in a confused rabble.

"They're not coming back," said Avi raising his head. He was tired, thirsty, and in pain from a dozen cuts and bruises. The dirt floor of the machine gun nest was littered with spent brass cartridges.

They watched the guerrillas organize a rear guard to retrieve their dead and wounded and gather fallen equipment. Sporadic shots rang out from the retreating guerrillas who turned and fired as they ran down the slope. A lone Arab on the opposite hill 800 meters away stood defiantly on a boulder clearly visible in the flare light with his hands on his hips, just out of the range of an M-16. Short and fat with a Russian sniper's rifle, a Dragunov, with its tell-tale skeleton stock slung over one shoulder, he cut a comic figure in a black checkered *kaffiyeh* and an oversized black *jalabiyya*.

"Coward," said Shlomo. "He kills only from a distance, not close up."

He took over the .50 caliber machine gun, sighted carefully down its barrel and squeezed the trigger. A cloud of dust erupted on the boulder beside the Arab. Shlomo corrected his aim but the sniper had slipped behind the boulder.

Silence hung over the settlement. The air was thick with cordite smoke. A flare rose and filled the sky with its ghostly white light. M-16 fire burst from the settlement above, followed by a long burst from what sounded like an Russian AK-47.

A woman from the settlement ran through the gate toward them. "Arabs in the *kibbutz*! The nursery!" she screamed.

Avi sprang to his feet. "Cover us Uncle," he said to Shlomo. "Follow me," he shouted to two settlers hunched against the sandbags in the machine gun nest, Racah and Meidav.

He grabbed an M-16 with a bayonet and ran through the main gate.

Ninety meters away between the generator shed and the soccer field, the sandbagged roof of nursery rose like the back of a beached whale. In the flickering white light, Avi saw four guerrillas in tiger fatigues, their heads wrapped in black *kaffiyehs*, run across the soccer field toward the nursery. They fired AK-47s as they ran. One of them carried a satchel charge. Avi and settlers who followed him returned their fire. Two of the guerrillas fell to the ground and lay still. The third and fourth, the one with the satchel charge, rolled behind a large piece of concrete pipe that served as a tunnel in the children's playground next to the bunker. Avi and his companions split in opposite directions to outflank the guerrillas. In the last light of the sinking flare, Avi saw a hand move behind the pipe and a small green spheroid arced toward the two men who had followed him.

"Look out, grenade!" Avi yelled as he dived for the ground.

A violent shock wave enveloped him. The ground came up and slapped him in the face before he heard the explosion that left his ears ringing. The flare sank to the ground and everything went black. He fired a burst in the direction of the concrete pipe and rolled to another position with a dry rustle of pebbles. He saw a stab of flame. Pain stung his left ear. He fired back out of instinct. In the glare of the muzzle flash he caught a glimpse of black, tan and brown stripes on tiger fatigues. A moment later came a thud and the sound of an Arab cursing. He fired again and rolled in the opposite direction. When the next flare flooded the compound with brilliant light, one of the guerrillas lay slumped over his AK-47 behind the concrete pipe. Avi saw the second man sprawled on the ground in the play ground beside a red toy horse mounted on an coil spring. His AK-47 lay on Avi's side of the horse. Suddenly, the man sprang up with the satchel charge in one hand. Avi saw him reach inside the canvas bag and twist the handle of the detonator's timer.

When the clockwork ran down, ten pounds of C-4 plastic explosive would ignite and pulverize everything within a radius of twenty meters.

"Now, *Al-Yahud* we both die," he said.

The man looked familiar, the arched nose, the wide mouth, the heavy lidded eyes, the thick black hair showing under the fold of the *kaffiyeh*, and the tiny gold ear stud in his left ear.

"You're the bastard who killed Bernstein," Avi said. He trained his M-16 on the guerilla's chest and squeezed the trigger.

Nothing happened.

Avi lunged at Sabah with his bayonet.

Suddenly a knife gleamed in Sabah's right hand. With a swing of his left hand, he tossed the satchel charge down the steps of the nursery's entrance. It landed against the locked wooden door of the bunker with a thud. His knife flashed toward Avi's neck.

Avi parried the thrust with the butt of his empty M-16. The point of Sabah's knife caught in the loose lapel of his fatigue jacket, then jerked up slashing his chin. A line of pain seared his face as the blade slicked through the muscles and sinews of his lower jaw and glanced off his clinched teeth. Dizzy with pain he propped himself up with his weapon, using it like a crutch with its butt resting on the ground. His mutilated hand clutched the handle of the bayonet below the blade where it engaged a lug on the muzzle of the M-16.

Leaping, Sabah aimed his knife at Avi's heart.

Without thinking Avi sat down suddenly still clutching the upright M-16.

Impaled on Avi's bayonet, Sabah shrieked, a reddish froth on his lips. With every breath he took the wound in Sabah's chest sucked and gurgled around the blade of the bayonet.

"I go to meet Allah, *Al-Yahud* but your children go with me," he gasped and spat bright red blood into Avi's face.

With an effort Avi pushed the dying man off him. How much time did he have left before the satchel charge exploded—ten seconds or two? He stumbled down the nursery's stairs with a tingling sensation running down his spine. At any moment, he thought, he might die. His hand closed on the canvas strap and flung the deadly satchel high in the air.

An immense blue light blinded him, followed by a violent shock and a sharp whistling sound. A harsh roar reverberated through the surrounding hills.

* * *

Rabbi Ben Yusuf and Shlomo Arendt entered the small bedroom and closed the door conspiratorially behind them. Shlomo's head was bandaged and his eyes were bright with excitement. The two men came and stood beside the bed where Avi lay on the edge of drugged sleep. The pale kerchiefed young woman who sat in a chair beside the bed looked up with large frightened brown eyes.

"The doctor said Avi should be left alone," she said reproachfully.

"He might like to know the children are safe," Shlomo whispered.

Avi opened his eyes and struggled to concentrate. His bandaged jaw throbbed where Sabah's knife had sliced it open. A medic had skillfully stitched the wound shut but he would be left with a jagged scar.

"How are you, nephew?" said Shlomo.

"I'll be fine," Avi said. "I'll go to Jerusalem for a full checkup in the morning."

"Would you like to know how it ended?" Shlomo smiled.

"Sure," said Avi but he didn't really care. All he could think about was Miriam in the chair next to the bed.

"Nine Arabs dead including the two you killed," said Shlomo.

"And our losses?"

"Dror, Racah and Meidav dead. Bernstein's dead too, of course."

They were his friends and he had seen them die, all except for Bernstein. "How did the Arabs get into the compound?" he said.

"They tied two ladders together over the back fence," said Shlomo. His fingers came together in the shape of steeple. "The attack on the front gate was a diversion."

Avi grunted with pain as he tried to sit up. "The Arabs will come again. We must be ready for them," he said. "Rest Nephew. The army has secured the perimeter and there's a tank in front of the main gate. We're safe for now."

"How long will the army stay?" said Avi.

"Until they are needed somewhere else," said Shlomo. "We requested a blockade of Ramallah and the surrounding Arab villages but the Prime Minister refused. He prefers to these coddle extremists."

"God gave us this land we will keep it, army or no army," said Ben Yusuf.

"And if Rabin settles with the Arabs and tells us to leave this Land?" said Shlomo.

"The roots of the Jewish people are entrenched in the soil of B'nai Ha'eretz. Not only will these roots not be uprooted, they will be deepened. We will never leave," said Ben Yusuf.

Shlomo seemed strangely subdued, even depressed by the Rabbi's words.

Ben Yusuf smiled at Avi and Miriam as he moved toward the door. "I want to take the worry from your hearts my children, and now Avi, you must rest. You have been through much and we need you to get well. There is work to do."

Twenty-Six

When Kallenborg and Asher stopped by the Shin Bet Message Center in Taggart Prison the next morning, the girl in army fatigues behind the desk handed each man a note and joked with Asher. It irked Kallenborg that she always had something to say to Asher, but was noticeably cool to him. He flushed and looked down at the blue squiggles of Hebrew on the small square of paper in his hand. He couldn't make sense out of it and showed the note to Asher.

"You have been summoned to the Fuhrer Bunker," Asher said with a grin. "Shlomo wants to see you." Then he read his own message and frowned. "See you later," he said and disappeared.

Kallenborg stopped for a drink at the water cooler before he went down the hall. He knew Shlomo's settlement, B'nai Ha'eretz had been attacked by the Lions of Allah the night before, and wondered if this had anything to do with the summons. Whistling softly, he knocked on his boss's door. The sound of a chair scraping on the other side was followed by the scuff of shoes and Shlomo Arendt's curt voice.

"Identify yourself," he said.

"Kallenborg."

The dead bolt was unlatched, the door opened a fraction, and Kallenborg looked into Shlomo's shrewd brown eyes. Shlomo opened the door wider to let Kallenborg in.

"Have a seat, Kallenborg," he said.

He wore a knitted *kippa* on his head and dressed in slacks and an open-necked shirt. A white gauze bandage covered his right temple.

"A present from the Palestine Authority," said Shlomo with a bitter smile. "If Arafat wants to prove his men are doing their jobs, let him produce the Lions." He jabbed at a thick folder of computer printouts with a blunt finger.

"I've been reading your MICA summaries, Kallenborg. They don't say much."

MICA was the computer system that Shin Bet inspectors filed reports on. Kallenborg looked away at the large topographical map of the West Bank on the white-washed cinder block wall behind Shlomo. He knew better than to try to mislead him.

"There's not much to tell, yet. It's too early."

"So what have you done so far?"

"It's all there. We interrogated the Goryeb woman several times. She says she knows nothing. Unfortunately, we cannot get much out of her because the Mossad will not let us use"—he paused delicately—"more rigorous interrogation techniques. We're keeping her under tight surveillance. She gave us the slip a few times but nothing's turned up. Yesterday she pulled the wool over Judge Weinberg's eyes and got him to release a young punk who we suspect is connected with the Lions of Allah."

Shlomo looked pained. "So I heard. What does your colleague from the Mossad think?"

Kallenborg shrugged. "You'll have to ask him."

"How's he making out with that old Fiat?"

Kallenborg said, "He says it's the worst car in the motor pool."

"Only the best for the Mossad," said Shlomo. He opened a drawer and handed Kallenborg a sheet of paper. "You might find this informant's report interesting."

Kallenborg read it quickly. "Your informant says there's a rumor circulating in the *souk* that we are watching the Goryeb woman and her office."

Shlomo nodded. "Put that together with no more messages and it sounds like blown cover."

A sly expression came over Kallenborg's face. "Asher's blown, probably," he said. "He does sloppy work."

Shlomo gave a dry humorless laugh. "Did he really fall on his ass right in front of the Goryeb woman?"

"In an alley behind her office," said Kallenborg.

Shlomo studied Kallenborg for a moment. "I've got a new job for you," he announced.

"You're not taking me off the Goryeb case?"

"Let this *chazerai*, this pig shit, slide for a couple of weeks while things cool down," said Shlomo.

* * *

After Shlomo's joke about the Fiat, it was a puzzle to Kallenborg why his boss had not arranged for Asher to have the Citroen instead. Shlomo's black Citroen *Deux Chevaux* was a real piece of *drek*, a noisy, smelly antique and the seats were made out of oversized rubber bands stretched over metal, canvass-covered frames. Although the Citroen was decrepit, Kallenborg noticed that, like all Shin Bet cars, it had a MICA terminal and radio data link. The keyboard flipped up to conceal the screen and make the terminal look like part of the dash board when not in use. Shlomo took the same road out of Ramallah that Asher had tailed the Goryeb woman on a few days before.

They headed west into rocky hills covered with thistles. A hazy patch of the blue Mediterranean Sea nestled in the hills in the direction of Jaffa. Kallenborg listened silently while Shlomo told him about a seminar he had attended at the Defense Ministry, and concluded the speaker was one of those liberal defeatists like Asher. Kallenborg's father, the General, used to shoot such people with his own officer issue Nagant, back in the Great Patriotic War.

"According to our speaker, *Yisroel* as a Jewish state will disappear in five years," said Shlomo. "Don't get excited, Kallenborg, that's what the experts have been saying since *Yisroel's* birth. The Arabs want their own state, but we're not about to let a hostile country exist within our own borders. To hold the Land, we placed settlements in strategic, defensible, positions in the territories. After last night's attack on B'nai Ha'eretz, it is clear we must arm the settlers."

"But they are already armed," said Kallenborg.

"I'm talking about heavy weapons. Rocket propelled grenades and mortars. Anti-tank weapons, shoulder fired heat seeking missiles."

"That's a lot of fire power," said Kallenborg. "Wouldn't the Army provide it when the need arises?"

"In a war, our Army's supplies last about a week. The Army needs its heavy weapons for itself."

Kallenborg was shocked. "One week in reserve? What happens when we run out?"

"The Americans used to re-supply us. But we know we cannot ask the U.S. for help to defend our settlements. The fucking anti-Semites would cut off military aid if their weapons are used to defend settlements."

Kallenborg looked at Shlomo through narrowed eyes. During the short span of years Kallenborg had been in *Yisroel* he felt like an outsider. Now Shlomo was confiding in him, something he'd never done before. Maybe he, Kallenborg, was finally making the grade with the people who counted.

"Wait a minute," he said. "*Yisroel* has missiles with atomic warheads."

Shlomo gave a dry chuckle. "Our Jericho missiles? Some of us want to live here without glowing in the dark."

Kallenborg remembered the reports of radiation pollution from the Ukraine, the pictures of the shattered Soviet atomic reactor at Chernobyl, the six-legged calves and bald-headed Russian children.

"So you're saying the speaker is right?" he said.

"I'm saying we need an alternative source of weapons that is free from the influence of American public opinion. Our European arms supply was cut off years ago, and now South Africa is getting particular about who they sell weapons to. The settlements will have to be defended by the settlers themselves. Fortunately, many are trained veterans."

"Who was the genius who gave this lecture?" asked Kallenborg.

"I was," said Shlomo.

Of course. He should have guessed as much. In silence they drove past an Arab woman walking at the side of the road with a clay water jar balanced on her head, and then a donkey ridden by a man in a dusty suit with his wife following behind on foot. Kallenborg wondered where this discussion was leading.

"What about my assignment?" he said.

"Someone's got to find us the weapons," said Shlomo.

"So?"

"That someone is you," said Shlomo.

The words hit Kallenborg with explosive force. His mind began churning with questions as he sorted out the implications. "How did the Shin Bet get this job?" he said. "Did the Prime Minister gave approval for it?"

"In principal, yes."

"I mean, why didn't the Mossad object? A special operation sounds more like their department."

A flock of sheep filled the road, and Shlomo braked to a crawl before he spoke again. "The Mossad would have been the Prime Minister's first choice," he said. "But our Mossad is never directly involved in any operation."

You bastard, thought Kallenborg. Either you don't know whether Rabin gave his approval or you won't tell me. Aloud he said, "Were they burned recently?"

"No, several years ago," said Shlomo. "It makes a good story. Would you like to hear it?"

Kallenborg nodded knowing he had no choice. The slow moving fetid river of sheep driven by two Palestinians wielding staffs passed by on both sides of the car.

Shlomo sounded his horn impatiently as he inched the Citroen forward. "Some crazy American and his wife, dropped by the Israeli embassy in Washington, D.C. They said their love for the Land of Milk and Honey was so strong, they said they wanted to help us. Would the Mossad like to see all the classified documents this crazy American had access to? He was an analyst in a Navy intelligence office that tracked terrorists. The wife would be their courier. Of course the Mossad is forbidden at least officially to spy on the U.S., so an old cutout originally set up to steal atomic secrets called *Lishka le'kishrei Mada* or Lakam handled the crazy American. When the U.S. found out about our windfall, there was hell to pay. The PM had to offer an official apology."

Kallenborg stared at Shlomo. "That was no crazy American. That was Pollard, and I heard the whole operation was unauthorized."

"There are no rogue operations in *Yisroel*," said Shlomo evenly. "The man in charge of Lakam was Rafael Eitan, a former Army Chief of Staff, the Mossad *katsa* who arrested Adolph Eichman."

"What happened to him?"

"He said others were responsible. Everybody who was involved in the Pollard case received promotions."

The last stragglers of the herd darted by. Shlomo shifted gears and roared through the village.

"Why were the Americans so upset?," said Kallenborg. "We know how to use Pollard's information better than they do. Our friends should have given it to us in the first place."

Shlomo regarded Kallenborg with a steady gaze. "You don't realize it but you owe *Yisroel* and Pollard one big debt. Some of that classified

Navy stuff we got from him was used to ransom thousands of Soviet Jews. *Yisroel* doesn't forget its friends, Kallenborg. Pollard got life sentence in an American prison, but we are still working to get him an early release."

So that was it, thought Kallenborg. Pay back time. Shlomo wanted him to carry out a semi-official operation for the good of his new country. If Kallenborg succeeded, he would be a hero. If he got in trouble, he was on his own and Shlomo would deny everything.

"This sounds like an interesting assignment," Kallenborg said cautiously. "Are you sure I have the right background for it?

Shlomo pulled off the highway onto a twisting dusty track that disappeared behind some boulders. "We are going to visit a settlement. Do you know what they are like?" he said.

"Sure," said Kallenborg. "Egg crates on top of hills."

"Settlements are *Yisroel's* security," said Shlomo.

"What do you mean?"

"Security is more than automatic weapons, mortars, tanks, air craft, an army, " said Shlomo. "Security is the desire to defend one's home."

Sitting on your ass in a foxhole in the middle of nowhere wasn't Kallenborg's idea of home. He had done enough of that in the Soviet Army before he joined the KGB. In another part of his mind he sorted through a mental list of contacts he had made in his career, searching for anyone who could help him deliver for Shlomo.

"Think of it this way," said Shlomo earnestly. "If people live in a place, they'll want to defend themselves. We have an obligation to defend our settlers—that's the only real security for all of *Yisroel*."

Shlomo's took on a conspiratorial tone. "B'nai Ha'eretz is cheaper and much nicer than where you are living in Tel Aviv. The new security highways and tunnels we built by-pass all the Arab towns and villages. In fact, you can live at B'nai Ha'eretz without ever seeing Arabs. And if you want to get in touch with your Jewishness there's no better way than Torah."

Kallenborg looked at Shlomo blank faced. "I'll get weapons for you," he said. "But don't ask me to live in a settlement. It's just subsidized housing in a bad neighborhood at the end of a long commute. I'd rather stay in Tel Aviv."

Shlomo threw him an irritated look. "Just listen and follow me around, he said. "But don't talk to anyone. I want you to know how a settlement is defended. Secrecy is essential."

Twenty-Seven

B'nai Ha'eretz was a fortress in a state of siege. A helicopter gunship flew low over the surrounding Arab villages while a radio controlled pilot less drone, loitered high overhead, its high resolution TV camera beaming pictures back to a communications truck parked in the compound. Platoons of soldiers combed the rocky hillsides and olive groves with metal detectors and guard dogs searching for weapons caches left behind by the retreating guerrillas.

Shlomo and Kallenborg drove past a needle-nosed Merkava tank parked beside the road next to the main gate. Shlomo wheeled around the wrecked Volvo fuel truck that lay just beyond the gate and parked the Citroen beside a flat bed truck. Police dogs, German Shepherds and Dobermans, barked anxiously from wire enclosed runs that had just been erected. Two soldiers struggled as they unloaded portable dog kennels from the flatbed truck. Inside one of the dog runs, a soldier groomed a Doberman bitch.

"After dark the dogs will be let loose in the compound," Shlomo told Kallenborg. "The Army is stretched thin. They can make a show of force for the Arabs for a week or two while they improve our defenses but then they will leave us."

Kallenborg noticed the two bearded men in black gabardine wearing fedoras, who acknowledged their arrival with dull glares, but did not interrupt their agitated conversation.

"Serving forbidden food and it stays open on *Shabbos*, Rabbi," said the younger man.

"And far worse, Etzel," said the Rabbi, "That hamburger stand in *Yerushalayim* symbolizes what is contaminating all of *Yisroel* and all of the Jewish people. When a Jew, a pure soul, eats an impure

173

animal, it destroys his soul. This causes our people to leave the homeland and to make mixed marriages. McDonald's will succeed where Hitler failed."

Etzel sighed. "McDonald's, Michael Jackson, Madonna. Is there no escape?"

"Ah, but *Yisroel* wants to be little America, Etzel." The Rabbi's voice was a harsh sneer.

"They want to live in comfort like the fat Godless Americans," said Etzel.

"We live where it's important to live," said the Rabbi, "Not where it's nice".

Shlomo gestured toward the Rabbi, "I want you to meet that man, Kallenborg. He is the future of our people."

"The Rabbi doesn't seem to be in a hurry to meet anyone. How effective are these defenses?" said Kallenborg.

Shlomo shrugged. "Until last night they did the job."

"What about the electronic fence?"

"The sentries don't trust it," said Shlomo. "The sensors cannot distinguish between a man and goat. No one can sleep if the men on watch shoot at everything that moves. And it wastes ammunition."

"Then what good is the fence?"

"To be honest, Kallenborg, we're counting on the dogs."

The Rabbi came over to them. "What have you brought us this time?" he said to Shlomo.

"Rav, this is Ya'akov Kallenborg, a security expert," said Shlomo. "Kallenborg, meet Rabbi Ben Yusuf."

Kallenborg extended his hand to the Rabbi who ignored it.

"Let me inform you about our situation, Mr. Kallenborg. There are over three hundred people living here, many women and children. The day before Tish B'av, we are holding a rally that will be attended by thousands of people from all over *Yisroel* and the U.S."

Tish B'av, the traditional Jewish day of mourning, marked the destruction of Judaism's two temples, first by the Babylonians and later by the Romans.

The rabbi was momentarily interrupted by the arrival of a jeep driven by a settler who brandished an automatic rifle. Sitting next to the driver was an Army lieutenant, his jaw covered with a thick wound dressing and surgical tape.

"If the Army cannot protect us from the Arabs, Mr. Kallenborg, the young men of Yeshivat Eyal will clean house for us," said Rabbi Ben Yusuf.

The jeep pulled up beside the Citroen and the young lieutenant got out stiffly. He was greeted warmly by the Rabbi as Shlomo beamed with pride.

"Please drop by my study before you leave, Shlomo," said the Rabbi over his shoulder as he and his companion left.

"Shalom," the young officer said to Kallenborg.

Despite his bandages, his eyes were full of good humor and easy confidence. His curly abundant hair under a colorful *kippa*, blue eyes, and freckled nose made Kallenborg unpleasantly self-conscious of his own shabby pale appearance.

"This is my dumbkopf nephew, Avi," Shlomo told Kallenborg. "He risked his life to save our children last night."

Kallenborg thought how different this Avi looked from the jumpy, depressed Soviet veterans he met who came back from Afghanistan.

He noticed the fingers of Avi's right hand were missing.

"Shrapnel?", he asked.

"No, Syrians, " said Avi.

Shlomo turned to Avi, as if to shut Kallenborg out of any conversation. "*Yisroel* has been asked to grant self-rule authority to the area around Ramallah. It's in the intelligence reports you never have time to read."

This was not good news, thought Kallenborg. The Palestine Authority in control of Ramallah would present a whole new set of logistical problems.

"I hope you have another reason for calling me up here, Uncle, besides nudging me about my homework," said Avi.

"What do you think the next step will be?" said Shlomo.

"If you are afraid all of Samaria and Judea will be put under the Palestinian Authority, that's not going to happen," Avi said.

Kallenborg heard a whistle blow out on the soccer field. Groups of boys wearing bobbing side-curls, short black pants, and high black socks streamed into the parking lot.

"Last night's attack proves the Army cannot defend us," said Shlomo. "They came only after *we* had beaten off the Arabs. What would happen if there were a big attack, not just a raid?"

"The U.S. will never let that happen, Uncle," Avi said.

Shlomo gripped him by the shoulder.

"*Yisroel* can never depend on another country for its own security. The Syrian Army has 5,000 tanks. Suppose Hafiz el-Assad wakes up tomorrow morning and says I think I'll go to war? His army could knocking on our door in an hour. The only thing that stops him from taking Jerusalem are these hills. Remember Egypt and Syria almost defeated us in 1973."

"Together they are very dangerous," said Avi, "but Syria is nothing without Egypt. Syria may provide support for Hizbollah forever but they cannot succeed at launching a conventional attack."

Shlomo kicked at the dirt while he studied the ground, but when he turned to face Avi, he smiled.

"You defended this place last night. Specifically, I need to know how to defend our settlements without Army assistance against aircraft, tanks and infantry for two weeks."

"What do you want me to do Uncle?"

Shlomo put his arm around Avi again. "Tell me nephew, how would you attack this settlement and how would you defend it."

Kallenborg felt a pang of jealousy. Then he felt foolish. What was he getting so upset about? Avi wasn't his competition. In fact, Avi was helping him.

* * *

Kallenborg waited in the Citroen while Shlomo met with the Rabbi in one of the apartment buildings. A smile twisted the corner of his mouth as he switched on the computer terminal in the center of the dashboard. The screen flickered as the high frequency radio in the trunk of the Citroen established a connection with MICA, the Shin Bet's central computer. In a few more seconds he was looking at the Christina Goryeb's official investigation file. The summary sheet listed a new report. She was seen by a police foot patrol entering the U.S. Consulate.

Let the Palestinian whore escape to America, he thought.

He'd looked forward to breaking her, but it would be even more gratifying to fuck Asher. Kallenborg whistled a tuneless little ditty as he keyed in the commands that would make Asher's life a little harder. When he was done, Kallenborg switched off the computer. He lit a cigarette, closed his eyes and took a nap.

Twenty-Eight

In his study, Rabbi Ben Yusuf sipped tea through a cube of sugar that he clenched gently between brown tea-stained teeth. He favored Shlomo with one of his sovereign smiles.

"The character of the Land does not lie in the old stones of the Western Wall," Ben Yusuf said. "It lies in the universal understanding that this place is special, that the peace that descends here every Friday evening cannot be experienced anywhere else."

Shlomo returned the Rabbi's smile, but he was thinking about his beloved Avi's narrow escape, thinking about Dror, Racah, and Deidav, still warm in their graves. For an instant he saw madness and rows of tomb stones in the Rabbis eyes.

The Rabbi studied the page torn from Shlomo's notebook. The numbers of men, location of strong points, weapons, amounts of ammunition, spare parts, fuel, food, water, and medical supplies marched across the paper in neatly ordered columns like Joshua's army assaulting the walls of Jericho.

"This is most impressive, Shlomo."

Shlomo took a long sip of tea and looked at Ben Yusuf. "I have some misgivings about the course we have taken, Rabbi. We drove those *mamzarim* off last night. We have many friends in the Knesset. The Likud is strong, they will keep us here no matter what."

The smile faded on the Rabbi's face. "If you have any objections, I'd better know what they are," he said abruptly.

Shlomo found himself speaking in stiff tones as though he were giving a briefing to his superior. "The goal of the Council of Jewish Settlements, is to keep Rabin and Peres from making good on their filthy deals with the Arabs, not to start a civil war," he said.

Ben Yusuf interrupted him angrily. "We will force their hand and make it impossible to remove us from God's Land." He smacked his fist into his hand.

"But if Rabin doesn't buckle, and there is civil war, the Arabs will destroy us," said Shlomo.

Ben Yusuf's eyes flashed. "Torah forbids Jews to withdraw from any part of the land of Israel," he said in a harsh voice, but then his manner became warm and full of encouragement. "But do not fear! Shlomo, we will succeed. Our show of strength on Tish B'av will bring down the government. Didn't our men block the main highway at Givat Ha'tamar and drive the police away with stones? We created such a commotion that Rabin's hands were tied. Arik Sharon warned Peres 'Do not uproot the settlers by force because they will defend themselves'."

Shlomo did not like to be pushed. "Did you know the Attorney General is thinking about charging our Council with sedition?"

Ben Yusuf glared at Shlomo. "Is that all that is bothering you? They can do nothing without the support of the Army. We will force the soldiers to chose between following orders and obeying God's Commandments. When orders are given to tear down Jewish settlements or military bases then the soldiers will disobey Rabin and follow our orders," he said.

"What if they don't?" Shlomo interrupted. "After all, many soldiers do not acknowledge the supremacy of *Halakhah*."

"With heavy weapons we will be able to stand up to the Army so they can't push us out with bulldozers like they did at Yammit. The soldiers will be forced to choose between killing us or joining us."

Shlomo was amazed at Ben Yusuf's grasp of strategy. This must be what was meant by visionary genius, he thought. Again he felt a thin shiver of fear. This time he recognized it as cowardice.

When we show them the steadfast righteousness of our cause, the soldiers will lose heart. They will begin to argue among themselves," Ben Yusuf continued calmly. "We will put pre-taped interviews in the hands of trusted reporters. The videos will show us, the brave men, women and children of B'nai Ha'eretz, faces shining with pride, pride at being part of God's struggle at the End Of Days." He shut his eyes for a moment. "It is a good thing to die for the Land God gave us," we will tell them.

"Excellent!" said Shlomo scribbling in his notebook.

The video tape idea had a lot of possibilities, he found himself thinking.

Ben Yusuf's voice became soft and he extended his hand like a symphony conductor. "Our people will gather around the interviewer in living rooms, supper tables, or in children's bedrooms, talking to them after their bed-time stories. Determined, well-armed men will practice with their weapons in an olive grove against a Bible landscape."

Shlomo pointed again to the list in Ben Yusuf's hand. "We'll need to equip at least 10 settlements in similar fashion," he said.

Ben Yusuf's wife, a plump, careworn young woman, entered the room holding a baby boy on one hip. In her other hand, she carried a plate of dates. She offered some to her husband. After he took a handful, she offered the plate silently to Shlomo. The baby regarded Shlomo and Ben Yusuf impassively with penetrating blue eyes.

Shlomo gnawed on a date. The course was set. The machinery was already in motion. And God was with them. The God of Abraham and Joshua.

Twenty-Nine

Two days later, Richard Goryeb filed off the blue and white El-Al Boeing 747 onto the tarmac at David Ben Gurion International Airport. He joined the other passengers from Los Angeles, New York and Dallas for the quick bus ride to the terminal, and waited in line at passport control. It was noon. His fellow travelers were part of a *Chizuk* mission, an annual tour of Jewish Americans who visited the settlements in the West Bank and Gaza to encourage the residents there. The 10 hour flight to Lod had been noisy with their singing, and redolent with the odors of the rich foods that the passengers brought with them. A blond haired grandmother had produced an entire smoked turkey. She sliced up with an electric carving knife, and handed pieces around to everyone on paper napkins. Richard felt uncomfortable accepting their food, but it would have called too much attention to himself to have refused.

Immediately in line behind him, a stout middle aged man from Dallas, Texas, lectured his teenage son. Richard gleaned from the conversation that the man's younger brother had immigrated to Israel, renounced his U.S. citizenship and now lived at a "Torah City" named B'nai Ha'eretz outside Ramallah. What a fool the younger brother was, thought Richard, to have given up his citizenship. Richard had waited years to become a U.S. citizen.

"If Rabin wants to give the Homeland of Israel to the Arabs, it will be over my dead body," the Texan said, in a loud swaggering voice. "Hundreds of us will take over hilltops in Samaria and Judea tomorrow. We'll block the highways with our bodies. We'll fill up the jails."

Richard doubted the speaker had ever put his life at risk or been inside a jail. Such foolish people, he thought. Their sentimentality allowed them to be used by both the settlers and the Israel. Richard turned to the Texan and asked in a deceptively gentle voice, "Do you plan to return to the U.S.?"

The Texan gave Richard a confused look. "Well, of course. What's your point?" Then he stuck out his hand. "I'm Ezra Kravetz, by the way."

"This is none of my business, Mr. Kravetz," said Richard. "But if I were you, I'd be careful about getting involved with the Israeli police."

"They won't bother us. We're Americans," said Kravetz. Then he smiled shrewdly. "So you live here. I thought you were a *sabra* even though you're dressed like an American."

Richard in his dark blue Brooks Brother's suit, blue shirt, and conservative tie, carried a grey Samsonite suit bag slung over his shoulder like an American businessman.

"I have dual citizenship," he said.

When he declined to explain further, Ezra Kravetz, returned to his son.

When Richard's turn came, he shoved his American passport under the thick bullet proof Lexan and watched the Israeli official inside the booth stamp it perfunctorily three times before returning it. With an ironic smile Richard tucked his passport safely back in his coat pocket and followed the rest of the passengers to customs. So much for their highly touted security, he thought. So much for the highly touted Israeli ability to spot an Arab face. He could have been a terrorist slipping into Israel but the official inside the bullet proof booth never gave him a second look. He remembered the humiliation of ID card checks, the constant threat of administrative detention and torture, how Christina's family looked down on him, how she had called him a coward for leaving.

When he received the letter from his daughter he had booked the first available flight to Israel. "Dear Papa," Aminah wrote in a neat schoolgirl script. "Mama was arrested by the Jewish police but they released her the same day. Now they watch our home and we are prisoners." He did not call Christina first. It no longer mattered to him what Christina wanted; she was an arrogant self-righteous fool who had endangered his children. She could stay in Palestine if she wished, but he would bring Aminah and Munah back with him to Springfield, Virginia.

The week before he had ridden his new horse, a chestnut thorough-bred named *Shammar*, on the C & O canal towpath beside the swift rapids of the Potomac River at Harpers Ferry. Now as he waited for a taxi, he gazed at the yellow Samarian Hills three kilometers distant. A two dimensional, pitiless landscape glared back at him. What was it about this place that drove so many people including his wife mad?

He thought about logistics. Car rental agencies did not allow their vehicles to be driven into the West Bank and he would take a Palestinian taxi to Ramallah. With delays at all the Israeli checkpoints, it would be evening when he arrived at Christina's precious house. He saw Ezra Kravetz, the man he had spoken to at passport control, board an Egged bus and reflected sourly that Kravetz's bus would not be delayed by Israeli checkpoints in reaching its destiny. Before leaving New York Richard had booked four return seats on a Tower Airline flight. They would need immigrant visas. Should he should drop by the Consulate first or go directly to Ramallah, and visit the Consulate later with Christina and the girls? The tougher problem was evading the Shin Bet surveillance. Why were the Shin Bet watching Christina? She must be representing a suspected terrorist. Some dangerous fool she thought was innocent. And of course she would have refused to cooperate with the Jews. In that case, the Shin Bet could refuse to give the children clearance to leave Israel until she cooperated with them.

What would he do then?

Richard smiled grimly as he walked to a telephone booth near the taxi stand. He dialed the number for Jan Pedders, the Jerusalem Bureau Chief of Reuters, a man he knew through his contacts with the State Department.

"Meet me at the Tower Air ticket counter at Lod, 2 p.m. tomorrow. I promise to provide you with an interesting story."

The Israeli government hated adverse publicity. If Richard had any trouble leaving Israel, it would be front page news.

Thirty

Two hours after Richard climbed into his taxi at Lod, Rabbi Ben Yusuf faced a TV camera and glared at the tall auburn-haired young woman in blue jeans and a brush jacket. In front of her was a big Hatachi TV camera with *Kol Yisroel*, the Voice of Israel, emblazoned on its side. She had just thrust a microphone in front of his face.

"I see you are wearing a wedding ring," Rabbi Ben Yusuf said to her sternly. "Why then is your head not covered and why are you not home with your children like a proper *bas Yisroel?*"

The reporter gave a small defiant toss of her thick reddish hair. "Do you have any message for the nation, Rabbi?" she said.

Now he favored the camera with his most benign smile.

"The cradle of our faith is Judea and Samaria. God gave this land to us in trust" he said in sober measured tones. "It is not ours to give away."

With a majestic nod, he walked slowly away.

Behind him he heard the red haired reporter say, "We're on the hilltop near Ramallah. More than 10,000 people are gathered here at the B'nai Ha'eretz settlement, the largest settler rally to date to protest Palestinian self-rule. This one is almost as large as the 'Peace Now' demonstration held last week. Below me you can see the parade winding its way up this rocky hill, as settlers and their supporters from all over Israel as well as *Chizuk* missions from United States converge on this soccer field. They're carrying banners, Israeli flags, and picnic baskets."

Every man the Rabbi passed was armed, some with Beretta and Eagle pistols in shoulder holsters, others with an M-16 or an Uzi slung from their shoulders. He paused for a moment at the edge of the soccer field to admire the huge banners that framed the view. "B'nai Ha'eretz: From Genesis to Eternity," declared the largest banner. "Hold The Land Until The Messiah Comes." Through the practical miracle of television these banners would beam his message throughout Israel and around the world. Most men wore *kippots* or else black fedoras and ear locks although a few were bare headed. Families picnicked on blankets spread on the soccer field or in nooks and crannies on the stony hillside. Guns were openly displayed on some of the picnic blankets. Vendors moved among the groups selling *kosher* apple juice and quarter pints of vanilla ice cream while teenagers passed out leaflets carrying Rabbi Ben Yusuf's picture. Long lines formed in front of portable toilets set up on the edge of the soccer field.

On a make-shift stage in the center of the field, the Tzaddiks' Yeshiva Band performed "Waiting for the Messiah" to a rock and roll beat. At its conclusion, a pot-bellied man in jeans with mutton chop sideburns stepped up to the microphone. He cleared his throat.

"Shalom, y'all," he said in a nasal twang. "My name is Moshe Kravetz, and I'm here to tell you how Torah changed my life. Back when I was living in Dallas, Texas, I searched for fulfillment and got nowhere. My name was Billy, and my life was empty and without meaning. I did not keep *Halakhah*. Why, I didn't know what *Halakhah* was, I was that ignorant and filled with darkness."

Scattered growls of disapproval greeted this revelation, and Ben Yusuf wrinkled his face in disgust. Moshe held up a pudgy hand and mopped his face with a yellow poka dot handkerchief.

"But then I came to *Eretz Yisroel,* and I met Rabbi Ben Yusuf, the man who saved my life. If you live the true life of Torah, the Rabbi told me, you will find fulfillment. So I made a little bargain with the Lord. I said: Lord, if you give me a life, I will follow your Torah. Well, the Lord kept his word and I have kept mine and now miracles happen everyday for me and my entire family, my wife, and our sons, Eli and little Menachem."

Cheers broke out, waves of applause, and Moshe Kravetz smiled broadly from ear to ear. He pointed into the crowd.

"Let's say hello to my brother Ezra and his family," he said. "Ezra's from Dallas too. He'll be demonstrating with us tomorrow. Hey Ezra, stand up and let the folks see you. Let's everybody give him a big hand."

Ben Yusuf felt a hand on his arm and turned. It was alert Etzel. "Who is that putz?", growled Ben Yusuf. "This isn't the Billy Graham Crusade."

"You remember him, our Texan," said Etzel. "He makes us look good on the television for the *non-frum*. Gives us a more folksy image."

The Rabbi lifted an eyebrow. "Better for the *kulturkampf*," he said.

The cellular phone in Etzel's pocket rang and rang.

"We want to hold this land, we'll need an army," said Etzel quietly. "See those people, Rabbi?"

"I am looking," said Ben Yusuf. "What I see is a mishmash."

"They are Joshua's Army—your Army to reconquer the Land!" said Etzel. "Unfortunately, many of them do not keep *Shabbat*. Right now, most of them are interested in affordable housing, but Torah will put fire in their bellies so they will fight for us. Will you excuse me, Rabbi, while I get the phone?"

On the stage, Moshe finished his testimony to a roar of applause. The loud speakers blared rock and roll music again while the next speaker was announced. Bibi Netanyahu, the popular silver haired leader of the Likud party and a fervent supporter of the settlements. Amid rumors of a video tape that featured his sexual conquests, Bibi had confessed he'd been unfaithful to his wife. The next day, a rash of bumper stickers on Israeli cars proclaimed 'I'm Bibi's Lover'.

Ben Yusuf's lips compressed in disapproval.

"Rabbi?" said Etzel cradling the telephone. "A group of settlement leaders want to meet with you. Do you have time?"Ben Yusuf looked at his watch and nodded.

* * *

The noisy hallway outside Samuels' apartment was packed with festive demonstrators. Etzel knocked on the door, and Samuel ushered them in, a plate of potato *latkes* in his hand.

"I just got off the phone with Alon", he said. "His people are living in trailers. He wants us to build houses for them before he'll go in with us.

Ben Yusuf munched on a *latke*.

"That's impossible," said Etzel. "We have no money."

"Alon says if we have money for weapons, we have money for his houses," said Samuels.

Ben Yusuf frowned. "It's Shlomo's money, not ours."

"I don't know," said Etzel doubtfully.

"You don't know, but I do," said Ben Yusuf. "If we build Alon houses, the other settlements will want something too. And what good are houses? We built them at Yammit, and the army tore them down anyway."

"Of course, Rabbi," Etzel said.

"Alon Michaux should want guns not houses," said Ben Yusuf firmly.

He and Etzel followed their host into the next room where several heavily armed men, leaders of religious settlements, sat around a television set. They argued in low voices as they watched the rally. *Matzo* ball soup simmered on a hot plate.

Ben Yusuf took an empty bowl and filled it with soup. He knew these men well. Strong, stubborn people. Hadump, the diamond cutter, from the Almog settlement, whose mother was an Arab convert. Evon, the one-eyed cook from Maale Shrom settlement, who worked in a trendy Jerusalem restaurant and pursued women, but studied Talmud. Labaton, from Ariel, the Russian physicist who saw into rock and metal as if he himself were an electron microscope. Orlev, from Kotel Ha-Ma'aravi, the rabbi from Flatbush Avenue, with grey hair and sensitive hands, a Cabalist scholar who preferred action. It was Orlev who drove away that Arab mob who stoned Ben Yusuf's car. Arba, from Zo Artzenu, the poet and writer of angry Kach pamphlets. Mori, from Tapuah, the farmer who grew up in Bensonhurst who spoke about purifying the Land with steel.

Orlev pointed a finger at Arba the poet. "Why waste effort fighting the government when our real problem is the Arabs? How many Israelis have they killed?" His finger traveled around the circle. "Beit Lid Junction makes 120 Jews dead since the peace talks started with the Arabs! The Prime Minister will fall if he keeps talking Arab self-rule in Samaria and Judea. Meanwhile our poor Alon and his people are still living in trailers. I still say fight the Arabs and build more settlements."

"But how can you build without money?", said Arba.

"The problem is the government," said Evon the cook. He worked the mechanism of his M-16. "We can handle Arabs."

Mori from Bensonhurst broke in, "Listen, the government promises us only we will live as 'protected citizens' under the final agreement with the Palestinians while they build new Jewish neighborhoods in

Arab East Jerusalem almost overnight. Meanwhile they have ordered all settlement construction halted in the territories. Now what does that tell us? Why, it tells us that the Prime Minister will exchange Judea and Samaria for Arab East Jerusalem."

"Rubbish," said Orlev. "Forget about Yitzhak Rabin. Soon Bibi will be in control, a good old fashioned Likud man. He will *futz* up the peace accords with so much smoke they'll be meaningless. He will wear the Arabs down, talk to them forever. They will get discouraged and leave."

Ben Yusuf wondered what Orlev knew.

"Bibi will cave in to the *non-frum* just like Rabin," he said. "He'll tell us that Israeli goods can't be sold in Europe unless he throws the Arabs a bone."

Orlev shook his head. "How are you going to fight the Army's tanks and jet fighters without heavy weapons. It's impossible."

"Our weapons are coming", said Etzel.

"So you say. I'd like to know something. Where are you getting them from?"

"We have friends," said Ben Yusuf curtly.

"Who are they? The Army knows you don't need anti-tank guns and rocket propelled grenades to keep protect yourself from Arabs."

Ben Yusuf glared at the circle of fierce touchy men seated in front of him. He sat forward in his chair. "The weapons will be delivered in good time, but for now we must show our righteousness with protest and demonstrations," he said.

"Protest won't work," said Arba.

"When *kedusha*, our tradition, is under attack, a storm of righteous outrage always succeeds," said Etzel. "Our numbers will get the attention of the *non-frum*. We will mass demonstrators at choke points to block the highways and take over military lands for new settlements. We will lie down like lambs when the police come for us and fill up the jails."

Ben Yusuf had no intention of going to jail himself nor did he expect his fellow settlement leaders to subject themselves to imprisonment but what better way for these tender new recruits on their picnic blankets to show their commitment to *Eretz Yisroel*.

Orlev interrupted him. "This isn't the U.S., Rabbi. The battle is different, the enemy is different, and the people are different. Many of your demonstrators are American volunteers. What will we do when Rabin's police breaks their heads?"

"Jews beating Jews will make Rabin look like Hitler, a pretty sight will bring the *non-frum* to their senses," said the Rabbi quietly. "In their hearts they know a divided *Yisroel* is like ripened fruit to Arab hands, and they will rally to our cause."

The men looked at each other and nodded.

Samuels broke the silence. "The Talmud says there is a *khokma* and an artistry to dealing with others who do not share your own way of thinking."

Ben Yusuf was about to reply when he felt a touch on his arm.

"It's time, Rabbi," said Etzel. "They're ready for you now."

* * *

Thunderous applause broke out as Ben Yusuf climbed the steps of the stage. A commando knife gleamed in his right hand as he raised his arms. As the hubbub died down, the thin bleat of a baby lamb could be heard.

Thirty-One

Forty kilometers away in Old Jaffa on the southern edge of Tel Aviv, Naomi Litvin opened the heavy wooden door of her office to greet Christina. Naomi's office, a small Arab villa, was all limestone pillars and tall windows with a clay tile roof.

"I brought Chaim Asher with me. I hope you don't mind," she said in a brittle sarcastic voice. She pointed at a grey Fiat that backed into a nearby parking space.

Naomi stared at her feeling flustered and embarrassed.

"I thought you didn't want to see him again," she said.

"I forgot to tell you he's the Shin Bet man who's been following me around," Christina said.

There had to be some mistake, thought Naomi.

Naomi protested, "But the Chaim Asher I know works on a *kibbutz*."

Christina gave Naomi a sad smile. "You really thought he is a simple farmer? Poor Naomi, your friend Asher moonlights as a Shin Bet officer."

"Why didn't you tell me sooner?" said Naomi. "I could have done something. You could have trusted me."

"I didn't want to get you involved. Besides, I'm leaving so none of this matters," said Christina.

Naomi closed the door behind her. Love affairs between Israelis and Palestinians were not uncommon, she reflected. Just impossible. "He's like all of us. His need to survive has made him wear two faces, Christina. We don't know which one is real. Forget about him."

"May we talk about these cases now," said Christina hefting her heavy brief case onto Naomi's work table. "My clients will pay you with goats, chickens or vegetables. Most have no money."

There was comfort in focusing on work, in knowing there was something she could do for her friend.

"I don't care whether they pay me or not," said Naomi.

* * *

It was mid-afternoon by the time the two women finished discussing Christina's cases.

"So I've got eight remand hearings and two interviews at Ketsiot," Naomi said with a smile. "In addition to my own cases."

"If it's too much, perhaps Jawad Boulous can help," said Christina. Boulous was the lawyer she had worked for before starting her own office.

"Don't be silly," said Naomi. "I can handle it all."

Empty coffee cups and a thick stack of legal size file folders littered the large double desk between the two women.

Christina rose to her feet. "Well, I suppose this is goodbye." There was a catch in her voice.

The two women embraced and held each other tightly for a few moments.

"I'll miss you," said Christina.

Naomi said,"Even with this business of Chaim Asher! If only—."

Her eyes sparkled.

"Come shopping with me, before I go to court," she said. "I have an hour to spare."

"I wish I could but there isn't time," Christina said.

"Then I'll come to the airport and see you off. What time is your flight?"

"We're leaving tomorrow, on the 2 o'clock Sabina flight to Brussels," said Christina. "I'll be looking for you."

* * *

When Naomi boarded the blue and silver No. 5 Egged bus for Dizengoff Square, she turned for a last look at Christina, who waved back to her. Once inside the bus, Naomi took a window seat near the front and shoved her brief case under the seat. The bus was almost empty when it started out but as it headed along busy Ibn Gvirol

Street toward the square at the heart of Tel Aviv, it rapidly filled with passengers. A sleepy young Palestinian workman carrying heavy canvass tool bag got on at the Hamelech Street stop. He looked around the crowded bus until his eyes rested on the only remaining empty seat, next to Naomi. He sat down beside her and held his bag on his knees instead of putting it under the seat. She shuddered without knowing why. Instantly she reproached herself and nodded to him pleasantly. She was not surprised when he silently looked the other way, since Israelis and Palestinians generally ignored each other in public places. He extracted a string of green worry beads from his denim jacket and fingered them with half closed eyes. A few blocks later Naomi heard him mutter a few unintelligible scraps of Arabic to himself and then a word that sounded like *"jihad."* Jihad, holy struggle, had different meanings depending on the context in which it was used. Giving money for the relief of widows and orphans was *jihad*. Giving one's life to Allah for his purpose was also *jihad*. Naomi stared as his thin brown hand slid into his bag. Deliberately she made herself calm. She had to warn the driver.

She rose to her feet and pulled the signal cord that ran above the windows. A bell sounded at the front of the bus.

"Excuse me, I'm getting off at the next stop," she said firmly in Arabic but the workman continued to ignore her. A faint whine came from the canvass bag. It rose swiftly in pitch, then became inaudible. Naomi threw back her head and screamed.

In front of the Tivoli Restaurant, the No. 5 bus vanished in a violent explosion. The blast smashed windows and hurled burned body parts and metal fragments in all directions.

Thirty-Two

About the time Naomi boarded the doomed bus, Shlomo Arendt sauntered past the large brown American Embassy and the ruined opera
house on Allenby Road where the first Knesset met in 1948. He dis-
liked Tel Aviv, the brash fast moving megalopolis dotted with tall new
buildings. The 'Big Orange' he thought with irritation. After the well-
kept restaurants, hotels, and cafes along Dizengoff Square, he found it
reassuring to stroll beside the curvilinear concrete shapes of 1930-
modern buildings of old Tel Aviv. Pushing on deeper into the neon-
decorated slum, past prostitutes and stalls that featured pornographic
books and movies, Shlomo found what he was looking for, a sign over
a shop that said Yafo Printing, business cards, catalogs, brochures,
invitations.

Inside, at the counter, he was greeted by a shy, bespectacled young
man wearing a blue and white *kippa*. The odor of printers ink filled the
room and the clatter of presses came through a door in the wall behind.

"May I help you," the young man said.

"I need business cards", said Shlomo.

The young man reached for a sample book. "These are our styles,"
he said.

Today was Tuesday. Shlomo opened the book, and found style
No.3.

"This suits me fine but six is also attractive."

The young man seemed confused. "Would you—I mean could I
have your name?"

"Herbert Samuel."

The young man vanished into the workshop. Shlomo sighed. He
hated these cloak and dagger routines. If it had been up to him, he

would have set up the forging operation in the basement of an unmarked government building. But the fussy old men above him cared less about security than with preserving the Prime Minister's ability to deny any connection with the Shin Bet's activities.

The young man was back. "Come with me, please," he said.

In a small room behind the presses, Shlomo found Knudsen sitting at a huge NEC MultiSync color graphics monitor. Knudsen and his wife belonged to a Christian sect in the U.S. who believed the return of the Jews to the Promised Land heralded the second coming of Christ. Knudsen burned with a zealous light. They conversed in English, since Knudsen's Hebrew was poor.

"I'll be off tomorrow," said Knudsen. "I'm joining Rabbi Ben Yusuf's march on the Knesset. We're marching on Rabin's office to protest his filthy deal with the Arabs."

"You can't go," said Shlomo angrily. "I need you here for a special job—."

"And it wouldn't be too cool if I got busted," said Knudsen. "Would it?" He gave Shlomo a wry smile as he reached for a cardboard folder. "The passports are ready."

He placed the passports in a row on the green blotter in front of Shlomo. "Soviet, Bosnian, and German."

Shlomo fingered the Teutonic eagle embossed in gold on the grey-blue pebbled cover on the German passport, then opened it. Kallenborg's ferret face stared back at him through various stamps superimposed on a background laced with fine blue geometric designs. He noted the convincing little tell-tales of authenticity, tiny bent page edges, a slight misalignment of typewritten letters, worn spots on the spine of the book.

"Why is the name and address handwritten on the Bosnian passport? Shouldn't that be typed?"

"You're the boss. But our East European expert says Bosnian typewriters stay broke nowadays."

"Impressive," said Shlomo. "I'm going to need more U.S. currency."

"You bet," said Knudsen cheerfully.

"Any problem with their new color-shifting ink?"

Knudsen shook his head. "We can still print the old style money. The new bills with security gimmicks won't be in circulation until next year."

"Seven hundred fifty thousand dollars in small denominations, fifties and twenties," said Shlomo.

Knudsen let out a low whistle. "Why so much funny money?"

Shlomo gave Knudsen a slight smile.

"Whatever, " said Knudsen. "Look, I figured this bogus stuff paid off Arab informers who didn't want *shekels*. No problem. It only circulates on the Arab black market and they're the losers. But seven hundred fifty thousand phony bucks? If that much stuff gets converted back into *shekels*, we're the chumps. That's a lot of inflation."

"Don't worry, it won't be used in *Yisroel*," said Shlomo.

Knudsen looked Shlomo in the eye. "This is kosher right?" he said.

"You bet," said Shlomo.

The dull thud of a heavy explosion rattled windows. Shlomo knew what the sound meant. Even before debris began to rain down, he was outside on the street running in the direction of the blast.

Thirty-Three

Slowly that evening, Christina pedaled her bicycle towards her beloved home on Shari' Yaffa, the major thoroughfare in Ramallah. Everything that met her eyes was bathed in the warm half-light of dusk. Golden light kissed the rough barked date palms lining the broad avenue, the busy thoroughfares with buses and cars, parked taxis at the curb, couples old and young strolling on the sidewalks and clusters of teenagers in blue jeans, and the golden hewn stone buildings themselves with window grills of iron lace. In the *Muntaza*, families ate supper and old men played *sheshbesh* under the park's lamp lights. The olive groves on hillsides and flocks of sheep seemed to radiate a soft inner glow.

Ramallah.

She would miss this place so much. As she rode through the twilight, she still savored her victory for Daoud Rubez the day before. It made up for the package of dynamite delivered to her office and its ultimate destination. She didn't want to think about the dynamite, about what it would be used for. There'd been no choice, she reminded herself. Hamad had threatened her daughters. No one she had been able to trust could help her, not her family nor Uncle Mukhtar. Richard, was too far away. Richard, who'd been right all along. She pedaled harder. Close to her house, she passed a sidewalk cafe with its metal shutters pulled down. She noticed the rest of the neighborhood shops were closed. Usually at this hour, they bustled with shoppers picking up foodstuffs for the evening meal on their way home from work. She realized she was the only person on the street. That could only mean only one thing: the border police had imposed a "floating" curfew. She pedaled faster toward home.

Every window in Christina's house blazed with light and she could hear the sound of festive music far up the street. Fahoum, the old man who was her gardener and houseman was waiting for her at the gate. She wondered why he was wearing his best white *jalabiyya* and skullcap.

"Mrs. Goryeb, you are home at last," he said and he placed a hand deferentially over his heart. "The radio reports a bomb blew up a bus in Tel Aviv. Twenty-one Jews were killed."

A cold knife twisted in Christina's stomach.

She wheeled her bicycle through the gate and Fahoum quickly chained the gate shut behind her. Candles glowed inside paper lanterns that hung among the shrubbery. The door to her house was open, and light flooded down the steps. A merry stream of chatter and laughter poured out of the house. Shrill feminine squeaks and screams rose and fell as she went up the steps and entered the vestibule. It was hung with red, yellow and green crepe paper. She gave her bicycle to Fahoum.

"What is going on?", she said, a touch of irritation in her voice. She wanted only to have a soothing bath followed by a quiet dinner. "What are all these people doing in my house?"

"Fatima is holding a party in your honor, Mrs. Goryeb", he said.

She instantly regretted her display of ire. Fahoum opened the big double doors and a swarm of people poured out to greet her led by a moist-eyed Fatima who hugged her. Guests in the vestibule called out Christina's name, kissed her cheeks, and pressed her hands, as they carried her along with them into the inner courtyard. Fatima's husband, Kamal, the carpenter, were there with Daoud and four more of their lively dark-faced sons. Najat was whispering into the ear of her husband, Hussein, the bearded surgeon, making him chuckle and laugh. Children in silly screaming groups played tag through the arches. On the stairs stood Janine, one hand on the shoulder of Jamal, her banker husband. Sitting regally on the wooden dais by the tamarisk tree Christina's mother, Leilah, radiated quiet charm and hospitality as she gossiped with several of her friends. Christina put down her brief case and surrendered herself to the happy occasion.

Leilah rose and gave Christina a regal embrace. "My fearless daughter," she said. To Daoud she said, "You are very lucky young man to have such a clever lawyer."

"Daoud conducted himself bravely," said Christina.

Fatima and Kamal beamed.

"What do you think about the bomb in Tel Aviv today?" asked Daoud, grim satisfaction in his voice.

Christina chose her words carefully.

"There will be many more arrests, I'm sure, and strict curfews will be imposed on us. Aren't we under curfew already? Which reminds me, Fatima, all our guests must sleep here tonight."

Daoud would not be deflected.

"The Lions of Allah did it," he said.

How did he know, Christina wondered, and what of anything did he know of her part in this wretchedness. Perhaps Abu Awad had taken Daoud into his confidence! The dismay in her face must have been evident for Daoud took her hand.

"Mrs. Goryeb, I am grateful for what you have done for me. It will bestow much honor on me and my friends if you will permit the *shabab* to serve as your personal guards during this time of trouble."

"No thanks Daoud," she said. "I'll be all right. Besides you need your job with Rosenbluth."

"Have you not heard? Israel's borders are closed to Palestinians. I can't get to work."

Christina was stunned. With the borders closed she would not be able to get to the airport. She did not want anyone, especially Leilah to notice how upset she was. Jamal approached Christina, holding out a glass of wine and chicken *shwarma*.

"For the guest of honor," he said.

She took them and took a bite of *shwarma*. "Thank you. I hope you won't mind living with us until the border opens again," she said.

Jamal shook his head and smiled. "I regret I can't stay, but I have business in Tel Aviv I must attend to tomorrow afternoon."

Christina said, "But the borders are closed."

"Only to Palestinians," Jamal said. "Remember, we have Israeli license plates." Jamal and Janine lived in Christina's West Jerusalem house and were Israeli citizens.

Jamal would take them to the airport, she thought.

As she nibbled on *shwarma*, Christina looked around the courtyard and saw a boy who sat in an open window and stared at her in a cool, insolent way. Christina recognized him immediately as the rude boy who'd burst into her office looking for messages, the boy who'd led her to Hamad, picked up the dynamite for him.

"Daoud, who is that boy?" she said.

"That is Rasul, Mrs. Goryeb. He is one of my *shabab* friends."

"Is he one of your close friends?"

Daoud shrugged. "Just someone I know. Do you wish to speak with him?"

"Oh, no."

So that was why the Shin Bet had been so interested in Daoud, she realized.

Suddenly Fatima appeared at her side.

"There's a telephone call for you Mrs. Goryeb," she said. "It's Mr. Litvin."

Yigael wouldn't call unless there was something wrong. She thought of Naomi's conscientious face and the knife twisted within.

"I'll take it in the library," she said, eager to escape.

She threaded her way through her guests to the phone on her desk in the library and picked up the receiver.

"Yes, Yigael, what is it?" she said forcing herself to be calm.

"Is Naomi there?" he said."

In his voice was anxiety and hope.

"No, she's not," said Christina.

"I'm a little worried. Have you heard about the terrible news: the bus bomb on Gvirol Street."

"She must be working late."

"I called her office, and she's not there. Where did you see her last?"

"Well we had coffee together at a sidewalk cafe."

"Where, Christina? Tell me at what time?"

She faltered. "About two o'clock this afternoon."

"The bomb exploded at two-thirty," he said.

"I'm sure she'll turn up," Christina said panic breaking through her voice.

"Have her call me if you hear from her," Yigael said and hung up.

Dear God, Christina thought, her hands shaking as she returned the telephone receiver to its cradle, not that bus! She could never forgive herself if Naomi had been on that bus.

Outside, the sounds of people enjoying themselves suddenly died down and the music stopped.

When she opened the door, she saw Richard. Through the press of people, he walked toward her, a wooden smile on his face. His eyes blazed with fury.

It was all very dreamlike, fragments of stopped time. First her mother's face, frowning and bewildered, her lips open in surprise. Then Aminah's and Munah's smiles, their joyous shouts and the clatter of their shoes on the tile floor as they ran to greet Richard. He bent down, threw his arms around his daughters and hugged them to himself tightly. My husband, she thought.

With a sad cold heart that she knew suddenly she no longer loved him, yet was counting on him to save their children and to help her escape the living nightmare her life had become. He was the only person who could.

The band began playing again and the party resumed where it left off.

"I'm very happy to see you," she said.

"I imagine you are," he said. The glitter in his eyes made her feel uneasy in front of the smiling faces of her family.

"We have something to discuss in private," he said in a cool soft voice. He took her arm firmly and steered her back into the library. Only after he had closed the door, did he take the envelope from his pocket and give it to her.

"Aminah wrote this to me," he said.

She unfolded the pale blue paper and read it quickly.

Richard interrupted her, his manner as imperious as a prosecutor. "What is the meaning of this, Christina?" he said.

"My law clerk, Abu Awad was passing messages for the Lions of Allah." Hastily she added, "This was without my knowledge, I assure you."

"I believe you, but you'll remember I told you not to hire him," he said, but his face remained dark and impassive. "What happened?"

"The Shin Bet killed him. Now they have me under surveillance," she said.

"I'm deeply disappointed that you did not tell me yourself."

"I was going to—,"

"But you knew I would come for my children, if you told me," he said.

"The Jews read our mail. Our phones are tapped."

"Christina, that's not good enough. If you'd wanted to contact me you could have."

"I didn't think I'd need your help," she said. "I was sure I could handle this myself."

His voice was remorseless, full of contempt. "Your pride has endangered our children. Tomorrow, I am taking Aminah and Munah to the Consulate to get visas and then I am driving to the airport at Lod to get on a plane and leave this stinking place."

He would make her pay, she knew. Palestine without her children would be intolerable.

"What about me?" she said.

To need him and not to love him was cruelty.

"In the past you refused to join me in Virginia," he said quietly. "What about your sacred cause—you've gone this far. Why not throw your entire life away? You'll make a wonderful martyr."

There was something in his eyes she did not know, could not comprehend, something stronger than wrath, deeper than sorrow, something gripped his soul until his eyes burned like hot embers. He looked down at her for a long time until her defiant gaze wavered, and he released her.

"Of course, you can come if you wish," he said. As she put her hand on the door knob to leave she turned to him.

"As it happens, I've already got our visas and reservations," she said. "We can leave whenever you want."

He gave her a smile of grudging respect.

"Then we have finally come to an agreement," he said.

Thirty-Four

Twenty-one Israelis were murdered in the Gvirol Street bombing. While Christina's guests celebrated in Ramallah, eight anxious men in shirt sleeves gathered around an oval glass covered conference table in Jerusalem's ultra-modern Knesset Building for the midnight meeting had been called by the Prime Minister. None of the eight acknowledged each other's presence, some taking elaborate pains to avoid eye contact. Sharett, the Prime Minister's Director General, conferred with his secure phone, while Ruppin, the Police Minister, glowered at a wilted bouquet of roses in the center of the table. Mekor, Director of the Mossad, toyed with an empty water glass. Each was accompanied by an aide, like Shlomo, with a brief case of papers. Shlomo still felt nauseated. The smell of seared flesh remained in his nostrils. His clothes were stained with the blood of the victims he had administered first aid to.

At long last, the Prime Minister walked in and took his place at the head of the table. With him was Brigadier General Daniel Ohr, the Deputy Defense Minister, who wore a summer uniform and his usual look of thoughtful concern. The Prime Minister, tie less as usual, glanced around the table instantly commanding attention.

"A group that calls itself the Lions of Allah claims credit for the bombing," he said. "What do we know about them?"

Shlomo's boss, Carmi Gillon, Director of the Shin Bet, felt obliged to speak first.

"We know very little, apart from the name. It surfaced in a case you asked us to help the Mossad with."

"What case was that?"

"The one involving the woman lawyer from Ramallah, Christina Goryeb."

The Prime Minister turned to the Mossad's Director. "Mekor, are they Hamas or independent?"

"We don't know yet. Hamas has a secretive and amorphous leadership. Some of its initiatives appear to be the work of isolated cells," Mekor said. "Furthermore the Lions of Allah could be a cell of Islamic Jihad, or Hizbollah. It's even possible the Lions do not exist at all. Five juveniles commit a violent act, then make up a catchy name and call themselves a brigade."

"They exist all right," said Gillon. "Graffiti in the Arab quarters says 'Lions love death more than Israelis love life'."

"Just punks stirring the shit," said Mekor.

"Mekor, the Goryeb case must be a no miss operation. I want a detailed report from you in an hour," said the Prime Minister. "And it better be good or I'll give that case to Gillon to handle. Now what about that bomb? Was it plastic or TNT?"

"Sticks of dynamite," said Gillon.

"Don't they usually extract dynamite from old land mines?"

"The sticks were stolen from one of the by-pass road projects."

"Then Mekor's probably right," ventured Ruppin. "Local free lancers."

"I can make my own assumptions," said the Prime Minister dryly. "What are your people doing, Ruppin?"

"Samaria and Judea are sealed."

"And the Shin Bet?"

"We are detaining all suspicious Arabs and interrogating them with utmost vigor," said Gillon.

Two blond mess stewards carrying a tray of cups and a silver coffee pitcher entered the room. They spoke to each other in Russian while they served everyone.

"Kindly remember to speak Hebrew!", said General Ohr curtly to the stewards.

"You never mind the lack of Hebrew when we had Arab mess stewards, Danny," said Gillon with a sly smile.

"Pay attention," growled the Prime Minister. "Here's how I view the situation. The Arabs want an iron fist? Good! We'll give it to them. The borders can stay sealed permanently if that's what it takes. This afternoon I called the Chairman of the Palestine Authority and told him if he doesn't arrest these lunatics, I will send the Army into Gaza and Jericho to hunt them down. Any discussion? Comments?"

"Soldiers don't make good cops," said Sharett. "Chasing Arabs down the back alleys in Gaza and Jericho will make our soldiers easy targets."

"The Americans won't like it," said General Ohr.

The Prime Minister looked irritated. "We must protect lives," he said.

"Suppose the Palestinians are unable to capture these scum?", asked Ohr. "Do we break off self-rule talks with them?"

"I haven't made that decision," he said firmly.

"Every Arab bomb shows the West they are murderers. Nobody would give a damn if we broke off talks and annexed the territories," said Ruppin.

As Shlomo listened, his excitement mounted. In one swift bold stroke the future of Eretz Yisroel could be secured. He looked at his watch. It was one minute past midnight.

"Today is Tish B'av," he said softly.

Ruppin nodded. "If we annex Samaria, Judea and Gaza, it will extinguish the fires of sedition brewed by the Likud. Otherwise, we must deal with Rabbi Ben Yusuf and his demonstrators as well as the Arabs."

"Get your heads out of the sand," the Prime Minister said. "We cannot annex the West Bank and Gaza without upsetting the West, and we cannot keep spending 25% of our national income on defense. There will never be enough money to build a real economy."

"The Americans supply the money. Three billion dollars a year is *bupkis* to the U.S.," said Ruppin.

The Prime Minister gave him a withering glance. "*Yisroel* was based on the idea that Jews would never again be dependent on *goyim* for their security," he said. "Now we are more dependent than ever on a foreign state which is half way around the world. Over 50 percent of American Jews marry *goyim* and their children will not be raised or vote as Jews. The only way we can stand on our own feet is to make peace."

"We don't need U.S. aid," said General Ohr. "Our economy is booming. I say we take care of ourselves. It's happened before, you know."

The Prime Minister slammed his fist down on the table and everyone winced.

"Our first priority is *aliya*! We need U.S. aid to absorb immigrants. If we don't bring more Jews here, the Palestinians will outnumber us. They will demand a separate Palestine or else the right to vote in the Knesset. And with their birth rate that will be the end of the Jewish State."

"So we don't let the Palestinians have a state and we don't let them vote," said General Ohr.

"We'll have no choice. Look at South Africa," said the Prime Minister. Apartheid has ended and that *kooshe*, Mandella, is on top."

Shlomo listened with disgust. He could already guess what the Prime Minister's decision would be.

"Do you think it's wise to keep the borders sealed indefinitely?", said Mekor. "Who will sweep the streets, empty the trash, wait on tables?"

"We can import Filipino or Thai laborers," said the Prime Minister.

"Another Lebanon," murmured Mekor.

"What do you mean?", said Gillon.

"With the borders sealed, the Palestinians in the territories have no jobs, no food," said Mekor.

"Better they starve than we should die from car bombs," said General Ohr.

"The settlers won't like it. They'll complain we're too soft on Arabs," said Gillon.

The Prime Minister gave a harsh laugh. "Too soft! I've kicked out more Arabs than anyone you can name."

"But the settlers are important to our security," said General Ohr.

"They're a cancer in the body of democratic *Yisroel* and a drain on our resources," said the Prime Minister. "It costs $20,000 a year to protect each settler. No, the only thing that's important is Jerusalem, no more East or West. We will continue to push the Palestinians for a united Jewish capital."

Shlomo was white-faced with anger. Why, the opportunity to annex Samaria and Judea lay ripe for the taking. The Prime Minister was a short-sighted as he was gutless. He, Shlomo knew what God wanted him to do.

Thirty-Five

The next morning Mekor woke up in Jerusalem to another bad day.

That dull ache throbbing behind his left eye was a sinus condition that flared up during the night when rain moved in off the Mediterranean. Antihistamines would dry up his sinuses but his doctor advised him to avoid them since they irritated his prostate. Pain killers were out of the question too. In the present crisis, his mind needed to be razor sharp. He was proud of his intellect, ate sparingly and followed a rigid regimen of exercise that began with a daily squash match with his Deputy, Gilda Sderot. It was too early for anyone else to be playing so they could talk shop.

They met every morning at 6:30 a.m. in the rotunda of the YMCA, one of the city's best known landmarks. Built in 1928, with funds given by a New Jersey millionaire, it was planned by the same firm that designed the Empire State Building in New York City, complete with a 152 foot art deco "Jesus Tower". Across the street was the King David Hotel, the right wing of which had been blown up by the Irgun in 1946 and rebuilt with a darker shade of limestone.

"Six-five. Pay attention, Mike, this game is the tie breaker," Gilda said briskly. She wore snug white shorts and her loosely brassiered breasts moved seductively under her blouse. He knew better than to try anything but she always put magic in his day.

Mekor drew back his racquet and tossed a small hollow, hard rubber ball into the air with his thumb and first two fingers. With one quick motion, he fired the ball toward the front wall of the squash court. The ball darted forward spinning backwards but instead of bouncing low as he had intended, it thudded against the metal tell-tale panel by the floor.

"Mike?"

"I don't fucking care. I'm beat," he said. ".The PM is all upset about the Gvirol Street bombing. Asks me stupid questions that have no answers. Acts so fucking naive."

"But you made up answers anyway," Gilda said cheerfully from the server's box. "I hope you didn't say too much." Her serve ricocheted off the side and front walls before hitting the floor.

He returned with a vigorous backhand drive. "You don't understand. Facts have nothing to do with politics."

She lobbed the ball high.

"Then I get to the office, and the Cray has crashed," he said.

The Cray 3 was the Mossad's main computer. It linked intelligence reports filed by field agents all over the world with incredible speed. Whenever the Cray was down the Mossad lost its star player.

"Your point," said Gilda.

"That was only the beginning," he said panting, still playing for sympathy from her. "My wife calls long distance from London. She says our Oxford son is living with a *shicksa* whore. Then she sticks the knife in deeper and says she hopes I'm not too lonely at night."

Gilda said without remorse, "But five minutes after she hung up, Netanya called".

Mekor made a lightning serve.

"How did you know?"

"I was here when you took the call, remember."

"Yeah. That's right. All pissed because I forgot our date at the Cinematheque. She doesn't know what's going on, thinks I'm a banker with a life. I'm raw meat."

Gilda laughed.

"You a banker? Mike, we have things to worry about."

"Like what?"

Gilda prepared to serve. From the tone of her voice, Mekor knew he wouldn't like what she was about to say.

"Chaim Asher."

"Why?"

"I don't think he's right for the Goryeb case," she said and fired the ball at the corner again.

They volleyed aggressively, each seeking the advantage.

"The PM considers the Lions of Allah to be our top priority. Personally, I'd use Ramon Boker," said Gilda.

"You already do. Just because Boker fucks you good doesn't mean he's our man. He'll be thinking about your lovely tits and ass when he should be sniffing around Goryeb."

"Please Mike be serious. The new psychiatrist, is concerned about Asher."

"Your friend, the exquisite Roz Berman?" Mekor chased down Gilda's foul ball.

"She's just completed Asher's annual psychiatric appraisal. Says he's a danger to himself and other personnel."

"So, he probably gave her wrong answers on purpose. That's what I do."

Gilda smiled coyly. "Dr. Berman doesn't believe you're the sex fiend you say you are!"

"What does she know?" he said.

"Mike, she says Asher's unsound. He pines after an *Yisroel* that no longer exists."

"I know, *kibbutzes, moshaves,* frugal living with meaningful relationships—"

"He told her that Menachem Begin murdered his family. That sounds pretty delusional."

Mekor said, "Asher's son died in Lebanon. Asher's wife committed suicide six months later. Lebanon was Begin's biggest mistake. Many Israelis feel the way Asher does."

"But they don't work for the Mossad. Did you know he circulated a petition after the Lillehammer and Noriega incidents? That shit he wrote about the Mossad being assassins for hire?"

Mekor frowned. This called for some delicacy.

"Asher's last assignment took him to the archive at Yad Vachem, the Holocaust Memorial, for a history lesson my generation would like to forget," he said.

"Okay, Boss, so explain Asher."

They began another fierce volley.

"Let's start with Asher's hatred of Begin. Remember the night Likud won the election?"

Gilda shook her head. "Mike, that was 20 years ago. I was a teenager then."

"How did your father vote?"

"He voted for Likud then. Of course, he voted for Labor in the last election."

"And my father voted for Labor in both," Mekor said. "He was a Histadrudt leader." The Histadrudt was Israel's giant trade-union. "When the TV predicted Begin would win, tears ran down his face. Then he picked up the phone. He and his colleagues began planning how to hide the Histadrudt's assets from Likud."

Gilda laughed. "Serves them right. You counterfeit Jews had locked us out of all the best jobs."

"Counterfeit Jews?" said Mekor with a note of irritation.

"You won't admit Eastern European Jews have no blood line to Abraham," she said.

Mekor gave her a belligerent look. "And yours do?"

Gilda could throw her Shepardic lineage up to him all she wanted. Yitzhak Rabin's Labor coalition had won the last election by promising prosperity and better jobs to Jews from North Africa, Yemen, and Ethiopia.

"My ancestors moved to Spain from Palestine after the Romans destroyed the Temple," said Gilda. "A thousand years ago, yours were pagan Slavs and Turks living in southern Russia in an empire called Khazaria. They converted to Judaism so they could remain independent of their Christian and Muslim neighbors. There's no other way to explain how so many Jews appeared in eastern Europe by the 17th century."

"Hitler didn't care about such fine distinctions," said Mekor, sourly.

The Khazars were a sore point, as far as he was concerned. Scraps of their history appeared in ancient Arabic, Hebrew, Armenian, Byzantine, and Slavic writings as well as the modern *Encyclopedia Judaica* which devoted an entire page to the Khazars. The Khazars wrote using Hebrew-Aramaic letters. A linguist from Tel Aviv University, a Dr. Wexler, had reconstructed Yiddish to show how it began as a Slavic language whose vocabulary was largely replaced with medieval German words. Kiev, the modern capital of the Ukraine, had been founded by Khazars. Of merely academic interest, thought Mekor angrily, except as ammunition for anti-Zionists.

Gilda interrupted his thoughts.

"'Fucking Fascists'—that's how Asher referred to Begin, Shamir, and their Likud Party," she said.

"You're talking about Asher's history lesson?" Mekor said with a slight smile.

"Let's don't talk politics, Mike." Gilda moved to the server's box, drew back her racquet then turned toward him. "So Begin and Shamir were tough and practical? That doesn't make them Fascists," she said and hit the ball.

"This isn't politics. Back before *Yisroel* got her independence, back in the 1930's, Shamir belonged to the Revisionist or militant wing of the Zionist movement. Begin joined later. The leader of the Revisionists was the hero of Russian Zionism, Ze'ev Jabotinsky, a brilliant energetic admirer of Mussolini."

"Benito Mussolini, the Italian dictator?"

"He wasn't anti-Semitic then. Hell, one of Benito's girl friends was even Jewish. Il Duce had a certain style that appealed to Jabotinsky. Jabotinsky's Revisionists wore brown shirts and staged large dramatic parades. As a young man in Czarist Russia during the *Pogroms*, he organized the first "Haganah", the self-defense Jewish organization in Odessa. That's what gave him the experience he needed to create the Jewish Legion in Palestine to fight against the Turks during World War I. The British repaid him with the Balfour Declaration which called for a Jewish Homeland in Palestine. Later, when the British reneged on the deal, Jabotinsky vowed to build a 'Wall of Iron' to run the Arabs and British out of Palestine. The Revisionists' military organization, the *Irgun Zvai Leumi*, killed hundreds of Arabs with booby traps and car bombs. Of course, the British and the Arabs didn't take it lying down. They were well-armed and matched atrocity with atrocity. In 1940 Jabotinsky died, and by the middle of World War II, Begin was head of the Irgun."

Gilda said, "But the Revisionists established self-defense *irguns* across Europe. Why they rescued thousands of Jews from the Nazis while the Labor Zionists in Tel Aviv did nothing. Did Labor want the Holocaust to happen?"

Mekor squatted as he retied a shoe lace. "Ben Gurion said the Land of Israel was more important."

"Okay, now tell me about Shamir." She whipped a serve into the right hand corner.

"He was nothing but a cold blooded assassin," said Mekor.

"Prime Minister Itzak Shamir?"

"When the Revisionists suspended operations against the British in 1940, Avraham Stern, Shamir and a handful of others broke away from the Irgun. They called themselves the *Lohamei Herut Yisroel* or Lehi. They robbed banks, assassinated British diplomats, and murdered more Arabs. They also executed Jews who they considered traitors. Shamir became the gang's leader after Stern was killed."

"But the Lehi were freedom fighters!" said Gilda.

Mekor spat the words out. "Itzak Shamir wrote the German Ambassador, in Ankara Turkey, 'We identify with you in principal. So why not collaborate with one another?'. In January 1941, the Lehi met with German diplomats in Lebanon and Damascus. Their proposal called for the establishment of the historic Jewish State on a 'national and totalitarian base, linked by a treaty to the German Reich' and the 'evacuation of the Jewish masses from Europe to Palestine'."

"Jews helping Nazis! That's incredible!"

"In your words, they were just being 'practical'. Shamir was arrested by the British as a Nazi collaborator. His Lehi plotted to assassinate David Ben Gurion when they believed the Labor Zionists had sold out to the British. Asher found Von Pappen's report to Hitler in the Yad Vachem archive."

"When did all this ancient history settle down?"

Mekor gave a grim chuckle. "But it hasn't. *Yisroel* is an argument not a nation. Did you know, for instance, that after independence in 1948, Ben Gurion ordered Yitzhak Rabin, then a young Army officer, to fire on the *Altalena*, a ship bringing arms to Begin's Irgun. Jew fought Jew in a pitched 10-hour battle for control of Tel Aviv. More than 40 years later, we're still arguing about the *Altalena*. By the way, 'Altalena' was Jabotinsky's pen name in Czarist Russia."

Gilda eyes widened.

"How did Shamir live down his past?"

"He worked for the Mossad as an assassin. In time he became Head of Special Operations. After he entered politics, he learned subtler tactics, but his policy of running the Arabs off the land remained unchanged. He pushed for more West Bank settlements and gave the settlers automatic weapons for self-defense. A weapon like an M-16 in the hands of crackpots like Meyer Kahane, Baruch Goldstein, and our latest—that Rabbi Ben Yusuf, makes them into bullies and vigilantes. Shamir was wary of the crackpots, but he let them serve his purpose and the Mossad was encouraged to undertake high risk operations. You might say we went overboard being 'practical'. A lot of our *katsas* became disillusioned, left the Mossad and went into business on their own."

It was a lot to take in, but Mekor could tell from Gilda's sharp intake of breath that she was making all the connections. Hell with a little more seasoning she'd be one of the best.

"So why send Asher to dig up this old dirt?"

"Another Lehi," he said quietly. "Do you remember Judge Dov Eitan?"

"He was one of the lawyers who represented Ivan the Terrible, the Nazi death camp guard," Gilda said.

"Soviet records showed the real 'Ivan' was executed by the Red Army in 1945 so this John Demjanjuk we tried was the wrong man. In the middle of the appeal to the Supreme Court, Eitan mysteriously fell out of a 15-story window in the Jerusalem Tower."

"Didn't Eitan commit suicide?" said Gilda.

"That's the official story. But after acid was thrown in the face of Eitan's co-counsel, Yoram Sheftel, the PM asked us to check into the possibility of another Lehi. The man who tried to blind Sheftel was a Torah Jew who said anyone who defended an enemy of God deserved to die, so I sent Asher out to take a closer look. He enrolled his team in a couple of *hesders*—you know those *yeshivahs* that combine Torah, regular school and play at being soldiers like Yeshivat Eyal at B'nai Ha'eretz? Eyal, by the way, was the motto of the Lehi—Only Thus!"

"Did Asher find any connection to Judge Eitan?"

"Just a smell, but no hard facts. But the *hesder* boys were a little disturbing. They believe that the kingdom of *Yisroel* is being rebuilt and the whole goddamn Army is holy."

"Oh, that's harmless," she said. "It's patriotism."

"Not so harmless if you consider that 40 percent of the Army's officers are religious. In the elite units the ratio is higher; at least two-thirds of the officers in the Golani Brigade are religious. We pulled the service records of these *hesder* boys. They are not the quiet, studious types. They are like Jabotinsky, brilliant and aggressive. Our most talented minds and they are everywhere in our military—even in the Shin Bet and the Mossad. Many have carried out intelligence missions, some inside Russia."

"So what are you worried about?"

"Mutiny. That they'll obey a rabbi like Ben Yusuf before they obey their commanding officers. Once that happens Israel's finished."

Gilda shook her head. "You are an alarmist." She entered the server's box. "I still think we should use someone with less baggage than Asher for the Goryeb case."

"No," said Mekor. "Chaim Asher is right for this job. Let's remember, this Goryeb woman isn't easily intimidated, and, her husband is close to the American government. If we lean on her too hard, he'll get the story into their papers and we'll look like *shmucks*. So get Asher in here."

Gilda sighed. "Okay, but I'm sending you an E-mail confirmation of this."

Mekor countered her serve with a low cross court shot that he sent thudding against the tell-tale.

"Eight all."

Mekor flashed his most disarming smile.

"Yeah, cover your pretty little tush."

Gilda's last serve zigzagged around the squash court like a demented bee.

Mekor missed it completely.

"Game and match," she said sweetly.

Thirty-Six

Kallenborg felt he had returned from the dead. He saw himself giving orders to his own hand-picked team of Shin Bet officers who in turn would lead squads of border police. With great enthusiasm he unfolded his newspaper at a table in a side walk cafe on Ben Yehuda Street in Tel Aviv, completely oblivious to the bustling street a few feet away. The Lions of Allah, his big case were banner headlines in the early edition of *Yediot*.

Below it was another story about an expected violence in a demonstration of settlers at the Knesset but Kallenborg was not interested.

All that was left was find out what the Goryeb woman knew, he thought. She was the connecting link. The first thing he'd do when he had access to MICA would be to reopen her investigation file. He had closed it to make Asher look bad but now he had the chance to break the case, to break her. Also finesse was called for, because Shlomo would not allow physical torture in her case. Still, the full range of psychological duress would be at Kallenborg's disposal. There were many choices. Isolation in a tiny airless cell? Sleep deprivation? Threats of harm to loved ones? That last one was always effective.

Kallenborg beamed.

He knew how to get to Goryeb. She had a big mouth but underneath she was soft.

A waiter brought him a bottle of Maccabee beer and *falafel*. He took a bite of the spicy vegetable sandwich, a sip of beer, and turned to the comics section of the paper where he became immediately absorbed.

When the shrill beep of a Citroen horn sounded at the curb, he looked up. Shlomo leaned out of the window of his black *Deux Chevaux* and beckoned for him to get in. Kallenborg paid his bill, picked up his paper and joined Shlomo. The Citroen pulled out into traffic, narrowly missing the fender of a charging cab. A few minutes later they crossed the Yarkon River and headed north out of the city on Route 2 in the direction of Haifa.

Shlomo's eyes were bloodshot and puffy.

"Up all night?" Kallenborg said.

"Let's hear your operational plan," Shlomo said brusquely.

A tourist bus was about to pull out into an intersection in front of the Citroen, and Shlomo pounded his horn.

Kallenborg was accustomed to such abruptness from Shlomo. He permitted himself a little smile. "I will personally handle the interrogation of the Goryeb woman. We will rough up one of her sisters. Goryeb will be forced to watch. She will tell us what we need to know about The Lions of Allah."

Shlomo shook his head vigorously, as he accelerated to pass a truck loaded with crates of vegetables.

"Forget about Goryeb. Your new assignment is arming the settlements."

Kallenborg tapped his paper. "What about the Lions of Allah?"

"She's not important. Your assignment is arming the settlements. Now what have you come up with?"

Kallenborg's face fell."But Goryeb is about to leave *Yisroel*. She was seen entering the American Consulate, day before yesterday."

"Shlomo shrugged. She's Asher's problem. Don't worry, if she escapes, I'll make sure the PM knows about it."

Kallenborg looked out the open window at orange groves with a spiteful smile. So be it. No one would ever find out who had closed Goryeb's investigation file on MICA and Asher would be covered in shit.

"Look, Kallenborg, the Prime Minister is counting on you."

Shlomo must want this badly, thought Kallenborg. He pulled out his pack of Players and looked over his small steel-rimmed glasses at Shlomo. "I know someone," he said.

Shlomo's eyes glittered. "Who is he?"

Kallenborg remembered the familiar broad, pock-marked face, and the shock of coarse black hair. The sure eye for the main chance.

"Nicholai Ivanovich Derevenko," he said. "A former Soviet Army Colonel."

"Where is he now?"

"He stayed in Kabul after the Soviets pulled out."

"For God's sake, why would any Russian want to stay in Afghanistan?"

"Derevenko has no family," said Kallenborg. "Opportunities for advancement in the Red Army are somewhat diminished since the collapse of the Soviet Union. And Afghanistan has lots of surplus munitions left over from the invasion."

"So your friend has found opportunity?"

Derevenko always found opportunity thought Kallenborg. Give the man shit and he'd turn it into a concession.

"He advises the Defense Minister of the *Mujahideen* central government."

Shlomo was properly impressed.

"Do you know how to get in touch with him?"

Kallenborg sucked on his cigarette.

Of course. He knew exactly where to find Derevenko. Two days before, Kallenborg had received a fax from a *concierge* at a Luxembourg hotel who forwarded communications for people who wished to conceal their whereabouts. It contained an innocuous message quoting prices on various scrap metals. However, Kallenborg had his own private KGB key that he used to decode the quotations. The message he read said: LETS DO BUSINESS. IRON FELIX WOULD APPROVE. REGARDS D.

Thirty-Seven

As Shlomo and Kallenborg drove to the medieval port city of Akko, north of Tel Aviv, Asher pulled up in front of Mossad headquarters on King Saul Boulevard in Tel Aviv. An hour earlier he had been sitting in his stake out near Christina Goryeb's house when his solitude had been broken by an insolent beep from the pager on his belt. Mekor's number appeared on its LCD display. Mekor wanted to see him in person, immediately the receptionist said when she took his call. The Mossad operated like a small, ruthless family business; its needs came first, night or day.

Asher climbed the broad stairs up into the lobby of the Hadar Dafna Building. On the ground floor of the glass and concrete office tower was a bank and on the second floor, a public cafeteria. He took the elevator to the third floor to the offices of the *Institute for Biblical Archaeology* and gave his name to the receptionist. As he waited, he studied the large back and white photographs that decorated the wall: a Roman amphitheater; the aqueduct at Caesarea; and some wrought iron nails that still pierced the ankle and wrist bones of a 1st century Esscene crucifixion victim. Through an open door he watched an archaeologist in a white lab coat catalog pot shards and wood fragments.

Asher wondered what Mekor wanted. Gilda must have complained, again, he thought with a mischievous smile. He was supposed to give her reports twice daily, but he avoided calling in on general principles. If he stayed in touch he wouldn't be able to take a crap without her grunting. What could he tell her about Christina Goryeb anyway? Didn't Gilda realize that trustworthy sources in the West Bank and Gaza were virtually nonexistent?

The only type of information available to Asher was seemingly trivial and unrelated pieces of data, recorded bit by bit on the computers of Aman, military intelligence, the Shin Bet, and the Mossad in huge on-line relational data bases. The delivery of a large quantity of rice and fresh lamb to a wretched hovel in the West Bank could be the tip off to a terrorist attack—the food might be for a celebration feast afterwards. A traffic citation issued in the West Bank to a Palestinian-American when he was supposed to be in Malta might reveal a terrorist traveling on a borrowed American passport. Such information came from undercover teams, telephone taps, prisoner interrogations, ID card checks, and informants. Informants invariably turned out to be Palestinian thieves and criminals who provided only items of gossip or rumor. Telephone taps run by Aman listening posts gave Asher few details of value about the Lions, since Palestinians suspected rightly that the Army eavesdropped on their phone conversations. He had hoped that prisoner interrogations and reports from undercover teams and police investigations might yield the clues he needed, but was disgusted to find they generated more false leads than solid fact. When Asher carried out a mission in a foreign country, he often relied on *sayanim*, Jewish volunteers who were private citizens of the foreign country where the operation was being carried out. The *sayanim* were the Mossad's secret weapon, the reason it could operate all over the world with a ridiculously small staff of 35 *katsas*. It was ironic, Asher thought, that one could recruit reliable men in Baghdad or Damascus or Cairo but was unable to find them in Ramallah, only a few kilometers from Jerusalem. On principal, he tried to avoid the brazen acts of buccaneering for which the Mossad was famous, but now there was no other choice if he was to find the Lions of Allah.

Mekor came out of one of the back rooms to greet Asher. His initial glance was critical, but then he broke into a sympathetic smile.

"Enjoy your vacation? Tailing Goryeb must be fun. Getting any? You can tell me."

Without comment, Asher walked past Mekor into his office and Mekor closed the door behind them. It was furnished with a teak desk, molded wood in and out trays, two chairs and a telephone. Mekor peered out through the weapons-grade Lexan window pane at Tel Aviv before shifting his attention to Asher.

"The Gvirol Street bombing has increased the importance of your case," he said. "I need you to get as close as you can to Goryeb. Find out what she knows about the Lions of Allah. Do not arrest her or hurt her. The PM is aware of her."

"So is the American Secretary of State," said Asher dryly. "Do I send her flowers or should it be candy?"

"Just get her to talk. Information right now is more important than time. The Shin Bet can round up enough of the usual trouble makers to quiet the politicians but we need solid information to find these *mamzarim.*"

"Get me better help than that twitchy Shin Bet thug," said Asher.

"I thought you'd find him amusing," said Mekor. "Anyway half your prayers are answered. Shlomo Arendt called and said he needs Kallenborg for something else."

"I'll need a replacement."

"No, you don't," said Mekor.

"Goryeb got away from me even when I had Kallenborg."

"So move in with her, then."

"Mike, how did you get so far with such a one track mind," said Asher.

But Mekor was right. Moving into Christina Goryeb's household was the only way he'd crack the case.

"Just remember she will be with her friend, but you will never be with your friend," said Mekor.

It was the familiar caveat that Asher himself gave to fledgling *kat-sas* at the Mossad's training school when he taught them how to recruit informants.

Gain her trust. Let her think you are her friend. But remember you are not.

* * *

The cars waited at a check point on Route 3 inside the West Bank. Asher hunched in his Fiat with one eye on Christina Goryeb while he keyed in commands on his MICA terminal. She sat in the back seat of a big black Mercedes Benz, three vehicles ahead that had a yellow Israeli license plate. Asher recognized Christina's two daughters and her sister, Janine. The driver, a man about forty-five, broad shouldered in good shape underneath his dark suit, looked like a prosperous business man. The woman opposite him in the front seat must be Goryeb's youngest sister, Najat. Asher glanced down at his computer screen and saw the Mercedes was registered to a Jamal Tawfik, a Christian Arab who was an Israeli citizen, Christina's brother-in-law. What a shame they were all so happy, Asher thought. A border policeman walked to his jeep. Clutched in his hands were the ID cards he had just collected from the occupants of the black Mercedes Benz.

They wouldn't be happy long.

Once that policeman verified Christina Goryeb's ID card on MICA, he would discover she was the subject of a Shin Bet investigation. Asher hoped the policeman wouldn't make a big deal out of detaining her. He gritted his teeth and prepared to get out of the Fiat.

A thin Palestinian boy in ragged jeans walked beside the line of cars selling the Arabic language daily, al-Kuds. Asher signaled the boy for a paper. Below a picture of a burned out shell of an Egged bus a small article caught his attention.

TEL AVIV—Naomi Litvin, a long time activist in the Peace Now movement is believed to be among the victims who died in the blast that tore through the No. 5 bus on Ibn Gvirol Street yesterday. Police detectives have identified the remains of a brief case in the charred wreckage as belonging to Mrs. Litvin. The results of DNA testing could be announced as early as tomorrow.

Asher pounded the Fiat's steering wheel with his fist. It was always different when it was someone you knew.

Someone Christina Goryeb knew as well.

He'd blinded himself to be obvious. His Christina was a liar, a mistress of deception, a ruthless political operative under careful disguise, protected by a web of privilege and family loyalty.

Asher watched as the policeman returned to the Mercedes, handed them their ID cards and a blue-grey booklet that looked like an American passport to the driver.

What the hell was going on? The policeman waved the black Mercedes on. Asher wrenched the shift lever forward. Its red emergency lights flashing behind its front grille, the Fiat roared up to the check point. Asher skidded to stop. He held up his pocket commission to identify himself to the policeman.

"Was one of the passengers in that black Mercedes a Christina Goryeb?"

"Yes it was," said the policeman.

"Didn't you run a trace on her?" he demanded.

"But she's clean," said the policeman.

"No, she's a suspect," he said. "Who's the American passport?"

"That was Richard Goryeb, the driver."

Asher stopped breathing. So Richard Goryeb was back in *Yisroel*. That meant Christina would have told her husband what was going on. Also Asher's plans were wrecked. All he could do was follow and improvise.

A quarter of a mile down the road at the Latrun intersection where Route 3 crossed the Jerusalem highway, Asher caught up with the black Mercedes. Its brake lights flashed briefly as it turned right toward Tel Aviv, then accelerated swiftly and merged into west bound traffic. Asher followed suit. He ducked in behind a garbage truck.

Fifteen minutes later, the Mercedes turned off on the road to the David Ben Gurion Airport at Lod. Of course. Richard Goryeb was taking his family back to America.

He would put a stop to that.

The black Mercedes slowed as it approached the airport's main gate and stopped at the check point. In the distance loomed the terminal building flanked by rows of aircraft hangers. A mammoth Sabena 747 jet liner touched down at the end of the main runway, smoke pouring from the herd of tires bunched under its fuselage. Lod's security was the best in the business.

Richard Goryeb's passport would get him through the Lod check point.

Christina wouldn't be able to waltz through here so easily.

Asher pulled up quietly behind the Mercedes and got out of his car. The raised trunk lid of the Mercedes hid him from view. One soldier poked around in the rear of the Mercedes with a flashlight while inside the shack another soldier busily checked IDs on his computer. He leaned against the Fiat's fender, lit a cigarette and waited. The slam of a trunk lid interrupted his reverie. The clack of computer keys had stopped.

"Please move on," said the soldier standing in the door of the shack and the Mercedes purred away.

Asher threw down his cigarette and walked up to the guard.

"There was a suspect in that car!" he said.

The soldier, a coarse-faced man, eyed Asher's pocket commission nervously.

"The computer says they're all o.k.", he said.

"In that case, your computer's wrong!" said Asher.

He got back in the Fiat and drove into the airport leaving the guard to figure it out.

The black Mercedes was nowhere in sight.

Goryeb would most probably drive to public parking.

Asher mopped his face with a handkerchief. He followed the signs to the lot. After he took a ticket from the dark skinned Falasha attendant in the kiosk, he drove slowly down the main aisle pausing at row intersections. At the fifth row he spotted Richard Goryeb leaning into the open trunk of the parked Mercedes. The women and girls stood behind him.

Richard Goryeb set a suit case on the pavement and then pulled out two more out of the trunk.

Relieved, Asher turned the Fiat in the opposite direction and found a parking place. Christina and her children would be easy to find. They would spend the next 2 hours waiting for pre-flight check in, baggage searches, and passport control. Nothing happened at Lod without a green light from the Shin Bet's computer. Time was back on Asher's side.

He keyed in the commands on his terminal and lit another cigarette while the cursor spit tiny orange letters across the screen. He ran his finger down a list of all files associated with Christina Goryeb, most of them ID card checks. Mid-way down he let out a low whistle.

No wonder Christina had a clean bill of health. Someone had closed her investigation file.

That putz, Kallenborg had tried to screw him.

MICA hadn't found any open investigation on her, which was why it kept flashing green lights whenever a security trace was requested.

Asher pounded on the keyboard and reopened the Goryeb investigation file. Then he called Mekor on his car's police radio. The Mossad communications center patched him through to Gilda.

"Where's Mekor?" said Asher.

"I'm acting for him," she said briskly. "Why did you call?"

He told her about Richard Goryeb and the road chase to Lod.

"Arrest the bitch, she's bolting," said Gilda.

"I can't do that without her husband creating an international incident," said Asher.

"Then kill her," said Gilda, her voice jolted in his ear. "You can make it look like the Lions did it."

"Have you lost your mind?" said Asher.

"What's the matter? You've shot people before."

Asher sat still for one long moment, surprised by his own feelings.

"You've been balling her, haven't you, Asher?"

Asher knew that if he refused Gilda would send someone else who would kill Christina. "I'm at the airport, Gilda," said he. "There're too many people around."

"Arrest them both, then," she said angrily.

"For what?"

"You'll think of something. Mike has faith in you even if I don't."

"Remember Goryeb's an American citizen."

"So what. I'll send Ramon Boker to help you."

Asher smiled thinly as he looked out the mud streaked windshield of the Fiat.

"Are you sure you can spare him?"

Thirty-Eight

At 2 o'clock that afternoon, the public address system at the Lod airport emitted a soft bonging chime. A woman's voice announced in Hebrew, Arabic, and English that the Sabena flight to Brussels and New York was ready for boarding at Gate 4 on the West Concourse. Christina forged ahead, pulling along her heavy grey Samsonite suitcase that slid behind her on tiny casters, pushing out of her mind Naomi's face and the small box of dynamite, while Aminah and Muna carried small blue overnight bags. Najat brought up the rear. She had come to see them off. Christina watched apprehensively as Richard spoke hurriedly in a low voice to a man with a weathered face and thinning blond hair who scribbled in a small notebook with the stub of a pencil.

The man with the weathered face wore olive drab trousers and a blue T-shirt. Richard had introduced him as Jan Peders from Reuters and Christina knew he was not there by chance. Their fate was in Richard's hands now, she thought, not hers. Behind them, a line of people zigzagged through a labyrinth of red plush ropes and chrome posts in front of the Sabena desk. Najat combed Muna's hair as they waited.

Richard looked at the gold Vacheron-Constentin on his wrist.

"We've been here over an hour already," he said.

"This is standard fare at Lod," said Peders. "Security is very tight."

"Will the plane leave without us, Daddy?" asked Aminah.

"It won't be much longer, sweetheart," said Najat.

Peders put away his notebook. With his battered Nikon he snapped a few pictures of Richard and Christina.

"Thanks for coming, Jan," said Richard as Peders started to walk away. "If anything happens, call the U.S. Consulate."

Peders gave him a relaxed smile. "I'll hang around until you board. I'm just getting a cup of coffee."

Something in his tone of voice set Christina on edge. She eyed the crowd that shuffled through the row of metal detectors guarding the entrance to the boarding area. Security personnel carefully scrutinized each passenger. She watched them yank a young man with scruffy two day beard out of line and hustle him away to an unmarked door. She took a deep breath to steel herself. Another gauntlet to pass before they could embark to safety.

Finally they arrived at the counter. Christina heaved the big gray suitcase up on the baggage scales and piled her daughters' little blue bags on top while a young airline clerk filed paperwork from the previous passengers. The clerk looked up, her fingers poised over the keys of her terminal.

"Your name?" she said to Richard.

"Goryeb." he spoke hurriedly but with precision. "There are four of us, Richard, Christina, Aminah and Muna."

The clerk pounded the keyboard. "One-way to Washington, D.C.?"

"Yes."

"Passports, please."

Richard hastily dug in his coat, and handed them to the young woman. She leafed through the passport booklets rapidly comparing information on the screen.

"One moment please." After she worked at the keyboard again she said, "I'm sorry, but I'll need to get the supervisor." She disappeared and then returned with a tall pale man with bulging eyes. There was a clatter of keys as he typed. He frowned suddenly.

"The system won't issue your tickets," he said in a less friendly voice.

Christina's heart sank. She could hear muttered complaints from people in line behind them. Richard jabbed her arm.

She reached into her purse and pulled out a thick wad of dollar bills, Jordanian dinars and British pound notes.

"I'm willing to pay the premium fare," Richard said softly.

The bulge eyed man looked at the money, then at Richard and worked at the terminal again. Then he looked up. "The override codes won't take. You need exit permits, for your wife and daughters. Go to Room 25C. It's the Shin Bet Office."

Christina touched the sleeve of Richard's coat but he ignored her.

"Perhaps, then you can write out our tickets by hand," Richard said as he piled the money into a messy stack on the counter in front of him.

"Sir, you don't understand," the supervisor said softly. "It is impossible for me to issue your tickets."

He glanced over Richard's shoulder.

Richard stared at him. "Give me back my passports then."

The supervisor made no attempt to return them.

Aminah and Muna suddenly brushed past Christina and stood behind her. She turned and looked up into Asher's familiar stark melancholy face.

He reached over the counter, took the passports from the supervisor. He picked up the stack of bills, and put them in his coat pocket.

Another younger man appeared at Richard's side. He had thick muscles underneath a blue blazer and open necked white shirt. "Would you come with me, please" he said and held his arm firmly.

"Take your hands off of me. I'm an American citizen," roared Richard as he struggled to get free.

That may be," said Asher, "but attempted bribery is a crime even in the U.S."

"Storm Troopers!" shouted Richard. "Heinrich Himmler would be proud of you."

He managed to get his arm free and swung at the young man in the blazer. The little crowd of people waiting in the lounge fell back with gasps and murmurs of alarm as the young man ducked under Richard's fist and grabbed his coat lapels. He kicked and punched Richard viciously, then wrestled him to the ground and pinioned his arms behind his back.

Christina felt sick.

"Take it easy, Boker," Asher said. Then he pulled out a badge and held it high for the crowd to see. "Shin Bet," he said in loud clear voice. "This is a security matter. Everyone stand back please, for your own safety."

"Why are they putting handcuffs on that man?" an American woman cried.

"They're Arab terrorists," said an old man, also an American.

Firmly, Asher took Christina by the elbow and steered her through the crowd toward the rear of the building where the taxi stands were. A sea of curious faces parted magically in front of them. As she passed through the crowd she spotted Peders, the Reuters man. He leaned against the snack bar as they passed by, his face expressionless.

Thirty-Nine

A grim-faced Chaim Asher led Christina out of the air conditioned airport terminal building holding her gently by the elbow. Najat and the two daughters trailed behind, dazed expressions on their faces. Aminah struggled to hold back tears, while Najat tried to comfort the sobbing Muna. He was relieved that the unfolding tragedy went completely unnoticed by the crowd of travelers passing by. He stood still for a moment squinting against the sun's glare. A stretch Mercedes *sharut* disgorged its passengers right in front of them.

Maybe we'll accomplish this without any brutality, he thought. Keeping his voice low, he turned to her.

"I think we can help each other, Mrs. Goryeb. Can we talk privately?" he asked.

Her angry eyes met his and her beauty broke his heart.

He wondered how she would thwart him now that all hope of escape was gone. The odor of exhaust fumes and traffic noise from taxis and buses was almost overpowering.

"My children and sister need to go home," she said firmly, but she looked surprised when Asher stepped to the curb and leaned into the taxi to speak to the driver. Then he stowed their luggage in the trunk.

As Najat climbed into the *sharut* with Aminah and Muna, Christina said, "Call the American Consulate. Tell them Richard and I have been arrested."

Three worried faces looked back at Christina from the *sharut's* rear window as it disappeared in traffic.

Christina glanced up at Asher.

"All right, Mr. Policeman, how do we help each other?" she said in a voice devoid of emotion.

Just remember, you will never be with your friend.

* * *

The vineyard was planted amid wheat fields on the sides of the Valley of Ayalon, a broad horseshoe valley in the Samarian Hills. Cutting through the valley was the Tel Aviv-Jerusalem highway. Asher feeling pleased with himself, and a sullen, silent Christina sat on a blanket on a low ridge overlooking rows of grape arbors. Stands of cypress and pines grew on the hillside that rose behind them. On a promontory that extended into the center of the valley rose the Latrun Monastery, where Asher had bought a bottle of wine and some white goat cheese for this impromptu picnic. Three monks with bared heads hoed weeds in the monastery garden. Above on the heights covered with wild lavender were a brooding mass of ruined parapets and turrets, the remains of a Crusader castle. He was determined to enjoy himself. The outcome he had dreaded had been averted, and now he had the plea-sure of her company, however unwilling it was. She sat silently on the blanket, her legs folded gracefully to one side and stared wistfully at a smaller road that ran between the monastery and a blockhouse like police station. It forked left to Ramallah. Somewhere on that road up in the hills, he knew, was the *sharut* taxi carrying her family to their home. His eyes followed the main highway as it climbed higher through green wooded hills to Jerusalem. The last leg of the highway was a steep gorge strewn with wrecked military vehicles, left as memorials of the 1948 war. He surveyed the remains of their meal on the edge of the blanket: a half empty wine bottle and a piece of large Druze-style flat bread. It was time to draw her in.

"My father brought me here when I was a child," he said. "This is one of my favorite places for picnics."

She still did not speak.

"You don't like the wine, Mrs. Goryeb?" he said gently.

She glared at him unafraid. "I don't care for the company."

Suddenly he felt very tired. "I am sorry to be the one to tell you this," he said. "Our mutual friend, Naomi Litvin is dead."

For a few seconds the vineyard was still and breathless that hot August afternoon. Choosing his words carefully, he said, "She was killed by the bomb yesterday in Tel Aviv."

At first he thought she'd been stunned to silence, but suddenly she twisted around. Hatred and disgust burned in her eyes.

"The Zionist liars who seduced Jews to steal our homes are the ones who murdered Naomi," she shouted. "You are punishing us for the Holocaust, a crime Palestine did not commit."

He had thought that she might be motivated to cooperate by the desire to avenge her friend, and he expected shock, tears, or outrage at the Lions, but not this fierce anger. Asher felt his cheeks grow warm.

She had seen through his ploy.

"I can never forgive the Zionists for making our young men into killers," she said bitterly. "If you set out to destroy people, of course they will strike back."

But Jews have at least as much right to this land as Arabs, Asher thought furiously. Jerusalem had been under siege in 1948. At the Latrun Monastery, the Arab Legion had cut the road, Jerusalem's life line to Tel Aviv. Three times his father's rifle company assaulted the Arab positions by the monastery; three times they were driven back. When it was over, two hundred-fifty dead lay in the fields, men who had survived Russian *pogroms* and Hitler's death camps only to be cut down clawing their way through dirt that no one wanted until Jews wanted it. Asher filled his glass with more wine. When his anger subsided he spoke gently to her.

"For better or worse, Mrs. Goryeb, we must live here together. It's the only way we can survive. The real battle in this land is no longer between Arabs and Jews but between fanatics of both faiths."

She sat still, an angry mocking look on her beautiful face but said nothing.

"I believe you have some connection with the Lions of Allah," Asher said. "The fact that you were at Lod, however, tells me you don't care too much for them. Did they threaten you or your family? That's the way it usually works. Cooperate with us or we'll kill you, kill your children, kill your sister?"

There was no mockery in her eyes now. They were naked, filled with something like desperation. She turned her head away.

Asher broke off a piece of flat bread. He looked directly at Christina. "I can offer you protection."

"Protection?" she said bitterly. "In exchange for what?"

"Information," said Asher.

"I don't know much."

"Any information will help," he said.

She lifted her chin, face flushed and met his eyes defiantly. "The Lions of Allah are using me. My office is their mail box. When I tried to stop them, they threatened to kill my children."

Asher took a bite of bread and a sip of wine. He chewed thoughtfully. "You don't believe me," she said.

It was a long uncomfortable pause for both of them.

"I believe you," he said finally.

Goat bells tinkled in the distance. Two monks came down a narrow rocky path toward them driving a herd of floppy-eared female goats through the wild mustard, thyme, and cyclamen.

After they passed by in the direction of the monastery, he said, "Have you hired a replacement yet for your law clerk, Abu Awad?"

"No. My sister is helping me now."

"I think you need a new law clerk."

Christina said, "My children and I need to go to America."

"That can be arranged," Asher said softly. "But first you must help me."

"So, your game is still threats and coercion," she said indignantly. "No, you listen to me. My husband is an American citizen. If we are not on that plane—if you do anything to prevent us from leaving—the American government will lodge an official complaint with your Foreign Minister and you will be front page news."

He said softly, "Your husband has broken our laws. As for you, it would be very easy to discredit your story, Mrs. Goryeb. What proof do you have that you are being blackmailed by the Lions of Allah? Any prosecutor could make a convincing case that you were a member of the Lions trying to escape to America."

Her face was taut. "Then, let my children go to America."

"I'll need your cooperation, first," he said.

"What do you want?" she said.

Asher watched the monks herd their goats into a little pen beside a milking shed on the end of the vineyard.

"I'm to be your law clerk. That way I can read the Lion's mail before they do."

She will be with her friend, he thought remembering Mekor's words. She doesn't know it yet.

"Fine," she said. "They'll kill us both."

Forty

Jerusalem's central prison near Zion Square off Jaffa Road was located in the Russian Compound, a collection of stone dormitories built by the Czar as a hostel for Russian pilgrims to the holy land. During the British Mandate one of the buildings was used as a police station and prison, a purpose it continued to serve for the Israeli government. In the courtyard around an onion-domed Russian Orthodox church small anxious family groups waited to learn of the status of relatives who had been taken to prison.

When Richard Goryeb arrived at the prison, as the sun set on Tish B'av, he was searched thoroughly by Boker in a corridor filled with police and army and border guards. A water fountain was mounted waist high on the wall.

"I'm thirsty," said Richard. "May I have a drink?"

Boker did not respond.

Either the man did not understand English, which Richard thought unlikely, or else he was deliberately ignoring Richard's request.

Richard bent over the water spigot.

Boker landed a terrific blow on the side of Richard's head. Richard felt his brain recoil against his skull, and his glasses fell off. Stumbling like a drunk, he tried to pick them up. Boker's foot came down hard on Richard's wrist, but he managed to grab his glasses before Boker could crush them. Boker grabbed Richard from behind, threw him to the floor and kicked him. Like a wounded animal, Richard crawled on hands and knees to escape, but Boker hauled him back to his feet, and dragged him through the hall, down a flight of stairs to a basement holding cell. The cell door opened and Boker shoved him in.

His white broad cloth shirt was torn and bloody where Boker had hit him. The crystal of his expensive watch was cracked. He shuddered as the door slammed shut behind him.

"I demand to see the American Consul," he shouted at Boker's receding back through the bars.

A score of sullen, bruised, American men, women and teenagers met Richard's eyes.

"Welcome to the American Gulag," said a familiar voice. It was Ezra Kravetz, the Texan who'd stood in line with him at passport control two days before. Kravetz's face was black and blue, and his clothes were torn, but he seemed oddly cheerful.

"I see they took it easy on you," said Kravetz with a wink. "Must have been the suit. Maybe these thugs don't respect Torah but they sure know good cloth."

Of all the rotten luck, thought Richard, to be stuck in the company of this nosy moron.

Kravetz's voice became low and conspiratorial. "I can't say you didn't warn us."

That morning Kravetz and his fellow Americans had demonstrated with a large crowd of Israeli settlers at the Knesset against peace negotiations with the Palestinians. Special riot police had savagely kicked and beat the demonstrators with night sticks. Kravetz's 13 year-old son, Isaac, had been clubbed to the ground.

"So these are the big strong Israelis held up to us soft American *olim* as good examples?" said Kravetz. "They are nothing but goons. Torah, *Halakhah, Klal Yisroel* mean nothing to them."

A cold shiver of fear ran down Richard's spine. If the Israeli police could treat American Jews this way with impunity, he wondered, what would they do to him?

"Don't confuse this country with America, Mr. Kravetz," said Richard, half to himself. "Israel has no constitution, no separation of powers, no checks and balances, no bill of rights, no First Amendment."

Ezra Kravetz shrugged.

"They have no soap or toilet paper in this pissant jail either."

"Pappa, I thought Jews didn't hurt other Jews. When are they going to let us out?" said Kravetz's son.

"Isaac, don't complain," said Kravetz. "This is a mitzvah."

* * *

Nicholas DeHart, Special Assistant to the American Consul, locked eyes briefly with the Deputy Defense Minister.

"Richard Goryeb?", asked Major General Danny Ohr.

DeHart recognized the soft tired voice of an overworked man in the service of his government, and he waited for the ritual denial.

"We are holding no one by that name," said the General. "As for the tale about his wife and daughters, I'm afraid that is utterly preposterous."

DeHart smiled a diplomat's smile. You are only an intelligence officer in the consulate, he reminded himself. Let's not overplay our hand. Peoples lives are at stake.

"I'm thinking of our mutual interests, General," he said smoothly. "We received these from Reuters this morning."

One by one, he spread five black and white photographs on the desk before General Ohr.

"The Reuters correspondent says one of the security officers who arrested the Goryebs identified himself as a Shin Bet officer to the people in the airport lounge."

General Ohr's eyes took on a hard foxy look but he remained silent.

"Mr. Goryeb is an officer for the National Association of Arab Americans," DeHart continued. He teaches at Georgetown University. The Administration consults regularly with him. Next year is an election year, and the President of the United States cannot ignore the concerns of his Arab-American citizens."

"I see your Arab-Americans have taken a page from our book about political action," said the General dryly. "I'll look into this."

"If you would release Richard Goryeb and his family to my personal recognizance, General, I will get them out of the country and do everything in my power to squash the story for you."

The telephone rang and General Ohr impatiently snatched up the receiver.

"Ohr speaking." He listened with increasingly visible irritation. "Reuters News Service? I have no time to speak to the press."

Jan Peders's timing could not have been better thought DeHart.

"Tell him we do not mistreat prisoners or employ torture," said General Ohr. He listened again. "In rare circumstances moderate pressure is used to obtain information we need to save lives."

After he hung up he mopped his face with a crisp white handkerchief.

"You see the situation, General," said DeHart spreading his hands apologetically. "Is there any way we reach an understanding?"

Ohr's face returned to stone.

DeHart studied the room. The desk was clear of papers. On its right corner stood a brass statute of a leaping Ibex antelope with long graceful horns that curved like twin scimitars and behind it was a blue glass vase that held a dried shock of wild wheat. On the left corner was an ash tray made of the base of an 8 inch brass Howitzer shell. Finally the General spoke.

"You can have Richard Goryeb. His wife and daughters are another matter—and this must be strictly between us, Nicky." The General glanced over his right shoulder. "Mrs. Goryeb is working for a terror cell we know very little about. She cannot leave until we eliminate this threat to our security."

"According to Reuters, she is being used against her will," said DeHart.

General Ohr gave a disingenuous shrug of his shoulders. "Let's be practical, Nicky. If Christina Goryeb is innocent as she claims to be, it is in her interest to help us. The Lions of Allah have murdered over 100 people. Unless we stop them more will be killed."

"At least let the Goryeb children go with their father. They are innocent by-standers," said DeHart.

Ohr looked at him shrewdly.

"They are not citizens of your country, Nicky. Their presence here will insure their mother's continued cooperation with us even if it is against her will."

Then it's going to take a Presidential phone call, thought DeHart.

As if reading his thoughts, General Ohr said, "Political pressure will only increase the risks for Mrs. Goryeb and her children."

* * *

Richard Goryeb was released from prison that evening. Nicholas DeHart and Lance Corporal Johnson, wearing civilian clothes, escorted him to a grey Ford Windstar that was parked in front of the Church of the Holy Trinity on the edge of the Russian Compound.

"Where are my wife and children?" said Richard when he saw the empty van.

"The Israelis won't release them," said DeHart.

"The bastards," snapped Richard. "Take me to Reuters. I can see the headlines now: *Children Ripped From Father's Arms by Israeli Security.*"

DeHart shook his head firmly as he opened the door of the van for Richard.

"No press—that's the condition of your release," he said.

Richard stood at the door, his face tense with anger. "I didn't agree to that. I didn't agree to anything," he said.

There was no one so much like God on earth as an outraged American citizen, thought DeHart. How quickly Richard Goryeb had adapted to his new country's ways.

"Mr. Goryeb, please," he said.

"Where's my passport?" demanded Richard.

"It's being reissued. You're flying directly back to the States. A jet is waiting for you on the runway at Lod."

"I'm not leaving without my wife and children," said Richard.

DeHart sighed. "Corporal, please help Mr. Goryeb into the van."

Richard half turned as a hand went firmly over his mouth and a hard arm clamped around his chest. He was shoved quickly into the van.

"I'm sorry we had to do that," said DeHart once the van was underway.

"You won't be able to shut me up," said Richard.

"I have a final word of advice," he said. "The Israeli government is extremely sensitive to adverse publicity. If any word of this leaks to the press, the Israelis will kill your wife and daughters and blame their deaths on the Lions of Allah."

Richard Goryeb sat very still. "They wouldn't dare," he said.

"In the intelligence business, Mr. Goryeb, it's happened before," said DeHart.

Forty-One

Mekor stuck his head into Gilda's office.

"Asher's got the Goryeb woman to cooperate," he said happily. "I knew he'd pull it off. The price is her children fly with her husband to New York, now. What she doesn't know is Danny Ohr just sent the husband back to the U.S. with his tail between his legs."

There was a piece missing thought Gilda, some unforeseen complication of the sort that occurred around Chaim Asher.

"Something's wrong isn't it?", she said.

"If we let the children go, we loose our handle on the mother."

Gilda frowned. "So we don't let them go."

"There's another problem." Mekor said.

"What is it then?", said Gilda.

"Goryeb wants her release guaranteed in writing by the PM, personally."

"Who does Asher think she is, the Queen of Sheba?"

Mekor said, "They're at Latrun. "Get your tush out there and find out what they've really got."

"You know I can't stand dealing with that limp dick; send someone else."

He pointed a finger at her playfully. "When did you get a chance to hold Asher's dick?"

That had been years ago, when Gilda had been recruited for the Mossad. Asher had not responded when she had made a play for him, and Mekor knew all about it. Intramural love affairs were encouraged within the Mossad family to keep Israel's secrets safe, but Asher kept himself apart. The grieving widower. From time to time there had been other women. Always foreign. Never Jewish for that matter.

"Mike, you know Asher takes too many risks. I'm not saying he's deliberately suicidal," she said.

Mekor just smiled."No, you can't use your pet *schmuck* and that's final. Nice try."

* * *

Driving down to the monastery in her shiny black BMW 735i, Gilda was livid, infuriated that Mekor thought her objections were merely personal. Asher was the one who was unprofessional. He ignored procedures, never called in on time, and seldom filed reports on the Mossad's computer although he exploited information filed by others with great skill. When he did, he neglected to say where he was going or where he had been. All this made it difficult for the computer to track Asher which was why he did it. If Gilda confronted him he would say 'What you don't know you won't pass on to the politicians, and the less they know, the safer we'll all be.' When anyone else pulled stunts like that, Asher wouldn't let them breathe. He was picky, prickly, and stubborn as a mule. Worse, Mekor never made him toe the line. One day he was going to get himself killed and she'd be stuck cleaning up the mess.

The monastery lay ahead on her right. Braking hard, she wheeled into the parking lot with a spray of gravel. She saw Asher leaning against the small grey Fiat, his arms folded across his chest. The Goryeb woman waited inside his car. He scowled when he saw Gilda and thrust his hands into his pockets.

She pulled up beside him and gave him her fish-eye glare, enjoying the way it made him look uncomfortable.

"Where's Mekor?" he said.

"He's busy. Get in," she said. She nodded at Mrs. Goryeb through the window. "You can get in too."

Asher opened the BMW's rear door and got in back. He sniffed the upholstery on the seat in front of him. "Real leather Gilda?," he said sarcastically. "I often wondered how you can afford this on your salary?"

Gilda ignored the insult. "I came to discuss Mrs. Goryeb's request for the PM's guarantee that she will be released if she cooperates. You should know better. We cannot involve the PM."

"Don't blow this, Gilda. Do you want Mrs. Goryeb's cooperation or not?"

Gilda turned to the Palestinian woman. She did not like what she saw. Christina Goryeb looked irritatingly self-possessed. She would not be easy to control.

"Mrs. Goryeb, you understand that politicians are cautious people?" The woman remained silent.

"Our Prime Minister doesn't like making commitments to anyone," said Gilda softly, "especially to people he doesn't know."

"Let my children go to their father in America. They are innocent," said the woman.

"Let us be frank, Mrs. Goryeb. The Gvirol Street bombing could have been prevented had you come to the authorities immediately. Innocent people were killed in the blast, children as innocent as your two daughters," said Gilda. I believe you knew Naomi Litvin?"

The woman gave Gilda a baleful cold stare.

"We need to know much more about the Lions, " said Gilda. "We will protect your children while you work with us."

"I've seen how *Yisroel* protects informers," the woman said bitterly. "When the mob drags collaborators from their homes, your police look the other way."

"Mr. Asher and others will be risking their lives to protect you," said Gilda firmly. "After this case is closed, your cooperation will be evaluated and then we will decide whether your children can travel to New York."

Asher stared at Gilda. "Let Mrs. Goryeb's children go to America," he said.

"Have you got shit for brains, Asher? Everything has a price," said Gilda.

"What price have you ever paid?" he said. "I have paid the highest— my family. If you don't let Mrs. Goryeb's children go after this is over, I'll get the story to the *Washington Post.* Our censors can't stop them from printing it."

Gilda fired back, "Just try that and you get your pension in the cemetery."

"I'm sure you'd plant me there yourself," said Asher savagely.

She gave him a long cool look. "This has been a difficult assignment for you, Chaim Asher," she said in a soothing tone. "You deserve a rest. We can find someone else to work with Mrs. Goryeb."

The Palestinian woman's eyes blazed. "Mr. Asher is the only one of you I trust. Unless it's him, I don't cooperate, and then you'll have nothing."

Gilda was amused as she watched the expression on Asher's face. Why he was in love with the woman, she realized with a shock. This was worse than she had expected. Mike had damn well better be right.

"Well, Asher," she said. "I see this Palestinian bitch has put lead in your pencil. Just be sure you don't fail us."

Forty-Two

The next morning at Lod the passengers on the Rome flight boarded their Boeing 737 jet aircraft at the Swissair gate.

"Here are your tickets," Shlomo said as he handed Kallenborg the grey ticket folder. "Go over your itinerary, one more time for me."

With a sigh of irritation, Kallenborg flipped through the folder. "Rome, Cairo, Karachi, Peshawar—."

Shlomo bore in. "You'll lay over 12 hours in Karachi before going on to Peshawar. Don't leave the airport building."

"I know what I'm doing," said Kallenborg. "This is not the first intelligence service I've worked for that sends agents abroad to hostile countries."

Shlomo ignored the bait. There was no time to waste.

"An American was killed by Muslim extremists last week in Karachi in broad daylight. Every foreigner in those places is a target," he said.

"Thanks for warning me," Kallenborg said, but did not sound particularly grateful.

"Good luck then," said Shlomo in a conciliatory voice. "I'm counting on you."

Kallenborg picked up his nylon bag and walked up the boarding ramp.

Farewell then, thought Shlomo. He had done his best. The mission was in the hands of God, and that was the Rabbi's department.

* * *

When Shlomo arrived back in Taggart Prison, a message from Ben Yusuf was waiting for him. AN IMPORTANT MATTER. DROP BY

FOR LUNCH. Mildly annoyed, Shlomo crumpled the paper in his hand. His plans to eat a sandwich at his desk and catch up on work were ruined. When the Rabbi called, he had to obey. It had to be something that could not be discussed over the telephone

At noon, Shlomo knocked on Ben Yusuf's apartment door in B'nai Ha'eretz, and was ushered into the Rabbi's study by the Rabbi's young, careworn wife. Ben Yusuf and Etzel in their black suits and knitted *kippots* sat behind a table stacked with volumes of the Talmud and commentaries bound in brown leather with faded gilt letters. Ben Yusuf smoked a pipe, and his *kippa* had slid lopsided on his head, a sign that he was engaged in higher thought, and temporarily unavailable. He bent over an open book and straightened his angular body for a moment, peering into space. Etzel noticed Shlomo and gently nudged the Rabbi. Ben Yusuf's brilliant blue eyes suddenly turned toward Shlomo, and a smile broke out over the Rabbi's face.

"*Nu*, you've finally come," he said.

"Rebbe, I came as soon as I received your message," said Shlomo apologetically.

Shlomo's showing of deference satisfied him. "When will our guns arrive?" he demanded. "Within a week might be asking too much, but perhaps two?"

"It will take at least a month, Rabbi," said Shlomo.

"A month? Where are you getting them from, the moon?"

"Almost as far, Rabbi—Afghanistan. I've dispatched a man to buy weapons from an arms merchant in Kabul. The country is littered with Soviet and U.S. equipment from the Afghan war. They sell to anybody for cash and no questions asked."

Ben Yusuf brushed a fleck of pipe tobacco from his coat sleeve and gave Shlomo an inquisitorial stare.

What is this, thought Shlomo, I'm studying for my Bar Mitzvah again?

"Afghanistan is a Moslem country," the Rabbi said finally. "Why should they help Jews?"

Shlomo spoke in a very low urgent tone. "They won't know it's us."

"Who's your man?"

The Rabbi must be getting anxious, thought Shlomo. "Ya'akov Kallenborg. You saw him with me and Avi last week."

"The unpleasant little fellow with thick glasses—are you sure he's a Jew?"

"He's a recent immigrant from Lithuania."

"And was a Litvak ever reliable?" the Rabbi said in an aside to Etzel.

"Kallenborg was in the Soviet secret police. His contacts make him extremely useful to us," said Shlomo.

Ben Yusuf threw Etzel a sidelong glance while he drew on his pipe. The bones in his angular face seemed to harden. "Sending several men would have been wiser."

"More men increases the risk of detection."

"Your Litvak could run off to start a new life somewhere else with the money," said Etzel.

"We have given him nothing but traveling expenses," said Shlomo.

"How will he pay for our guns if he has no money?" said Ben Yusuf.

"The first payment will be sent to Kabul when I receive a coded telegram. The money will be hidden in a diplomatic pouch carried by a Danish attaché."

"I don't like *goyim* doing our holy business," said Ben Yusuf. "Why should this Dane help us?"

"He has no choice," said Shlomo.

"You're blackmailing him aren't you?" said the Rabbi with a smile.

Shlomo nodded the relief of a student who has pleased his teacher with a clever answer.

"The greater good subsumes the lesser evil," the Rabbi said approvingly to Etzel.

Shlomo never quite understood how the Rabbi's mind worked. He needed Ben Yusuf to bring in the faithful. The charismatic Rabbi could rouse the masses, but he needed Shlomo to start the parade.

Now Etzel chimed in. "What about transporting the weapons from Kabul to Yisroel? Your Kallenborg can't possibly do that by himself," said Etzel with a smirk.

You miserable shit, thought Shlomo.

"The arms merchant will deliver our weapons to Karachi. He will receive a second larger payment from another courier, once all the guns are there. It has all been arranged," said Shlomo.

"I suppose your Kallenborg and the Karachi courier will charter a ship and sail home to Eilat with the weapons," said Etzel.

It was then that the Rabbi came to life. "Who is this courier?"

Why is he asking this, thought Shlomo.

"Arbel is the one I had in mind," he said. "After all, he is in the Navy reserve."

Ben Yusuf stared out the window as if he expected to see the Messiah walking across the parking lot on his way to Jerusalem from Galilee. "Arbel is very good in his own way, but something may go wrong. This mission is far too important to depend on one man."

"Golani is going with Arbel," said Shlomo. "Golani is young but he has proven himself, and he is eager for the opportunity."

"We need another man, a man we can trust like family to keep an eye on your *shaigetz* tool."

"Do you have someone special in mind?" said Shlomo.

A stab of alarm passed through him.

"Your nephew, Avi," said the Rabbi.

NO, NOT AVI, he wanted to shout. Not Avi, who was like his son, as precious to him as Isaac was to Abraham. It could not be.

"No," said Shlomo firmly. "You may not have him. He has done enough already. Besides he is my sister's only child. There's no one left to carry on our family line should anything happen."

Ben Yusuf's voice became low and guttural, his most persuasive voice.

"*Eretz Yisroel* is the only thing that matters. Only The Land of Israel can provide a sanctuary for the World's Jews. If we breach our covenant with God this time, he will abandon us forever. We can't afford to fail."

Avi was the best man they had.

The bastard was right, thought Shlomo. If their plan didn't succeed, they'd quickly be suspect, infiltrated, and jailed like before when they tried to blow up the mosque on the Temple Mount. He fixed his eyes on the red and green checkered linoleum floor. He was in too deep.

"I'll ask my nephew," he said very quietly.

"No," said the Rabbi. "You'll tell him."

* * *

It wasn't until *Shabbat* morning that Shlomo saw Avi. Ben Yusuf had honored Avi by asking him to make a blessing over the Torah before the selection for the week was read. The synagogue at B'nai Ha'eretz was filled. One hundred fifty men dressed in black, heads covered with prayer shawls sat in blue vinyl seats in a large auditorium like room. The women sat apart in a large balcony at the rear barely visible behind a diaphanous curtain. Shlomo watched with a mixture of pride and foreboding as Avi climbed the steps to the podium and touched his lips to his prayer shawl. Avi chanted the blessing in a strong clear voice and then stood beside Ben Yusuf as the cantor read aloud from the scroll. It lay before them on the center of the podium covered with dark wood. When Avi was about to rejoin the congregation, Ben Yusuf turned and clasped both Avi's hands with a congratulatory smile. Shlomo felt a chill in the air although it was not cold, a restless stirring that seemed to come from within the synagogue. He shivered and focused his attention on the tattered prayer book lying open in his lap imprinted with its dense rows of Hebrew characters. The book his father had given at his bar mitzvah. *God is a shield to his chosen people. Blessed are thou oh Lord our God, shield of Abraham.*

After the service Shlomo followed Avi outside.

"May I have a word with you, Nephew? There is an important matter we need to discuss."

Avi's wife, Miriam, a pale kerchiefed young woman in a black dress followed both men at a discrete distance.

"Do you remember the sound advice you gave me about the heavy weapons we need?" said Shlomo.

"Oh, our little plan to stop Hafez el-Assad?" said Avi with his good natured self-depreciating smile.

"I need a job done, a matter of utmost importance to our security. I can give it to no one but you."

Avi's blue eyes filled with amusement. "Come, come, Uncle. With all the men in the Shin Bet at your disposal?"

Shlomo said "You are the only one I trust."

Avi's smile faded.

"I want you to meet a man in Karachi," Shlomo said in a low urgent voice that assumed compliance. "You will pay him a sum of money and he will hand over the weapons we discussed. Then you will rent a boat, put the arms on board and sail them to Eilat."

Avi drew lines in the dust with his shoe as Shlomo spoke. "I have news for you Uncle. Miriam is pregnant. We haven't told anyone yet. You are the first to congratulate us. You'll have to find another man."

"Avi," Shlomo cried. "I have no one else to turn to."

Below on the soccer field workmen were taking down the rented grandstands on the soccer field where the settler rally had been held two days before.

"Oh, I see, Uncle. You've gone into business for yourself," Avi said quietly.

"Avi!" Miriam called.

"Excuse me, Uncle, " he said. "I must rejoin my wife."

As he turned to leave, Shlomo touched his shoulder.

"The business Rabbi Ben Yusuf and I are in, is the business of saving *Eretz Yisroel*. For the sake of your child. And his children. And all the Jewish people. Without the hills and mountains of Samaria and Judea, *Eretz Yisroel* is defenseless against an invasion by Syria, Iraq, and Iran. The American *goyim* will never shed a drop of their blood for Jews." He put his face next to Avi's and whispered furiously. "*Esau sone l'Ya'akov*. Esau the Goy hates Jacob the Jew. Remember the Holocaust, Nephew. Jewish leaders begged Mr. Roosevelt to bomb the railroads to the death camps and the gas chambers but he refused."

Avi smile was patient but strained. "I know there were anti-Semites in America, but Mr. Roosevelt wasn't one of them. Militarily it wasn't possible. And, if they had bombed the gas chambers what if they had missed and killed Jews?"

Shlomo shook his head. "Even you believe their stinking lies? The West never gave a shit about us. After the war, we were the ones to rescue the few Jews left alive, and bring them to Palestine. Jews still behind barbed wire in camps in 1946—never forget that, Nephew!"

Avi's broad shoulders sagged as though under the weight of 5000 years of Jewish history.

"Very well," he said.

Shlomo hugged his nephew and looked at him with pride. "A good *Shabbos*, Avi," he said. "And to you, too, Miriam," he said.

The pale young woman said nothing but her glance was cold.

* * *

That evening, Miriam and Avi ate their Shabbat meal at her parent's apartment with the families of her brothers and sisters. Miriam sat next to Avi at the long Sabbath table draped in white cloth and laden with food. Loaves of braided *challah* lay by four white candles that stood in candlesticks in the center of the table. She slipped two fingers under her wig to rub the tense spot at the back of her neck. She dressed like a proper *bas Yisroel*, her hair cropped short after marriage and covered by a scarf or a wig as did all the women at B'nai Ha'eretz. The Torah commanded that the sight of her hair, arms, legs, and knees were for her husband's pleasure alone. Miriam did not mind. She wanted nothing more than to raise her children and make a warm Jewish household for her family as her mother and grandmother had done before her. If anything should happen to Avi, she would surely perish thought Miriam. Her beloved husband, her happiness would be gone. She worshiped the ground he walked on. How grateful she had been to her father who'd arranged her marriage through a *shotchun*, a marriage broker and had cheerfully sent her to her wedding with a large dowry. When Miriam's father, a physics professor in Yeshivat Eyal, entered the room, everyone fell silent. He wore a black suit and tie and a *kippa*.

"What are we waiting for?" he said with a smile. That was the signal for Miriam's mother to light the candles and recite the Shabbat prayer. He chanted the *Kiddush* over a glass of wine in a low voice and made the blessing over the *challah*.

"You can bring the soup now," he said.

Miriam's mother and widowed older sister brought out a thick soup in which floated noodles and chicken feet. Esther's, Ohad had been killed by Arab gunmen in an ambush outside Jericho.

Avi's growing child was alive in her belly. She had placed Avi's hand on her stomach that morning and together they'd felt the child's kicks. Perspiration beaded on her forehead and beneath the faint downy hairs of her upper lip as she watched Avi suck the meat from the clawed toe of a chicken foot while he spoke to Michael Arbel.

There was something new and strange about the square set of their shoulders and the hard gleam in their eyes. Both men had been happy and carefree, before Uncle Shlomo spoken to Avi that morning, but now they were as alert as the police dogs that prowled outside in the compound at night. Avi looked troubled, and the freckled golden olive skin of his cheeks was stretched taut across the bones of his face—her same handsome Avi, yet how different he looked.

"How long will we be gone?" said Michael Arbel.

"Perhaps a month," said Avi.

Avi's place is with me, she thought and blushed furiously. She put her hand on her husband's shoulder.

He turned to her with an indulgent smile.

Her voice was a nervous murmur.

"Avi, I know it's not my place to say this but I don't have a good feeling about this special job you are doing for Uncle Shlomo."

"There's no danger. Michael and Golani are going with me."

Emboldened by the new life within her Miriam became more insistent. "Golani has not started a family. Why does it have to be family men like you and Michael? There are a hundred other men who could go."

"We cannot refuse the Rabbi and Uncle Shlomo," said Avi.

Miriam broke into tears. "Uncle Shlomo and the Rabbi are using you." As she sobbed she could feel Avi's arms wrap gently around her. Surely he would find a way to stay with her.

"It will be better, Miriam. Soon it will be better," he said quietly in her ear. "I must do this for *Eretz Yisroel*."

At the head of the table her father began to sing a lilting catchy version of *L'dor va'dor*.

To all generations we would proclaim thy greatness, and to all eternity declare Thy holiness. And may the praise of Thee, our God, never leave our mouths.

Forty-Three

Israel's retaliation for the Gvirol Street bombing had begun. Gilda sat in the back of a bouncing jeep with an Uzi cradled in her arms, exhilarated at the prospect of following troops into battle. She wore new combat fatigues and a heavy steel helmet. Far away below Mount Hermon, artillery fire flashed sullenly, like the eyes of a marauding lion. The flickering light silhouetted low clouds in the pre-dawn gloom, tingeing their edges with orange.

Operation Sampson would feature an assault on an Arab guerilla stronghold in south Lebanon. Mekor arranged for her to follow the Army's advance as a VIP observer.

A Hizbollah communications bus had been captured at al-Fawqa in the Bekaa Valley almost intact, a major intelligence coup. She knew Aman, army intelligence, always kept the best stuff for themselves. If she reached al-Fawqa before them, she could keep them honest.

"Sayret Matcal commandos caught the Arabs with their pants down," said Gilda's driver, corporal Zimmerman. He twisted his head to speak to her. "Literally, most of them were taken in their underwear."

"Let's hope they didn't have time to destroy their code books," she said.

In the foothills of Mount Hermon, they refilled the jeep's fuel tank and ate a field kitchen breakfast under a tent. The air reeked of sweat and canvass preservative. Men in battle fatigues ate hastily at rows of wooden tables. They washed their mess kits in a large metal trash can filled with boiling soapy water and rinsed them in another. Gilda flashed her VIP credentials to butt in line ahead of an infantry platoon. The men behind her stared resentfully as she held out her mess kit.

They found al-Fawqa two hours later. The stone buildings of the village perched on the side of a green ridge above plowed fields of rust-red dirt. Mount Hermon's snowy fingers stretched down from the sky in the background.

Directly ahead signs of battle greeted them, great clouds of red dust and diesel smoke thrown up by the Merkava tanks, the intermittent thud of explosions punctuated the steady pop of gunfire. Two Iroquois helicopters swooped down to pick up wounded soldiers wrapped in bloody field dressings, strapped in litters. A hospital corpsman crouched beside each litter holding aloft sacks of blood serum and thin plastic iv's. Four soldiers, a graves registration detail, heaved long black plastic bags into the back of a truck, the dead, the latest of Israel's heroes whose reward would be burial in Yad Vachem. This was the real thing, she thought. Dirt, blood, confusion and the stench of burned cordite.

At al-Fawqa they stopped beside a stream bordered with wild grape vines. The street was littered with the bodies of dead Arabs and their belongings. Flies circled over dark pools of blood drying in the dirt. Gilda reported to the Israeli command vehicle, a large desert-tan truck parked by a well.

Brigadier General Arnon Aluf stood face to face with an angry red-faced British colonel who wore the blue beret of the United Nations Peacekeeping Force. His finger jabbed at a map that he held under the General's nose.

"This is outrageous, Aluf. You have already advanced 60 kilometers into Lebanon with three mechanized infantry companies. You are not pursuing terrorists. You're attacking civilians."

The general shook his head. "No English," he said with a thick accent. He turned to his aide, a major, and asked in rapid fire Hebrew, "So now we're attacking civilians? Can you believe this candy-ass limey liberal?"

The major gave the general a guarded smile. "He's so naive," he replied in Hebrew.

Gilda looked up just as a pair of rockets whistled down from the olive grove on the ridge above the village and exploded like a thunder clap. Everyone dove under the command truck.

"What do you think about your poor civilians now?" shouted General Aluf in perfect English.

"What are you going to do when they graduate from *katyushas*?" snapped the British colonel.

The General's aide crouched beside the command truck and spoke calmly into a walkie-talkie to a forward observer. "We're taking fire in quadrant 9-F. Call in air strike. Repeat, air strike."

Four F-15 Strike Eagles roared over the horizon like pre-historic birds of prey, talons extended. They came out of the south, screaming in a low level and banked sharply left, clearing the ridge by a few meters. The first run calibrated the fighters' computer systems for the terrain, to be sure they didn't fly into the ridge. The thunder of the F-15's afterburners as they came in the second time was deafening and terrifying. A great sheet of oily flame rose from the olive grove where the *katyushas* had come from. A herd of burning sheep ran out of the trees trailing inky black smoke. They fell to the ground thrashing and bleating.

Gilda and corporal Zimmerman crawled out from under the command truck to watch the war. They asked the major for directions to the captured bus. When the major saw Gilda's VIP ID, he insisted that she be delivered to her destination in a tank.

The interior of the Merkava Mk 3 was hot, noisy and smelled of lubricating oil. Shock resistant light bulbs glowed in wire cages. Gilda and her escort rode on canvas seats behind the gun crew in the rear of the tank. The tank's roaring 1200 hp diesel, placed in the nose of the lumbering vehicle, improved their chances of survival in the event of a hit from point blank range. After a bumpy 10 minute ride, the Merkava wheeled suddenly on one track and clanked to a stop. The rear ramp eased down with a whine of hydraulics and they walked out.

The captured communications bus was a dirty blue Syrian Karnak tour bus parked under a huge oak tree. A sagging arc of wire strung between the tree and some Roman columns had served as its short wave antenna. Nearby were two burned out tanks with faded Syrian markings. One was a Panzer IV, a German World War II antique. The other tank was a Russian T55.

"Shit," said Gilda.

Aman field men were already at work interrogating prisoners in a small tent, one at a time, while the others waited in the now blazing sun under guard. Ordinance experts checked the serial numbers on enemy weapons.

Inside the bus, she saw a lean heavy-eyed face. She recognized him as Mark Ambrache, an Aman electronics expert and one of her old lovers from her pre-Mossad army intelligence days. He bent over a workbench with a screw driver removing a hard disk from one of the wrecked computers. When he saw Gilda he leaned back against the bench, arms folded on his chest, bulging crotch presented.

"I should have guessed I'd run into you here," she said. "Still getting the shitty end?"

He put his arms around her. "What is the Mossad's brightest young light doing in this dump?" he said.

"Just looking around," she said sweetly.

"Help yourself. I've already got what I'm came for."

The interior of the bus was littered with smashed computers, radio gear and overturned furniture. The guerillas had started to destroy their records when they realized they were being attacked. Gilda followed a dark trail of blood to a pile of half-burnt papers in the back of the bus. Someone had been shot while trying to dispose of his secrets. These were the most sensitive documents, she realized, the ones the Arabs would try to burn first. Fortunately, the blaze had been put out by Israeli commandos. She knelt and began to sort through the mess. Her jaw dropped in amazement when she saw that the blackened manila folders contained intercepts of Shin Bet and Army radio messages, some of which appeared to be decoded.

"Mark, the Arabs are cracking our digital communications. They're more advanced than we imagined," she said.

He gave her a superior smile. "Not really. I've found only partial decrypts of routine traffic over here. They cabled these eight PCS together running Linux to make a poor man's super computer. It'll take a lot more power to crack our important codes," he said.

At the bottom of the half-burned pile she found a small black plastic box. The outside of the box was partially melted. When she opened box she found that it contained 3fi inch micro disks. None of the disks seemed harmed. Each bore a colored label on which was written a single Arabic word, "Bab" or door. One of the disks had an additional line of faint Arabic. She held it up to the light trying to read the impression the pencil had made in the label. She made out "Allah" preceded by some characters. Were they "Anwar" or "Assad"? It was Lions, she realized.

The Lions of Allah.

She hoped that she held the code key to the Lions of Allah's messages in her hand.

Now all the Mossad needed was a message to decode. Asher and his Palestinian bitch had better come up with one by the time she got back to Tel Aviv.

She caught Mark's male scent as he peered over her shoulder. "Holy shit. Aman is going to want a copy of that," he said.

"You'll get it. What else did you find?"

"They're writing code on bare metal. This is an EPROM burner." He patted the box under his arm, happily.

Then he showed her the tiny plastic rectangle cupped in the palm of his hand. The orange and blue chip looked like a common garden pest standing on two rows of 16 metal legs.

"Interesting," she said.

"Why would Hizbollah need to program chips in the field?" he said.

Gilda returned his gaze feeling the sexual tension. He was almost as good a lay as Boker, she thought as she gripped him passionately. She kissed him full on the lips before releasing him.

"Hope you didn't get married," he said. He stared at her breathing heavily.

"This bus didn't belong to Hizbollah," she said.

"How do you know?" he said.

She gave him a thin smile as she stepped out the door.

"Trust me," she said.

Forty-Four

Asher, dressed as a Palestinian, rode down al-Fajr Street on a rickety green bicycle that looked like it was made of castoff parts. It was his first day as Christina's law clerk. A battered cardboard suitcase was strapped to the luggage rack. In the wire basket between the handle bars a grey kitten with yellow eyes was leashed by a short piece of string. The kitten, borrowed hastily from a new litter of kittens at Gan Geneva, was part of his cover. A strange man with a kitten would seem less threatening to people he met on the street. Although his face was calm, he was filled with a suffocating sense of dread.

He pumped the pedals of his bicycle and wondered if he could successfully pass for a Palestinian at close range. The aura of a Shin Bet officer was all the authority he had needed in the West Bank, but now the political situation in Ramallah was changed as Palestinians anticipated the coming of self-rule. Israeli soldiers on patrol were now ordered to stay out of the side streets and back alleys, and to keep to the main roads and intersections. Here he would operate alone as he did when he worked in foreign countries as an Israeli spy.

Asher's deeply tanned *sabra* features had enabled him to pass as an Arab many times in missions abroad. Furthermore, his Arabic was excellent, and he wore disguises convincingly. Nonetheless, he was apprehensive that Christina's neighbors would remember his face from the times he sat in his Fiat near her house, openly advertising the fact that she was under Israeli surveillance. No doubt some of them would have seen him dressed as he was today in a *jalabiyya*. Besides it took more than fluency in a language and acting skills not to raise the suspicions of people who lived with you at very close range day in and day out, especially children. The biggest problem would be Christina's family who hated him. Her children were present the two times he had arrested her, once in her home and once at the airport. Her sister Najat had seen him too. He would need to secure all of their cooperation and silence.

Even in the early morning hour, the air felt oppressive, hot with the scorching promise of a noon of glaring blue sky and pitiless bronze sun. The silence that greeted Asher that morning was tense and sinister. The street lay silent. No cars drove by. No street vendor raised the ocher dust with his push cart and shuffling feet. There were no sounds of women's voices in the neighboring courtyards nor the pleasant sounds of breakfast being prepared. Buildings, streets, trees—everything in Ramallah seemed to hover in anticipation of an ambush.

Asher was relieved to see lights glowing behind the partly closed wooden blinds when he arrived at Christina's office. The door was unlocked. He entered cautiously pushing his bicycle ahead of him and smiled slightly when he saw Christina. Her back was to him as she busily cleaned out the clerk's desk by the door. She wore a blue cotton dress with a full skirt, a color that looked especially pretty against her dark hair and smooth olive skin. When she turned around he caught her eye. She defiantly tossed a box of paper clips onto the pile of odds and ends in the center of the desk.

"Why aren't there more people outside?" he asked.

"Today is *Mawoulid An-Nabawi*, the Prophet Mohammed's Birthday," she said sharply.

A real Palestinian would have known that, thought Asher ruefully. "I thought Ramallah was a Christian town," he said.

"My office is in a Muslim neighborhood," she said. Her face softened when she noticed the grey kitten. "What a beautiful little creature. Does he have a name?"

Asher thought quickly. "Khalil," he said, and untied the kitten's string.

Khalil was Arabic for Abraham.

Christina took the kitten in her arms and stroked the side of his face. He arched his little back and raised a paw playfully. She shook her head.

"He doesn't like Khalil," she said. "He looks more like an Anwar."

Anwar, meaning Lion.

"Anwar it is, Mrs. Goryeb."

"You may leave your bicycle in the back hallway," she said.

When Asher returned, he found Christina seated in her chair behind the large desk in the rear of the office, Anwar the kitten perched on her shoulder. Framed diplomas and bar licenses hung on the wall above her head. She pointed to the clerk's desk. "Please sit down, Mr. Asher. We need to discuss what you expect of me, and how we will keep up this ridiculous pretense that you are my law clerk."

He had expected to control this meeting, but her business like manner threw him off, for it was she who was controlling the conversation.

"If I need you to do anything, obey my instructions without hesitation," he said. "Our lives may depend on it. Otherwise you may carry on as usual."

She raised her chin. "My clients will know something is wrong. Usually my clerks are university students, much younger men than you."

Six file rooms at Mossad Headquarters contained shelves packed with bogus identities just waiting to spring into life. Asher had chosen his with care.

"I'm Achmed Bikfaya, an unemployed school teacher," he told Christina.

"From what village?"

She was cross examining him now.

The folder Mekor had handed him contained a color photograph of a rooming house in Jenin, a street map marked with its location, a description of the neighborhood, and a detailed personal history. Bikfaya was a perfect tenant who paid his bills by mail, lived quietly and was never around much. Asher had Bikfaya's old Jordanian passport, his worn black savings passbook, his latest rent, phone and electric bills and copies of tax returns that the Mossad had dutifully filed for a man who never existed. Jenin was a West Bank town 60 kilometers to the north which made it unlikely that Bikfaya's neighbors might run into Asher. The cover was computer resistant and plausible, although not totally unbreakable.

"I'm from Jenin," he said.

"Why are you out of work?"

"There is not much demand these days for a geography teacher. Students today wish to learn English, mathematics, and the sciences, but not geography," he said.

The harsh sunshine coming in the windows burnished her olive skin, accentuating the swell of her breasts under the thin cloth of her dress and the haunting beauty of her face. He noticed she was staring at him, a quizzical expression on her face.

"What are you thinking about?" he said.

"Where you will sleep," she said, and then looked embarrassed by her words.

He laughed, gratified to have pushed her off balance.

"Why I'll curl up at the foot of your bed with Anwar."

"There is a vacant room in the servant's quarters of my home," she said firmly.

"What have you told your family?" he said.

Christina shivered.

"I told them not to speak to anyone about you."

"If we are to succeed, we'll need more than your family's silence. They must be participants who cooperate just as convincingly as you."

"I'll speak to them this evening," she said, resentment in her voice.

It occurred to him how devastating it was for her to have him invade her home.

"No, it would be better if I speak to your family myself, and I'd prefer to do it at supper." he said.

She got up and crossed the room to a table that had a long necked pitcher of coffee on an electric hot plate. She poured herself a cup of coffee. Her movements were as graceful as Anwar's. "Would you like some?"

"Yes, thank you." Her hands as she held the cup were slender and strong.

Suddenly he was annoyed with himself for being so distracted with her movements that he had momentarily forgotten his reason for being here.

"I'm going to befriend Hamad," he said.

"What do you mean befriend?"

"I want to discover where he lives and win his confidence."

"You are an insane man," she said in a cold voice. She seemed about to speak again and then turned away and stroked the kitten.

He recognized fear in her voice. What he proposed made him uneasy too. He felt like he was standing at the top of a very high ladder.

"Where did you see Hamad?" he asked her.

"In the *souk*."

"Any particular shop?"

"Hamad is the kind who is suspicious of his own mother," she said. "This is not going to work."

"I don't need a letter of introduction, just his address." said Asher.

She shrugged and reached for a pen.

He watched her while she wrote some lines of Arabic on a piece of paper.

"Follow these instructions and you will find a carpet dealer's shop. I met Hamad in a warehouse across an alley behind the carpet shop."

* * *

Sayian's carpet shop was closed when Asher arrived in the *souk* at mid-morning. The shop's iron shutters were pulled down and there were no lights in the windows. He planted himself across the street in front of the Arab League Cafe, his back to the carpet shop. He studied its image reflected in the cafe's front window. Other stores were open and the narrow street was beginning to fill with people, a reassuring sign. He would not be conspicuous in a crowd of shoppers. He expected Sayian would open for business if he hung around long enough. He took a seat at one of the cafe's marble top tables on the sidewalk. As he sipped a cup of sweet tea, he checked out the neighborhood. Men at the adjacent tables played cards or backgammon, and carried on animated conversations. A few seemed to be just watching the world go by. Asher noticed a sharp-eyed boy wearing a *kaffiyeh* and a faded Mickey Mouse T-shirt who went from table to table hustling games of backgammon. When the boy's turn to play came, he shook his dice cup with an arrogant sneer. The former occupants of Asher's table had left a half-finished game of backgammon behind. Asher pushed the board away, hoping the boy would pass him by.

Behind the carpet shop's roof rose another flat-roofed stone building with boarded up windows, which had to be the warehouse Christina had mentioned. Beside the carpet shop, a high wall broken by a heavy iron bound wooden gate enclosed a courtyard. Set into the gate was a door with a sliding metal grill at eye level through which visitors could be scrutinized before they were admitted. Asher watched as light flashed behind the grill. A man's face appeared briefly and was gone. A moment later the gate creaked opened. An elderly Palestinian man emerged leading a donkey with a pack saddle on which hung heavy coils of hemp rope. Explosives could have been hidden in the donkey's load, thought Asher. The gate closed behind the straining animal.

He knew infiltrating the Lions of Allah would not be easy. He suspected they usually recruited only relatives or long-term friends. Groups like the Lions devised harsh trials to weed out spies from among people they didn't know or had only recently met, as a condition of admission to full membership. Israeli intelligence had learned during the *Intifada* that the passing such tests might well mean killing a Jew. It would be impossible for Asher to find full acceptance in the midst of the Lions. But he could work the fringes, picking up what he could. In the high-strung world of the Lions, he could pose as a criminal trafficking in stolen Israeli goods or a man seeking revenge against the Israelis for the death of a loved one, or else a fool.

Asher opened a dented silver tobacco case and sprinkled green home-grown tobacco over a scrap of newspaper, rolled a cigarette and licked the paper shut.

First he needed to make contact. At that moment Asher felt a tap on his shoulder.

"*Sheshbesh*?" said a voice.

It was the young backgammon hustler. His dark eyes stared at the board on Asher's table. His face was smooth, fine featured, and spiteful.

"Be more respectful with your manners," Asher said sharply in the manner of a Muslim elder.

Startled, the boy stepped back but only for a moment.

"But that's a good move," he cried and pointed to Asher's board.

Asher remembered Christina telling him the Lions used young boys as couriers.

"A mere boy can play with men?" Asher said.

The boy met Asher's eyes. "The mind of a boy is sharp as a sword."

Asher shrugged. With great deliberation, he repositioned the black and white checkers on the board for a new game.

"A *shekel* a game?" said the boy.

Asher reached in his *jalabiyya* for a 10-*agorot* coin.

"That's not worth my time," the boy grumbled but he sat down to play.

Asher glared at the boy in silence.

They rolled to decide who would go first and the boy won. With rising irritation, Asher, who had played backgammon often, saw the luck of the dice go against him. The boy threw the same combinations of doubles over and over, blocking the progress of Asher's checkers around the board at just the right times. The young cheat must have been using crooked dice, he thought.

Asher's threw down his silver tobacco case when the boy won.

"What a *khazuk* you gave me," he said. "What a shafting!"

The boy treated Asher to a mocking smile.

Asher wanted to snatch the dice out of his hand. "What is your name?" he said.

"I am Rasul," said the boy.

Asher suspected that this the same Rasul who picked up messages for Hamad at Christina's office.

"Is there something wrong?" said Rasul.

"Let us see if you are lucky again, boy," Asher said.

They played four more games and each time Rasul won. At the end of the last game Asher stubbed out his cigarette on the marble top table. He rose to his feet and exclaimed"Allah save me from this devil." Then he tossed five coins on the table and turned to go.

"Wait," said the boy.

Asher stopped.

"What is this?"

The boy held up one of the coins, a Syrian *piaster*. The *piaster* was bait. Asher pretended to frown and replaced it with another 10-*agorot* coin.

"You have the way of a *fellahin*," said Rasul, "but I can tell you are noble and tough. Have you been to Damascus?"

Asher stared at the boy but said nothing.

"Perhaps you would like to play *sheshbesh* tomorrow?" said Rasul.

It was time to leave. Asher went leisurely on his way, hoping that Rasul would follow.

* * *

Asher was not disappointed. A half an hour later he looked over his shoulder as he entered Christina's office and saw a familiar figure in a

Mickey Mouse T-shirt staying close to the shadow of the wall across the street. The ruse had succeeded.

Christina greeted Asher from her desk, one hand resting on Anwar, the kitten, who purred in her lap. An old woman with black hair who sat in front of Christina cleaning a long stemmed pipe with a rusty piece of wire.

"You have to help me, Mrs. Goryeb," said the woman. "The Jews confiscated 50 *dunams* of my land in East Jerusalem."

She turned and peered suspiciously at Asher.

"*Hajja* Nabulsi, this man is my new clerk, Achmed Bikfaya," said Christina.

Hajja, a Muslim title given to women who had completed a pilgrimage to Mecca, signaled Asher that he was expected to be deferential toward her.

"I am honored to make your acquaintance," he said gravely and she seemed appeased.

As he sat down at the clerk's desk he glanced through the blinds. Rasul stood outside the open window, looking in. Asher calmly rolled a sheet of paper into the typewriter on the clerk's desk and began to hammer furiously at the keys.

Christina looked at Asher with amazement. "Mr. Bikfaya, what are you doing?"

"Preparing the *Hajja's* protest," he said solemnly.

"Protest?" Christina's voice carried a tone of mild reproof.

"The *Hajja's* protest to the Courts of the Jews regarding the illegal confiscation of her land."

Christina looked puzzled. "Are you always so efficient at your work?"

"Is that not why you hired me, Madame," he said.

He wished there was some way to warn her that Rasul was eavesdropping on their conversation.

The little bell hanging over the office door jangled and Rasul swaggered in.

"What good will a protest do?" the boy sneered. "All the Jews do is talk about peace while they steal our land and run us into the desert."

Hajja Nabulsi rose unsteadily from her chair, her face contorted and purple with anger. Waving a cane at Rasul she snapped, "What do you want, meddlesome boy?"

"You must leave at once," Asher said. "You are disturbing our work.
Rasul laid Asher's silver tobacco case on the desk with a flourish.
"You left this behind at the cafe, Mr. Bikfaya," he said.

Asher patted the pockets of his *jalabiyya* and grimaced. He gave
Rasul a 10-*agorot* coin. "Thank you for your trouble."

Rasul seemed in no hurry to leave. He dawdled at the mail table,
ran his fingers through the envelopes and dropped one to the floor
which he picked up and put back in the pile. He sidled up to Asher's
desk again and their eyes met.

"*Sheshbesh?*" he said.

Asher adjusted the paper in his typewriter.

Hajja Nabulsi grumbled insults in a Samarian dialect that Asher did
not understand.

"Mr. Bikfaya, I will thank you not conduct your personal affairs in
my office," Christina said in a firm voice.

"*Sheshbesh?*" said Rasul in low whisper.

"Yes, yes," said Asher.

"Tomorrow?"

"I'll be there. Now go."

Rasul snapped his fingers and his face lit up with triumph.

* * *

That night Asher watched by the light of a tall silver candelabra placed
at either end of the dinner table as Christina went through the motions
of presiding over her family. Her two daughters, Muna and Aminah
entered the dining room with sulky, averted eyes. Christina's mother,
Leilah, an imposing woman with steel blue eyes, wore a maroon *abaya*
trimmed with gold thread. There was a hint of strain at the corners of
her mouth when she saw Asher.

He nodded at them pleasantly from his chair next to Christina. A drop
of sweat ran down into his eye and he wiped it away with the back of
his hand. His legs felt tired and rubbery. Still, he had accomplished far
more than he thought was possible on his first day undercover, and
Mekor would be pleased with his progress. One task remained—to
assure that Christina's family would not betray him. One careless remark
by any of them, or even a change in behavior could spread gossip in the
neighborhood, and might draw unwanted attention from the Lions.

Fatima, the cook and the rest of Christina's servants stood in the archway.

"Shall we say a blessing?" asked Christina looking around the table. They all bowed their heads except for Asher who lowered his eyes.

The servants disappeared when she finished the prayer to eat in the kitchen and the cook, Fatima reappeared a moment later in the archway pushing a trolley loaded with food. There was a stack of fresh flat bread, three kinds of salad, bowls of *baba ganoush* and *humus*, tall blue and white china pitchers of bitter coffee and sweet tea, little glass bowls of sugar and cream, a big brass platter of roast lamb resting on a thick bed of brown rice, and a fruit bowl piled high with bananas, oranges, grape fruit, plums, and another bowl of green and red melon balls. Asher hoped the lavish meal would make Christina's family more receptive. He helped himself to lamb and rice which he began to eat with his fingers, in the manner of an country school teacher.

Muna Goryeb gave a little titter of laughter. "The Jewish policeman eats with his hands."

Anwar sprang up on the table and began to eat daintily from Asher's plate, his erect tail brushing Asher's cheek.

"The kitty's hungry," giggled Muna. "May I hold him, please?"

Aminah made a face. "A cat shouldn't be on the table," she said.

"We know our manners in this household, Mr. Bikfaya," said Christina in a stern voice.

He was momentarily caught off guard. So involved with assimilating the habits and persona of Achmed Bikfaya had he become that he had ignored the silverware laid beside his plate. Asher wiped his hands on his napkin and gently removed Anwar from the table.

Fatima had finished serving and retired to eat in the kitchen.

"Mrs. Goryeb, may I speak to your family?" said Asher.

"Yes," she said with a wary look.

"I expect you are all wondering why I am here."

"We know who you are," said Aminah who radiated hostility.

Asher decided to ignore Aminah for now.

"Muna, who do the servants think I am?" he said.

Christina answered for her youngest daughter.

"The servants were only concerned about your status in the household. From the looks they gave me, when I told them you would live here—."

She broke off with an embarrassed smile but Aminah's eyes flashed. From this Asher inferred that the servants believed he was Christina's lover.

"What did you tell them?" he said.

She smiled. "I told them no one must obey you."

"So in this house I am the lowest of the low?" said Asher in a joking manner.

Muna laughed loudly but Aminah was not amused.

"Why should any of us help a Jewish policeman?" she said. "You are our enemy."

Asher looked calmly at the older girl. "Tell me, Aminah. The bombs that are killing so many people in Israel, do you think they can harm you too?"

Aminah studied Asher coldly.

"Everyday there are new Jewish neighborhoods being built in the hills around Jerusalem. The Jews pull down Palestinian homes to make way for them. The Lions of Allah make the Jews pay for stealing our land," said Aminah.

"Suppose your mother happens to be near a bomb when it explodes?" said Asher. "Or maybe your Grandmother, or even your little sister?"

"Remember what happened to my friend Mrs. Litvin," Christina said. Her eyes suddenly glittered with tears and she looked away.

Aminah's hard expression softened. "I could not bear it," she whispered. "If anyone I loved were killed it would be unbearable."

"Shells and bullets don't care who they destroy," said Asher. "These Lions of Allah who Jews have also threatened to kill your mother."

Aminah turned to Christina in alarm.

"Is this true?"

Christina nodded.

"The Lions have threatened to kill us unless I do what they want," she said. "They care as little about our lives as they do about the lives of Jews. They are madmen, not patriots."

"They want war," said Asher.

"The only way to a better life in Palestine is to trust reason, not madmen," said Christina.

Aminah shivered. "But our lives would be better with my father in America," she said. "I miss him so much."

An army jeep passed by on the street with its siren wailing. Muna and Aminah glanced at each other with large frightened eyes. These were children; Asher did not war on children. He wished he could put his arms around them the way he used to comfort his David.

"I promise you," he said, "next Christmas you will be with your father. In America."

* * *

"Would you like some tea, Maman?" said Christina after the girls had finished and retired upstairs to finish their homework.

"Thank you."

Beyond Christina in the guttering candlelight, Leilah's face was a foreboding dark smudge. She sat up straight on the end of her spine, eyes gleaming like a hawk's.

"Mr. Asher, is all this really necessary?" she said.

Before Asher could speak, Christina replied.

"Unless I cooperate with Hamad, he will kill the children. If we do not cooperate with Mr. Asher, the Jews will blow up our house. If we assist him, the children will be safe."

She spoke calmly, as though the subject had been discussed quite enough before and she did not wish to talk about it again.

"When the Jew is through with us he'll throw us into prison and we'll rot there," Leilah said to her daughter, as though Asher wasn't there. "Even your husband won't be able to get us out. Why do you trust this Jew?"

Asher found himself admiring the woman's ferocity and pride even as he felt the force of her disdain.

"I believe he is fair," said Christina. "He threatened his own superiors with exposure in the American press in my presence."

As Leilah sipped her glass of tea, Asher watched her expression change from that of truculent old woman intent on spinning intrigues of her own to that of a matriarch determined to preserve her family and its prestige among their people. Finally she spoke.

"Go to America with your children, Christina. My life is almost done, I'll stay in Palestine. Your life and the children's are more important."

She treated Asher to a stiff smile.

"I hope you do nothing foolish Mr. Bikfaya, or whatever it is you call yourself. There will be disastrous consequences if you miscalculate," she said.

Asher looked from one to the other. Christina sat immobile as statute, while her mother busied herself with her embroidery. They would cooperate he thought but at the same time he was ashamed. He did not enjoy bullying women or children.

Later than evening, while he took his shower in the servant's communal bathroom Asher reflected on the work he had done in the past four months. The pieces of the puzzle were falling into place. In April, when he was given this assignment, he had taken over the Shin Bet's botched investigation. He had started with virtually no knowledge about the Lions of Allah. Worse he'd been saddled with a stupid, brutal partner who was on the verge of destroying their only lead, Christina Goryeb. He had correctly deduced that she was being blackmailed by the Lions and prevented her from leaving Israel. If he could unravel the Lion's operation, the Mossad could roll it up and put them permanently out of business.

Once Asher had done his job, a team of specially trained *katsas* from the *Kidon* or Bayonet Unit would be brought in to assassinate the Lion's leader and their master bomb maker. Someone like that bug-eyed Strabo would do the dirty work, Strabo who wore a *yarmulke* woven from human hair to match his own so he could keep *Halakhah* while working uncover. Asher had been with Strabo in Cyprus when they'd ambushed two PLO gunmen. "I just wanted to get it over quick so I could get back to the soccer match on TV," Strabo had said.

* * *

In his role as Achmed Bikfaya, Asher lived in Ramallah relinquishing completely his old life and habits. Jerusalem was only a few kilometers away, but he did not go there or to Tel Aviv or his *kibbutz*, Gan Geneva. He became a familiar sight on al-Fajr Street as he trudged to the mosque near Christina's office with his prayer rug under his arm or poked around the *souk* shopping for fruit, tobacco, newspapers or used books printed in Arabic. He opened an account at the Arab Bank, and applied for a library card in the Islamic Heritage Center. Most important for his cover, he mailed letters to imaginary friends in Jenin. Asher mailed his letters in the *souk*. The post office was a narrow cubby hole in the back of a dry goods store that was cluttered with bolts of brightly colored cotton. These letters were filled with Achmed Bikfaya's boundless self-pity at having been fired from his teaching job, and his hatred for the Zionist Oppressors. He wrote that he was let go for having made remarks that were critical of Yasser Arafat's Palestine Authority when Jenin was placed under Palestinian rule. "Imagine!", he wrote. "An educated man like Achmed Bikfaya, reduced to working as a clerk for a woman lawyer, a Christian to boot." He also referred to an outstanding loan from the friend and enclosed five dollars in U.S. currency, with a promise to pay more. The money was visible through the cheap paper of the envelope.

By the time he mailed the third letter, the girl at the window knew him by name. She stared at the envelope with a greedy eyes. She looked all of fourteen years old and was breast feeding a baby.

"A stamp, Mr. Bikfaya?" she said.

Asher knew that as soon as his back was turned, she would rip open the envelope to steal the money. She might read his letter too. Hopefully she would gossip about its contents.

As he came out of the dry goods store, he saw a slim young man in a jeans and white shirt leaning against a wall in the shadows of the alleyway, silent, patient and watchful. The man did not notice him immediately but as Asher moved into the bright sunlight, the man turned away quickly and pretended to urinate against the wall.

Asher turned in the direction of the Jerash Hotel. At little farther on he zigzagged across King Abdullah Street, dodging traffic to see if the man would follow him. The street was full of people, women in shapeless black *abayas*, and men wearing trousers, jeans or *jalabiyyas* undone at the necks. Asher stopped a Greek Orthodox priest and pretended to ask directions. Out of the corner of his eye, he saw the young man was still behind him, accompanied now by an older heavy-set man in sunglasses. Asher walked briskly without looking back, past crowded cafes, shops and stalls, searching for a vantage point from which he could look back undetected. He wished he had the Beretta but knew it would blow his cover if he had to use it or was caught with it.

Asher crossed a busy intersection, and walked into the lobby of the Jerash Hotel. He found himself in an spacious room with a white mosaic tile floor filled with dingy red-plush drawing room furniture.

Tall gilt mirrors lined the walls. An old French elevator inside an ornate wrought-iron tower had been installed in a stairwell next to the counter. The desk clerk gave Asher a suspicious look. Asher was about to ascend the stairs nonetheless, when he saw the barbershop. Through the plate glass windows of the barbershop he could see the *souk* outside. If the two men were tailing him they would have to pass by these windows. It was not an ideal vantage point, but it would do. Asher walked in boldly and sat down in an empty chair that faced the windows. The barber, a thin Palestinian man with blotchy skin sat in the adjacent chair reading a newspaper. He smiled at Asher in a self-deprecatory way.

"What will it be, Sir," he said to Asher.

"Give me the *al-Fatah*," said Asher. It was a popular West Bank hair-cut and besides he needed a haircut anyway. Asher looked out the window again and smiled as the two men dashed by. A moment later, they entered the lobby. Their footsteps made a hollow echo on the tiny hexagonal floor tiles.

"Good morning, Mr. Bikfaya," said the heavy-set man in the wrap-around sunglasses. He wore a baggy grey suit and soiled Nikes. Asher recognized him as Hamad from Christina's description.

"May your day be bright," Asher said using the traditional Arabic response to Hamad's greeting.

Hamad waved a pudgy hand in Asher's direction. "Forgive this intrusion, but I am particularly anxious to meet you," he said.

The young man guarded the door behind Hamad with a large Eagle pistol.

"I shall not detain you long. May we talk?" Hamad sat down in on a wooden bench by the window and crossed his legs. He frowned as he lit a cigarette. "I am one of Mrs. Goryeb's clients. She handles certain complicated business for me," he said.

The barber busied himself at the sink, rearranging the bottles of hair oil and shaving lotion. Hamad snuffed out the match with his fingers and stared at Asher as if expecting some sort of response.

"*Effendi*, I'm only Mrs. Goryeb's clerk," Asher said. "I know what she lets me know."

"Let us hope so," said Hamad. "Information which passes through Mrs. Goryeb's office must be handled with discretion. If my competi-tors find out my trade secrets I could be harmed. Your employer depends on my enterprise. My lack of success will have consequences for her and for you."

In a flash of insight Asher realized that Hamad couldn't trust any Palestinians outside the Lions. That was why he had to blackmail Christina after Kallenborg tortured Abu Awad to death. Now he was forced to recruit Asher. Christina had been telling him the truth all along.

Hamad inhaled deeply on his cigarette. "Tell me about yourself, Mr. Bikfaya," he said.

Now his smile exuded goodwill.

Asher told him Achmed Bikfaya's story in a few brief sentences. "*Effendi*, on my honor and between men, I am a poor man who must work to eat, I do my employer's bidding. I have no interest in your affairs," said Asher.

"Discretion is essential to me. That is why I had to meet you," said Hamad. "Otherwise I'll have to take my business elsewhere."

"Better a wise stranger than 10 stupid brothers," murmured Asher.

When he met Hamad's gaze he was unpleasantly surprised to find the eyes were cool and intelligent, not at all the eyes of a madman.

Forty-Five

Derevenko's last message had said "12 Noon Sajjar Grill."

It was an old sun dried mud-brick restaurant in Kabul, dingy and dilapidated like the other buildings in the surrounding neighborhood. Inside, Kallenborg waited fretfully in a hard wooden booth. Physical exertion in the thin cold mile-high air, even walking down the street, taxed him. His blue eyes and blond hair drew hard-eyed stares from passersby, and he felt naked without a gun. Still, it was good he had not brought one. He'd been searched at every checkpoint, just as Shlomo had warned him. Kallenborg's hired body guard, a sulky-faced boy in a sheep skin jacket, silently hunkered down with his AK-47 assault rifle in one corner on the hard packed clay floor.

Kallenborg ordered a cup of hot *dudhchai*, a sweet milky tea and reflected on Kabul's peculiar lack of amenities. At his hotel, the desk clerk informed him that alcohol and night life were nonexistent in Afghanistan outside of special bars where non-Muslim foreigners could buy weak beer provided they signed a form declaring they were not Muslims and paid a small fee in addition to the cost of the beer. The desk clerk also persuaded Kallenborg to purchase a *shalwar qamiz* to avoid offending the faithful, and the hospital-green garment, which consisted of baggy pants and loose long shirt, provided little warmth.

An elderly man with broken teeth delivered Kallenborg's tea. Most of it slopped out on the floor getting there. The big pendulum clock that hung crookedly over the cash register said five minutes to twelve.

"Is that the correct time?" Kallenborg said, remembering his Pashto phrase book.

The old man nodded wearily and shuffled away to the counter. He changed the figures on Kallenborg's bill, sat down on a stool and stared out the window.

Kallenborg looked across the dusty booths, the rickety tables with bent wood chairs, and past the reversed blue neon Pashto script behind the front window. The shops of Kabul's bazaar across the street were full of Western goods: refrigerators, VCRs, crockery, clothes, toiletries and toys. He wondered who had money to buy such things. And where were the women? Apparently, they were kept out of sight behind the walls of all the flat-roofed mud houses.

After ten minutes he ordered another milk tea.

The restaurant door opened. Two men in grubby robes and black skull caps entered and claimed the front booth. From a few scraps of overheard conversation, Kallenborg he guessed they were merchants.

Still no sign of Derevenko.

Was it possible that he had discovered who Kallenborg really worked for? Not that Derevenko would care, but his *Mujahideen* boss might be seriously displeased if he caught Derevenko dealing with an enemy of Allah, like *Yisroel*.

Kallenborg sipped his tea. Easy enough for Derevenko to check Kabul's passport office. He would find no Ya'akov Kallenborg registered there, but he would learn that a German relief worker named Werner Ault had registered in the past 24 hours. Suppose Derevenko asked at the telegraph office for messages for Werner Ault and received a fax written in Hebrew sent directly from Jerusalem? Damn that turd, Shlomo! He finished off the cold tea and ordered another.

With the third cup of tea in front of him, he looked up at the clock again and checked it with his own watch. Both said twelve forty-five. Derevenko was not coming. Kallenborg took another sip of tea and gagged.

A faint alarm went off in his head: Look out. Watch your back.

He spun around.

There was no one there. He noticed a crude sign tacked to the splintered door behind him. Probably the door to the toilet. When the front door opened again, two more men entered. They had the same empty black eyes and impassive faces Kallenborg had noticed the day before at the Torkham border crossing. The two men paused at the door. One stared at Kallenborg's dozing body guard, while the eyes of the other glided around the room and eventually locked on Kallenborg.

He braced himself and waited. His arm itched unbearably. He wanted to scratch, but it would look like he was reaching for a gun. If these men were after him, there would be no escape.

They slipped into the adjacent booth.

Kallenborg heard the gurgling roar of an antiquated high-tank toilet flushing. He stiffened, then turned quickly. The door to the toilet creaked open and there stood Derevenko grinning broadly. The big nose and those deep set eyes as shrewd as an elephant's. His pockmarked cheeks and coarse black hair streaked with grey. The Nagant pistol in his hand was pointed at Kallenborg's head.

"You are getting soft, Ya'akov," he said in Russian. "I could have killed you."

He stuck the gun in his belt under the black *shalwar qamiz* he was wearing.

Kallenborg rose to his feet. He gripped Derevenko tightly, kissing him on both cheeks. They slapped each other on the back, and swore at each other in Russian with vicious affection.

"What business brings you to Kabul, Ya'akov?", said Derevenko, "Or should I say Werner?"

Kallenborg had his story ready. "I have customers for some of your surplus," he said.

"I forget who is your employer these days."

"Peruvians."

Derevenko looked surprised. "Marxists?"

"I didn't ask," said Kallenborg. "They could be."

"Don't guerrillas steal from their own military? Why come all the way to Afghanistan to buy my worn out goods?"

Kallenborg shrugged.

"Are you hungry?," said Derevenko cheerfully. He placed his Nagant on the table. "The food is terrible here. Thus, I like it."

Kallenborg eyed the pistol longingly while Derevenko ordered curried mutton, *dhal*, and fried rice. An unaccountable wave of homesickness struck Kallenborg, a longing for his old life in Russia, for the respect he'd enjoyed as the son of a Hero of the Soviet Union.

"My father used to carry a Nagant. I haven't seen one of them in years."

"What was 'Iron Felix'—I mean the great General Kallenborg—like to his son?" said Derevenko.

"A real piece of shit," said Kallenborg. "Just as he was to everyone else."

Derevenko smiled.

"My employer needs heavy arms. Stingers, anti-tank rockets, mortars," said Kallenborg.

"Keep talking." Derevenko's shrewd eyes remained fixed on Kallenborg as he ate.

"They must be delivered to the dock at Karachi within two weeks where they will be loaded on a ship."

Derevenko eyebrows lifted.

"South America is a great distance, " he said. "Why not rent an aircraft and fly the goods out of here?"

Kallenborg realized he had no choice but to be truthful with Derevenko.

"My employer is the Israeli government," he said.

Derevenko belched.

"Israel can get all the weapons it needs from America," he said.

"Not anymore," said Kallenborg. "I was ordered to come here."

"I'd heard rumors you landed in the Middle East," said Derevenko. "That much I believe. I would have never guessed Israel."

Kallenborg cursed himself for not thinking of a better cover story while Derevenko chewed on a rib.

Finally Derevenko grumbled, "What do you need?"

"Here's the shopping list," said Kallenborg handing him a piece of paper.

Derevenko licked his fingers and put on heavy black rimmed glasses. "I wouldn't wipe my ass with Israeli *shekels*," he said when he finished reading.

Kallenborg said, "Don't worry, you will be paid in U.S. dollars."

"Let me see them."

"The money will be sent to me by courier."

"What?" roared Derevenko, "You come to me with nothing and ask for my help?" His hand rested on his Nagant.

"Nicholai Ivanovich, calm yourself, please," said Kallenborg. "You know how dangerous it is to travel in Afghanistan with cash. The money will be brought to me by diplomatic pouch."

Kallenborg helped himself to curried mutton and fried rice.

"And, you should know Israel has no diplomatic relations with this country," said Derevenko.

"That's not a problem. My boss will arrange everything."

Derevenko stuck the pistol back in his belt.

"Getting arms to Karachi is not easy," he said. "It is impossible to bribe officials at the border. You'll need porters to carry the goods over the mountains to trucks in Pakistan. From Peshawar, it is a 700 mile journey to Karachi. An avalanche might wipe out the porters, or a truck could fall off a cliff. A driver might steal the goods for himself. Still worse, Pakistani intelligence might find out. There is much risk in what you propose, my friend."

His open-handed gesture implied such difficulties were not entirely insurmountable.

"For such trouble you'd deserve a generous commission," said Kallenborg.

Derevenko smiled broadly.

"What the hell! I've done crazier things," he said. "My price is $750,000 in U.S. dollars or the equivalent in British pounds."

Kallenborg nodded. "I'll pay half in a week. You'll get the other half when the weapons are delivered to the dock."

Derevenko wiped his mouth on his sleeve.

"This must be entirely between ourselves." he said. "If my boss finds out I sold guns to an Israeli, it won't go well for either of us."

"Not to worry. We'll do more business if this works out," said Kallenborg. "I'll make you rich yet."

"I am rich already, but more never hurts." Derevenko's eyes lit up. "Let's celebrate!" He reached under his shirt. His hand came out with a big bottle of vodka and a small container of powdered coffee. He filled both their cups with vodka and ladled in a generous portion of coffee. "A toast to our new business venture," he said. "To Ya'akov, son of 'Iron Felix' Kallenborg."

They were still drinking two days later.

* * *

The Defense Ministry was located in one of Kabul's few modern buildings left standing by the war. Outside the Minister's door, a soldier typed haltingly on a manual typewriter. The Minister's office was a small room with dirty walls. The Minister, a short portly man in his fifties, wore rimless glasses and a badly tailored grey suit.

"Six hundred fifty thousand," said Derevenko.

"What?", said the Minister of Defense. His voice was soft but deep.

"U.S. dollars."

Derevenko watched as the Minister wrote it down in his notebook. He wrote down everything in wire bound notebooks that were stacked neatly on one side of his desk.

Without looking up, the Minister spoke. "On whose behalf is this man Kallenborg acting?"

"He's an Israeli," said Derevenko.

The Minister stopped writing.

"As long as we get cash for our goods, why should we care who buys them?" Derevenko said. "Besides, this Israeli promises to buy more."

The Minister's eyes were alive with interest. "U.S. dollars will help us more than worthless military junk." He dismissed Derevenko with a wave of the hand. As Derevenko rose to his feet, the Minister said, "Oh, one more thing, Nicholai".

"Yes?"

"I am pleased you told me about this. Continue to keep me well advised."

Forty-Six

ZIONIST AGENT YA'AKOV KALLENBORG BUYING LARGE
QUANTITY OF MORTARS, STINGER MISSILES, MACHINE
GUNS, ROCKET-PROPELLED GRENADES, ANTI-TANK
MINES. SHIP LEAVES KARACHI TWO WEEKS. DETAILS TO
FOLLOW—M.

Ayoub Khan, re-read the telegram from Kabul and set it on the desk
in front of him. He'd met the Minister only once, at a Pan Arab League
conference in Baghdad. Back then the Minister was an obscure officer
in one of the groups of Islamic rebels who were fighting the Soviet
puppet government in Afghanistan, and Khan was a Ba'athist socialist delegate from Syria.

Ayoub Khan fingered his mustache thoughtfully. This telegram
from Kabul tantalized him. It held interesting possibilities. He
would show it to the President, but surely there was some additional
advantage to be gained. In his official capacity as the Head of the
Mukhabarat, Syria's secret police he was obliged to reveal the telegram's contents to President Assad. But what would be the consequences? The President might turn it over to the Americans to
demonstrate Syria's good faith and Israel's lack of peaceful inten-
tions. Most important, it would place the Americans in Syria's debt.
The Americans would be grateful. They would complain to the deceitful Zionists, of whom they were surely growing tired. However, in
the end, the Americans would do nothing since it did not concern
their precious oil.

Ayoub Kahn had few illusions about the man he served or Assad's
commitment to the Pan Arab cause. Assad was a cunning despot who

stayed in power by allying his fellow *Alawi* Muslims with other Syrian minorities against the fundamentalist *Sunni* majority. Assad was a gatekeeper of a gate that he did not own. Syria was a portal through which flowed millions of dollars of aid from Iran and other Muslim countries to guerilla fighters operating against Israel. Groups like Hizbollah, Hamas, and Islamic Jihad, were careful to consult with Damascus before undertaking any military action against Israel. When civil war broke out in Lebanon two decades earlier, Assad revived the old Pan Arab dream of uniting Syria and Lebanon by ordering his Army to occupy that country. The Syrians never left, and Assad had played the game of pitting Soviets against the U.S.

The demise of the Soviet Union, and the Gulf War with Iraq ended all that. Now Syria found itself in an uneasy partnership with the U.S., encouraged to establish peaceful relations with Israel. President Assad's official position was that although he himself preferred the status quo rather than accede to Israel's conditions, there was no alternative to peace.

Unofficially, he let it be known Syrians were not sheep.

Ayoub Khan reached in his coat pocket for his box of Tic-Tacs, shook out a breath mint and slipped it under his tongue. After a moment's hesitation, he buzzed his orderly and asked him to contact his cousin, Hamad. He believed Hamad's little group called themselves the Lions of Islam. He corrected himself, they were the Lions of Allah.

After he made a duplicate of the telegram on his personal copying machine, he picked up the phone to call the Executive Secretariat at the Presidential Palace.

"Add another item on the Senior Staff Agenda," he told the duty officer. "Call it 'Insight From Kabul'".

* * *

Hamad Taleb arrived in Damascus thirty-six hours later, exhausted from the circuitous journey. The first leg had been a long bus trip, south from Ramallah to Eilat, where Hamad crossed the Israeli border into Jordan. He stopped in al-Aqabah to confer overnight with one of his lieutenants before proceeding north to Damascus. He met with Ayoub Khan for evening prayers at the Umayyad, the Great Mosque.

As the two cousins entered, they passed a line of foreign tourists wearing paper slippers. The 2,000 year old building was originally a temple to Jupiter and later a Byzantine church but the huge orange and red stain glass window over the monumental doorway, so admired by the tourists was purely Islamic design.

Ayoub Khan wore a *jalabiyya* over his suit, his head was covered with a fine lace prayer-cap, and he held a pair of expensive hand made shoes in one hand. The marble tiles felt cool to his bare feet. Hamad's *jalabiyya* was plain and in his hands were modest sandals. The men spoke quietly as they washed their faces, hands and feet at a low fountain sheltered by a wooden gazebo-like structure at one end of the open courtyard.

"These are weapons an army fights with," Hamad said, after his cousin showed him the copy of the telegram from Afghanistan.

"They would be so easy for you to take, Hamad," said Ayoub. "You could put them to good use."

The vast pillared hall to their right echoed with voices of other worshipers arriving for evening prayer.

Hamad whispered, "We could halt a column of tanks or shoot jet fighters out of the sky. But why aren't you taking them yourself, cousin?"

"Syria remains well armed. We have no need of more."

Hamad studied the telegram carefully. "But neither does Israel," he said. "America keeps them well supplied."

"To be truthful cousin, I am somewhat puzzled," said Ayoub Kahn. "Unless... ," said Hamad.

The two men stared at each other.

"A group of Jews is preparing for civil war?" said Ayoub Khan.

"Jews don't kill each other," said Hamad. "They kill us."

"If Jews have turned on each other, the Americans will not be able to help," said Ayoub Khan.

A flight of birds swooped out of the darkening sky to settle in the galleries of the courtyard.

"Remember those settler rallies we saw on Israeli television? The settlers fear Rabin will trade their settlements to the PLO."

Hamad said, "With weapons such as these, their settlers could easily defend themselves from the Israeli Army."

"Peace with the PLO is driving the settlers to revolt. The revolt will spread all over Israel, and Jew will kill Jew," said Ayoub Khan.

Hamad's eyes glittered. "Then we'll kill the winners, and drive the rest into the sea."

The two cousins lingered, enjoying the sense of peace, the play of people across the stones, the glow of the sunset on the columns and mosaics.

"We shall make sure these Jews get their merchandise," said Hamad. "I will send instructions to my men."

Ayoub Khan placed his hand lightly on Hamad's arm. "You must use this information wisely, my cousin," he said.

"Assad doesn't know about the Kabul telegram?"

"The President doesn't know that *you* know."

A sly smile played on Hamad's face. "I always thought you were his man."

"I look out for his interests but I also look out for yours," said Ayoub Khan. He looked away and nodded pleasantly at two Syrian Army Officers who went past.

"Assad is angry with me. I make war without his permission, and this is an embarrassment and an insult."

"Then this can be an opportunity to redeem yourself."

Hamad's eyes flashed. "I will not place my men under the orders of that toothless old beggar. We both know Assad will use this telegram to curry favor with the Americans—which is why you came to me," he said grinning suddenly."

"It would be a mistake to under estimate the President," said Ayoub Khan.

At that moment the high young voice of the Umayyad's *muezzin* came from a niche in a recess above the hacked face of a Roman statute. "*Allahu akbar! Allahu akbar!*"

Forty-Seven

The rusty green 1952 Chevy sedan with two flat tires was still in front of the office. Christina eyed it and moved away from her office window.

"I'm sure there is a bomb in that car," she said fretfully. "Hamad knows who you are."

"Please notice the two flat tires, Mrs. Goryeb," said Asher. Patiently, he typed a pleading on the old Adler, copying Christina's handwritten draft. "I imagine a mechanic will come this afternoon and make repairs."

"Don't be so sure," she said. "The Lions are cunning."

Asher didn't look up.

"They could have put the car there to test us," she said.

"What do you mean?", Asher said with sigh.

"Most Palestinians will ignore a derelict car," said Christina. "Most Israelis will not, fearing it is booby-trapped."

"Then by doing nothing we will avoid confirming the Lion's suspicions," Asher said.

She remembered Hamad's mocking words. 'Your office on al-Fajr Street is still safe. It is safer than ever.' Word of her new law clerk was all over the *souk*. Although Rasul came periodically during the week and checked the table, no messages had come for Hamad since Asher started working in her office. She felt Asher's gaze on her as she sorted nervously through the letters.

"It is sometimes better not to care so much," he said.

The deep sadness in his voice caught her.

She had grown oddly accustomed to his presence during the past few weeks. The lines between prisoner and jailer blurred between them at times. He was constantly at her side, passing himself as her clerk in the office, in the streets, handing her papers in court, or holding her basket in the *souk*, his public manner deferential. He wore a shirt and tie beneath an open *jalabiyya*. There was no trace of the Israeli security officer in his gestures or speech. Nor was there any trace of the man who'd made love to her on the beach at Gan Geneva. Instead, he was grave. She had the sense that all of his emotions were held in check, and that the strongest of these was grief.

Asher had stopped his typing and stared at the wall.

She remembered the row at Latrun in Gilda's car. *He has lost his family and I have failed to protect mine.*

* * *

Faces flickered on the torrent of years. Tears and kisses mingled on tender faces, faces that brightened and faded slowly, faces gone and faces nameless, all lost in the dim, dark well of souls that knew no tears or time or laughter, love or passion or regret. Ardah and David. Asher's finger traced the letters that passion and heartache had cut in stone. The *kibbutz's* graveyard was like a deserted village, two hundred limestone markers in a field inhabited by moths and butterflies that his grandfather had reclaimed from a malarial swamp. In its soil lay three generations of those who loved and toiled at Gan Geneva since the first *aliya* in 1902.

Beloved sleepers in the Land.

A memory of swimming in the waves toward a time softened ruin on a grassy hill upon which a gentle surf broke and ebbed. Of dozing in the sand with a naked sun bronzed girl. Of that wild taking and the linking of their joy.

"Ardah and I met in the Army," he said. "She was so beautiful. Eyes were the color of topaz. We thought we were grown, but we were children."

His words loosened her own.

"Richard and I knew each other from childhood," she said. "We shared the same dreams for the future. My mother didn't want me to marry him because his family was poor. As if that mattered."

Asher said, "We had only one child. Our David. Such a perfect baby. Everyone wanted to cradle, to hug him in their arms. My little man, I called him. He wanted to touch the clouds with his own hands. At 17 he wanted to be a paratrooper. He was too young for the Army. We refused to give our consent but he begged us."

"Richard wanted us to live in America," she said, "And I refused. If I ever left Palestine, I told him, my soul would die. If only I had bowed my head, acquiesced to the loss of my home, my daughters would be safe and happy." She paused, and then added," Naomi Litvin might still be alive."

It was a relief to speak Naomi's name to Asher, to speak of regret, to admit her mistakes.

"We gave our David permission," said Asher. "The Lebanon War was madness. Everyone knew it, yet the children of Likud called Menachem Begin, Israel's King and Ariel Sharon, their greatest hero. Our David was killed in that evil war. It should have been me."

"I called Richard a coward with no honor. But it is I who have no honor left."

"Ardah shot herself with my pistol six months later," he said.

He felt Christina's presence beside him, her hand resting on his shoulder. Without thinking, he reached up and took it, felt the warm current of her melt the stone at the core of his being. He pressed his face to her breasts. Uncontrollable, violent sobs shook him. Passionately, she returned his embrace, heard again the crashing waves, voices laughing, and the soft notes of the mandolin.

Come then, my love, my darling, come with me.

Eyes half open, lips parted, aroused, her breath came in little gulps. Asher's lips touched her mouth, warm and tender. He felt her yield to him, as she had that night at Gan Geneva, her skin welcoming his touch. Suddenly she pulled back.

"Oh Chaim, we can't. I shouldn't—" she said.

Christina struggled to compose herself. Distractedly, she shifted through the pile of letters on her desk.

"Well then, Mrs. Goryeb, we'd better get back to work," he said, slipping almost without effort back into his role. His eyes sparkled.

"Why Mr. Asher, you're the most conscientious law clerk I ever had," she said, her voice brittle in the attempt to match his levity. "Your Arabic is as flawless as your typing. You know how to interview people, how to put them at ease and quickly gain their confidence. Of course, given your particular background, you would be naturally good at these things."

He chose to overlook the jibe. "I'm pleased that I can be of genuine assistance to you." He gestured toward the page in the typewriter. "Can we talk about this case?"

"Certainly," she said, eager to return to solid ground.

Asher fidgeted with his tie. "With all due respect, I don't see how a court will take this petition of yours seriously."

"Why not?", said Christina sharply and she caught herself.

"Your client Abdul Khaliq claims that the settlement of B'nai Ha'eretz has extended its fence line by 20 meters into his land. How can he prove the land is his? He doesn't have a deed. We don't even know what the boundaries are."

"There will be testimony from villagers that his family has been grazing sheep there for as along as anyone can remember," she said.

"It seems to me a judge might say no one owns the land or, at best, the property was abandoned," said Asher.

Yes, he was serious, she thought. She gritted her teeth. "That's what a thief would say."

For a second his eyes flashed, but then he seemed to shrug off her words. "There is enough room in the Land of Israel for everyone," he said. Then he bent over the typewriter and began typing industriously.

The bell over her office door jangled and a stout woman in a black *abaya* and *esharb* entered.

"May I help you," said Christina, rising to her feet.

The woman smiled hesitantly, came in and handed a palm-sized transistor radio to her. Christina nodded mutely but her knees felt like rubber and as soon as the woman left, Christina handed the radio over to Asher. He was on his feet in an instant.

The bell jangled again.

Christina looked at Asher and he slipped the radio into his pocket.

When she opened the door Daoud Rubez stood smiling in the doorway, a picnic basket in one hand.

"Mrs. Goryeb, I've brought your lunch," he said. His smile faded when he saw Asher.

"I was expecting to see your Mother," Christina said awkwardly.

"I'm helping her today. Rosenbluth doesn't have any work for me again this week."

"Thank you Daoud, you can leave the basket there." Christina indicated a spot beside the door.

Daoud put the basket down but he remained in the doorway.

"You may go, Daoud," said Christina.

Daoud inclined his head toward Asher. "Who is this man?"

"This is Achmed Bikfaya, my new law clerk, " she said. "He's a retired school teacher. Your mother must have told you about him."

Asher gave Daoud a severe nod.

Daoud studied Asher. "Mrs. Goryeb usually hires law students," he said. "What is your village?"

"I am from Jenin," said Asher.

Daoud looked doubtful. "My mother wants to know. Is everything all right?", he said to Christina.

Asher rested his hand on the door. "We have important business to discuss," he said in his school teacher's voice.

Daoud looked Asher in the eye. "I am addressing Mrs. Goryeb. Is everything all right?" he repeated.

"You may tell your mother she has no cause for concern," said Christina.

Daoud looked from Christina to Asher. "Good day, Mrs. Goryeb." He turned on his heel and left.

Asher waited until Daoud was out of sight and looked up and down the street. Then he closed the front door and locked it. He turned out the lights, and drew the blinds. From a desk drawer he removed a small notebook computer and a wallet-sized tool case. "Where can we work without being interrupted?"

"There's a storeroom under the floor," said Christina. She showed him a trap door next to the back wall. Grasping a heavy iron ring, he lifted the door to reveal stone steps that led down into darkness.

The storeroom was confining and dusty but she felt more secure there than in the office above. Asher spread newspapers on top of a crate to create a makeshift table. He placed the radio and the notebook computer on it and handed Christina a flashlight.

Asher turned the radio over. "Keep the light focused here," he said. He removed the cover to the battery compartment and pried out three AAA batteries. A slip of folded paper fell out. He picked it up and handed to Christina. Tiny groups of numbers covered the paper.

"That's a dummy message," he said producing a 35mm camera. "But we had better photograph it anyway."

"How do you know?"

"See that." He showed her a miniature socket with two rows of metal pins. The socket was hidden under a deep recess in the battery compartment. "Inside is a computer chip that can be used to store a message. If the Lions can read it so can we."

Asher zipped open his tool case.

"Was the message to Abu Awad hidden in a radio like this one?"

Asher did not answer. Of course it was, she realized. As she watched Asher connect the notebook computer to the radio with an electronic cable, she felt a perverse pride that her people, called hewers of wood and drawers of water, could make such an ingenious device.

Asher switched on the notebook computer and began typing commands. Technical jargon flickered across the flat glowing screen. "Uh-uh," he said. "We'll need a password." A spot of light blinked beside a large right arrow symbol: ">". Asher typed more commands and the screen began flickering again. "Perhaps our little computer can guess what it is."

"Suppose you are not successful?"

Asher's smile narrowed. "Then we'll take the chip to the experts, and I'll replace it with an identical one."

"The Lions will know their container was tampered with," said Christina, "Your substitute won't have a message."

"Maybe the Lions will assume the sender made a technical mistake, their message was not written into the chip," he said.

"Hamad is no fool," Christina said. "Do you have any idea what will happen if he realizes this radio has been opened? He will come here with his pistol."

"And I'll protect you, Christina," said Asher.

Everyone had offered to protect her, she thought with a flash of anger. Daoud Rubez with his *shabab* friends. Richard had tried, and now this impossible man! But would anyone be there when the time came?

"You and your precious information! I won't be able to clear my name, my children will be trapped in Palestine, and the Lions will be seeking their revenge while I spend the rest of my days trapped here with you."

Asher's fingers stiffened on the keyboard for a moment. Then he was the self-absorbed professional once again.

"We'll have to figure out the password ourselves," he said calmly.

For the next few minutes, he tried various Arabic expressions without any success. Then he turned to Christina. "We must think like Hamad. What would Hamad use for a password? Think. Anything."

Christina hesitated and shook her head.

"Concentrate. When you met him what was he doing?"

"Talking with some other men in a warehouse."

"What else do you remember?"

"He had a pistol. A Marakov."

"Good. Let's try Marakov," said Asher. He typed the name of the pistol. A moment later he said, "No good."

"That game they were playing," said Christina. "*Sheshbesh!*"

Asher typed *sheshbesh* but the screen did not change.

Christina looked at him sharply as a new thought occurred to her. "Hamad called me *Khantarish*," she said.

He looked amused. "*Khantarish?*"

"It seemed to be his favorite expression."

Asher's fingers flew over the keys. When the screen changed, to rows of numbers mixed with letters, he looked up at her with new respect. "Excellent, Mrs. Goryeb. *Khantarish* is the password! Why you could work for us."

"But I already do," she said in a dry voice. "Only it's not exactly by choice."

It took him only a few seconds to copy the contents of the chip to a micro disk which he slipped the disk into his pocket.

"What does the message say?" said Christina.

"Our experts will have to decode it. I'll give them the disk this afternoon. Meanwhile we must get back upstairs."

As they returned Christina heard the whine of a winch and tiptoed to the window. Now the Chevy had its front wheels hoisted off the ground. Two men in filthy *jalabiyyas* were checking the lifting chains, preparing to drive off in a battered Ford tow truck.

"I told you not to worry," Asher said happily.

He put the transistor radio on the mail table, switched on the lights, and unlocked the door but left it closed.

Christina watched the men get into the tow truck, and drive away with the Chevy. On the opposite side of the street, a boy squatted on the sidewalk. It was Rasul. He looked carefully in both directions and jumped up.

"There's a courier out there from the Lions," she said in a loud whisper. "He is coming this way."

"Not a moment to spare," murmured Asher.

When Christina looked down, she saw she was still clutching the dummy message from the radio.

Asher snatched the slip of paper from her hand and sprinted to the mail table. "Quick", he whispered. "Keep the boy busy."

Christina moved instinctively to the door and gripped the knob. The moment she felt Rasul's tug, she heaved the door open and dashed out at full speed. The astonished boy was knocked off his feet when she tripped on the threshold. Stunned she lay on the sidewalk, trying to collect her senses.

"Oh, it hurts, it hurts so much!" she cried, grabbing her side. "I think I've broken a rib."

Rasul picked himself up. Looking resentful and embarrassed he edged toward the open doorway.

Asher suddenly appeared, the very soul of Palestinian solicitude and dignity. "Oh Mrs. Goryeb, Mrs. Goryeb," he said sorrowfully in Arabic. "What has happened to you?" He glared the boy. "Ill-tempered oaf! Where are your manners?"

Rasul slunk through the door and emerged with the transistor radio in one hand.

"Almost a craven Zionist!" cried Asher harshly after him. He was on his knees beside Christina putting her arm over his shoulder. As he lifted her she felt him shudder. The shaking continued as he tenderly carried her through the doorway to her chair.

"Are you all right?", she said.

He didn't respond. She opened her eyes, looked up and saw a broad smile. Asher was convulsed with silent laughter. She started laughing too, wildly laughing. The absurdity of Asher's masquerade overwhelmed her. She felt beyond tears or fear. Jew and Palestinian, spy and prisoner, jailor and lover, her world was turned inside out and she couldn't stop laughing.

"Oh Chaim," she gasped. "Say something serious."

His mouth found hers and kissed her again and again as if it would devour her with hunger. He kissed her mouth, her eyes, her forehead, her hair, her cheeks, her chin, her throat and again and again her mouth, which melted into his with a taste of passion and discovery.

Forty-Eight

In his permanently reserved suite in the Lev Yerushalayim Hotel, Mekor was enjoying a noon time tryst with Netanya, his current mistress. He lay naked on the bed, covered to the waist by a sheet. He watched as with tantalizing slowness, Netanya removed a leopard-print Hermes scarf and her black linen Chanel suit, Mekor's latest peace offering. Slung across the back of the chair was the expensive black handbag he'd bought her for her last birthday. Netanya could spot fake Chanel at twenty paces, and although her age was perpetually 35, her birthdays seemed to fall every six months. Her enthusiastic lovemaking, made it easy for Mekor to overlook such minor deceptions.

Reaching behind her back she unhooked her black satin bra and removed it. Her breasts were firm and beautiful. She bent over the bed to remove her panties, dangling them full in his face. They smelled of Shalimar. Then she straightened and slapped him, hard on the right cheek.

"Ouch," said Mekor, all in injured innocence.

"So, Mishka, why did you stand me up at the Cinematheque?" she said.

"I told you. It was an emergency directors meeting. Some big loans went kaput on us. We had to move quick to get our hands on the collateral."

Her dark pubic hair was tangled thatch framed by the black straps of her garter belt that held up black net stockings. She climbed onto the bed and lay on top of him. She was still wearing her Manola Blahnik spike heeled sandals.

She looked at him reproachfully. "Such an emergency, you couldn't telephone, Mishka? You left me standing there all alone like a cheap whore." She rolled over and pretended to sulk.

"Never cheap, my dear," he said.

His fingers lightly inscribed her wide pink nipples, tracing across her lush satin curves until she began to breath more heavily. Without a word he bent down to press his lips to the tip of her left breast. She giggled softly at the sensation. He teased it gently with his tongue, his lips applying a sure, patient suction, coaxing its growing hardness. She lay back her eyes shut, her arms clenched behind her neck. He reveled in the sensual smoothness of her nakedness turning and writhing under his caresses. When his penis was hard he knelt behind her, pulled her up on all fours and moved the head of his penis back and forth between her moist inner lips while he watched the reflection of their intertwined bodies in the mirror on the wall. Her face was contorted with pleasure.

"Fuck me," she groaned. "Fuck me now. Fuck me until I cry."

He cupped her breasts in both hands, pinching her nipples and shoved his penis deep into her hot, slippery vagina.

"Take it," he said.

Suddenly her vagina tightened.

"Did you see that?", she said.

She pointed a long blood red manicured nail at the door.

"See what?" said Mekor.

"The door knob just turned," she said.

He looked quickly around the pastel room, across the kitchenette with its stove, refrigerator and microwave, and focused on the connecting door to the adjacent suite. A dead bolt lock secured it. She squeezed his swiftly deflating penis again.

"There!", she said. "It turned again."

They watched the glass knob on the door rotate silently, moved by an unseen hand on the opposite side. As Mekor reached under the bed for his 9mm Beretta, his eye fell on the tiny pager by the reading lamp. With his free hand he groped for his portable secure phone and dialed Gilda. In a moment he heard the faint beep of another pager through the thin wall. He put on his bathrobe and moved to one side of the connecting door, pistol raised.

"Gilda?", he said softly and drew back.

"Gilda?" said Netanya, "Who the hell's Gilda, and where did that gun come from? You told me you were in banking."

"The *falafel* market must have crashed," he growled.

When he unlocked the door, Gilda stood in the doorway, her brown leather purse slung over her shoulder.

"*Falafel*, my tush," said Netanya.

She wrapped the sheet around herself and stalked into the bathroom.

"Such a great tush, too." he said, watching her go with regret.

"So that's why you didn't answer your pager!" said Gilda. "Put your shorts, Mike. We got big problems back at the bank."

"What's up?"

She handed him a piece of computer paper.

"Read this," she whispered. "We've just decrypted the message Chaim Asher intercepted."

Mekor picked up his cigarette and sat on the edge of the bed. The message was from Damascus. It was long and detailed. The part that concerned him most said:

CEASE OPERATIONS AGAINST CIVILIANS UNTIL FURTHER NOTICE. OBSERVE AND REPORT. ZIONIST AGENT KALLENBORG TWO OTHERS SAILED KARACHI AUGUST 10 ABOARD SHADOW OF THE PROPHET WITH LARGE SHIPMENT HEAVY WEAPONS. PRESUMED DESTINATION EILAT AND JEWISH SETTLEMENTS IN OCCUPIED PALESTINE. KALLENBORG CLIENTS WILL REVOLT ONCE SETTLEMENTS TRADED TO PALESTINE. AFTER JEWS TURN ON EACH OTHER, LIONS OF ALLAH TO LEAD DEFEAT OF ZIONIST ARMY—H.

* * *

In the shade of a wild olive tree on a steep hillside, Christina and Asher ate lunch, dipping pieces of flat bread in bowls of mashed peas. At the bottom of the hill lay the village of Ayna Nub, the slim minaret of its mosque rising gracefully from a cluster of mud and rock buildings. In preparation for Abdul Khaliq's law suit against B'nai Ha'eretz she was locating the boundaries of his sheep pasture. Christina gestured angrily to Asher at a row of posts and three strands of shiny new barbed wire that cut across the hillside below them.

"This tree is a marker, Chaim," she said. "Notice, the tree is at least 20 meters behind that new fence. This is proof that the settlers have stolen this man's land."

Asher didn't move his head.

"We have company, Christina," he said in a low voice.

When she turned in the direction he was looking, she saw two men with binoculars on the hillside about a hundred yards above them. They wore loose-fitting army green fatigues. M-16 automatic rifles were slung casually on webbed straps across their shoulders. A phalanx of white apartment houses jutted on the ridge behind them.

"What do you think they will do?" said Christina.

"I don't know. But if we don't leave, they will probably come down here."

"I'll leave when I've finished my job," she said. "There's still one more marker to find."

Asher looked at her with raised eyebrows, but said nothing. He dipped another piece of flat bread into his bowl.

Stony ridges stretched all around them in empty silence. The cloudless sky was a sweltering dome of glare and heat from one horizon to another. Flies gathered around the edges of their bowls. Christina brushed them away mechanically, her energy drained from the effort to keep her emotions under control.

She found herself increasingly aware of his body. Her gaze wandered to the base of his throat where she longed to place her lips. The sight of his strong hands at the keyboard of her old Adler reminded her of the gentle sureness of his touch. Her loneliness and the danger they shared increased her desire. At night she woke up, sweat drenched, from dreams in which he ravished her. She tried to dismiss her disturbing thoughts. Once this nightmare ended, she told herself, the desire would vanish and she would be herself again, Richard's wife. Asher had made no further advances since he kissed her in the office, but there remained between them an odd closeness, as though they had known each other for years. If they knew how she felt towards Asher, her daughters would be shocked, their trust in her shattered, her family would be disgraced.

Christina turned her attention to the men hunkered down under the date palms by the well. A young man in jeans approached them, holding a long necked pitcher at his side. Sunlight flashed from a crown of tiny brass coffee cups balanced on a tray on his head. In the midst of this pleasant scene an old Buick jalopy with a steamy radiator pulled up at the end of the road. A woman wearing a black *abaya* and white head shawl got out of the car. She walked briskly up the dusty path toward Christina and Asher. Two Palestinian women, who were returning to the village turned to stare at the woman. When she reached the new fence, she dropped to her hands and knees and crawled under it.

"Who do you suppose this is?", said Asher.

"Someone with troubles, a new client probably," said Christina irritated at the thought of interruption.

"The fellow she's with kept the engine running," said Asher. "Must be in a big hurry."

"Perhaps he's afraid he won't get it started again."

The woman was panting from the exertion by the time she reached them. Christina recognized her as the hateful woman who Asher called Gilda.

"Are you fucking crazy, Gilda?," Asher said to her. "I told you where we were going, I didn't issue invitations. See those characters down there in the village? They find out you're a Jew, we'll get our throats cut. Why didn't you just page me?" He patted his *jalabiyya*. "I've got a secure phone."

"It's not secure anymore," said Gilda with a grim superior smile. "Here's your new code key." She handed him a piece of black plastic molded in the shape of a key.

Asher's jaw dropped. "What happened? A mole in the temple?"

"Worse than that," said Gilda. She looked at Christina. "Can we talk privately?"

Christina glanced at Gilda with equal suspicion.

"The villagers will get suspicious if we leave Mrs. Goryeb here alone," said Asher.

Gilda lips compressed in a thin line. "There's no time." She handed Asher a folded piece of paper. "Read this. It's the decrypt of your Lions message." She turned to Christina. "Keep your mouth shut about this."

Christina's face remained a frozen mask.

Asher turned to Gilda. His eyes burned. "You Nazi," he said softly. Christina silently applauded.

"Just read the decrypt first," Gilda said. "Then you can call me names."

Asher spread the paper on his knees. He looked up at Gilda utterly bewildered. "Is this the same Kallenborg?"

"We think so. Ya'akov Kallenborg left *Yisroel* on a Swissair flight to Rome last month. He has not been heard from since."

"Ya'akov Kallenborg works for Shlomo Arendt," said Asher.

"Shlomo says his man Kallenborg went on a scheduled two week vacation to Italy. When he didn't return, Shlomo reported him AWOL."

"I know this Kallenborg," said Asher. "He likes to be comfortable. Off duty, he hangs out on the beach at Tel Aviv or smoozes in a cafe. It is hard to believe that shmuck would buy weapons for a settler revolt on his own."

"Damascus wouldn't have stopped attacks on our civilians if they didn't believe Kallenborg is genuine," said Gilda.

A flock of scrawny sheep picked at the dry grass on the village side of the fence. A boy sat on a rock, spinning a wooden top on a cord stretched between two strings. He tossed it humming high into the air and caught it again on the cord.

"Kallenborg isn't AWOL," said Asher. "Shlomo put him up to this."

"Do you know that for certain?", said Gilda.

"Just a hunch. Shlomo lives right up there in B'nai Ha'eretz." Then he shrugged. "What are we so upset about? This is probably an official operation. The PM's support for peace with the Palestinians in the Knesset is weak. The settlers have powerful friends who are sentimental about Samaria and Judea."

"Mike checked it out with the PM," said Gilda. "He didn't know the Shin Bet was in the arms business. We're under orders to stop the arms shipment and find out what's going on before he talks to Shlomo's bosses."

Asher gave a low whistle.

"Then this is a rogue operation."

"A rogue operation with support," said Gilda. "As you say, the settlers have powerful friends."

"Where did they get the money?"

Gilda shook her head slowly. "Maybe private donors in the U.S. We don't know whether it's just Kallenborg and his boss, or the entire Shin Bet or maybe all our armed forces, even the Mossad itself. The cost alone indicates a big operation."

Now Asher understood. "So that's why you couldn't use the phone."

"We couldn't take the risk," said Gilda.

"But you trust me," said Asher.

Gilda shrugged. "If you were dirty, you would have decoded the Lions message first and fed us innocuous pap later." She turned to Christina. "And Asher would have shot you."

Asher is not like you Gilda, thought Christina, but she understood what Gilda meant.

Steam hissed loudly from the old Buick as the radiator boiled over. A disgusted middle-aged man in a thread bare *jalabiyya* got out and opened the trunk. He took out a plastic bucket and topped up the sputtering radiator from the well. The villagers on the red carpet laughed at something he said to them.

"You brought Mekor with you," said Asher.

"Who can you go to for help if you don't trust anyone?", said Gilda.

"So, the three of us are going to stop Kallenborg, a settler revolt, and the Lions of Allah all by ourselves," said Asher.

"Mike's assembling a team. But he needs time to figure out who he can trust."

"How much time do we have?"

"Maybe two, three days at the most. We'll take care of things in Jerusalem. Mike wants you to take charge of the field operation."

"If Eilat is Kallenborg's destination, why not send a couple of Navy missile boats down the Gulf of Aqabah or the Red Sea to intercept his vessel?"

"I told you we can't trust anyone."

A long sustained burst of automatic rifle fire came from the hillside above them. Gilda dropped to the ground instantly. Asher pulled Christina down with him.

"It's a security patrol from B'nai Ha'eretz. They think we're Arabs," he whispered to Gilda. "That new fence you crawled under is their perimeter wire."

"You mean we're inside a settlement's outer perimeter?", said Gilda. "This place is a bloody mine field!"

"Not mined yet, it's too new," said Asher.

"Some consolation," said Gilda.

The firing continued without interruption. Christina could hear bullets buzzing off the top branches of the olive tree.

"They're getting our range," said Gilda. "We've got to get out of here."

"The clips hold only 20 rounds," said Asher. "Be ready to run, and don't stop until you reach the big rock on the other side of the fence."

Abruptly the firing stopped.

"They're changing clips," he said, rolling forward and was on his feet. He yanked Christina up with him. "Go, go, go."

They raced madly down the path from the olive tree. Christina's legs flew beneath her, the rush of adrenalin seemed to propel her effortlessly down the hill. She came to a skidding halt beside Asher who was crouched at the fence. Gilda's *abaya* had snagged on the barbed wire, and he tried to free her. A shot suddenly broke the stillness. There was the simultaneous thud and spray of dirt in the grass to Christina's left. She dropped to her knees and began to crawl through. Then her *abaya* caught on the barbed wire too.

She closed her eyes and waited to die.

"Fuck!" screamed Asher.

He tore Gilda's robe and shoved her under the fence. A line of bullets kicked up dirt toward him as the automatic rifle fire began again. He reached over, freed Christina, and they both slid under. He caught her hand. Now they were up and running for the big rock. Ten more steps, Christina told herself. The firing was almost continuous now. Suddenly she was off her feet, plummeting to the ground face down with eyes closed tightly. When she opened them again, she was in the shelter of the rock. Bullets ricocheted harmlessly off the top of it. Asher and Gilda lay next to her, panting. The shepherd boy was there too.

The firing stopped and a voice above them called out in Hebrew, "That will teach you filthy Arabs to stay off our land."

"Fucking fanatics," said Asher. His eyes were screwed tightly shut in pain.

"Are you hit?" said Christina.

"Just a flesh wound," he gasped. His right ankle was covered with blood.

"Now you know how it feels to be a Palestinian," she said.

Forty-Nine

In the subdued lighting of the *Midrasha*, an underground command bunker run by the Mossad, north of Tel Aviv, Mekor listened impassively to the familiar gravelly voice. The Prime Minister's words were blurred by the whirring of a ventilator fan so that Mekor had to strain to hear him.

"All my life I've fought Arabs," said the PM angrily. "I'm too old to learn how to fight Jews. How big is this latest rebellion? Is Likud behind it?"

"Bibi's certainly stirring the shit," said Mekor.

Binyamin "Bibi" Netanyahu, the leader of the Likud Party was increasingly popular.

A slow smile spread over the PM's face. "Ah yes, The Star of Zion! That smooth bastard with his phony American accent!"

Mekor said nothing.

"Do you know what will happen when I order the Army to disarm these rebels? Bibi will call for another vote of confidence in the Knesset. This time, we may lose."

"Bibi's been talking to our Arab parties," said Mekor. "For what that's worth."

The five small Israeli Arab parties held the balance of power in the Knesset between the Labor and Likud parties.

The PM looked perplexed. "What can they give each other?" Our Arabs want fewer settlements, Likud wants more."

"The Arabs are just twisting our tails to show us how weak we are without them," said Mekor. "I don't think Bibi's involved with our rebels, but some of his followers are."

The *Midrasha* conference room smelled of electronic gear and stale sweat. A large circular table of dark wood and comfortable chairs filled most of the space. Vaulted concrete walls slanted down to a thick wine-red carpet on the floor. Through the glass wall in front, Mekor and the PM could look into the War Room below, with its rows of softly glowing computer terminals and huge situation screens. It was here in the *Midrasha* that Israel's prime ministers held numerous secret meetings with Jordan's King Hussein during the past twenty-five years. The King never made concessions; his advice, however, eased tensions between Israel and Jordan.

In the Middle East, thought Mekor, appearances counted for nothing. Your enemies could be your secret friends, while your friends attempted to destroy you.

The screens displayed live pictures of the late afternoon streets of Baghdad via Ofek 3, Israel's spy satellite that orbited the earth every 90 minutes. An expanding red circle slashed across the center screen and zeroed in on the side window of a large black Mercedes limousine. The image jumped, as the sullen mustachioed face of Iraq's Chief of State came into focus. A perpetual enemy.

"Fuck you, Saddam!" said the PM happily. He turned to Mekor with a smile. "Who needs spies when we've got this?"

Mekor shrugged. "Miracle machines can't show you where your enemy is if he's underground or inside a building. They can't tell you what's inside his head," he said. "Only spies can do that. I need some men I can trust. Right now there are very few I'm sure of."

"The Army is administering loyalty oaths," the PM said dryly.

"A lot of good that will do," said Mekor. "The rabbis have ruled that oaths to the government are invalid."

"Pull your personnel records, and see who is a yeshiva boy and who is not," the PM said.

"That doesn't always mean anything either. What matters is how a person interprets Torah. Most observant Jews are not rebels."

The Prime Minister took another cigarette from his half filled pack of Lucky Strikes. At 73, he still smoked four packs of Luckies a day. "Those pious shmucks still think we're God's Chosen People," he said, eyes narrowed. "We can't risk civil war. Find these traitors, Mekor. Lift up their rocks, dig them out of their holes, pull them clawing and screaming out into the sunlight. It's the only way we will survive."

Mekor was secretly amused. At bottom, for all his fierceness, the PM was a very sentimental man, a man who had spent a lifetime concealing his feelings. Mekor was one of the few people outside of his wife to whom the PM would open up; Mekor's father and the PM had grown up together in Jerusalem. Mekor knew also that if he ever lost the PM's trust, the old man would simply turn his back and never speak to Mekor again.

The Prime Minister finished his cigarette in silence.

They went outside, and climbed in a jeep. A bottle of Fleischmann's 90 proof whisky and a fresh pack of Lucky Strikes lay on the seat between them. The Prime Minister, who looked ten years younger than his age, drank his liquor straight out of the bottle without showing the slightest sign of intoxication. Even when drinking, he had more brains in his big toe than most sober men had between their ears, thought Mekor. A hard man, the kind who would live to be a hundred.

As the Prime Minister drove, his Shin Bet body guards followed in a second jeep at a discrete distance. They went past an airfield where two *Lavi* jet fighters swooped low, practicing touch and go landings. The Prime Minister stopped for a company of soldiers in fatigues who jogged by, their automatic rifles held at high port. At a tank depot lined with needle-nosed *Merkava* tanks the PM turned off the main road, and Mekor could smell the sea. The jeep bumped along a sandy lane for a short distance until they arrived at a deserted beach.

The Prime Minister smiled gleefully as he shifted into four wheel drive. Stilt-legged ibis and doughty little sand pipers scattered at their approach, uttering cries of alarm. The jeep bounced over a low sand dune and splashed through a tidal pool that lay on the gleaming expanse of sand. The men drove in silence for several minutes. When the PM began to speak he was thinking out loud, and did not attempt to converse.

"I used to think like our friends in Likud, the 'Fighting Family'. We had no choice. Kill or be killed. No reason to be concerned about the Palestinian people, they would easily find a home elsewhere in the Arab world. But when I was Defense Minister during the *Intifada* I realized the Palestinians were staying put on the West Bank. This is a no-win game. I want to survive. I want Israel to survive. Anyone who harms a

Jew, I would kill. But people are not superior merely because they have endured evil. Even we Jews. We are no longer a beleaguered people, destined to be singled out no matter what we do. Israel is not an army with a country. It must be a nation like any other in the world."

A huge crimson sun sank on the horizon under a ominous bulwark of marbled cumulus. The circling birds watched the jeep drive on. It shrank until at last it was just a dot in the warm haze. The sea birds resumed their wading, hunting tiny fish and crustaceans trapped in the pools by the receding tide.

Fifty

Two men in a khaki Land Rover sped toward Aleppo, Syria, on M1, a four lane divided highway from Damascus. They passed through fields of blood red dirt planted with sugar beets, barley, wheat and cotton. Tattered pieces of brightly-colored plastic bags and bits of trash littered the roadside.

Hamad said to his cousin who was driving, "I hope you appreciate the risk I'm taking."

"President Assad does not make idle requests," Ayoub Khan said sternly. He looked crisp and cool in a clean, pressed Syrian Army uniform that had no rank badges. "This is the opportunity you've been looking for."

Hamad wore a white *kaffiyeh* and a thread-bare army jacket over a black shirt and jeans. He had altered his appearance by shaving off his beard and wide mustache. He had not eaten since leaving Ramallah the previous day. From the safe distance of Ramallah, it had been beneficial to enjoy President Assad's support, but a face to face with this cold, calculating man was not an opportunity Hamad relished. He hoped this would be the last time.

"You probably don't realize that every time I cross at Aqabah, the Shin Bet's computers remember," said Hamad.

"Then use a different passport, my cousin."

Hamad shook his head. "It's not that simple anymore."

Ayoub Khan looked mildly chagrined.

They passed the exit sign for Hama. Ayoub Khan slowed before turning off on a winding road that descended into a deep cleft in the plain.

"I did not expect President Assad to live here, in Hama," said Hamad.

That President Assad, renown for his caution would choose to live in this place, considering his own part in its bloody history, was astonishing to Hamad. In 1982, as a young *Ba'athist* socialist in the Syrian Army, he had seen President Assad crush the rebellion of the Muslim Brotherhood in Hama. The riflemen of the Muslim Brotherhood had no chance against Assad's Russian MiGs, tanks and heavy artillery. The cost was 25,000 lives.

"He has a summer home in Hama," said Ayoub Khan with a bland smile.

"But this was the home of the Muslim Brotherhood," said Hamad.

Ayoub Khan chuckled grimly. "It's perfectly safe now, my cousin. The Brotherhood's survivors are loyal to the President," he said. "Besides we hold their loved ones."

At the bottom of the canyon, a muddy brown river overhung with lilac, poplar, and willow trees twisted its way through a sunken city untouched by the modern world. The Land Rover drove past old Arab houses, mosques built of black and white stone, and a *souk* lined with stalls. Women dressed in somber robes from head to toe passed by them on the street with only their eyes visible. Others covered only their heads and faces with dark hoods tucked into buttoned-up overcoats, even though the morning heat was already fierce. Hamad's eye was arrested by the sight of a woman in a green summer dress, with stockings and stylish high-heel shoes, who wore a black plastic bag over her head as if all tricked out for her own execution.

Ayoub Khan parked the Land Rover in front of an ornate Mameluke villa with a walled courtyard. At the gate four Syrian army corporals in gleaming black Corfam boots and paratroop jump suits, stood guard, their M-16s loaded and at the ready, slung across their stomachs. The tallest corporal respectfully escorted Ayoub Khan and Hamad along a gravel path through a side garden brimming with asters and violets to a terrace at the rear of the house overlooking the river where several white wicker chairs had been placed on a lawn around a low table.

"Inform the President we are here," said Ayoub Khan to the corporal.

As the cousins waited, Hamad watched small boys jumping into the river from four huge ancient water wheels, called *norias* across from the villa. Made of wood and mounted on wooden blocks upon stone piers, the *norias* groaned. They turned at various speeds like gears of some gigantic clock, lifting water into canals borne on arches that irrigated gardens of chickpeas, tomatoes and cucumber. Wheels within wheels, he thought gloomily. Plot and counter plot.

"Good morning," a high thin voice said behind him. Hamad jumped to his feet with alacrity to face President Assad. Assad's bulging forehead rose like a cliff above a craggy beak of a nose and thin grey mustache. The eyes below the forehead were keen and wary. His movements were precise and economical, and his hands had a peculiar elegance about them. He wore a dark, handmade, Italian suit.

"I am pleased that you came," he said inclining his head toward Hamad. " Will you accept some coffee?"

A mess boy filled their cups with the hot thick over sweetened liquid and offered them a bowl of olives.

"It is a great honor to meet with you again, Mr. President," said Hamad with a low bow.

Ayoub Khan sipped his coffee discretely, Assad's man, the claims of kinship superseded.

From here on in, Hamad would be on his own. If he incurred Assad's displeasure his cousin would be the last person whose support he could count on.

President Assad gave Hamad a long penetrating stare. "How long have you been fighting Zionism?" he said.

"All my adult life," said Hamad.

"In how many organizations?"

Obediently, he ticked off on his fingers as he spoke. "Al-Fatah and its attack arm, the Fatah Hawks, which split off from the Fatah Revolutionary Council, the Palestine Liberation Organization, the Democratic Front for the Liberation of Palestine, which was born out of the Popular Front for the Liberation of Palestine, then Hamas and Islamic Jihad—."

Assad interrupted him. "Yet you have not succeeded in destroying the Zionist state."

As if it's all my fault, thought Hamad resentfully.

Assad's eyes glittered.

"But their destruction may be imminent. We have word from Kabul that the Zionists are preparing to fight among themselves. Two weeks ago a Shin Bet officer was spotted in Kabul buying heavy weapons for Israeli settlers on the West Bank. A settler's rebellion is the fulcrum we need to push the Zionists into the sea," he said. He looked at Hamad expectantly. "Kabul has sent word to all our brothers. Through a coordinated effort we can defeat the Zionists."

A surge of hope went through Hamad. Assad meant to replace Arafat who he loathed with his man, Hamad Taleb.

Assad looked pained as if he had read Hamad's mind. "That is why you will meet with the Chairman of the PLO and persuade him to join us. A delicate mission to be sure, but essential. If you can persuade the Chairman to join us, our success is assured."

Anger pulsed through Hamad. Was this some sort of punishment?

"Don't make me soil myself by going to him. The PLO sold our birthright for American money so their Chairman could shake hands on television with the American President and the Israeli Prime Minister," said Hamad. "He is not a man—a man fights until he is victorious or dead."

Assad sucked on an olive. "Do you know why I selected you?"

A boy swimming in the river hung onto a cross beam on the nearest *noria*. It lifted him 15 meters into the air before he leaped and cannonballed back into the river.

Hamad looked at the dregs in his empty cup and saw an inauspicious future.

"To be truthful, there are others I would have sent before you," said Assad. "However, you were the Chairman's choice. It seems you are the only one of my associates he trusts." Assad's eyes remained fixed on Hamad.

So be it. Could there be any question of refusing Hafez al-Assad?

"If that is your wish Mr. President, I will go," said Hamad quietly.

"I know you will not disappoint me, Hamad Taleb," said the President. He indicated with a curt nod that the meeting was over. "You will visit me on your return."

Ayoub Khan gently nudged his cousin. "We leave now."

But Hamad didn't hear him. The boy who had been cannonballing off the *noria* had wedged himself within the angles of its framework. He went round and round, with one dip per revolution as Hamad watched the great wheel turn.

Fifty-One

At Al-Ladhiqiyah on the Mediterranean, Ayoub put Hamad on board a white two-masted schooner, the *Jeanne-Marie*. High on a yard arm above her spotless teak deck floated the red, white and blue French tricolor.

"If you succeed, the President will be very pleased with you," said Ayoub holding his cousin at arm's length. "He directed me to place three Syrian Commandos at your disposal. They are already on board."

"Otherwise, I'm expendable?" said Hamad.

"You'll find marriage and fatherhood have made Arafat softer," said Ayoub. "Just play him off against his own men, cousin."

He gave Hamad a farewell hug, and Hamad felt his misgivings evaporate.

Captain Argent, a heavy set man in his fifties in white ducks and black mesh singlet, showed Hamad around the *Jean Marie*. Argent ran a charter service out of Rhodes for foreign tourists. He told Hamad that outside of three men who had come on board earlier, there were no other passengers. The *Jeanne-Marie* was 30 meters long and had a great cabin aft paneled in mahogany with a turquoise carpet and comfortable dark blue leather cushions on long bench seats. The sun shone through curtained portholes which added a touch of gay light to a sober masculine room. The long center table cluttered with papers and charts. Captain Argent proudly opened lockers containing fishing gear, spear guns and an array of scuba diving gear. He took Hamad forward through a narrow passageway that provided access to a communal bathroom and five small passenger cabins. He assigned the fourth cabin to Hamad.

"Besides the three men who boarded earlier, you are the only passenger," the captain told Hamad. "How curious."

Hamad said nothing.

"Pity to take a vacation without a woman," said Captain Argent.

"This is a business trip," said Hamad.

The Captain asked no more questions after that.

After supper the Turkish crew hoisted the jib sails and the *Jeanne-Marie* slipped out of the harbor on a gentle evening breeze bound for Rhodes. A day out from Al-Ladhiqiyah, the Jean Marie turned due south toward Egypt.

* * *

In pre-dawn darkness, as the *Jeanne-Marie* cruised off Gaza in international waters, Hamad and the three Syrian commandos landed on the beach in a black rubber Zodiac powered by an outboard motor.

A flash light pointed directly in his face and strong hands gripped his shoulder.

"Welcome to Gaza, we've been expecting you," said a gruff voice in guttural Arabic.

Four leather-tough officers of the Palestinian Authority's National Security Forces hustled Hamad out of the rubber boat. They wore green berets and khaki uniforms and smelled of *arak*, apple tobacco and gun oil. Staggering in knee deep surf toward shore, Hamad heard the muffled whine of the Zodiac's motor behind him. He turned to see the commandos racing back toward the distant lights of the *Jeanne-Marie*.

Hamad watched the Zodiac disappear in the waves.

"Don't worry. Your friends will return for you," said the Palestinian officer at his arm.

"Take your hands off me," Hamad said and tried to jerk himself free from his captor.

A second officer, an older man, patted Hamad down for weapons, then handcuffed Hamad to his own wrist. The old officer's smile revealed a mouth full of bad teeth.

The sky had turned the faint rose-grey of dawn. The once beautiful beach Hamad remembered from his youth was awash with hunks of concrete, scraps of wood, shards of glass mixed with bottles and plastic cups, trash bags, bread husks and chicken bones and cobs from roasted ears of corn sold by street vendors. Twisted metal skeletons of washing machines and cars protruded from the piles of rubble. The two Palestinian officers propelled Hamad past the bloated carcass of a donkey and into a big new camouflage-green Chevrolet Blazer that waited on a narrow road. In the back seat of the Blazer, a nurse wearing a white *abaya* and the arm band of the Red Crescent Society, Islam's equivalent of the Red Cross, examined Hamad briefly. She checked his blood pressure, listened to his heart with a stethoscope, and peered in each eye with a tiny penlight.

"He is well," she murmured to older officer who seemed to be in charge.

"What is this, an interrogation?" said Hamad. No one spoke to him.

The Blazer drove through a warren of dark alleys and twisting trails that were more potholes than pavement. A grimy landscape of sheds and shacks, lean-tos, apartment blocks, concrete refugee shelters and small mud-brick mosques crawled past the Blazer's open windows. Men, women and children, countless numbers of children, choked the streets on their way to work in Gaza's sweat shops and factories. At the intersection of two nameless alleys, a geyser of yellow-brown sewer water streamed through a hole in the pavement. The older officer caught Hamad's look of disgust.

"The Eternal Fountain," he said. "We'd be lost without it."

The mob eddied around the geyser slowly, and the Blazer stopped moving. Hamad counted a score or more of Palestinian policeman directing traffic who shouted, screamed and waved their hands in motions variously commanding and imploring. The police had no more effect on the people than Hamad's swats at the large black flies that alighted on his arm. How Gaza stank of foul water, decaying garbage, donkey manure and unwashed human beings, mainly of human beings. He looked in embarrassment at his companions who sat unperturbed in their comfortable seats watching the sights of human misery unfold. He turned to the man he was handcuffed to, the officer with the bad teeth. "What happened to all the money the West pledged?" he said.

"They insult us demanding we account for every penny, so we refuse to accept it," the man replied.

"Surely Palestinian Americans give freely without strings?"

The driver, a younger officer said over his shoulder, "We can't spend their money because the Jews won't let us import building materials."

The Blazer pulled into a parking lot beside a former Israeli government building and they all got out. At the entrance a reedy boy and an old man in vaguely matching uniforms sat in the dirt drinking tea. Amiably they waved at the older officer who led Hamad inside. High on each door post was a bare spot in the paint where the Israelis had pried off their *mezuzahs*. Hamad tried to peer in each doorway they passed by on a wide hallway. Tables, desks, chairs, filing cabinets, electrical and plumbing fixtures, wiring, even iron pipes were all gone.

"No furnishings?" said Hamad.

"Our newest friends, the Israelis, stripped the place clean," the officer said.

He led Hamad through an open doorway into a small room filled with more uniformed men, and shoved him into a small metal folding chair. As Hamad looked up at the long table covered with masonite, he realized he had intentionally been given a chair meant for a child.

The haggard face, rubbery lips and scruffy 3-day beard of his former leader, Yasser Arafat, Chairman of the PLO, looked down at Hamad from a fan of tiny black, white, green and red Palestinian flags. Arafat wore his trademark checkered *kaffiyeh* and army green brush jacket. Positioned on either side of him were various aides. The fat generals and the slim boy gunsels of the Fatah Hawks lolled in chairs behind Hamad, their AK-47 automatic rifles propped against the walls.

Hamad sprang to his feet determined to show these sons of pigs and monkeys he was no coward. His raspy tenor deepened as he began to speak.

"I bring greetings from the President of Syria," he said.

The Chairman's hand fluttered contemptuously.

"An emissary from our friend Hafez al-Assad is most welcome," he said. He motioned to the officer standing next to Hamad that he could remove the handcuffs. Then he shook his head sorrowfully.

"Hamad, my brother, why have you have failed me?"

Hamad was ready for this ploy but it irritated him. He had hoped Arafat would be in one of his blood-struggle-and-victory moods, small eyes flashing, calling for Arabs to unite.

"Mr. President, I am here to discuss an important proposal," he said. Arafat preferred to be called 'Mr. President'. Chairman of the Palestine Authority, was the hated title the Jews had twisted his arm into accepting.

Arafat beamed. "Tell us about this proposal from the President of Syria."

"The Jews are preparing for civil war," said Hamad.

Arafat only shrugged. "Hardly an original idea."

"Word of it comes from an impeccable source."

"I've heard this all before," said Arafat. "European and Russian Jews despise other Jews from Algeria and Morocco, who in turn look down on those from Yemen and Ethiopia. And the *sabras* feel superior to everybody. President Assad sent you here to tell me something I already know?"

"Syria wishes to help free the people of Palestine from the shackles of injustice," said Hamad.

Arafat growled "Allah be praised! The last time we had Assad's help, he chased us out of Beirut, all the way to Tunis."

Derisive chuckles came from the men behind Hamad. Many of the older ones were veterans of the Lebanon War.

Hamad said in a loud voice, "The state of Palestine must be born on the land of Palestine, not in Lebanon, not in Tunis, not here, but in Jerusalem!"

Scattered cheers broke out and Hamad felt momentarily elated.

Arafat quickly raised his hand. When the men had quieted down he said, "I make the speeches here. Just tell me what Assad wants."

"President Assad wishes to join with you in a *Jihad*, when the Jews start fighting each other," said Hamad. "I am instructed to request you should not tell your new friend the Prime Minister of Israel about his little problem."

The room was very quiet. All eyes were on Arafat.

"Do you think I am like a child and deeply unaware?" he said scornfully. "This report from Kabul may be true, but then again it may not be. However, in the meanwhile, why should I bother the Prime Minister with mere gossip?"

Good, thought Hamad. The shipment of arms would be allowed to reach its destination. The settlers would have their arsenal. Civil war would spit Israel like a rotten melon.

"Then you will join with us as well?" said Hamad.

A crafty expression settled over Arafat's face. "I will do whatever is in the best interest of the Palestinian people."

"When will you decide?" said Hamad.

"When the time comes," said Arafat with smile. "Be patient."

"This is no time for patience," he cried. "This is the time to strike. The Jews will never give us a state. Force is the only thing they can understand."

The Chairman's shook his head. "Peace has given us the beginnings of our state. Fighting only gives the Zionists an excuse to grab more land."

"Do you really think they will give you anything?" said Hamad contemptuously.

"The Americans will force them to grant it," said Arafat. "In a few years there will be more Palestinians than Jews in this land. Kindly remember that Nelson Mandella is now the President of South Africa. If the Jews don't give us our own state we'll demand full Israeli citizenship and fornicate our way to victory at the voting box."

Arafat stood up, the signal that the meeting was over.

The officer behind Hamad stepped forward and handcuffed him again, this time fastening both his hands behind his back. Hamad was hustled downstairs to the basement and thrown into a windowless cell only half a meter in width. Lying face down on a dusty concrete floor, he realized he was in a former Shin Bet detention cell.

"We'll turn you over to your Syrian keepers at dusk," growled the older officer as he slammed the door shut. "You will not have a chance to spread Assad's poison to your Hamas brotheren."

Better to have stayed in my father's rope business and not become a politician, Hamad thought as the sound of the officer's footsteps receded into the pitch blackness. Better not to have sought glory.

The report of his meeting would not please Assad. Maybe he could convince Assad's goons to put him ashore in Lebanon. Otherwise he'd have to count on deceiving Ayoub Khan and hope his cousin had no sources inside the PLO to report Hamad's failure.

* * *

Ayoub Khan leaned against side of his Land rover and played with a tooth pick as the *Jean Marie* docked at Al-Ladhiqiyah. A few meters away, a band played loudly while a pale blue French liner, her rails lined with tourists, backed slowly into the adjacent berth. He eyed the noisy crowd of street vendors waiting for the tourists with their push carts filled with fruit, postcards and cheap knickknacks. Ayoub Khan would have preferred the privacy of a broken down wharf on the far side of the harbor, but he knew the sight of the luxury schooner tying up at such a humble place would have attracted unwanted attention.

Hamad came up the schooner's gangplank, sweating and obviously edgy. The three Syrian commandos followed wearing casual jeans and sports shirts.

They exchanged hugs. "Well, did Arafat agree?" said Ayoub Khan.

"He was most agreeable to our plans," said Hamad.

"You're quite sure?" Ayoub Khan's eyes were on Hamad's face.

"Yes, I swear it. Arafat agreed to everything."

"The President will kill us both for lying to him if you are mistaken." Ayoub Khan's laugh was genial to show he was only joking but his eyes were cold.

Hamad wiped his face on his sleeve. "Arafat will join us once the Jews start fighting each other."

"This is good news indeed," said Ayoub Khan with relief. "Let us tell the President."

At that moment the leader of the commandos, a soft spoken soldier named Husam stepped forward, and whispered in Ayoub Khan's ear.

Ayoub Khan turned to Hamad. "You asked twice to be put ashore in Lebanon?" he said.

Hamad turned deathly pale.

The band struck up the *Marseilles* for the benefit of the French tourists and the crowd on the dock burst into cheers.

Ayoub Khan gave Hamad a stern look.

"You have lied to me, cousin. I gave you valuable information and you have wasted it. The President does not employ failures."

"No, I swear by Allah I'm telling the truth."

"Hamad, if you're lying to me, I will do what must be done."

Hamad pulled himself together. "You have nothing to fear, Ayoub," he said bravely. "I'll tell the President myself." He opened the Land rover's door and took the passenger's seat. Husam slipped in behind Hamad in the rear seat.

Ayoub Khan now behind the wheel, did not look at his cousin. "You have dishonored our family but we will be merciful."

He removed a handkerchief from his uniform blouse, folded it into a square and placed it on his shoulder while Hamad looked on in wonder. Then he motioned to Husam who drew a small 22 caliber Beretta.

Husam killed Hamad quickly with one bullet, just behind the right ear. The slug made a moist rattling sound as it bounced around inside Hamad's skull and he slumped sideways with his head resting on the handkerchief. A trickle of urine ran down the side of his seat to collect in a puddle on the floor.

"Take him back to his people, Husam," said Ayoub Khan quietly. "Let it be said that Hamad Taleb was a martyr, murdered by the Mossad."

Fifty-Two

The first drops began to hammer on her wooden deck like hailstones. At 3 o'clock in the morning on the Indian Ocean in monsoon season the rain squall swept over the *Shadow of the Prophet*, as she beat through the heavy chop that had set in from the southwest. She was a big sea-going dhow, 80 tons, with a short raked mast near the bow, a cargo hold amidships, and a pilothouse, engine room, galley and crews quarters aft. Her huge lateen sail was furled, and its boom lashed down on the deck. Four truck loads of weapons packed in army green crates in the hold made her ride low in the water. The crates contained 35 MM mortars packed in Cosmoline and 500 mortar shells, 75 TOW anti-tank rockets, ten Stinger missiles, 100 Russian rocket-propelled grenades, and thousands of American anti-tank mines.

There was enough weaponry to defend B'nai Ha'eretz from a entire German Panzer division, thought Avi uneasily. He crouched by the pilothouse holding one hand over his mouth. Why, they could hold off the Army itself. Did Uncle Shlomo really need to get this stuff this way? Was he planning more than defense against the Arabs? Avi wished he'd kept a closer eye on Rabbi Ben Yusuf and the men who surrounded him. He hunched his shoulders against the wave that swept over the deck.

If he'd had any excuse he'd throw the whole rotten boatload into the sea.

Damp salt spray stung his eyes. Avi was no sailor. Food smells from the galley combined with diesel fumes from the booming exhaust stack nauseated him, and the swaying movements of the *Prophet* as it paused in the trough between waves were sickening. He watched for an opportunity to go below, when a wave wasn't showering the deck with spray. When his chance came, he lifted the hatch, stepped over the boarded up companionway, and ducked inside.

The Somali helmsman looked around at Avi impassively before returning to his task.

Avi stood under the closed hatch, and waited for his eyes to adjust. In the dim shifting light cast up by the ship's illuminated compass, the turbaned helmsman resembled a genie from an Arabian fairy tale. Behind him, Avi could make out the man Uncle Shlomo had sent him to meet in Karachi, Ya'akov Kallenborg, who slouched on a wooden bench. He had met Kallenborg once before at B'nai Ha'eretz when Shlomo had asked him to help make up the list of weapons, and his impression of Kallenborg had not been favorable.

Over the ponderous beat of the one cylinder engine came Kallenborg's cutting voice in bad Yiddish.

"What's the matter, Avi?"

"Can't sleep," he said.

"How are Golani and Arbel?" said Kallenborg.

"In their bunks, hugging buckets. Puking their guts out."

Kallenborg laughed. "Arbel, sick? He's the only deep water sailor in this outfit."

Avi looked around warily at the helmsman. Kallenborg was the one who insisted they converse in Yiddish since they were supposed to be passing as Bosnian gunrunners. Avi thought this was idiotic although the Arab crew seemed to ignore their conversations.

A match flared suddenly.

"Have a smoke," said Kallenborg, and offered a cigarette to Avi.

Avi searched his pockets for his own cigarettes. He sat down on the wooden bench with Kallenborg.

"Still pissed?", said Avi in a conciliatory voice.

"What do you think?", said Kallenborg. "Three weeks in hell with that drunken Russian Colonel, and his stinking savages. I had to pack the weapons out of Afghanistan on trails, no wider than your foot. We got in a shootout with bandits. Once we got to Peshawar, and hired the trucks, I thought we could relax but that was only the beginning of our troubles. We ran out of gas on the Grand Trunk Road around Mardan. At Quetta we were surrounded by a mob of religious fanatics. They would have pushed our trucks over, except that Derevenko convinced them we were transporting dead plague victims. Two trucks broke down half way through the Swat Valley and we got stuck in some verminous hole of a village until spares arrived. On the back of an elephant, yet! At which point our drivers decided they hadn't been paid enough so Derevenko had to shoot one as an example. I could go on, but I'm sure it would bore you."

"Take it easy," said Avi. "Uncle Shlomo knows you did an outstanding job."

"I thought Shlomo sent you to Karachi to bring me the rest of the money, not take over my operation. I'm tired of stopping Arabs for ID checks, chasing curfew breakers down narrow alleys, squeezing confessions out of them while young punks with nothing but family connections get the opportunities. I'm 45 years old. My father was a fucking legend at 45."

"So who was your father?" said Avi.

"'Iron Felix' Kallenborg, Marshall and three times Hero of the Soviet Union," said Kallenborg with bitter pride. "You may have heard of him.

"Amazing," said Avi who had not. He tried not to smile. "Hey, Shlomo's the boss. "These are his orders, and I didn't want to be here either. My wife Miriam is pregnant. I should be with her now, not stuck out in the middle of the ocean." He extracted a dog-eared snapshot from his wallet and gazed at it hungrily. "A face like an angel."

"Without that kerchief she wouldn't look bad," said Kallenborg with a faint sneer.

"She's the finest woman in the world," Avi said quietly.

The helmsman grunted as the *Prophet's* wheel kicked, and the spokes slapped through his palms before he brought it under control.

"Storm's getting worse," said Kallenborg pointing through the spray smeared glass of the pilothouse.

The rain had stopped but the wind was increasing. Holes appeared in the clouds through which the full moon shown intermittently. The *Prophet* bucked and plunged over powerful waves the size of houses. Every second or third wave broke clear over her bow.

Whining, self-pitying bastard, thought Avi.

"It's not a matter of family connections, Kallenborg. You don't have the language skills to carry off an operation. They wouldn't have given you shit in Kabul. That Russian, Derevenko, fronted for you while you were on the road, remember? You couldn't have chartered this *dhow*, or fixed things with Pakistani customs officials to get the weapons out by yourself."

"All you did was grease some palms," said Kallenborg.

"It takes more than grease," said Avi. "Back when we unloaded the trucks at the dock, the customs agents got suspicious once they saw us lugging so many crates with rope handles on board."

"They believed my story about smuggling arms to our Muslim brothers in Bosnia," said Kallenborg.

"What rubbish!"

Kallenborg shrugged. "There are over 2,000 Afghan soldiers in Bosnia. Around here Muslims consider the war in Bosnia to be part of the Holy Struggle. Does the Captain know our destination is Eilat?" He gave Avi a twisted smile.

"He thinks he's headed for al-Aqabah," Avi said.

"We'll shoot the crew when we approach al-Aqabah," said Kallenborg.

The man was a psychopath, thought Avi.

"It won't be necessary to shoot anyone," he said. "For a little more *baksheesh*, they'll go to Eilat willingly."

Kallenborg raised his eyebrows.

The pilothouse hatch opened and the Captain joined them. He was a large man in a loose khaki shirt, and a dingy officer's cap. He greeted Avi and Kallenborg courteously in a deep bass voice. Proudly, he produced from his shirt pocket what looked like a pocket calculator but was in fact a global positioning system or GPS, a miniature radio receiver that determined its user's precise longitude and latitude from signals emitted by satellites in the sky. Developed by the Americans, these devices flooded the *souks* of the Middle East after the Gulf War. When the Captain tapped on a keypad and a tiny orange screen glowed. He studied the tiny screen thoughtfully. Then he rapped the old brass barometer on the wall. "Head another two degrees west and watch out for shipping," he told the helmsman. "They won't see us."

"Where are we?" said Avi.

"Entering the Red Sea," said the Captain.

Avi turned to Kallenborg. "We're almost half-way home," he said. I'll be with Miriam in another week."

"How did you learn Arabic so well?" said Kallenborg.

Kallenborg might have intended sarcasm, thought Avi but he could not keep envy out of his voice.

"I was a Syrian POW," said Avi.

* * *

The ocean raged at dawn. A subtle brightening of the thick lead-colored clouds was the only indication of daybreak. Two sailors worked the hand-operated bilge pump on deck as if their lives depended on it. Mile-long giant green combers swept straight up at them from the southwest.

"The waves are too rough for the size of the load she's carrying. This tub is leaking like a sieve," said Avi.

"You exaggerate," said Kallenborg. "The ship's not overloaded."

"Son of a whore!", screamed the helmsman.

A wall of white rose steeply and hung over them. The *Prophet* poked her nose into the smoking mountain of foam. Kallenborg put his hand on a beam to brace himself. The *Prophet* groaned in every seam as tons of water engulfed her. A foaming wash creamed against the pilothouse glass. Then slowly she emerged. Water streamed off the windlass in the bow, the cargo hatch cover, and gunwales, and ran out the scuppers into the sea.

"Another wave like that and we all die," the Captain told Avi. "We must heave to and lighten the load."

"None of it goes, do you hear me!" Kallenborg shouted. "None of it!"

"It's my ship," the Captain roared back. "Too much cargo in her hold. Lighten the load!"

Avi's face tightened. "Something has to go." he said.

"Yes, the big man said. "Those big boxes on the top and quickly."

Avi nodded. At least some of the cargo would have to go. He would never see Miriam again if the ship floundered and sank. He listened as the orders were given in Arabic to alter course. Bells jangled from the engine telegraph and the beat of the engine slowed. The bow angled away from the crests of the waves instead of heading into them.

Kallenborg seized Avi by his shirt collar.

"We can't throw the weapons away! What are you going to tell your precious Uncle Shlomo?"

Avi tore himself away and stumbled out on deck into the wind and spray. He helped the Captain and the crew winch open the hatch to the cargo hold.

Kallenborg refused to help. Instead he leaned against the side of the pilothouse. Avi felt the Russian's eyes burning at him.

A lean sailor with a wispy beard struggled to push a crate of anti-tank mines up to the Captain, who braced against the wind and shouted to a brawny seaman with an ear slit deeply from a knife fight. The three of them formed a human chain. When the wind blew the Captain's loose khaki shirt up, Avi noticed his rust streaked 9mm Tokagypt. Kallenborg's eyes were riveted on the old pistol.

Forward, at the bilge pump two sailors labored wearily at the pump handles. Immense waves rolled in endless succession from the horizon, tossing the *dhow* in dizzy arcs as they passed under its keel. In the hold Avi and the sailor pushed another crate up to the men on deck. A wave swept the deck and doused the struggling men with sea water. Avi fumbled as he tried to grip the wet crate with his mutilated hand. Down in the pilothouse, the helmsman struggled to keep the vessel under control. The engineer stuck his grizzled head out of the engine room door to see what was going on. Another crate went over the side.

Kallenborg lunged for the Captain.

"Stop you fool," Avi yelled. He relaxed his grip on the crate he was lifting and started to climb out of the hold.

The Captain reeled, let out an grunt of surprise and staggered forward. Kallenborg stumbled backward and fell to the deck. He seized the Captain's foot with both hands and twisted it hard. Howling in pain and rage, the Captain dropped the gun and fell to the narrow deck. Avi managed to get his head and shoulders over the lip of the hold and lunged for the gun which lay next to Kallenborg but Kallenborg's hand closed on the Tokagypt first. Avi and the Captain lay sprawled on the deck, momentarily dazed. Then they scrambled to their feet. The slit-eared sailor circled the hold to Kallenborg's left. Something in the Captain's hand gleamed in the early morning light. A knife blade flicked toward Kallenborg's face and drew a scarlet line down his cheek. He shot the Captain in the chest, squeezing off three rounds in quick succession from the Tokagypt. The Captain jerked as each bullet thudded into his body. His cap fell off as he slumped to the deck and was whipped away by the wind.

From the side, the slit-eared sailor jumped Kallenborg, knocking the Tokagypt out of his hand. The pistol tumbled into the hold where Avi and the thin sailor fought for possession of it.

The two men struggled. Avi could hear the man's breathing, and smell him. He was six inches taller than Avi, muscular and at least 40 pounds heavier. Avi clawed at the sailor's eyes and kicked hard at his shin, hoping to break the bone. The sailor twisted and dodged. Suddenly Avi broke free and threw a vicious low punch to the sailor's belly. He gasped, blinked his eyes but kept on coming. Avi struck again, this time aiming for the bridge of his nose. The sailor side-stepped and Avi's fist hit nothing but air and he fell among the slippery crates. When he got to knees the sailor was holding the gun.

"Kallenborg!", screamed Avi.

The muffled crack of a pistol cut through the roar of the waves.

Gasping for breath, Kallenborg backed slowly away from the slit-eared sailor who advanced toward him with the Captain's knife. He glanced over his shoulder and saw the sailor with the wispy beard clamber over the lip of the hold. He was holding the Tokagypt.

"Oh shit!", said Kallenborg.

He turned and ran blindly toward the stern. Just past the engine room door he tripped over a capstan and fell headlong to the deck. A shot rang out. The top of the gunwale next to Kallenborg's head exploded in a shower of splinters. Desperate, Kallenborg squeezed between the capstan and the gunwale but there was very little cover. He peered around the capstan. How many bullets were left, he wondered? One or two at most. The two Arab sailors slowly advanced on the pitching deck. If he could dodge them, he could stay alive a little longer.

Abruptly, the gloating looks faded on the sailors faces. An ear-splitting burst of machine gun fire erupted behind Kallenborg. The two sailors jerked and screamed. Their limbs flailed in a grotesque dance as streams of bullets ripped into their clothes leaving bright red stains. When the firing stopped they lay still in pools of blood mixed with sea water.

Kallenborg felt weak and light headed.

He lifted himself on one elbow. Beside him Golani and Arbel were crouched on the deck holding Uzis. They didn't look too steady either.

"What happened?" said Golani in his ear.

"Fucking Arabs jumped us," Kallenborg said. "The Captain ordered his men to throw the weapons overboard to lighten the ship. Avi tried to stop them but they shot him."

"My God!" said Arbel. "Where is he?"

"In the hold, but look out. There are more Arabs."

"How many are there?", said Golani.

"Four," said Kallenborg. "Two forward by the pumps, one in the pilothouse, and one in the engine room."

The two sailors manning the pumps had flattened once the firing started. Now as Golani and Arbel approached with Uzis ready they groveled on the deck and begged for their lives to be spared. Kallenborg followed. He shouted to the sailors to get back on the pumps and bent down to pick up the Tokagypt. Something else on the deck caught his eye, a small army green plastic rectangle. The Captain's GPS. Kallenborg stuffed it in his pocket.

A big wave smashed into the *Prophet*, rolling her over on her beam, out of control. The gunwale and deck dipped under a wave and the hatch cover started to float away. Only the foot-high lip of the hold kept her from filling with water. Clutching the pistol with one hand, Kallenborg hung onto the backstay rigging with the other, and peered at the pilothouse. In a moment the turban of the helmsman poked up from behind the wheel. Slowly the bow came around. The *Prophet* righted herself and began to ride the waves again.

Kallenborg joined Golani and Arbel who stared down in the hold at Avi. There lay Avi in a dark pool of blood, bone fragments and brains. The back of his head was missing, blown completely away. Golani began to retch quietly.

Kallenborg was filled with a wild joy.

"I'll take the pilothouse," he shouted. "Golani, you cover the Arabs at the pumps. Arbel, seize the engine room."

Arbel hesitated.

"Snap out of it!", yelled Kallenborg. He rushed the pilothouse, threw up the hatch and pointed his pistol at the helmsman. The Somali helmsman looked back at him without fear.

"Get back on course," snapped Kallenborg in his rough Arabic. "If you leave your post again, I'll shoot you like a dog!"

After a moment the helmsman turned and coolly rang the engine room telegraph. Kallenborg crouched in the open hatch. The engine's beat picked up. He breathed a sigh of relief. The engineer must be cooperating with Arbel. The fight was over but they had still not won the battle with the sea.

He stood on the pilothouse roof and addressed Golani. "Get that hatch on the cargo hold again," he shouted. "Be sure the tarp is securely tied down."

"Where do we put Avi?"

"Throw his body over the side. Throw all of the dead Arabs over the side too."

Golani didn't move. "Who put you in charge?", he said.

Kallenborg glared down at him from the pilothouse. "Avi's dead," he screamed. "I'm in command!"

"No you're not," Golani yelled back.

"What do you suggest? Call Shlomo on the radio? We're about to be swamped."

"Kallenborg!"

Arbel's firm voice coming from behind startled him. Kallenborg turned sharply catching his breath.

"We'll all be in charge," said Arbel.

Kallenborg found himself between Golani and Arbel, both of whom were armed with Uzis. He had a rusty old pistol and one bullet left. Outflanked and outgunned, again.

Kallenborg smiled weakly. "We'll be swimming back to Israel if we don't get the cargo hold covered," he said.

"We'll do it," said Arbel. "But we're taking Avi back to be buried in Israel." He climbed down in the hold and lifted Avi's body tenderly in his arms. His eyes were filled with tears. Then Golani, who was crying too, helped him find a piece of canvas to wrap the body in. They emptied one of the weapons crates and placed Avi in it. Arbel searched the Arab sailors for weapons and ordered them to secure the hold. They threw the bodies of the rest of the dead overboard.

Golani and Arbel were a bunch of weak sisters, thought Kallenborg. What did they expect? This was war. Avi was just another soldier who got killed in action.

Fifty-Three

Hopes ran high in Ramallah. The August air was charged with rumors. Foremost was that Israel would agree to withdraw from the town and the neighboring town of El Bireh by Christmas. If this was true, it meant that the Palestinian Authority would govern wide areas of the West Bank, ending 28 years of Israeli occupation.

Christina did not believe the rumors. Construction of new Jewish neighborhoods by the Israeli Ministry of Housing in East Jerusalem continued unabated. Palestinian applications for building permits were repeatedly denied. Demonstrations by Jewish settlers in the surrounding hills were now frequent despite violent confrontations with Israeli police. Some settlers near Hebron, tried to establish new settlements on stony hilltops, moving mobile homes in which to live. "Facts on the ground," the settlers called them. It was a tense and troubled time.

Disheveled hair touching her cheeks, Christina bent over her desk and tried to compose a letter to Richard.

"When I received your telegram that you and the children are still well I was overjoyed," he had written. "I pray daily for your safety and dream of your joining me. The deceitful Zionists are thieves and can never be trusted. My friends at the State Department are ready to help. The air of Virginia has cleared my head. If your letters stop I shall talk to the Press. The Jews can lie all they want. The U.S. is beginning to see the light."

She glanced at Asher who sat on the divan with Muna, a chess board between them. The wound to his ankle was worse than he would admit. Rock splinters from the settler's bullets two days before had nicked the tendons of his heel, forcing him to walk with a cane. He'd refused to see a doctor but he did let Najat, a nurse, clean and bind up the wound. He seemed to be enjoying himself despite the snide remarks Aminah made about his game. Her older daughter was curled up in an arm chair with a book, and wore Richard's supercilious pout. The expression on Richard's face that said 'I'm right and you don't know what you are talking about.' Once she had loved him for his clear-sightedness, his refusal to romanticize failure or folly. He was still right. She no longer loved him but she needed him. For the children's sake she needed him. For their sake she'd will herself back to loving Richard. In America, though, not here.

It was as if Chaim and Richard existed in two separate worlds. How could she love them both? One man was her cavalier, her companion and guardian in the most dangerous adventure of her life. The other Richard, the father of her children, was a memory and a sadness, a duty and an honor. The old image of escape flashed into her mind. But even if her letter to Richard did get past the censors who read her mail, would he be able to help them in time?

Muna moved her knight and threw Asher a challenging look. She shared the same rich brown eyes and delicate olive complexion of her mother as well as the same thoughtful expression when confronting an opponent.

He started to move his bishop.

"You're in check, Mr. Asher," said Muna.

"So I am! I didn't see your rook behind the knight."

"Now I take your bishop!," she said.

Asher emitted a soft groan, and Christina's eyes met Aminah's.

"Aminah says you're our jailor, Mr. Asher," said Muna.

"Do you think I'm your jailor, Muna?" he said.

"You're a cowboy," she giggled. "Like the ones on television."

"I have no horse, nor hat. So tell me, Muna, what makes me a cowboy?" said Asher with a ghost of a smile.

"You have a holster and a gun," she said.

Christina noticed Asher's jacket had fallen open, exposing a pistol in a shoulder holster. After he buttoned his jacket he studied the board. Muna moved her rook.

"Now your king is trapped, Mr. Asher!"

Asher studied the board. "Checkmate," he said finally. "You win."

320

He looked up at Christina. "I taught my son, David, to play chess when he was younger than your daughter. I haven't played in a long time."

He was a father with no son.

Christina flashed a severe look at her younger daughter.

"Muna, I need to remind you again that Mr. Asher is our secret," she said. "If anyone finds out, we will be in great danger." She shifted her gaze to Asher. "Is it really necessary to carry that weapon in my house, Mr. Asher? It upsets my daughters."

He considered her request. "I suppose it's not necessary here. Actually, I loathe firearms."

"Don't you carry one in your home?"

Asher laughed. "You must think every Israeli is armed to the teeth?"

"But you are armed," said Christina, sharply. "Every one of you in Jerusalem and Tel Aviv carries a pistol in his pocket."

"Not everyone," said Asher. His eyes were distant. "And Israel wasn't always like that."

"In that case, I wish we could turn the clock back," she said. She wanted to say turn the clock back 30 years when Palestine was not occupied by Israel. "There were shortages then, the stores were empty. Why, where I grew up in Jerusalem, we saved even scraps of tin foil and pieces of string. But—"

"I too would like to return to the old Israel," he said. "Because then those mad men from Brooklyn who insist on living in your land wouldn't be here."

How dear Naomi Litvin had tried to convince her that many Israelis did not support the settlers, but Christina knew better. Scratch any Jew, even slightly, and one would find an ardent Zionist. Asher was not being candid with her. He simply telling her what he thought she'd want to hear.

"The settlers are the logical result of the Zionism, she said. "Your whole philosophy is nothing more than an invitation for them to come here."

The muscle along Asher's jaw line twitched.

"The religious Zionists are the ones standing in the way of peace. Here, let me put this pistol away," he said.

With an aching heart, she watched him limp up the stairs to his room and sighed. How hopeless it was to think that picking a fight with

Asher over politics could ever erase the memory of his lifting her up in his arms and carrying her into her office. Christina blushed and looked down at her younger daughter who stood at her elbow, forgotten.

"Muna darling, why aren't you wearing the little gold ear loops your father sent you last week?"

"Aminah borrowed them. She takes everything of mine!" Muna cried. "I can't find them anywhere."

"Then, don't loan her your things," said Christina.

"But I didn't! She goes into my room, and takes things without asking, and never gives anything back."

"Aminah?" said Christina.

"I don't know where they are," said Aminah in sullen tones.

"You must ask your sister first before you borrow her things. And you must always return them. Now, both of you go look for Muna's ear-loops."

Asher entered the room just as the girls left. He looked at them with an expression of vague disapproval.

"Please excuse my daughters' foolish behavior," Christina said. "Confining them to the house makes them irritable. During the day they're safe at school. But I can't let them out on the street after school, not with this business going on."

"They want to see their friends?" he said.

She was heartened momentarily.

"Would it be out of the question for each girl to invite a friend over?" she said.

Asher appeared to think it over, but then he shook his head. "I'm afraid so."

Christina sighed and looked away. "Will that awful Gilda woman be coming here?" she said.

He gave her a sidelong glance.

"In fact, she will be here tonight."

"Must you meet with her in my home? Wouldn't it be safer somewhere else?"

"I have to stay where you are."

"How can you protect us and find these guns at the same time?"

"That's my job, Mrs. Goryeb," he said.

The bell rang outside on the gate in front of the house. Fahoum, shuffled out to open the iron gate.

"At least I haven't been completely taken by surprise. I suppose that is your associate," she said.

When Fahoum returned, he announced apologetically that a woman and three men wanted to see Mrs. Goryeb.

"The lady is well-dressed," he said with a tone of respect. "The men look like laborers."

"A contractor seeking Israeli work permits, perhaps?" said Asher.

"Show them in, please," said Christina.

Gilda brushed past Fahoum. The three men with her wore torn jeans and dirty denim jackets. She wore business clothes, an expensive looking dark suit, nylon stockings, and spike-heeled shoes.

"I have an urgent matter to discuss with Mrs. Goryeb," she said in Arabic.

The nightmare had returned again, thought Christina.

"Thank you, Fahoum," said Asher. "You may go now."

The old man ignored him and looked at Christina but she did not respond. She wasn't going to cooperate with Asher's ridiculous charade.

Finally Fahoum said, "I will tell the cook to bring coffee." He disappeared in the direction of the kitchen.

Asher gestured toward the study. "Madame, gentlemen, please come this way," he said. As Gilda and the men walked past them, Asher whispered to Christina, "These are your new clients."

"I will help you fight the Lions," she said, keeping her voice low. "This other business of yours is not my concern."

"If you do not play your part, your servants will suspect something," he said gently. "Please consider the losses for all of us, should we fail."

Gilda and her three men were already seated when Asher entered the study with Christina. The book-lined room was illuminated by a single bulb in a green glass shade. Christina reluctantly took her place at the head of the long oak table in the center of her study. Asher closed the door. The three men regarded her with unfriendly curiosity.

"Why is this Palestinian present?" said the eldest. He was in his early fifties, short with piercing dark eyes that missed nothing and a lined face fixed in a permanent scowl.

"Please, Abdallah Zrake, everything will be explained," said Gilda. "Can we begin?"

"As you wish," he said.

Gilda turned to Asher. "Here's your team. Their loyalty is unquestioned, each has a distinguished service record. Abdallah Zrake, is a surveillance expert, Salim Darazi, has experience with explosives, and Tareq Hakim will handle your communications. We're giving you a fully equipped surveillance van, with all the gear you will need for this mission."

Asher nodded at each man as Gilda spoke his name. "Thank Mekor for me," he said.

"It was my idea to use our Druze *oters*," said Gilda. She looked around the table and caught each man's eye before she continued. "Two of them worked with you before, haven't they?"

"Abdallah and Salim were with me in Lebanon," said Asher.

"Good, then you are familiar with each other," she said. "Our survival depends on this mission. If we fail, Israel will be destroyed by civil war."

"Please spare us the speech," said Asher.

She gave him a dirty look and resumed. "We have information that an Israeli named Ya'akov Kallenborg purchased a large amount of heavy weapons in Afghanistan. He is transporting them to Israel by sea, and we believe he will attempt to land at Eilat. You must destroy those weapons before they reach Kallenborg's clients."

"You want us to blow up a ship in Eilat harbor?" said Salim.

"Yes," said Gilda. "Furthermore, the destruction of Kallenborg's arms must be made to look like an accident."

"So tell me, who are these clients of Kallenborg?" said Zrake.

Gilda paused.

"Israeli settlers," she said.

Zrake's mouth curved a little but he did not smile.

"And who is this Kallenborg?"

"He is working for the settlers," said Gilda. "We cannot tell you more than that."

"Where is his ship?" said Salim. "Can you tell us that?" He was tall and sinewy, a younger man with a short beard.

"We know its name and the date it sailed from Karachi," said Asher, "That's all."

Salim tapped at his tooth with a finger nail. "We could work out its position. Look up the ship's name in a shipping registry and find out its size, speed and so forth."

"According to our information, it is called the *Shadow of the Prophet.* However, Lloyds world-wide listings show nothing by that name," said Gilda.

Salim laughed. "Most likely, she's a fishing boat or a *dhow.*"

Asher looked at Gilda. "What about satellite imaging of small craft in the Red Sea and the Gulf of Aqabah?"

"We've studied many boats but none can we identify as Kallenborg's, she said."

"Have you picked up any radio signals from Kallenborg?" said Tareq Hakim.

"Again, the same problem," said Gilda.

The Druze exchanged doubtful looks.

"It shouldn't be hard," said Gilda. "Eilat is a small harbor surrounded by mountains. Only three roads provide access to it, two from Israel, one from the port of Aqabah across the bay in Jordan. And, the entrance to the harbor can be watched easily from the beach."

As Zrake started to speak he was interrupted by a knock on the door. Fatima entered carrying a pitcher of coffee and a tray of *kanaffi*, a delicious Palestinian treat made of hot cheese and honey. Everyone stopped talking. To break the awkward silence as Fatima served coffee, Gilda told a story about a rabbi and an Arab shepherd.

Christina found the story distasteful, patronizing. Everyone else laughed politely at Gilda's joke except Asher whose disapproving expression seemed to mirror her own thoughts.

"Enough about sheep and rabbis," Zrake said after Fatima left. "Chaim Asher, I want to know more about this Kallenborg."

"Kallenborg is a Shin Bet security officer. His boss, Shlomo Arendt, is heavily involved in the settlement movement," said Asher. "They are running a rogue operation."

"I am not surprised," said Zrake with a sardonic smile. "So be it." He gave Christina a curious look. "Are you sure this Palestinian can be trusted?"

"Mrs. Goryeb has as much to lose here as we do," said Asher.

"When do we leave for Eilat?" said Zrake.

"The sooner the better," said Asher.

* * *

After Gilda and the men left, Christina tried to compose herself, but her eyes filled with tears.

"Why does this trouble you so," said Asher.

"My name and reputation in Palestine were my life, and you've stolen them," she said. "Sooner or later it will come out that I collaborated with you. Then I won't be safe anywhere, not even in America."

"We can protect you in America, too" said Asher.

What a master of deceit he was, she thought bitterly.

"You've turned my home into a police station," she said, "You've used me and my children."

He looked pained, but his manner was casual.

"Christina, I hate this as much as you do. Perhaps more, in fact."

"I don't believe you," she said, "you're too good at this. You enjoy playing with people's lives, you love the excitement and danger."

"I enjoy none of it," he said. "This evening, when I was playing chess with your daughter, I remembered how I taught my son to play when he was about her age. Tonight, I am feeling like a father again. That is what I enjoy, what I enjoyed."

From the direction of the stairs, she could hear the angry voices of her beloved daughters. "These horrible wars are destroying all our children," she said quietly.

The loud voice was Muna's. "I'll scream if you come near me, I will! Get away from me! Don't you dare hit me!"

"Here, take your miserable ear loops, you little traitor," Aminah sneered.

"Traitor! You are calling me a traitor?"

"Yes! Disloyal to Daddy, disloyal to Palestine, plays chess with the Jewish policeman!"

"But I won!" cried Muna.

"You're so stupid. He let you win. He just wants to win you over so you will defect and be a good little Israeli," said Aminah.

"Mother!" cried Muna as she dashed into the study, arms rigid at her sides, fists clenched. "Aminah called me a defector."

"Aminah!" said Christina. "I need to speak to you this instant."

Aminah entered the study, her face pink with rage. "Why do you always blame me, my Mother?"

"This is a difficult time for us all, but you make it far worse by picking on your sister," said Christina. "I need your help."

Aminah's eyes rested on Asher and a malicious light flared in them. "My father wouldn't stand for this one minute." She put her hands on her hips. "If he were here, he would throw you out on your ear." Christina gently laid her finger across Aminah's lips.

"Be quiet, Aminah, before you embarrass yourself further."

Aminah pulled Christina's hand away. "I'm not finished," she said glaring at Asher. Her body quivered with insult. "You are vile."

For a tense moment, there was silence. Asher finished the last of the cold coffee in his cup.

* * *

The dream was vivid with comic danger. She and Asher were shopping in the *souk*. The narrow aisles between the stalls were choked with people who clamored and argued with one another in shrill tones, yet no one seemed to notice they were both completely naked. The stalls were erected against the sides of orange and white Egged busses. As they paused at a stall piled high with purple egg plants and plump red tomatoes, the vegetables changed into miniature faces of Israelis she had known. Naomi's face stared from among the tomatoes, pleading and pensive. The merchant under the awning made a smarmy bow and said in perfect Hebrew, 'Have you brought me my mail?' It was Hamad. A terrible image of an exploding Egged bus flashed before her eyes.

The kitten Anwar woke Christina. He stared at her with his large soulful yellow eyes and pawed her again, his little claws pricking the tender skin of her forearm. Through the open window came the raucous braying of a donkey stabled in a nearby courtyard. The clock on her night table said it was past mid-night.

Anwar padded silently out the door of Christina's bedroom. "I'm no fun so you'll find someone else to play with," she said. She slipped quickly out of bed and put on her robe, intent on catching Anwar before he disturbed anyone else. At the end of the hall she saw a slight movement by the door that led to the stairs to the roof. The kitten scampered through the door and she followed him. It was lovely on the roof with its view of the stars. Many Palestinian families slept on the flat roofs of their houses to escape the hottest summer heat. She found Chaim Asher outside a stone gazebo overgrown by vines. He lay on a sun bleached chaise lounge smoking a cigarette, his head uplifted to the sky. She sat down beside him on the other chaise lounge.

Asher did not seem surprised to see her. The tip of his cigarette glowed in the dark. She moved closer.

A crescent moon which had reached its zenith a week before, floated up from the horizon. The sky built a starry vault pillared with distant clouds over the Samarian hills.

He pointed at the sky. "There are 50 billion galaxies in the universe. Each has a billion stars. Do you suppose that the Creator of the Universe really cares where any of us live?"

He was right, thought Christina. And Richard was right. That was the great tragedy of this land. What folly to sacrifice lives for a piece of land and for being right. She was part of the folly.

"I was responsible for Naomi's death. As surely as I'd killed her with my own hands," Christina whispered. "A package of dynamite was delivered to my office the day before the Gvirol Street bombing. Rasul picked it up."

He listened to her, his face was drawn and pensive. "The choice was the sure death of your children against the chance that the Lions might not use the dynamite effectively. In war there is no moral way, only a choice among horrors," he said.

Christina broke down. The sobs seemed to come from her deepest soul and she was powerless to stop them.

"I love Palestine but everybody is driving me out," she said.

Asher took her tenderly in his arms and she buried her tear streaked face on his shoulder. He held her tightly until the sobs subsided.

She was not prepared for what he said next.

"My people are the most oppressed people in the history of the world. We deserve a place of peace and safety we can call our own. Yet when we get power, we have become the oppressors. The Holocaust never gave us the right to dispossess you," he said softly. "Forgive me, Christina."

As Asher spoke she stepped back astonished. Yes, his dream of Israel had vanished along with her dream of Palestine. He had sacrificed his son and his wife for a handful of dust. She could see all ages in his face, the ardent teenager, the idealistic young adult, the complex, passionate mature man he was, and how he'd be when he was old. Full of hard won wisdom, passionate still, implacable yet tender. She was filled with longing and desire.

For one more night, let me believe that Chaim and I are the only lovers left in this land of the damned. No one need ever know.

He kissed her forehead lightly, and put his arm around her, his right hand rested on her shoulder. She felt the warmth through the thin cloth of her robe. He bent to kiss the soft sensitive flesh of her neck. Then he took her in his arms, laid her gently on the chaise lounge and kissed her roughly on the lips. She felt his hardness against her. His hand pushed aside her thin robe and found her left breast. Her nipples firmed and she raised herself to meet his caresses.

That night she gave herself to him joyfully and without regret.

Fifty-Four

A hot westerly breeze filled the *Prophet's* lateen sail, heeling her over sharply as she plowed through four foot waves. Kallenborg could smell death through the thick cloth smeared with soap that covered his mouth and nose. The stench of Avi's decaying body in the hold was overpowering, even at sunset, when the fierce heat of the Red Sea cooled. Kallenborg leaned on the pilothouse and watched a formation of pelicans soar low over the waves, fishing. His reverie was broken when a SAAR-4 missile boat shot out from between two rocky islands at 50 knots dead ahead of the *Prophet* scattering the pelicans. He could just make out the small blue and white flag with its six pointed Star of David beating at the masthead and the silhouettes of officers on the bridge staring at him through binoculars. It circled the *Prophet* once and disappeared in the direction of Eilat in a cloud of spray.

By God he had done it! He had navigated over 2,500 miles of open sea, surviving mutiny and storm. He had cheated death. "Iron Felix" would have been proud of him at last. There was, of course, one small remaining problem.

Shlomo did not know Avi was dead.

The following afternoon, they would dock at Eilat and the stinking corpse in the hold must be gone. They had been under strict orders to maintain radio silence; the radio was to be used only to contact Shlomo when the *Prophet* was close to Eilat. Kallenborg did not relish the prospect of presenting Shlomo with the corpse of his precious nephew. He noticed the wind now blew on his cheek from a different direction. Gradually, the *Prophet's* bow turned West. The edge of the sail began to flutter and one of the Arab sailors surreptitiously tightened the sheet.

"Jumaane! What's going on?" Kallenborg shouted to the helmsman. There was no answer. He could hear Golani and Arbel arguing inside the pilothouse.

"So we should throw Avi into the sea, and let the crabs and eels pick his bones? Is that what you want?" said Arbel.

"I tell you, *Halakhah* requires the body to be buried within 24 hours," said Golani.

"He should be buried in a hero's grave in Yad Vachem," said Arbel.

Kallenborg clattered down the steps into the pilothouse.

The two men sitting on the bench behind the Somali helmsman acknowledged Kallenborg's existence by switching over to English.

"You think I don't know American?" Kallenborg said angrily.

Golani gave a sarcastic chuckle. "Is your American as good as your Hebrew?" he said.

Kallenborg snatched the GPS from the chart table beside the helmsman, and pressed a button. A small LCD screen displayed the longitude and latitude of their current position. He pressed the NAV ROUTE button, checked the *dhow's* compass, and his face darkened. He shoved Jumaane away from the wheel and took the helm himself. The spokes slipped through his fingers as he brought the *dhow* around back on course toward the Gulf of Aqabah.

The helmsman regarded Kallenborg placidly.

"We were headed for Suez, you idiot!" Kallenborg said. He looked at Golani, and his eyes flashed with anger. "Ten minutes ago I told him the new course into the mouth of the Gulf of Aqabah."

"I follow only your orders, *Hawaja* Kallenborg," said the helmsman in a sing song voice and pointed to a worn notebook beside the compass.

Kallenborg saw he had forgotten to write the new bearing down for the helmsman. He glared at Jumaane. Resting his hand on the Nagant in his belt, he snarled, "Get on deck!"

"Take it easy, Kallenborg," said Arbel. His Uzi was within easy reach.

Kallenborg stalked out of the pilothouse, shouting over his shoulder, "Go off course again, Jumaane, and you're a dead man." At the top of the steps he stopped and eavesdropped through the hatch.

"That guy makes me nervous," said Arbel. "It's almost like he's looking for an excuse to shoot Jumaane next."

"Jumaane's shipmates killed our Avi," said Golani. "I saw him spit on Kallenborg's cigarette this morning when he wasn't looking."

"Still, you don't shoot Arabs out of hand," Arbel continued. "We are Jews, not the Gestapo."

"*Hawaja* Arbel," came the helmsman's voice. "The man you call Kallenborg took my captain's gun from him. That's how the fight started in which your friend was killed. Your Avi's death was not our fault."

White hot rage gripped Kallenborg. He drew his Nagant and charged down the companion way. Arbel blocked his path.

"Calm down, Kallenborg and put that thing away," said Arbel.

Their eyes locked.

"The bastard is trying to split us up, don't you see," hissed Kallenborg.

"You're upset," said Arbel coolly. "Take a seat." He pointed at the bench with his Uzi.

Kallenborg sat down reluctantly.

Arbel regarded him with keen eyes. "I've been thinking about Avi."

"So have I", said Kallenborg.

"Shlomo's going to ask us questions. A couple of things about Avi's death don't make sense."

"Very well," said Kallenborg. "Let's talk."

"You said the Captain jumped you during the storm."

"And I got this to prove it," said Kallenborg. He pulled his face cloth down to reveal the festering scab on his cheek where the Captain had knifed him.

"Here's what puzzles me. Why would he jump you in a storm?" said Arbel.

"To steal the weapons, of course," said Kallenborg.

Arbel was watching his face closely.

"Not in the middle of a storm. Shlomo will never believe that. If the Arabs were trying to steal our arms, they would have ganged up on us the first night out, killed us, and sailed back to Karachi."

Golani turned to Jumaane, "You were there. What did you see?"

"We were sinking, *Hawaja*. The Captain throws some cargo overboard. Then Kallenborg fight with him. Suddenly everybody fighting."

Arbel gave Kallenborg a bleak smile. "So you attacked them."

"I had to, don't you see? They were destroying the mission," said Kallenborg.

Arbel shook his head. "Did you think that maybe the Captain was right to jettison some cargo."

"He wanted to dump everything," said Kallenborg. "Our whole operation was jeopardized."

"Fine," said Arbel. "You'll be the one to tell that to Shlomo."

"Don't worry, I'll tell him," snapped Kallenborg.

So he was left holding a sack of shit yet again. He went on gamely, "Shlomo's going to be more upset about Avi's body. We should stop and bury him. We could bury Avi's body on that island over there." He pointed out the pilothouse window.

"That's Egypt, you poor shmuck! If an Egyptian patrol searches this wreck, we'll be as dead as Avi," said Arbel. "No, we'll bury him in *Yisroel*. It's the only right thing to do."

Fifty-Five

Salim Darazi awoke listlessly. He felt sand on his cheek and remembered he was still in Eilat. Tareq Hakim sat beside him, hugging his knees, his attention focused on the beach.

"What time is it?", asked Salim.

"Eleven o'clock," said Tareq in a low voice. On his wrist was a heavy gold Rolex.

A businessman's watch, thought Salim. Not that anyone would mistake the baby faced Tareq for a businessman.

The sun glared through the thin nylon beach tent. A shadow moved in front of Salim's face. He shifted his head and peered out. As he raised himself up on one elbow, his heart skipped a beat. Facing him was a girl with blue-green eyes, long dark hair and a skin diving mask pushed back above her forehead. She wore a black net bathing suit through which Salim could discern the soft white skin of her breasts, rosy nipples and the dark triangle between her thighs. Flippers and snorkel dangled from her left hand. She stood not more than ten feet away, ankle deep in the emerald water of Eilat's Coral Beach. She seemed to be inspecting the piece of red coral stone that she held up in her right hand. Lying snugly between her breasts was a small diamond encrusted Star of David pendant.

"Shalom," Salim called to her.

She looked up startled, glanced at him, then turned away with faint disdain. They watched her wade out across the shallows to deeper water, where she balanced awkwardly to pull on her flippers. She looked back at them for an instant, then she paddled slowly away in the direction of the Tour Yam jetty up the beach.

Abdallah Zrake sat cross legged on the other side of Salim, smoking a filter-less Camel cigarette. A thick gold chain hung from his neck. "Our Salim has a wondrous effect on women," he said to Tareq.

"Rich Jewish girls don't speak to Arabs," said Salim.

Zrake turned his head to exhale. "How does Venus know you are Druze? Maybe she wanted you to pursue her."

"Stop pretending, Zrake. We don't have Jewish faces. To women like that we are no more than stupid, filthy Arabs," said Salim.

Zrake scowled. "A million Israelis are Arabs. We vote in the Knesset. We stopped herding goats fifty years ago," he said in a fierce voice. "We grew up with Jews; we protect them. We are Israelis with rights." He paused and in a gentler tone said, "What is troubling you."

"My brother was refused entrance to the Technion. I received the news last night."

Zrake looked concerned. "I'm sorry about your brother, but there are other engineering schools."

"The Technion is the best!", said Salim.

"The entrance examination is difficult, many are turned away," said Zrake.

"Many Arabs are turned away, you mean," said Salim.

"Is your brother a born meathead like you?", said Tareq.

"My baby brother is the student in the family," said Salim. "We sacrificed a lot to prepare him. Even I sent everything I could spare. I had no money for women. Now he won't be able to find work, unless he wants to be a construction worker for Israeli settlements. All our sacrifices were for nothing."

"Your brother must try again," said Zrake.

"Why bother?" said Salim.

He lay on his stomach and stared at the shimmering white buildings of al-Aqabah across the bay for a long time. Finally he said, "I think I'll go to al-Aqabah tonight and see what real women are like."

Zrake and Tareq exchanged looks.

"Is that wise?" said Zrake.

"We've been rotting in Eilat for a week," said Salim. This is a waste of time."

"You must be patient. Patience is the key to good surveillance," said Zrake.

"Maybe your job is to watch. Me, I blow things up," said Salim smacking his fist into his palm."

Tareq gave Zrake a knowing smile.

"There is nothing you can miss so much, eh?", Zrake said. "But one can catch up on it so quickly."

"Maybe for you two," said Salim. "But I am no monk."

Zrake smoked another cigarette, his eyes distant. Finally he shrugged. "Tareq go with him and see that he stays out of trouble. I'll take the evening watch. We have a job to do, so be careful. You'd better leave now if you want to get visas."

* * *

The sun sank in a fiery blaze behind the Eilat Mountains when Salim and Tareq got into a taxi in front of the Queen of Sheba Hotel. Salim remained silent during the half mile ride to the Jordanian border. At the crossing, a hefty Israeli border policeman leaned into the taxi.

"Let me see your ID's," he said.

They dug in their pockets and handed over their ID cards.

He stared at Salim. "Nationality?" he said.

"You can read," said Salim. "The card says Arab."

"Get out, both of you," the policeman said. He searched them thoroughly and disappeared into the guard booth.

"And Zrake calls us 'Israelis with rights'?" said Salim.

"Just cooperate," said Tareq. "We're all on the same team."

Twenty minutes later the policeman returned. There was a subdued air about him as he handed Salim and Tareq back their cards. "Why didn't you tell me?", he said with a good natured growl.

Salim and Tareq looked at him blankly.

"Get out of here." The border policeman opened the taxi door for them.

On the Jordanian side, their Israeli passports and Jordanian visas received only a cursory glance, and they were waived through. Tareq looked back at the tall chain link fence topped with razor wire and electronic sensors that marked Israel's border with Jordan. He had been outside Israel many times before, of course, but each time he knew he was in a different world.

Al-Aqabah streets were lined with date palms and old stone buildings. A few modern high rise structures loomed by the beach. As the taxi drove into the city they could see clusters of tourists along the sidewalks, Israelis, British, and Dutch.

"Where do you want me to let you off?" said the driver.

"We are looking for a good time," said Salim. "Fine cooking, excellent wine, beautiful women."

"There's not much nightlife since the morals police cleaned up the city," said the driver but when Salim handed him some bills, his face brightened. "I know just the place." He took them to the *souk* and as they got out, he said "Ask for The Blue Gazelle," and pointed down an alley. "It doesn't look like much but the food is superb. Tell them Fairouz sent you."

They slung their jackets over their shoulders, and strolled leisurely, sniffing the warm dry desert air. They stuck their heads in small shops that overflowed onto the sidewalk, haggled with merchants for practice but did not buy their cheap jewelry, silver inlaid copper trays, hand-tooled leather saddles or worn copies of Playboy and Penthouse magazines. They laughed as they watched two boys working the street in tandem. One offered "genuine American" condoms to a tourist and the other, came right on his heels, hawking hand-painted pictures of the Blessed Virgin Mary on black felt. At The Blue Gazelle they ordered a meal and glasses of *jot* and watched a fleshy, middle-age belly dancer gyrate to a dirge of keyless quarter notes played on a one-string fiddle, electric lyre, and drum. Salim drank several more glasses of the white liquor.

At ten-thirty their waiter brought them their bill. "We are closing," he said.

Salim's face fell. "So soon? We were just getting started. Can you recommend another place?"

The waiter looked doubtful. "All the bars and clubs close at this time by order of King Hussein. Unless you are looking for something more discreet?" He gave Salim a wink.

"Women?"

"Only the most beautiful," said the waiter.

"Are they clean?"

The waiter stepped back. "But, of course."

Salim gave Tareq a slow smile. "How long has it been since you had a woman?"

Tareq grinned foolishly and sipped his arak.

"Just as I thought," said Salim. "Where are they?"

"Madame Sharaz's," said the waiter. "Here are directions." He slipped a card furtively into Salim's hand. "Give them this."

Outside Salim tried to read the card under a street lamp. His hand was unsteady.

"Can you make sense of this?", he said, handing it to Tareq.

Tareq studied the writing on the card. "The establishment is nearby," he said. He removed his watch and stuffed it in his pants pocket.

Farther on down the cobbled alley, a merchant pulled down the metal shutters of his shop with an echoing clatter. The alley twisted through an archway and wound around in a maze of stone walls and crooked corners. They went past cooking smells and the murmur of voices from courtyards concealed by the walls.

Suddenly a steep stairway rose out of the dark. A tall man with a black pointed beard came silently down the stairs toward them. He wore a striped robe and a green *kaffiyeh*. They stood aside to let him pass. As he came abreast, he held their eyes for an instant.

"*Salaam aleikum,*" he said.

"And upon you be peace," murmured Tareq.

He waited until the man disappeared around a corner. "This isn't a good idea!", Tareq said.

"What's the matter?"

"Think of where we are!"

"I'm not afraid."

"That's because you're drunk," said Tareq.

Salim stumbled up the stairs.

Tareq shook his head and followed. They entered a dusty courtyard where a lonely lemon tree grew. A door, its wood aged and dried, blocked their path. Salim knocked. An obese woman in a dirty *abaya* opened the door and looked at them knowingly. Salim offered the card. She took it and held out her hand, palm up.

"Two hundred dinars," she said.

Salim rummaged through his pockets and pulled out the money. She nodded and led them inside. The woman disappeared, leaving Salim and Tareq alone in a small, dimly lit room, a blackened kerosene lamp in an alcove its only light. A threadbare rug, heaped high with stained pillows, covered the floor.

Salim collapsed onto the pillows, a sigh of contentment in his drunken throat.

Tareq wasn't so relaxed. He looked around warily.

The shabby curtains closing off the room from the rest of the house parted and an adolescent girl entered, her perky newly-rounded breasts in marked contrast to the old torn T-shirt she wore.

That was all she wore.

From his vantage point on the pillows Salim licked his lips in anticipation as he peeked up her T-shirt at the exposed pubic hair that surrounded her moist young vagina.

"Two lumps for me," said Salim as the girl offered him a lump of hemp resin.

She placed them in the *nargileh's* fire pot and handed him the pipe. Salim took a long, deep hit and held it in his lungs until he thought his head would explode. He exhaled loudly.

"This is strong stuff, my brother, you'd better start with one lump," he said.

Tareq shook his head. "I'll take two, also."

As the girl prepared Tareq's pipe she regarded both men with predatory eyes. To Salim she looked sexy.

"No woman for me?" Tareq asked.

"We'll share," Salim said.

"How?"

"You've never had a twosome, Tareq? Oh, the things I'm learning about you."

"Well, I'm first."

"Oh, Tareq, Tareq...where's the fun in that? We do it together."

Before Tareq could respond the curtains parted again and an even younger girl, her naked breasts just beginning to bud, entered the room.

"Ah good...," Salim said. "Now I won't have to play teacher. Or will I Tareq?" He grabbed the first girl, pulling her T-shirt over her head to reveal the hard pink nipples of one recently virginal.

She slid against him, expertly unzipping and unbuttoning his clothes until his erect penis was exposed. She bent over it, mouth open. But Salem pushed her face away, twisted her around roughly, and tried to mount her. She wasn't ready for him. Twisting her pelvis from side to side, and back and forth, she made him thrust and lunge, playing him in a sexual game of hide and seek.

Salem stopped the game to take another hit on his pipe. The room spun around him, its colors kaleidoscopic. He felt something warm and wet moving down onto his cock. This time the girl wasn't using her mouth. She'd lowered herself onto his hard penis, slowly squeezing her vaginal muscles, until he had to stop her or burst. He lifted her off him, spun her around, and mounted her, pinning her down with his powerful hands.

Tareq's girl took the pipe from his hand and coaxed him down onto the pillows. She placed the pipe stem into his mouth, kneeling in front of him, licking her lips, caressing her breasts, teasing him. Although younger, she seemed more experienced than Salim's girl.

Following Salim's lead, Tareq sucked the hashish deep into his lungs and held it. He'd never smoked before. A paroxysm of coughing wracked his body. The younger girl laughed and slapped him on the back.

Salim looked up. His girl was now back on top, riding him like a pony. He waved to Tareq, giggling. "My brother, Tareq, I had no idea this was your first hashish." The girls giggled too.

"I learned to smoke in Lebanon," Tareq lied and gave another hacking cough.

"At Lebanon? I was with the Christians at Sidon by the coast," said Salim. "Where were you?"

"Balbek with the Jews," said Tareq.

At the mention of "Lebanon" and "Christians" and "Jews", the two girls lifted their heads. They exchanged glances, eyes narrowed.

Tareq noticed. "Enough talk. We didn't come here to talk," he said.

He grabbed the younger girl and swung her onto a pillow. She sprawled before him, legs spread wide, arms above her head, there for his taking. The hash made his head spin. He felt disembodied, he was all sensation, no thought. Her body undulated beneath him, hips moving, her hairy mound thrusting toward him, enticing him, seducing him, welcoming him. He wanted to suck her breasts, lick her navel, run his tongue between her legs, parting them, teasing her clitoris, making it hard, making it stand up an beg for release.

She grabbed his head and held it tightly between her thighs, rocking against his tongue, pushing, straining. It was then that he realized this wasn't a fantasy.

This was real.

His head was between her legs, his tongue was pressing against her hard red clitoris... Realization made him hotter, made him harder. He could feel she was about to come against his tongue. He pulled away. She made an angry noise, baring her teeth in complaint.

He covered her mouth with his. She could smell her musk on his lips. The scent excited her. She licked his lips wanting more. He pushed himself into her. She rubbed against him, pumping, working for that orgasm. Then suddenly, unexpectedly, they exploded together in a burst of ecstasy. A miracle. Two strangers merging as one, floating up to the clouds, in throbbing, thrilling pulsating ecstasy.

And then it was over. Tareq felt himself falling, falling, falling back to earth. Something cold pressed against his neck, a bright line of fiery pain encircled his neck. A primeval warmth strangely familiar, flowed down his chest. He let out a gasp. It was his own blood. The girl had cut his throat.

Lost in his own drug-induced dream, Salim heard Tareq's screams of ecstasy and then the gasp and smiled, too lusty to stop and look. He sucked hard on his girl's nipples as he thrust deeper inside her. She whimpered in pain. That only aroused him more. He pushed her legs back until her knees were bent behind her ears and forced himself even deeper inside her. He felt as if he had the largest most powerful cock in the world. His girl groaned in agony. Salim felt omnipotent, if he wanted, he could go on fucking forever. His only reality was the tight, moist, young vaginal walls, clutching at his throbbing, thrusting penis.

She pulled her head away from his and signaled to her friend for help. The younger girl left Tareq's lifeless body, the blood still flowing from his neck, and kneeled behind Salem, gently fondling his balls.

He turned in surprise. The younger girl smiled at him. Poor Tareq, he thought. One good fuck and he was gone and now he Salim must satisfy two women. Oh well, who better...?

He was still congratulating himself when he felt the sharp hard steel of the knife sawing across his neck muscles. The younger girl angled it expertly between the vertebrae. He died instantly as she cut through his spinal cord and his body collapsed in a heap. She continued to work with the knife until his severed head tumbled onto the young breasts he had just been sucking, covering them with blood.

* * *

Zrake squinted against the sun and cursed himself for falling asleep. The cries of children playing at the Aqua Sport summer camp filled the air. He consulted his watch. 8:30 a.m. Then he got to his feet and emerged from the tent. Where were Salim and Tareq, he fretted? They should have been back by now. He swept the harbor with his powerful 40mm Nikon binoculars. Brightly colored tents marched on North Beach in uneven rows, all the way to the Jordanian border. Nothing moved out on the red-tinted green waters except pleasure craft, sailboats and a few motorboats, leaving the North Beach marina. The same missile boats and rusty ex-British sub were tied up at the nearby naval station. The same Japanese freighters were moored at the adjacent port facility. Winches groaned and thudded as they unloaded cargo. Close by, a Tour Yam glass-bottom boat packed with sightseers left the jetty. Across the sandy highway, people went in and out of hotels and restaurants. All was calm as usual.

Zrake's binoculars stopped on a large crowd of people in front of the Club Mediterranee about a hundred yards away. A municipal police car with flashing lights stopped on the beach beside the crowd. Soon it was joined by an unmarked white Peugeot. A man in plain clothes got out. He looked like Shin Bet.

Zrake decided to go over and have a closer look. As he approached he heard shouts and an angry muttering.

A voice cried, "See what happens when we open up the border with Jordan. Fucking Arabs. Everyone of them should be killed."

"What's going on?" Zrake asked a man on the edge of the crowd.

"Arabs murdered two men last night—cut their throats," the man said.

The woman next to him said. "A child found the bodies covered with beach towels. His dog smelled them." Her lower lip trembled. "They took him to the hospital in shock."

Zrake pushed through the crowd with a sinking sensation in the pit of his stomach. It couldn't be them. But where were they? Why hadn't Salim and Tareq come back?

Then he saw the corpses, their naked bodies supine. Tareq's throat had been cut, yet his face was peaceful. Something had been jammed down his throat. Salim's severed head lay face down, resting on his genitals. Zrake trembled, nausea welled up in his throat. Across the chests of both men was a crude cardboard sign printed in English and Hebrew. It said: "SO DEAL THE LIONS OF ALLAH WITH TRAITORS."

The Shin Bet man kneeled on the sand, face grim, jaw muscles twitching. Zrake strained to see what he pulled out of Tareq's mouth. Another Shin Bet officer gruffly told him to move back. Still he lingered just long enough to see that it was a plastic Israeli ID card. The officer gently lifted Salim's head from his lap and turned it around, face up. Jammed in his mouth, too, was an ID card. Then Zrake could see no more. The scene was completely blocked off from view.

He stumbled away, stopping at a trash can in the beach parking lot. He bent over it and dry heaved.

Straightening up, Zrake took a long, deep breath of the tangy, sea air. The sky was blue, clear and unclouded. Gulls wheeled overhead. Waves rolled lazily into shore. The knot of people surrounding the corpses broke up as the Shin Bet officers shooed them away.

"Death all around us," Zrake thought, "and yet life goes on as if nothing happened."

He unlocked the battered white van. Inside, he located one of the team's secure phones, inserted his cryptographic key, and dialed Chaim Asher's number in Ramallah.

"Chaim, this is Zrake. I have very bad news."

Fifty-Six

Christina looked up from the pages of *al-Kuds*, at Asher. His face was lined with tension and there was a faint note of panic in his voice. Two men had been found murdered in Eilat. The Lions of Allah claimed credit. She felt sick with dread.

"I need replacements now, Mike," he said into his secure phone. "Yes, I saw Ben Yusuf on TV. So, our favorite rabbi holds another rally. What does that pious shmuck have to do with my replacements?"

Asher was sweating despite the cool morning air in the office. His wounded ankle, swathed in bandages, gave off an unhealthy odor. The ankle must be killing him, thought Christina.

Christina returned to her paper. Now she knew for certain. Those were Asher's men, the men who'd been in her house.

"It's falling to pieces, Mike," said Asher. "Get me somebody to send down there fast."

So it was the two young ones, Christina thought. The one with the baby face and red checkered *kaffiyeh*. The handsome one with nervous fingers.

After Asher hung up, he stared out the window for a long time. He seemed cornered but not defeated.

"Chaim, you must see a doctor about your ankle," she said. "If the infection gets worse you could die of blood poisoning."

"I'm all right," he said stubbornly.

"You are afraid you'll be taken off my case aren't you? Please don't endanger your life on my account," she said.

Finally he said, "We must go to Eilat."

Her eyes widened.

"You want me to risk my life for the Boers of the Levant? Oh no, Chaim. Even you cannot ask me to do that."

"*Yisroel* is not South Africa, Christina. And Salim and Tareq died because they were thoughtless and got sloppy."

"I cannot leave my children," she said.

"Najat can care for them."

"You promised us round the clock protection from the Lions," she said angrily.

"Then, Mike will hide the children while we're gone."

"Don't put my children in a prison."

The thought of Aminah and Muna in Gilda's hands tied her stomach into a hard knot, but Asher was their only chance to get out of Israel. Their fate was bound to his. She prayed this would be the right choice since it was the only choice. If Asher died, his masters would forget her children ever existed. Hamad would not.

"What do you need me to do in Eilat?" she said.

"Help me get about, drive the car, keep an eye on the harbor," said Asher. "You are the only one I can trust."

Christina gave Asher an ironic smile. "You mean I'm the only one left you can bully."

He held her hand tightly for a long time.

* * *

The trip took a little over an hour by air. Christina looked down as the nine passenger Arkia turbo-prop lost altitude. The Negev stretched below, 60 percent of Israel's land area, an endless mosaic of shapes, clumps of camel thorn, dust clouds, sand, and wind carved volcanic hills. Suddenly she saw a narrow highway with tiny cars and trucks. The plane bounced around in thermals rising from the desert floor, and then it swooped over low hills dotted with sturdy flat-roofed buildings. There were muffled thuds as the landing gear extended and locked in place. Finally they settled down on a dusty runway with a bump. As the aircraft taxied to the terminal building, the pilot came on the intercom.

"Arkia welcomes you to Eilat. Be careful of the heat. The temperature is 110 degrees."

The passengers, a party of students and tourists, looked at each other and grimaced.

Christina slipped on her dark glasses as she emerged from the aircraft. She felt the sun burn through her thin linen dress. She turned and helped Asher down the steps. He wore an open necked white shirt, tan slacks and leaned on his cane. Waiting for them at the foot of the aluminum steps was the scowling Zrake. His shirt was rumpled and sweat-stained, and he looked like he hadn't slept in days.

"*The Prophet* has just entered the harbor," he said.

Asher reeled as if struck by a fist.

"Damn! There's not enough time," he said. He grunted with pain and leaned over his cane with his head down.

"Are you ill, Chaim?" said Zrake.

"I feel like shit but I'll live. It's my damn ankle."

Zrake squatted at Asher's side and gently touched the bandage protruding over the top of Asher's shoe. Christina noticed the laces were already loosened.

Zrake peered at the door of the aircraft. "Did you bring anyone else with you besides her?"

"No one," said Asher. "Mrs. Goryeb has kindly agreed to help us."

For the first time Zrake looked at her with respect.

"Mr. Asher is very persuasive," said Christina dryly.

Carefully, using a sharp knife, Zrake slashed the leather of Asher's shoes.

"Thank you, that feels much better," said Asher wiping his forehead with a crumpled white handkerchief. "Now, let's get going."

Christina watched Asher hobble after the rest of the passengers who filed hurriedly across the airfield to the terminal to get out of the searing heat. Zrake, stood beside her looking worried.

"I'm afraid we'll have to watch out for him," said Zrake.

"Mr. Asher seems to know what he is doing," said Christina.

"A mind eaten by hate can do stupid things," said Zrake.

Their eyes met.

"He hates the people who are stealing our country," said Zrake.

When the two of them caught up with Asher, he was hunched over his cane again, sweating profusely.

* * *

346

The airport lounge was not air conditioned. There was a ticket counter, empty benches, a baggage claim area, and a snack bar. Two security guards were eating lunch at their posts beside a metal detector and x-ray machine.

"Do you need aspirin?" said Christina.

"My ears are ringing I've taken so much," said Asher.

Zrake put Asher's arm over his shoulder and half carried him to the rear of the building, through some double doors and out into the parking lot. They stopped beside a white Ford Econoline van. Zrake pulled back the van's sliding door revealing the cargo area. It was fitted out with tool lockers that lined both sides.

"What did Gilda give us?", said Asher.

Zrake pointed to various compartments. "Disguises, camouflage suits, bullet proof vests, concealed video cameras, RF bugs and debugging devices, night-vision goggles, and STU-3 secure phones."

"What about weapons?"

"Four Galil automatic rifles and two Shtutser sniper's rifles."

"And grenades?"

"Fragmentation, percussion and phosphorus."

Asher crawled in back.

"Mrs. Goryeb will you please drive us," he said.

Christina took the keys from the reluctant Zrake. Although she had never driven a van before, this one had an automatic. The engine started immediately.

Zrake sat next to her.

"Turn left at the exit, stay on Derech Ha'Arava," he said. "The docks are a mile away."

"How much time do we have?", said Asher.

"They may be unloading now," said Zrake. "When I first spotted the *Prophet*, a pilot boat with three armed men went out to meet her."

Eilat harbor spread out before them, a shimmering brass bowl edged by dark red mountains under a sky of iron. Past the airport the street sloped down and became a narrow two lane highway that ran beside a wide beach. On the right were hotels and shopping complexes filled with restaurants. Few people ventured out on the sidewalks.

An air horn thundered directly behind them. Christina looked in the side mirror. A military truck was right on the van's rear bumper. Irate male faces glared down from the cab. Another long blast sounded.

347

"Let them pass, Mrs. Goryeb," said Zrake.

She slowed and pulled over. Three 2fi ton army trucks rumbled by, their wagon beds covered by drab green canvass roofs. As they passed, the canvass curtains at the rear of the last truck, parted and two men stared at them. Christina gave a gasp. She recognized the members of the B'nai Ha'eretz watch patrol, the ones who had tried to fix her sister's Vauxhall the time it broke down when Asher was following her.

"What's the matter?" said Zrake.

"Those men are from B'nai Ha'eretz," she said.

"Did they recognize you?" said Asher.

"I'm not sure," she said. "No, I don't think so. They're ignoring us."

"Good. Then follow them."

"Chaim, what do you have in mind?" said Zrake.

"After they load their trucks, we'll blow them up," said Asher.

"With what?" said Zrake.

"One of these." Asher held up a smooth fat hand grenade.

"Phosphorus? We'll be too close. Besides there are three trucks."

Ahead was a sign pointing to the New Tourist Center. Christina eased her foot off the gas pedal, pulled into a parking lot in front of a row of night clubs and restaurants, and killed the engine.

"What are you doing, Christina?" said Asher.

"You're both insane," she said quietly, "This is a suicide mission." She reached for her handbag on the seat and opened the door.

"Please stop," said Asher.

Zrake grabbed Christina's arm. As he did, his hand knocked the handbag spilling its contents on the floor. A package of nylon hose lay on top of the untidy pile.

She pulled the door shut and began to pick up her belongings.

Zrake stared at two flat cellophane packages in her hand.

"What I really cannot understand is what someone like *you* is doing here, Mr. Zrake," said Christina. "If some crazy Jews want to kill each other why do you, an Arab, want to risk your life?"

"The packages, please," he said.

"You want my nylons?"

He nodded.

She gave him the two packages. Zrake tore open one wrapper and held up a stocking for Asher to see.

"Here is our timing device," he said happily.

"You can't fuse a grenade with that," said Asher.

"Pass me a grenade," he said.

Zrake bound a stocking tightly around the grenade Asher handed him. "The fuel tank on an army truck has an oversize filler opening. You can drop a grenade directly in the tank. Without a pin, the arming handle is restrained by the stocking until the gasoline dissolves the nylon. The explosion will turn the truck into a fireball," he explained.

"How long does it take for the nylon to dissolve?" said Christina.

"It is not precise," said Zrake.

Asher shrugged. "Gasoline should dissolve the nylon." he said. "Mrs. Goryeb, please drive on."

Christina did not take her foot off the brake pedal.

"The men in the trucks will be killed," she said. "You may even kill innocent bystanders. Isn't there a better way to handle this?"

"Mrs. Goryeb," said Zrake in a gentle voice. "You asked why I, as an Arab, should care if the Jews kill each other? I will tell you: If there is civil war in *Yisroel*, we will all be much worse off. No amount of killing will drive either the Arabs or the Jews out of this land. But if we help the Jews to live in peace, we Arabs will also live in peace."

Asher spoke again. "The men in those trucks are stiff-necked rebels who are endangering many lives. If they must die so that the rest of us can live in peace, so be it."

She thought about the price of civil war, the laughing, teasing boys playing marbles in the dust of courtyards who would be homeless or imprisoned. Tall serious young men who would never court sweethearts, never have jobs to support families or who would die. Whole villages bulldozed. Their inhabitants would rot in refugee camps, consumed with hatred and despair. She thought about dear Naomi Litvin, her grieving husband Yigael, and her "Peace Now" friends. She thought of Chaim Asher playing his mandolin at Gan Geneva. She started the engine again and pulled out into traffic.

* * *

Five minutes later Christina saw the derricks and masts of ships rising above a row of white corrugated iron warehouses. She could smell the tangy odor of creosoted pilings mixed with fuel oil. The trucks that passed them earlier were now drawn up in front of a bar beside a sentry box that guarded an opening in a chain link fence. Two girl soldiers were talking to a stocky man in a black T-shirt and army trousers who had jumped down from the first truck.

"That's Shlomo Arendt," said Asher. "Pull up behind them."

Christina maneuvered the van behind the last truck. The bearded face of a settler stared down at them.

Zrake leaned out of the van.

"What's going on?" he said with a dead pan expression.

The man gave them a furtive grin. "Same shit, different day," he muttered and vanished behind the curtain.

"What shall I do about the guards?" said Christina.

"Show them this," said Asher. He handed her a Shin Bet pocket commission. A badge was pinned on one side of the leather holder. Asher's picture stared back at her from the other side. "Spread your fingers over the photo but let them see the badge. Act like you own the place."

One by one, the army trucks moved forward and were waved under the raised barricade by the guard. She held up her hand when the white van approached the sentry box.

"Shin Bet," said Christina briskly. She flashed the badge the way Asher said.

The guard glanced at her log book. "You're not on my list," she said. "Are you with them?" She nodded at the trucks disappearing behind a warehouse.

"Rush job," said Zrake.

"Someone should have called ahead," said the guard.

"So, what else is new?" said Zrake. He looked bored.

The guard took down the van's license plate number and passed them through.

Christina felt a thrill of excitement. She tried to give Asher the pocket commission.

"Keep it," he said. "You'll need it."

With growing confidence, she drove down a narrow road behind the warehouses. It was lined with stacks of steel shipping containers and wooden crates.

Zrake pointed to a spot next to a fork lift truck. "Please park over there, Mrs. Goryeb."

She braked and wheeled the van around so that it pointed in the direction they came from. Then she backed into the spot he indicated.

"What if any one asks me what I'm doing here?" said Christina.

"Show your badge, tell them this is a police line and order them to move away," said Asher.

He handed several grenades to Zrake. Zrake bound each one with nylon hose but did not pull its pin. He put them in a canvass bag that he slung over his shoulder.

"I'll start a fire," Asher said. "Shlomo's men will be too busy putting it out to see you drop off our little tokens of esteem."

"How will we communicate?" said Zrake.

"Wait," said Asher. He located two walkie-talkies and gave one to Zrake and stuck one in his belt. Then he showed Christina how to tune the van's radio scanner to the walkie-talkie channels. "Now we'll be able to hear each other."

A vast tangle of shadows swept over van, blotting out the sun. Christina looked up at a giant overhead crane with a room-sized cargo container hanging from its hoist.

"The crane operator can see us," said Zrake.

"What can we do to blend in better?" said Asher.

Zrake reached for a bag on the van's floor, and he pulled out a pair of denim overalls. "Put these on," he said. "We'll be dock workers searching for lost crates." Zrake took another pair of overalls for himself. He handed Asher a metal hat and tinted safety goggles. "Lean on the cane. Everyone ignores a cripple," said Zrake.

As they left, Christina turned off the engine. She was alone in the van.

A hoarse voice rang out from the direction Asher and Zrake had gone, "Shalom! Shalom!"

Her skin crawled. She knew that voice. It was the same insolent voice she had heard months before, when a Shin Bet officer beat on the door to her home in Ramallah.

Fifty-Seven

The *Shadow of the Prophet* glided across the hot gleaming surface of the harbor. Close in by the dock, the helmsman put her on her heel and left her standing into the dry breeze from the desert. The lateen sail undulated slowly like a huge dorsal fin, tall and ragged. Men with deeply sun burned faces stood on her deck. As they came nearer, Asher could see red blistered lips and dark hollow eyes. The men wore filthy, salt-crusted *jalabiyyas* or faded jeans. Shaggy hair stuck out from under slovenly draped *kaffiyehs*. Overhead, a few sea gulls circled and screeched.

Asher recognized Kallenborg who stood alone on the roof of the pilothouse, a sinister bronze-skinned apparition in a T-shirt and dungarees, a sneering god of war. Kallenborg waved to the heavily armed men who stood on the dock in front of the waiting trucks.

"Shalom!" cried Kallenborg. "Shalom!"

The men on the dock were silent.

Asher was in agony. The climb to the top of the mountain of crates had left him light-headed and dizzy. Now he sat with his back to a crate, clutching the wad of papers he hoped would be mistaken for bills of lading. There was no place to hide but he was in a good position to serve as a lookout. He could see the narrow aisle where Zrake would be working beside the trucks, and he also had a clear view in both directions of the pier below where the trucks were parked. He would have an unobstructed view of the *Prophet* when it docked. Thirty feet away he saw Shlomo Arendt, pacing back and forth on the edge of the pier like a small impatient bull.

On the *Prophet's* deck, sailors crouched beside heavy mooring hawsers. They threw thin lines over to the dock where the waiting men caught them, pulled over the hawsers, and drew the Prophet in close to the pier. Shlomo charged down the gangway to the *Prophet's* deck as soon as his men could shove it in place. Kallenborg and two men dressed like Arabs came forward to greet him.

"Where's Avi?" said Shlomo.

The two men pulled off their *kaffiyehs* and looked at each other.

"Ask Kallenborg," the taller one said.

"Golani! Where's Avi?" demanded Shlomo.

Golani turned to Kallenborg.

"If you don't tell him, I will," he said.

"Avi gave his life for *Eretz Yisroel*," said Kallenborg in a flat toneless voice.

An inhuman shriek erupted from Shlomo lips. He grabbed the railing of the gangway and tried to rip it loose from its mountings. The taller man put his hand on Shlomo's shoulder.

"Golani, Arbel, why didn't you idiots save him?" he cried.

"We weren't there in time," Golani said.

"We didn't know until it was too late," said Arbel.

"Arbel, for God's sake, what happened?" said Shlomo. "What really happened?"

"Kallenborg started a fight with the Arab crew."

Shlomo didn't wait for the rest of the story. He fell on Kallenborg like a fury.

"Murderer!" he screamed pushing Kallenborg. "Filthy, lying Litvak scum!"

"You got your guns, didn't you?" said Kallenborg.

"You murdered my boy," said Shlomo.

"Your precious Avi was helping the Arabs throw your guns overboard," said Kallenborg. "Without me you would have ended up with nothing."

"We can always get more guns, fool!" Shlomo shouted.

Asher's lips curved in an involuntary grim smile. Now Shlomo would know how it felt to pay for *Eretz Yisroel* in blood, thought Asher. He moved behind the crate and ran his finger over its black stenciled markings for the benefit of anyone who might be watching while he spoke quietly on his walkie-talkie to Zrake.

"They're all tied up. Shlomo's chewing Kallenborg out for something and the rest of them are away from the trucks lapping it up. You can deliver the presents now."

"Okay," came Zrake's voice on the walkie-talkie pressed to Asher's ear.

With an effort Asher managed to stand. Reeling with waves of pain, he stumped along on his cane from crate to crate, reading the numbers stenciled on their sides. He caught sight of Zrake, head bent over his clip board, moving between the trucks and Asher's crates. When Zrake came level with the first truck, he leaned against its fuel tank. One hand fumbled behind his back open the oversized filler cap while the other dipped into the canvass bag where he kept the grenades. His shoulders hunched as he removed the grenade's pin and dropped it in the gas tank.

Zrake replaced the filler cap and moved on to the second truck.

Cautiously, Asher turned around. No longer were the men standing on the edge of the dock with their eyes on Shlomo and Kallenborg. Instead they clustered in angry little knots. Muttering with expressions of disgust, they tied handkerchiefs over their noses and mouths.

"You left his body to rot? You have no respect for the *Halakhah*, you don't even *know Halakhah!*"

Shlomo's voice trembled with rage and pain.

Asher's eyes returned to the second truck but he could not find Zrake! "What are you doing?" he said into his walkie-talkie.

"There's a lock on the cap," said Zrake. "I'm trying to find something to snap it off with, a piece of pipe, anything."

"Pick it open. They'll suspect something if it's gone."

"I don't have a pick."

Asher gritted his teeth and reached in his pocket. His fingers closed on a paper clip. "I'll bring you mine. Go on to the third truck."

He looked back at *Prophet's* deck. Another man, a settler, was on the gangway speaking urgently to Shlomo. His face looked familiar. It was Ben Yusuf's chief lieutenant, Etzel Meyerson.

"Pull yourself together, Shlomo," Etzel said. "We've got to load these trucks and get out of here."

With visible effort Shlomo controlled himself. "Get out of my sight," he said to Kallenborg. Then he spat in his face.

Kallenborg gave Shlomo a terrible look and wiped the spittle off. He stared coldly at Etzel, then at Golani, and then at the men on the dock, as if memorizing their faces for future reference. Suddenly Asher realized that Kallenborg was looking past the men directly at him. He rested on his cane and looked down at his wad of papers. Then he moved behind the crate out of Kallenborg's line of sight and started inching painfully down the pile of crates. He was spurred on by the sound of orders being shouted aboard the *Prophet* to winch up the main hatch. At last he reached the pavement and made his way to Zrake who crouched by the second truck.

The padlock on the fuel tank was new, made in China, coarsely machined but strong.

"There were no locks on the other two trucks," said Zrake.

Asher took the paper clip out and bent it rapidly until it broke into two pieces of wire. From the larger piece he fashioned a pick and inserted it into the lock.

"Someone is coming," whispered Zrake. He felt in his overalls for his pistol but did not draw it.

Asher could hear footsteps. He blinked, wiped the sweat out of his eyes and concentrated on his hands. Using the shorter piece of wire as a lever, he exerted a slight pressure on the key cylinder while he manipulated the loose fitting tumblers inside with the pick. He worked frantically but couldn't get them to align correctly. He was about to give up when—

Thank God!

The cylinder turned grudgingly and the shackle fell open.

Zrake's eyes lit up. In one quick movement, he lifted the gasoline cap, dropped in a grenade and closed the cap.

Asher secured the padlock's shackle again.

* * *

Back in the white van, Christina listened to Asher and Zrake conversations on the police scanner. She heard Asher say, "Let's get out of here." She had a fair idea of what was going on, but she could not hear much over her channel beyond abbreviated conversations, footsteps, and faint sounds of shouting in the background.

A muffled command rang out, "Stop those two." Then came the sound of running feet and Asher's labored breathing from the radio's speaker. Seconds went by without another sound. She dug her nails into the palm of one hand.

She recognized Asher's voice. "Shalom, Kallenborg."

"What are you doing here?" Kallenborg's voice was full of venom.

"I don't like guns stuck in my face," said Asher.

"Then lie face down on the ground, hands behind your back. Your friend too."

There were scraping sounds and a grunt of pain from Asher.

She heard Kallenborg say "I don't like guns either," and guessed that he had searched Asher and Zrake and found their weapons.

"Kidnapping us will land you in even more trouble, Kallenborg," said Asher.

"No, I just redeemed myself," said Kallenborg. "Shlomo doesn't like people who spy on him. What were you two doing to those trucks anyway?"

"Kiss my ass," said Asher.

There were thuds and cries of pain from Zrake.

Christina turned the scanner off. She felt sick. She rested her forehead on the steering wheel and tried to think, to concentrate.

A man's voice startled her.

"Are you all right?" he said through the open window of the van.

A fat sweaty-faced workman was looking at her. She nodded at him and started up the van. She drove down the road toward the only symbol of authority in a world turned upside down, the sentry box.

But whose truth would the guard believe? Her story or Kallenborg's. He was a Shin Bet officer while she was an Israeli-Palestinian. Moreover Shlomo Arendt would be on Kallenborg's side, not hers. From the way Asher had reacted to seeing him, she knew Shlomo had to be someone important.

Christina put her foot on the brake and backed the van into a side alley. She picked up the secure phone Asher had left behind on the seat beside her. Except for the plastic key stuck in its side, the instrument resembled a portable telephone. The familiar Bezek dial tone hummed in the receiver when she put it to her ear. She hung up in dismay. Asher and Zrake took their orders from Gilda and Mike but Christina had no idea how to contact either one of them. She stared at the phone's mouth piece and then slowly put it back on the seat. Her head felt empty like a big hollow cotton sphere.

* * *

When the first truck roared past the front of the alley, Christina ducked down behind the wheel. The second truck back-fired as it passed, and her eyes opened wide. She sat up as the third truck go by. The settlers were leaving! Asher and Zrake had to be on one of the trucks.

Was it too late to save them? Were they bound and gagged hoping desperately that she would find a way to rescue them? Or had Kallenborg murdered them?

With a shudder she pushed this thought out of her mind. She eased the van's transmission into "Drive" and pulled out of the alley. It was mid-afternoon with the sun right in her eyes. Brake lights flared in the distance as the trucks approached the sentry box. Christina fumbled around on the seat until her fingers found Asher's pocket commission. She slowed down so that she would be at the sentry box just as the last truck drove out on the highway.

The young woman on duty stepped forward and raised her hand. She looked into the white van and then her eyes came back to Christina. "What happened to those two men who were with you?" she said.

"They're in the trucks with the rest of the men," said Christina with a wry smile. "I get to drive home by myself."

The soldier gave her a sympathetic look, and motioned her to drive on.

Fifty-Eight

Inside the truck's gas tank bounced a fat little grenade wrapped in a stocking. Asher lay in back and stared at the canvass roof of the army truck; his mouth taped shut and his hands bound with thin plastic handcuffs. Kallenborg had flung him on top of a case of mortar shells. "Don't forget your cane, old man," he'd said scornfully. Zrake, next to him, was trussed up in a similar fashion.

How much longer it would be before the truck exploded?

Asher was already nauseated. The thought of the grenade rocking obscenely back and forth made him sicker. The odor of death that came from one of the long green boxes overpowered him. In the suffocating heat, the stench, exhaust fumes and reek of canvass preservative combined into a vile mixture. He would probably choke to death if he threw up.

And he ached in every joint. The thin handcuffs were drawn up very tight, cutting off his circulation, causing extreme pain. Every bump and pot hole in the road over which the truck ran was magnified by its rigid tandem axles and rock-hard suspension. Before he realized what was happening, he retched. Instinctively, he tried to turn over on his stomach but could not. He took a deep breath through his nose, and thrashed around wildly, first banging his face into Zrake's shoulder, then smashing into the box next to him, trying to rub the filament tape away from his mouth. The tape edge that ran under Asher's nose hooked under the box's hinge. He strained his neck muscles. The tape's adhesive tore at his mustache before it pulled free, and vomit spewed out of his mouth all over the side of the box.

He was free!

No, not free, but at least not totally helpless. When the spasms subsided, he worked the rest of the tape over his chin by pulling it against
the box hinge. He turned over and looked at Zrake. "Let's get your
tape off," he said.

Zrake's eyes flashed.

Shouting to make himself heard over the roar of the truck's
exhaust, Asher twisted and pushed himself so that he could get his
face next to Zrake's, and started biting and tearing the tape away
from Zrake's mouth.

"Thank you, but I am not a woman," were the first words out of
Zrake's mouth, once Asher removed the tape.

"At times like this, one should not always be so particular," said
Asher. "Hold still."

It was hopeless. He continued to chew at the plastic handcuffs on
Zrake's wrists but the thin plastic was tougher than steel.

"So Chaim, will I see my grandchildren grow up?" said Zrake.

His eyes were clear and calm.

Asher stopped.

"You're right. We've got to tell them about the grenades."

"I hope they can hear us," said Zrake. A thick wall of munitions
boxes rose to the ceiling in front of them.

"Yell as loud as you can," said Asher.

"What shall we shout?"

"*Reemon betokh ha'benzeen!*" Grenade in the gasoline.

They shouted in unison, for five minutes but no one in the driver's
cab seemed to hear them.

"Maybe we can attract attention behind," said Zrake. Canvass curtains tied securely across the back of the truck hid both of them from
view. He touched a finger-sized hole in the canvass where the curtain
rubbed against the tail gate.

Asher craned his neck and peered out at the desert through the
hole. "How incredible—our white van is following us," he said.

"You're sure?"

"It's about a quarter mile behind. I didn't think she gave a damn
about us."

"If we could dangle something from the truck, we could attract
Mrs. Goryeb's attention," said Zrake.

Asher twisted sideways, put his hands on his cane, and rolled over.

Zrake took the cane from him and held it by its tip with both hands. He maneuvered the crooked end over the edge of the tail gate and began to swing it back and forth in clumsy arcs.

"The van is coming closer," said Asher. "She flashed her lights," he said.

Zrake signaled with the cane, again.

* * *

"The lights flashed again," said Asher, "but she's keeping her distance."

While Zrake waved frantically, the cane slipped from his fingers and fell onto the highway below.

Asher stared through the hole. "Now she's speeding up." A smile began to spread over his face. "She passed us," he said.

"May she have courage," said Zrake.

"Courage she has," said Asher. "She could use some luck."

"We could all use some luck," said Zrake.

Over the roar of the trucks came the distant trumpeting of air horns. Their own truck's horn blared, in response. Then a submachine gun stuttered one long burst.

Asher put his eye to the peep hole just in time to see the white van career off the highway through the desert camel thorn. One side was pimpled with an ugly rash of bullet holes and a window was shattered completely. The van slammed into a low sand dune and stopped.

"Murderers", Asher said in a broken voice. A cold icy numbness gripped his heart and spread throughout his body. Oh God! They had killed his Christina. He felt like giving up, he had no wish to live. He wanted to scream, to shout, to do anything to vent his rage but he remained immobile. Why had everything gone so wrong?

Zrake avoided Asher's eyes.

Asher stared at the army green canvass, at the cases of mortar shells, and the long green box that smelled of death.

Fifty-Nine

Bits of laminated safety glass covered the front seat. Truck tires receded on the highway toward the Dead Sea over 100 kilometers away. Christina raised her head warily and saw their dark shapes vanish. She opened the door and shook the glass out her clothes. Tiny chunks of glass fell out of her hair and ran down her neck.

What next?

She knew that Asher and Zrake were in the last truck. At any moment the grenade in its gas tank would turn the lumbering vehicle into a raging fireball. The other grenades in the other trucks would explode and Kallenborg, Shlomo Arendt, and the settlers in the other trucks would die too.

She brushed off the driver's seat with her handbag, and slipped behind the driver's wheel. With a prayer on her lips, she turned the ignition key. The motor coughed but did not start. She tried again but failed. On her third attempt, the engine caught, ran and settled down to an uneven idle. She started to back away from the sand dune in front of the van but the wheels spun. Then she remembered, she must partly deflate her tires to drive on sand. She knelt at the rear of the van, beside a tire and noticed her stocks had unsightly holes in them. She touched the fabric.

Asher and Zrake had not known how much time would elapse before the nylon stockings dissolved. Would it take one hour or twenty-four?

This time the wheels gripped the sand and she drove back onto the highway. There were two roads to Jerusalem. Route 40, preferred by most Israelis, followed a northwesterly track to West Jerusalem. Route 90, the one taken by the settler's trucks, ran due north to East

Jerusalem and Ramallah. They must be bound for the B'nai Ha'eretz settlement. But she would be forced to drive slowly until Paran, the next town, where she could find a garage and reinflate the van's tires to normal pressure.

There was one way left to save them. She picked up the secure phone.

Sixty

Christina drove into the outskirts of East Jerusalem. The van's yellow license plates allowed her to breeze through military checkpoints past long lines of waiting Palestinian vehicles. The darkening sky matched her mood. As she wheeled through sharp turns on the narrow two lane blacktop, she could make out Palestinian villages and Israeli settlements on surrounding hills and ridges. In the long shadows below the villages, Palestinian farmers bent over their crops in small wheat fields and vineyards. Flocks of sheep and goats foraged in olive, grape and plum orchards. Near the settlements, surrounded by security fences and necklaces of mercury vapor lights, the land was not being worked. She had caught up with the settlers' trucks an hour earlier. Now she pursued them, but at a safe distance.

Suddenly as she rounded a bend, she saw the three army trucks grinding up a steep horse-shoe turn in second gear. She skidded to a stop and backed the white van out of sight behind the slope of the embankment. A flicker of red and smudge of black smoke on a far hillside caught her eye. She looked around, studying the lonely hills, the rocky gorge, the road junction shaded by olive trees.

Daoud Rubez had chosen well. This would be the perfect spot for the ambush.

In a deep inset between two ridges, another road came down out of a shallow gorge and joined the main highway. On the corner, under the olive trees, was a vegetable stand as well as a bus stop. A large crowd of Palestinians strolled in the roadway, waiting for a bus. A couple of skinny dogs nosed around looking for handouts. A man led a goat on a rope. Another man balanced a crate of chickens on his hip. Horns blared, as the three trucks approached the bus stop, forcing them to slow to a crawl. After the last truck had gone by, a Palestinian bus rolled out of the side road and drew up at the bus stop. There was more confusion as passengers got off to join the crowd.

The men of B'nai Ha'eretz would not be able to see the burning tires until they rounded a sharp bend about 100 meters farther on.

Christina smiled. She doubted the bus was mere coincidence. The van's tires squealed as she sped along the winding road toward the intersection. As she eased past the waiting bus, Daoud Rubez with two boys, all of them wearing black checkered *kaffiyehs*, stepped out of the crowd.

Daoud put up his hand and signaled her to stop.

"Your two friends are in which truck?"

"The one with fastened curtains," she said.

Daoud flung open the door on the passenger's side and stood up leaning out. The two other boys got in through the van's sliding door. Yelling slogans in a rhythmic Palestinian singsong orchestrated by hand-clapping cheerleaders, the sea of faces in front of Christina bobbed and twisted as a rising tide of fury gripped the crowd. She beat on the van's horn and inched the van forward while Daoud called to the crowd to make way. They made little progress.

"We'll have to go on foot," Daoud said.

They left the van in the middle of the road and joined the crowd. Everyone headed for the steep hillside that the trucks had disappeared around. She could see high on the hill against the sky, the silhouettes of young boys hurling stones. Daoud and the two other boys ran too and Christina followed them. The whole crowd surged forward waving a forest of sticks and clubs.

Sixty-One

Some men run in the teeth of danger, some men stand and fight; Shlomo Arendt never ran. Shlomo in the lead truck saw the wall of sooty red flames dead ahead. He braced himself as Etzel slammed on the brakes, heard shouts from the hillside above, the thuds of rocks on canvass and metal and the sound of breaking glass.

"It's an ambush!" said Etzel.

"Somebody must have tipped off the Arabs," said Shlomo squinting out the window. "We've been betrayed." He kicked open the door and sprayed the hillside with bullets from his M-16. "We'll teach those fucking Arabs a lesson!" he growled.

From the rocky ridge above, swarms of small boys hurled stones down. Kallenborg and the rest of the settlers jumped down from their trucks and opened fire on them.

"Etzel," shouted Shlomo. "Get that fire out. He wheeled and stared at the crowd of Palestinians gathered on the road behind the last truck. "Get some gas down on that mob, Kallenborg!"

Kallenborg disappeared behind the lead truck and came back toting a grenade launcher. He aimed it and fired a volley of tear gas into the crowd. Pop-pop!

The leaders of the crowd, laborers and students wearing checkered *kaffiyehs*, excited adolescents, and howling women with raised fists ran toward the trucks. Christina, Daoud and his friends pushed their way forward. Out of nowhere a gas canister dropped at Christina's feet. Instantly the sickly strong gas mushroomed over the pavement and she was choking with tears in her eyes. Daoud kicked the canister violently out of the road and grabbed her hand.

"Here, put this over your mouth," he said.

He gave her a rag wrapped around an onion cut in half. She followed his instruction and miraculously the choking stopped. Through streaming tears she could make out the back of the last truck which loomed over them out of the thick gas. Its curtains were fastened.

"We want that one," she said.

Daoud started to climb up but Christina put a warning hand on his shoulder.

Combat boots beat a staccato on the pavement toward them. Daoud slid under the truck, pulling Christina with him out of sight of the settlers and Shlomo's men.

Silhouetted against the flames, the men of B'nai Ha'eretz pulled on gas masks and heavy work gloves while behind them Shlomo dashed to the rear of the convoy followed by Kallenborg. Fusillades of stones rained down on the two men forcing them to crouch beside the last truck.

Shlomo lifted his mask. "Keep the gas thick," he said.

Kallenborg nodded and fired more tear gas grenades into the dense fog of gas until the stones stopped flying.

"That'll hold them," said Shlomo. "Wait here."

Kallenborg raised his M-16 and fired a short burst at a small boy who rose from behind a low boulder.

"Don't kill any of the bastards unless you have to," said Shlomo. "We don't want a stink in the newspapers." He headed back toward the men working on the barricade.

The boys on the hillside blew whistles and shouted to each other as they took up new positions in the boulders around the Kallenborg's truck. Through the tear gas came the distant sound of hand clapping and chanting as the crowd reformed. Then wild ululating cries echoed among the boulders above the truck. A thick volley of stones pelted Kallenborg. When a rock glanced off his grenade launcher and hit him in the face, he threw down the grenade launcher and scrambled up the rocky hillside after them with his M-16 blazing, leaving the truck unguarded.

Christina, lying on her stomach under the truck whispered "Now!" Then she and the three Palestinian boys crawled out of their hiding place and scrambled to their feet.

She scanned the hillside for Kallenborg. He was no place to be seen but erratic bursts of automatic rifle fire came from the boulders.

Peering cautiously around the end of the truck, she spotted Shlomo, busy with the other settlers spraying foam on the burning tires. She motioned the boys forward.

Daoud and his assistants clambered up the back of the truck with knives in their hands. With swift stokes they slit open the canvass and disappeared inside. Christina waited, not daring to breath. Moments later they emerged, dragging Asher and Zrake after them.

Their eyes were glazed, their lips were cracked and bleeding. Gags of filament tape that they had managed to work loose flopped at their chins. Asher's was encrusted with vomit. One side of his face had a nasty purple bruise where Kallenborg must have hit him. Daoud quickly severed the plastic handcuffs that bound their hands.

"Thank God you're alive!" said Christina.

"This is indeed a miracle," said Zrake with a dry smile. He kept looking from Christina to Daoud and the other two boys and then back to Christina before his puzzled eyes settled on the crowd.

Asher stared at her without saying a word. The fond look in his eye was enough.

Daoud clasped Asher's hands warmly. "Mr. Bikfaya, it is a honor to save a friend of Mrs. Goryeb from the Zionist oppressors," he said.

Christina started, then remembered that "Bikfaya" was Asher's cover name that she used when she had introduced him to Daoud at her office. It seemed a lifetime ago, no two lifetimes.

She gave Asher a warning look.

Daoud hugged Asher tightly. "Allah be praised. I should have never doubted."

The gas clouds began to drift away on the afternoon breeze.

"I remain totally confused," said Zrake.

"I think Mrs. Goryeb and her friends have saved our worthless lives," said Asher. "But we better get out of here if we all want to keep them."

A muffled voice behind Christina said, "Raise your hands." She turned.

It was Ya'akov Kallenborg. He removed his mask and pointed his M-16 directly at them.

Asher, Zrake, and the three boys turned around slowly. They too raised their hands.

Kallenborg stuck the barrel of his weapon in Asher's neck.

"Would you care to explain yourself?"

The shouts of the crowd were louder now and rocks began to fly again. Out of the tear gas appeared the running shapes of the young stone throwers.

"Get in the truck, all of you," said Kallenborg.

"There's a grenade in the gas tank," Asher said. "It could go off any second. We'll all die if we don't get out of here immediately."

"Bullshit," said Kallenborg and jabbed Asher again.

"We don't want to die," said Asher calmly.

"You're are interfering with a Shin Bet operation."

Asher remained silent.

Christina, standing at the back of the truck with her hands raised, could still see Shlomo. He was with another settler beside the first truck. The fire was extinguished now, and Shlomo's men were hauling the last of the melted tires to side of the road. She realized that Shlomo was staring at her. He raised his M-16 and fired a long burst over the heads of the crowd.

"Etzel get the trucks rolling!" he cried and ran toward Christina firing his M-16 again in the air. "Kallenborg, we're pulling out," he yelled as he jumped in the cab. He sounded the truck's air horn to signal the other trucks to start moving.

Kallenborg pointed his M-16 at Christina.

"For the last time, get in or I'll shoot all of you," he said.

"You can't. There're too many witnesses," said Christina.

"Ever the lawyer, eh? They're just filthy Arabs."

The truck jerked forward with a clash of gears and a powerful roar. A rock struck Kallenborg in the shoulder and then another in the head. He wheeled fired a burst and then lunged for the receding tailgate.

"Wait," he yelled. The tail gate was inches away from his outstretched fingers. Kallenborg tore off his gas mask and sprinted.

Asher's tired face creased with a smile as he saw Kallenborg jump and haul himself on board the accelerating truck.

"Let's get out of here," he said. He grabbed Christina's hand and leapt over the embankment. Then Zrake and Daoud too leaped. Christina and Asher lay face down beside them.

A tremendous explosion shook the ground. Asher held her tightly to shield her. He held her as the deadly fireworks display went on and bits of flying steel whizzed through the air. At last the only sound she could hear was a crackling roar of flames from the shattered hulk of the third truck. When she opened her eyes she found Asher looking into her eyes.

She managed a weak smile. "Have I earned my freedom now, Mr. Policeman?" she said.

"Of course," he said. "But forgive me if I wish I could keep you with me for a little longer," he said.

Stinking black smoke from the burning truck hung over the crowd as it slowly dispersed.

Sixty-Two

Dry heat lightning forked silently over the hills outside Ben Yusuf's study as he read the words of Moses de Leone in the *Zohar*. It was late afternoon and everything was hot and still at B'nai Ha'eretz. He had thrown open the windows in a vain attempt to find a cool breeze. The book-lined study was a private sanctuary into which Ben Yusuf retired every night to read and work. Row upon row of Talmudic references bound in green, brown, red and black covers rose to the ceiling. Some of these volumes were over four hundred years old. They called to him across the centuries, a symphony in Yiddish, Russian, Lithuanian, German, and Spanish. Against their cries sounded Hebrew, like a bassoon playing a didactic counterpoint. It was to the *Zohar* that the Rabbi turned for purity and strength in times of crisis. Its angular hooked letters imprinted on yellowed paper contained divine secrets, a code for speaking to God. Ben Yusuf closed his eyes. His lips moved silently pronouncing mysterious names and words, each full of magic portent. His head slumped on his chest and he dozed fitfully. The sun set and darkness fell. Suddenly he felt the presence.

"Is it you, Lord?" he said.

IT IS I.

The voice was deep and personal. Ben Yusuf broke out in a cold sweat.

A pin prick of light flashed out of the darkness and burst into flames. The flames became a man's arm, hairy, muscular and hard. The arm burned with a vivid white fire yet was not itself consumed. Its hand pointed directly at Ben Yusuf.

THE PROMISED LAND WILL BE CLEANSED WITH FIRE.

Then the arm vanished. Ben Yusuf opened his eyes. He heard the trucks grinding up the hillside toward B'nai Ha'eretz.

370

Samuels burst into the room. His eyes glittered. "Rabbi, our guns are here," he said.

The two men went to the window and peered out into the tranquil evening. Headlights bobbed up and down as two trucks roared through the main gate and stopped at the far end of the compound by the soccer field with a hiss of air brakes. Ben Yusuf and Samuels hurried downstairs and strode across the wide expanse of asphalt to Etzel.

"Just two trucks?" said Ben Yusuf.

"I thought Shlomo said there would be three," said Samuels.

Etzel paced back and forth shouting orders to the men unloading the trucks. The gleam of panic was in his eyes as he turned to greet Ben Yusuf.

The Rabbi shook his hand. "Did everything go well?"

"Shlomo's dead," said Etzel. "We have been betrayed. The Arabs ambushed us about half an hour from here."

"Shlomo's dead?" said Ben Yusuf wonderingly to Samuels. "How can that be?"

"His truck exploded," said Etzel. "The Arabs threw a grenade under it."

The Rabbi was oblivious. He was thinking of the auspicious sign he had just received, and was filled with ecstasy.

"I have seen the flaming hand of God," he told Etzel. "God spoke to me. He commands us to cleanse the promised land with fire."

"You saw a flaming hand?" said Etzel, eyebrows raised.

"The hand pointed directly at me. The Prophecy is fulfilled," said Ben Yusuf with a tremor of awe in his voice. "Etzel, the time of redemption has arrived. Shlomo Arendt will be raised up."

Etzel put a hand on Ben Yusuf's arm. "Take it easy Rabbi," he said nervously.

"I tell you, the prophecy of *King Moshiach* is fulfilled. GOD IS WITH US!" shouted Ben Yusuf raising both arms to the sky.

The men stopped unloading the trucks and stared at the Rabbi.

Etzel waved at them. "Get back to work. Unpack those mortars and anti-tank weapons. We've got to prepare our defenses. The Army is going to be all over us any minute," he said.

In the gas tank of the nearest truck, the last strands of nylon dissolved, freeing the arming handle of the grenade. The explosion came first. Next there was a vacuous belch like an enormous beast regurgitating a piece of rotten viscera. Suddenly a bright blue fireball engulfed the men and the trucks. It rose swiftly and became a tremendous roiling tongue of orange, red and purple flame that licked the evening sky.

The earth shook.

Sixty-Three

A government spokesman said the trucks were part of a routine Army convoy that had parked over the settlement's fuel tanks to unload defensive munitions. The Israeli government hushed up the whole B'nai Ha'eretz affair to avoid a national referendum on Yitzhak Rabin's peace negotiations with the Palestinians. A Shin Bet investigation traced the cause of the explosion that caused the death of Rabbi Ben Yusuf, among others, to a faulty wiring in a fuel tank gauge. In a highly imaginative, malicious account, the *Jerusalem Post* reported the fiery deaths of Shlomo Arendt and Ya'akov Kallenborg as a suicide pact between two lovers, and not as rumor had it, the result of a Palestinian ambush.

* * *

On the evening of November 4, 1995, three months later, Prime Minister Yitzhak Rabin delivered a speech from a terrace before 100,000 supporters at a "Peace Now" rally gathered in Malchei Yisroel Square outside Tel Aviv's City Hall. Afterward, he walked down the steps of the terrace into the restricted area where his bullet-proof Cadillac limousine waited for him. A number of irregularities occurred that night; routine precautions overlooked. It was customary to light the areas where he would walk, but the parking lot that night was dim. Members of the public loitered within the security perimeter that was usually guarded by dozens of policemen, yet now the policemen were absent. Although Ichilov hospital was just 500 meters away, the ambulance that was usually posted near his car when he made public appearances was missing. Unperturbed, buoyed up by the success of his speech, Rabin walked toward his limousine. His wife, Leah, followed a few steps behind with Foreign Minister Shimon Peres. As Rabin reached the limousine, the Shin Bet bodyguard, who was supposed to cover his rear, turned away in a moment of inattention. A short, dark handsome man dressed in street clothes and a *kippa* on his head, a young man well-known to the security detail as a former member of the elite Golani Brigade, lunged forward and fired three shots at Rabin's back.

The 9mm Beretta was so close the muzzle flash burned Rabin's shirt. Two hollow-point bullets tore through Rabin's lungs, spleen and chest. The assassin told the Shin Bet officers who pinned him against a concrete wall, "Srak. Srak," or "they're not real, they're not real."

Another officer repeated this to Rabin's wife. He told her not to worry because the shots came from a "toy pistol".

Yigal Amir, a religious Zionist, proudly admitted to killing Yitzhak Rabin and was sentenced to life in prison without the possibility of parole. He attracted a following of teenage girls who chatted with him on the phone in his cell.

Carmi Gillon, Director of the Shin Bet, and a bitter foe of the settler movement, was forced to resign his office.

Orthodox rabbis who had called Rabin a traitor and murderer, now publicly searched their souls. Political opponents who remained silent when Rabin had been publicly vilified now offered their condolences to Leah, his widow, and shook her hand.

At Yitzhak Rabin's funeral, prominent Arab statesmen joined other world leaders in eulogizing him as a hero of peace. Yasser Arafat who did not attend the funeral for security reasons, wept openly and mourned him like a lost brother. Ordinary Palestinians did not.

* * *

The Lions of Allah disbanded after the death of their martyred leader, and a small boy swore revenge.

The day Christina Goryeb had left for America, one of the Lion's former spies, a maid at the King David Hotel, spotted her with her lover. They were in the company of a man who appeared to be an Israeli security officer. Rasul discovered the lover's name in a small notebook she'd left behind in her law office. Years passed. He learned

Hebrew. He took a job as a lavatory attendant in the Tel Aviv post office. He became friends with a gang of Israeli mail thieves. Patiently, he waited for the opportunity to take his revenge. He was prepared to wait a lifetime.

* * *

Yasser Arafat continued to meet with the Israelis in an attempt to gain control over more territory, as if through small concessions a nation could be assembled from tiny shards of land. Each humiliating attempt failed, confirming what Rasul and ordinary Palestinians knew all along. There would be no peace between Palestinians and Israelis until there was an end to Israel's military occupation of the West Bank and Gaza.

* * *

On July 4, 2000, Arafat's Palestine Liberation Organization announced it would declare Palestine an independent nation on September 13. In response, the U.S. President convened the last peace conference of his administration at Camp David. The talks ended abruptly when the Israelis proposed to give up *de-facto* control of the Temple Mount in exchange for the right to build a small synagogue on the northeast corner of the ancient site. Palestinians poured into the streets demanding Israel withdraw from their country and return to its original borders drawn by the United Nations in 1947.

For the first time, Arab citizens of Israel threatened to join their cause. Throughout the Arab world, supporters rallied in support of the Palestinians. The Israelis were divided and demoralized.

Rasul now was elated. Israel appeared to be on her knees with neck outstretched, waiting for the headman's sword.

He would be that sword.

A Bir Zeit University student helped him obtain Christina Goryeb's address off the Internet. The post office gang acquired the address he needed for the lover's post card. Baiting the trap was easy.

Sixty-Four

My Dearest Christina,
   What joy to learn you have indeed returned. If you are free on Thursday, meet me at the King David Hotel for lunch. I'll be in the lobby at noon.

Your Adoring,
Chaim.

With fierce satisfaction, the young Palestinian man in the waiter's uniform paused to read the message he'd written on the postcard before slipping it in the mail box behind the concierge's desk. Then with a furtive glance that reassured him he was unobserved, he returned to the hotel's kitchen.

* * *

Christina Goryeb received the postcard at her home in Ramallah in the evening of the following day, September 26.

Her hands shook as she held the post card. After all this time to actually see him again. "It's from Chaim," she told her sisters. "He knows I'm here already. He wants me to meet him tomorrow for lunch in Jerusalem."

Janine took the card from her, read it hastily, and then frowned.

Their Mother's frown, thought Christina.

When she'd told them about her Chaim Asher, they had been sympathetic as expected, although she sensed in Janine a careful withholding of judgment.

"Is this wise? Think of your husband, Christina. Think of your daughters."

Christina gave Janine a bitter smile. "My marriage is over. Richard has an American mistress, one of his little graduate students. With our daughters away at school, he is less discrete. Don't look so shocked. Americans divorce each other all the time, and we're Americans now."

"I had no idea," said Janine.

"I didn't want to burden you," Christina said. "It has been so lonely for me in America."

Najat gave Christina a worried look. "Do you think it is safe for you to go to Jerusalem tomorrow? There may be violence."

"What violence?" said Christina.

"Have you forgotten Ariel Sharon's visit to Al-Aksa Mosque and Dome of the Rock?"

"Of course I remember!" said Christina. "That old criminal hopes to start a riot to topple the peace negotiations."

"Stay home, Christina," said Janine.

Christina's face softened as she thought of Chaim. "We will not be in any danger. We won't be near Al-Aksa where all the trouble will start. Besides, I have no way to contact Chaim. He didn't give me a phone number."

* * *

Her face flushed with excitement and her heart beat with odd little jerks. As the taxi pulled up under the portico of the King David Hotel, the grizzled Jerusalem cabbie turned to Christina. "You'll have a ring-side seat for Sharon's visit to the Temple Mount this morning," he said with a cocky smile. "It's about time the Likud showed the Arabs who's boss."

Christina said nothing.

A uniformed footman held the door of the taxi while she got out. She wore an expensive lavender sun dress that accented her golden brown coloring, a dress originally bought for a Georgetown garden party that she chose not to attend, once she'd found out that Richard's young mistress would also be there. With mounting excitement she walked through the heavy revolving doors into the King David's spacious lobby where she was greeted by its familiar old-world grandeur, luxury no American hotel could ever provide. She realized she was early as her eyes swept around the crowd of people who were there.

She paused for a moment to admire the broad, fluted pillars that rose from the lobby's gleaming marble floor, decorated with a mélange of ancient Semitic symbols, azure Stars of David among brick red Assyrian, Hittite, and Phoenician motifs. The walls were a cream and beige symphony of good taste, illuminated by discrete gilt edging and soft yellow light from Art Deco lamps. Bowls of flowers on glass topped writing tables were a gracious addition.

Chaim had not yet arrived.

She sank into one of the gold and blue Greco-Syrian style chairs near the entrance, suddenly nervous. Who would she find waiting for her? She knew he'd changed. He was now a man who wrote imploring letters in Arabic. She remembered Mekor said Chaim was no longer with the Mossad. What if he'd retired because he'd lost an arm or leg? Suppose he'd been tortured or mutilated? Do I ever know this man, she thought. She remembered the time he cried over the deaths of his wife and son, sacrificed on the alter of Zionism. The night of bright stars on her rooftop when he formally, shame-facedly apologized to her for what his beloved Israel had done to her homeland. That was the man she waited for, the man she loved. A man with a cane walked slowly toward her, his features obscured by an auburn beard and sunglasses. Was that Chaim? No, his movement was that of an older man. He turned away from her to join a family reunion.

"Christina!"

When she turned around she saw him. Her Chaim, striding briskly toward her. Infinitely sane. No sign of injury. His eyes, glinted at her with that familiar expression of bemused enjoyment. He wore blue jeans and a soft white shirt and a broad olive drab strap was slung over his right shoulder. She could feel his strength as if it were a powerful scent. It made her a little dizzy.

Impulsively, she threw her arms around him and kissed him but drew back when she felt the Uzi submachine gun.

"Why are you carrying this awful thing? Mekor told me you were a civilian, now," she said, vexed.

He made a dismissing gesture with his hand. "I'll explain everything. But this is a miracle! I never expected to see you again."

She kissed him again, a longer kiss, full of hunger and he pressed her close to his heart.

When they separated, he took her hand and placed it on his arm, a gesture of playful gallantry. He escorted her through the hotel's shopping arcade to the outdoor restaurant that overlooked the terraced gardens at its rear. Their terrace which looked out at the familiar walls and homes of 'Jerusalem the Golden' punctuated by its minarets and golden domes, and beyond it were the Mount of Olives, Mount Scopus, and the Judean Hills.

As they sat down, she couldn't help but notice their young waiter. Something was familiar about the young man's voice but she couldn't place it. From his accent she realized he was Palestinian, a local men who worked in the hotel. Poor but smart, she thought, like the young Palestinians she'd defended a lifetime ago.

Chaim ordered a bottle of Carmel wine while she looked at the menu.

"What would you like to eat?" he said.

"Something I can't get in America."

"Let's have *falafel*," he said.

"Oh Chaim!" she said. "Only you would invite me to lunch at a five star hotel, and order Israeli junk food."

"So you don't like the cut of my dinner jacket?" he said touching collar of his shirt.

"I think it's perfect," she said and placed her hand on his.

Their waiter poured wine into their glasses. He took their order and turned to Chaim. "If you will permit me, Sir" he said and reached for Chaim's Uzi. "I must check that weapon with the concierge. Hotel rules."

Chaim shook his head, calmly. "Then you'll have to make an exception. I'll be happy to discuss the matter with your concierge."

As the waiter withdrew, Christina gave Asher a cold smile. "Forgive me Chaim, but why did you humiliate that young man? He was just doing his job. That weapon makes you look just like one of those bullying settlers."

"That is why I carry it," he said.

"So if you're not working for Mekor who are you working for?"

"I watch the settlements for Peace Now," he said quietly.

"Chaim, that is lunacy" she said. "What if you're recognized?"

"Shlomo Arendt and Kallenborg are dead. The others never got a good look at me."

He spoke matter-of-factly without any trace of the agonized passion that filled his letters.

"But why? You wrote that you hated surveillance work," she said. He gave her a curious stare. "When did I ever write that?"

"In just about every letter you wrote me in the last three months." She stared at him in sudden confusion. He looked calm, so self-possessed. "Chaim," she said firmly. "You haven't forgotten the letters you wrote me, have you? They were the most beautiful, passionate— She stopped, aware their waiter had returned.

With an ingratiating smile the young man placed two plates of *falafel* before them. "Will there be anything else?" he said, pointedly ignoring the Uzi beside Asher's chair.

Christina smiled uncertainly at Chaim. "*Kanaffi* for desert?"

"Excellent!" said the waiter. "We have the best."

* * *

Angrily Rasul stood with his back to Christina Goryeb and her lover as he polished wine glasses on an adjacent table one at a time. The lover was armed. He had dared not conceal a weapon on himself as the hotel security men searched the Palestinian staff when they came to work each day. Nonetheless, unarmed he would force the whore and her lover to walk to a secluded spot on the grounds of the hotel. He would bind and gag them, and cut her throat. She would bleed to death. The lover would be forced to watch. Rasul, would shoot the lover with his own Uzi. Now, it would look like a murder suicide. The murder of the noted Palestinian peace activist by a Jew would make headlines in every capital in the Middle East. He felt a thrill of excitement as the cell phone in his pocket rang. It signaled the sniper was in position.

* * *

Chaim looked up from the postcard with narrowed eyes at Christina. "I never wrote this," he said. He dug in his pocket and handed her another postcard.

She felt sick to her stomach as she read it.

Chaim, I'm in Jerusalem for a few days. Will you have lunch with me? I'll be in the lobby of the King David on Wednesday at Noon. Fondly, Christina.

She shook her head. "Both of these were written by the same person. Oh, Chaim, someone is playing a monstrous, practical joke on us."

His lips hardened into a thin line. "I was suspicious at first. Then I assumed your handwriting had changed, perhaps you'd injured your hand. And, when I saw you get out of that taxi alone, without anyone following you, I felt foolish for doubting you."

"Sir?"

She looked up at the slender waiter's haughty features. There was guarded contempt in his eyes, an expression she'd not seen before. Again the flash of recognition ran through her mind, but also a shiver of dread. He was someone she'd known long ago, someone she'd feared.

"Are you Chaim Asher?" The waiter held out a tiny black Swedish cell phone.

Asher accepted the instrument with a puzzled frown. His face seemed to turn to stone as he listened. He took a deep breath, looked up sharply at the waiter who handed him a pair of binoculars. Then he nodded once slowly and looked through them at the golden dome of the Muslim shrine that rose half a kilometer away on the Temple Mount above the Old City of Jerusalem.

"There's a sniper on the Dome of the Rock," he said softly. "He says he will shoot us and all the people in the restaurant unless we do exactly as he says."

For one horrifying moment she saw a needle thin beam of brilliant red light flicker on Chaim's temple and vanish.

A laser gun sight, she thought.

The waiter gave her a scornful smile. "Do you remember me, Khantarish?"

That rude boy, the Lion's messenger.

Her mouth felt like dry cotton. "You are Rasul," she forced herself to say.

"I am gratified you remember me," said Rasul.

The gloating look in his eye made her tremble inside.

"Rise to your feet, slowly," said Chaim to Christina. He seemed to be obeying instructions he received from the sniper over the cell phone.

She did as he said and he rose also.

"Take my hand and walk beside me," said Chaim.

Christina glanced at his eyes, trying to read them for any message, but they were blank, his face expressionless. As they started off, she looked back over her shoulder.

Rasul stood beside the table in his apron, black eyes darting around as he pretended to write up their bill. Satisfied that no one was watching him, he bent down and picked up the Uzi. She saw him carry it surreptitiously toward a small lattice work pavilion where clean plates and cutlery were stored. He entered the pavilion and slipped out the other side carrying a round plastic tray with two glasses of iced tea. In a moment, his head reappeared over a hedge bobbing in the gardens of roses, rhododendrons and azaleas that extended behind the pavilion.

I must not show fear, thought Christina. She tried to imagine the sniper. Another young man, desperate and vengeful, like Rasul. Why doesn't he kill us now? she wondered. Suddenly, she realized Rasul wanted to kill them himself. This was personal revenge. Their only hope for survival was delay, delay by any means until the Israeli police could be alerted. She looked at the faces of the diners around the tables that moved past her they walked by. Who among them would have the courage to call the police? A fat man wearing a green beret; a small boy with thick glasses blowing spit wads through a straw at his sister; a group of silent nuns in Coptic robes. The girl burst into tears, the man cuffed the boy and the nuns frowned disapprovingly.

In a few more steps, we will be in the garden, thought Christina. There they would face a double threat from Rasul and the sniper. She looked around at the crowded tables. Think quickly. She had to tell someone. That ominous red beam played across the face of an old man who sat smoking a cigarette and stopped on the neck of a young African-American woman who was changing her baby's diaper. When the woman looked up and smiled at Christina, her courage deserted her. Chaim tugged at her hand and she turned. A group of Palestinian businessmen suddenly blocked their path immediately ahead. They wore robes and *kaffiyehs*. Sunglasses hid their eyes.

In their midst, an Israeli woman dressed in the blue uniform of tour guide looked directly at Christina. She said in loud voice, "And, this is where Paul Newman and Eva Marie Saint had a drink in the motion picture, *Exodus*."

That voice, thought Christina, momentarily stunned. She stared back at the woman. Yes, she was.

Gilda Sderot!

The Palestinians smiled broadly as they crowded around Gilda. Mekor's men disguised as Palestinians, she thought. *Oh thank God!* For a moment she was euphoric. But when she heard Chaim speak to the sniper on the cell phone, she knew nothing had changed.

"If you shoot, you'll hit your countrymen too. Rasul will be very angry with you if Palestinians die." Asher said.

She felt his hand squeeze hers several quick squeezes. He was signaling her. She had to get word to Gilda.

As Chaim shouldered his way past the last of Gilda's men, Christina found herself face to face with Gilda. "There's a sniper on the Dome of the Rock and another man in the hotel garden with an Uzi," Christina murmured.

Gilda gave no indication that she heard Christina. "You're interrupting our tour," she said officiously. "Please get out of the way." She turned on her heel and walked briskly away, the men rapidly dispersing into the crowd behind her.

* * *

12:15 p.m. He'd worked all night coordinating intelligence for Ariel Sharon's tour of the Temple Mount. Reports of planned violence by Palestinian and Israeli extremists were common knowledge. From his command post on the roof of the King David Hotel, Mekor watched the garden below. In fifteen minutes the Likud opposition leader's cavalcade was scheduled to pull up in front of the Al-Aksa Mosque beyond the garden where a line of border police armed with rifles, batons and shields were holding back an angry crowd of Palestinians.

"Gilda, what the hell's going on?" Mekor said into his wrist microphone.

"We're putting on flack jackets. We can't rescue them until you take out that sniper on the Dome of the Rock," said Gilda in his ear piece.

Mekor turned to Strabo, the marksman from the *Kidon* unit. "Do you see him?" he snapped.

Without a word, bug-eyed Strabo, quickly crawled behind the nearest air conditioner ventilating stack. Resting his long-nosed Shtutser rifle on the stack, he peered through his telescopic sight. A high blue-tiled facade jumped into focus. Another long-nosed rifle and a checkered *kaffiyeh* peeped coyly over the top of the parapet. But a heavy wooden ladder blocked his view of the sniper's head. Overhead an Israeli army helicopter armed with missiles hovered in the sky, part of the security screen for Sharon's visit.

"The angle's wrong. I can't get a clear shot," he said to Mekor. "But we've got a perfect opportunity to destroy the mosque with a missile."

"Not while I'm in charge," growled Mekor. "If we harm Dome of the Rock, we'll be at war with every Arab country in the region!"

Gilda's voice came over the radio. "There's another terrorist in the garden. It's the waiter who gave Asher the cell phone. We put a tracer on his phone. The sniper's controlling Asher through it."

Mekor's mouth went dry. His tongue felt like it was spot-welded to the roof of his mouth. Something was going to happen that afternoon, but he still had no clue as to how or when. Too many questions and no time to find answers. Asher and Christina, seated in the garden on a high backed white bench, were in plain view of the sniper, but where was that waiter? He scanned the brick lined pathways that crisscrossed the hotel's garden. Empty!

"He's disappeared," Mekor said angrily. "Gone, fucked off."

Strabo popped his chewing gum. "Mike, are we going to sit on our asses all day?"

Mekor pointed at the stone tower that rose across the street above the Jerusalem YMCA. "Pack up, we're moving." He switched his radio to a different channel. "Get me the border police at the Western Wall," he ordered.

* * *

12:17 p.m. The call reached the desk-duty man at the Western Wall station.

"Lieutenant Yotam Melman?" The voice was deep and cigarette scorched.

"Speaking," said Melman as he glanced at his watch.

"This is Major General Mekor Ivry."

Hurriedly, Melman cleaned away the scraps of a meat loaf sandwich he'd eaten for lunch and sat a bit more erect as he listened.

"Melman, you are sitting on the most delicate spot in Israel," said Mekor and he explained in detail what he wanted Melman to do.

When he had finished, Melman said he'd put all his men on the job. "Use no more men than necessary," said Mekor. "Contact me immediately when you eliminate the sniper."

Melman memorized the code word Mekor gave him.

* * *

12:19 p.m. The pulsating song of cicadas filled the garden with a shrill, crackling howl. Beads of sweat ran down Asher's forehead and into his eyes. Christina's face had an imperious, tragic look, her eyes pools of shadow. Ancient royalty, readying herself for death, he thought.Finally she spoke. "We never had a chance to live together," she said, "but it appears today we'll die together." She took Asher's hand and clasped it tightly.

"I love you with all my heart," he said.

The nights he'd lain awake thinking of her. "You know, I've been following your brilliant career," he said with a light chuckle. He dug in his blue jeans for his wallet and extracted a worn piece of paper which he unfolded and smoothed out for her to see. *Christina Goryeb, Advocate for Peace*, said the caption under her photograph.

"It's not the career I chose," she said. "I wanted to be an honest lawyer like my father, and live with my family in our home."

She pushed a damp curl of hair away from her forehead with one hand. Her lips were dry, her mouth burned with thirst. Abruptly, the cicadas stopped singing. A hot stillness cloaked the level lawn in front of her, bordered by beds of roses, oleander and crocus.

"Not yet!"

Christina turned her head. The angry whisper came from a gardener's tool shed to her right, half hidden in a tall privet hedge. "There is a helicopter overhead. I cannot kill them until it is gone." A start of horror ran through her as she recognized the voice as Rasul's, and that he was talking to the sniper.

"Rasul is in that hut," she murmured to Asher.

The red laser beam flashed suddenly in her eyes as a warning. Without thinking, she put her hand up to ward it off and realized it did not come from the Dome of the Rock, but from farther away at a higher elevation. She traced the scintillating light to its source, a window in a Palestinian slum on the hillside above the Old City of Jerusalem, the one the Israelis called the City of David. She nudged Chaim and he followed her gaze.

As the sniper's laser shifted to his face, the cell-phone on the bench beside him rang. He picked it up.

"Silence, Al-Yahud," said the sniper.

* * *

12:23 p.m. Black robed Orthodox Jews chanted and swayed before the massive chalky-yellow stone blocks of the Western Wall as Lieutenant Melman walked alone past them. He'd telephoned ahead to his counterpart, a detective sergeant in the Palestinian mosque police, to ask for a meeting but had said nothing about the sniper. A handpicked squad of six border police armed with Uzis waited in the station for Melman's summons. He broke into a trot when he reached a long flight of stairs leading up to the vast stone-paved platform, all that was left of Herod's Great Temple. At the top he was met by the agitated Palestinian detective.

"What is this information you received?" the detective said angrily.

Melman lied. "A Christian fanatic is on the roof of the Dome of the Rock."

"What!" cried the detective. "Another arsonist?"

Eight years before, a deranged Australian tourist had set fire to Al-Aksa Mosque, severely damaging it.

"We assume so," said Melman.

The Palestinian's smile was knowing and bitter. "Why did you wait so long to tell me?"

Melman looked straight into the man's eyes. "If we really wanted to destroy Dome of the Rock I wouldn't be here, warning you, would I?" Then he radioed his men.

The detective stared at Melman angrily then he issued orders over his walkie-talkie in rapid fire Arabic.

Melman's men arrived out of breath and sweating from sprinting up the long stairway. In a moment, they were joined by five mosque policemen in green uniforms armed with M-16s.

"We don't have much time," said Melman to the detective.

"Follow me," said the detective.

He led them through a line of policemen in front of the Al-Aksa Mosque and headed across the Temple Plaza toward the glittering dome.

Suddenly, one of Melman's squad, a young private, popped up in front of him and saluted. "Lieutenant, I request another assignment. My rabbi forbids me to step on the Holy of Holies." His head bobbed tightly; he was blinking.

Melman felt a coldness run down his spine. "Go on back to the station," he said curtly. He turned to the other men. "Anyone else with a rabbi problem?" No one else spoke.

The ancient shrine was empty and quiet when they entered. The detective pulled off his shoes and gestured at the Israelis to do the same. A sublime light filtered down from above, illuminating thick red carpets that covered the floor. Floral designs decorated the walls, ceiling and arches. The huge, flat grey boulder rose two meters high in a circle of marble columns under the dome. This was the Holy of Holies the young soldier had been afraid of.

Just a large piece of rock, thought Melman. But it was the Foundation Stone, where according to tradition, Abraham had built an altar and bound Isaac as a sacrifice to God. The rock from which, Muslims believed their Prophet had leapt to heaven. Here, the young Jesus amazed the priests with his knowledge of the Bible.

"This is the way to the roof," shouted the detective. He pointed with his pistol to a side arch and pounded up a rickety wooden spiral staircase with a speed that surprised Melman. His men unslung their Uzis as they ran. Three floors up they arrived at a small nail-studded door, arched and water stained. Its hinges and lock were cracked and rusty, but a new padlock and chain had been stapled into the woodwork and stone frame.

Melman thought his heart was going to burst from his chest.

"Shoot it off," he gasped and stepped back.

The detective braced himself on both feet and fired. Bits of wood and metal, and spent flattened slugs flew in all directions. The door buckled and swung drunkenly inwards. Melman flipped his Uzi's safety to full auto and charged forward. He was the first one out on the roof, the detective on his heels. Directly beside the door Melman saw the sniper's ladder leaning against a tall stone parapet. He wheeled and emptied his submachine gun into the crouching figure at the top. Before he could jump out of the way, the sniper fell backward and crashed down on top of him. He caught the sniper in his arms, surprised he should weigh so little. A child? He let the body drop. His eyes shifted to the pieces of the rifle at his feet. Its barrel was a broom stick polished with pencil lead to look like metal.

"Our sniper is a mannequin with a wooden rifle," Melman radioed Mekor.

"A fucking decoy!" said Mekor. "Search the entire area."

* * *

12:30 p.m. "I heard gunfire," said the sniper to Rasul over the cell phone. "Do you see anything?"

Rasul put his eye to the crack in the planked wall. His two hostages sat stiffly on the wooden bench ten meters away. Behind them in the distance rose the golden contours of Dome of the Rock, its sloping lower roof hidden behind tall blue tiled walls.

"Nothing," he said. "What do you see?" he said.

"Sharon and his party are getting out of their cars in front of Al-Aksa," said the sniper.

"It must have been El-Fatah firing into the air to frighten the Jews."

"I could kill Sharon so easily myself." The sniper's voice was soft and wistful. "The entire Likud Knesset faction, as well as the Mayor of Jerusalem are in my gun sight, like rats in a trap."

"That is not our plan, Yassin," said Rasul. "Killing these leprous scum will only harm our cause."

"Yes, but my revenge is sweeter," said Yassin.

Rasul wanted to grab the fool by the throat and shake him until his bones rattled. "If you kill Sharon, it gives the Zionists the excuse they have been itching for to take back all we have won from them. They have a modern army. We have only our blood and a few rifles." He pulled back from his spy hole and paced back and forth in the hut, his eyes bright with fury.

Asher eavesdropped on their conversation with growing agitation. The sniper no longer had his weapon trained on them, he realized. Suddenly, he saw Gilda and her men on the edge of the restaurant terrace. The men were still disguised as Palestinians. Gilda wore the black gown and white head shawl of a Palestinian women. A police whistle sounded two shrill blasts and the bogus Palestinians trotted purposefully toward them. Asher's whole body tensed. He sprang to his feet, dragging Christina up with him.

"Run!" he said in a low urgent voice.

* * *

Rasul cocked his head, listening. With a muttered curse, he pressed his eye to his spy hole. For a split second he was stunned with surprise. The whore and her Jew lover were surrounded by the robed Palestinians he'd seen earlier. They held Uzis like his. Just as he'd feared—they were Israelis disguised as his people.

His hand clenched the cell-phone. "You fool!" he screamed at Yassin. "You let them get away." He stripped off his waiter's uniform and changed into the disguise he'd hidden in the hut earlier, a *yarmulke*, dark glasses and Israeli army fatigues. He picked up Asher's Uzi from a mound of burlap sacks and peered through the spy hole one last time.

* * *

Full of anger and despair, Yassin rested his Russian Dragunov on the stone window ledge and sighted. The rifle's cracks was lost among the staccato reports of Israeli riot guns and the shouts of the Palestinian rock throwers gathered at Al-Aksa Mosque.

* * *

Christina heard deadly thuds on the backs of the men who shielded her. Then she was thrown face down on the grass, struggling for breath under the weight of their bodies. Asher's face was pressed next to hers, red eyes, streaked with dirt.

"Lie still," he said. There was no emotion in his voice, just the familiar business of combat.

She felt neither pain nor joy nor hatred, only amazement that Israelis would die to protect her.

* * *

Through powerful binoculars, Mekor watched the yellow-and-blue muzzle flashes. The sniper was a kilometer away, still within killing range. There was a set, hard look in his eye as he turned to Strabo. "They say you're good, Strabo! Let's see you prove it," he said.

* * *

The stone window sill exploded in a shower of splinters. Yassin ducked down just in time as more bullets screamed through the window. Their hot, brutal breath sent shivers of fear down his spine. He saw three Israeli jeeps roaring up the hill from Al-Aksa towards him. A pounding of soldiers' boots echoed in the alley behind the house.

Yassin slung his rifle over his shoulder and opened a back window in the dim attic. Shots rang out below as he climbed out on the tile roof. A bullet grazed his shoulder and he spun around. His foot slipped on a lose tile. He tumbled down the roof, slamming into a chimney before he stopped. Dizzily, he picked himself up and ran to the end of the roof. Pain burned in his shoulder. The air was full of tear gas now. He could hardly see. With a desperate leap he landed hard on the next roof, managing to stay on his feet this time. With gathering confidence, he ran lightly across the crumbling tiles, flitting like a bat from rooftop to rooftop as the shouts of his pursuers faded behind him. He too would escape, blending back into the crowds of Palestinians who inhabited the narrow twisting streets of East Jerusalem.

* * *

"The terrorist who took my Uzi is in the hut," said Chaim in a low voice.

The dead man lying on top of Christina stirred and leapt to his feet. She heard him fire a long burst from his machine gun and tensed. There was no returning fire. Another agent jumped up and sprinted toward the hut with his machine gun blazing. He kicked the door open and looked in.

"The bastard's gone," he shouted.

Chaim helped Christina up, sweeping her tenderly into his arms. There were tears in his eyes.

"It's over," he said.

"Was anyone hit?" said Gilda.

"Nothing but bruises," said the man who'd fallen on top Christina. With a tired smile, he pulled off his *kaffiyeh* and robe to reveal a soldier's helmet and a bullet proof vest

"Thank you for saving our lives," said Christina.

* * *

Two blocks away, Rasul emerged from an alley. Across the busy street, an Israeli jeep revved its idling engine. The driver who wore an army Captain's uniform looked carefully around. Satisfied Rasul had not been followed, he gave the all clear signal by lighting a cigarette. Rasul dodged between two oncoming cars, and jumped in the jeep. The engine roared and the jeep shot forward.

The driver did not speak.

Rasul spat on the floor. Yassin had ruined his plans, he thought bitterly. He gave the driver a brave smile. There would be other opportunities. There would always be other opportunities.

Sixty-Five

Our last picnic, Christina thought as she packed their basket. The roast lamb was cut into thick slices and wrapped in waxed paper. The flat bread was fresh, baked that morning. There was a container of humus and another of eggplant salad. She added a bottle of his favorite wine, Carmel, and a bag of pomegranates to the picnic basket. She dreaded the return to her unwanted public life in America and the ashes of her dead marriage.

They'd been together one month in the bungalow he'd rented for them at Caesarea. It was the off-season but the Mediterranean was still delightfully warm for swimming. He'd rented a Vespa motor scooter so they could explore Caesarea together. They were like young lovers, freed from their burdens of nationality and obligation. There was no guilt or recollection of it. They'd earned their pleasures. I could live with this man forever, she thought.

Chaim would never leave Israel. She wasn't a Jew. They could never live together.

She had just closed the lid of the basket when she heard him come in. He held her tightly as he always did. It always hurt, but she didn't mind, for she had almost lost him.

They never talked about the future.

He picked up the basket and said, "My God Christina! You've packed enough food for the rest of our lives."

"What's the news?" she said although she didn't want to know. It couldn't be good.

He always tensed up when they talked about the news.

"Sharon's show on the Temple Mount was pure provocation and Arafat's no better. The uprising is spreading. Even our Arab-Israelis are in revolt." His voice was harsh, anger laced with sorrow. "Our hopes for peace have been set back 50 years."

"Chaim, what are we doing here?" she cried.

Finally he spoke.

"Too many prophets of too many gods in too small a country."

She looked into his eyes. "I need to go home," she said sadly, "And I don't know where home is anymore."

He released her abruptly. "What do you want? What do you want me to do?"

"This is not our home. This is just a beautiful dream."

"You still have a house in West Jerusalem, in Rehavia?" he said. "We will live there."

She shook her head. "My sister, Janine and her husband live there. It's her home now. I couldn't put her in that kind of danger. Najat has taken our Mother's house in Ramallah."

"You can't go back to Ramallah. Arafat's men are executing traitors."

"I am not a traitor," she said firmly. "It is our own countrymen who have betrayed us." There would never be peace, she thought. The best of her people and the best of his would always be outnumbered by those who reveled in strife.

She stared out the window at the ancient ruins rising amid banana groves, palm trees and tropical undergrowth. The southern half of the sky was filled with dark, threatening clouds. The day was still beautiful.

"It's going to rain," she said.

"I think the storm will miss us," said Chaim confidently. As if he could control the weather, she thought.

They got on the Vespa and headed north over winding sandy lanes for the beach. The sky darkened. As the first rain drops fell on them, they passed by Caesarea's East Gate. A gust of wind pelted them with stinging marble-sized drops. She felt soaked to the skin. Chaim turned the Vespa around and parked beside the square, vaulted gatehouse. As they dismounted the clouds burst.

Inside the stone gatehouse they watched the storm. The rain came down in heavy sheets. Within minutes the dry moat was awash with water.

At last the downpour ended and the flood receded. The little Vespa fired the first time Chaim pumped its starter pedal.

The sun returned and wraiths of steam rose off the roads as they drove. Sitting sideways on the motor scooter's rear seat, the basket on her lap, her eyes half closed, Christina did not see the spectacle until Chaim stopped the motor scooter beside a Roman aqueduct half buried in sand.

She looked around, speechless.

Brilliant rainbows arched over the Mediterranean in glowing bands of color just offshore. The stripes of the larger, upper rainbow were reversed and dimmer than the one below. And above the second, a very weak third rainbow hovered, a rainbow weak as hope but still visible. The sign of the Covenant in triplicate.

"This is miraculous. God's joke on us," she said.

Chaim gave her an amused look. "God has nothing to do with it. The first rainbow is cause by sunbeams bouncing inside raindrops like a prism," he said matter of factly. "The second is a reflection of the first, the third, a reflection of the second."

"Improbable but not impossible, like us," she said.

She felt his arms slip around her back sure and hard. She felt again the rushing current of warmth that left her limp. He bent her head back across his arm and kissed her, softly at first, then with a growing intensity that made her grip his back. His lips molded hers. Her thigh pressed against his groin. She felt a familiar hardness and in herself the mounting excitement but also hunger.

She pulled herself away, laughing. "Chaim, you're insatiable," she said.

"I adore you. Better get used to me," he said.

She stopped laughing.

"How will I?" she said with bitterness. "You can never leave Israel and I cannot live here. Not even for you."

His voice was level, serious this time. "I really do not care what country we live in as long as I have you. We will find a way to live together. I cannot lose you again."

They would be their own country, she thought, joy bursting inside her like a wave.

WHAT DOES THE LORD REQUIRE OF THEE?
ONLY THAT THOU DO JUSTICE, LOVE MERCY, AND WALK
HUMBLY WITH THY GOD.
—MICAH

Biography

Benjamin Eric Hill

Washington lawyer Benjamin Eric Hill was raised in the Middle East, served in Vietnam and has written for numerous publications including the Washington Post and the Village Voice.

Printed in the United States
18887LVS00001B/222